CONFESSIONS OF FELIX KRULL
CONFIDENCE MAN

Thomas Mann

CONFESSIONS OF FELIX KRULL

CONFIDENCE MAN

[THE EARLY YEARS]

Translated from the German by
Denver Lindley

VINTAGE BOOKS
A Division of Random House
New York

Vintage Books Edition, *February 1969*

 Published in the United States by Alfred A. Knopf, Inc., New York, and Random House, Inc., New York. Distributed in Canada by Random House of Canada Limited, Toronto. By arrangement with Alfred A. Knopf, Inc.

Originally published in German as *Bekenntnisse des Hochstaplers Felix Krull: Der Memoiren erster Teil.*

Manufactured in the United States of America

[1]

BOOK ONE

CHAPTER I

As I take up my pen at leisure and in complete retirement—in good health, furthermore, though tired, so tired that I shall only be able to proceed by short stages and with frequent pauses for rest—as I take up my pen, then, to commit my confessions to this patient paper in my own neat and attractive handwriting, I am assailed by a brief misgiving about the educational background I bring to an intellectual enterprise of this kind. But since everything I have to record derives from my own immediate experience, errors, and passions, and since I am therefore in complete command of my material, the doubt can apply only to my tact and propriety of expression, and in my view these are less the product of study than of natural talent and a good home environment. This last has not been wanting, for I come of an upper-class though somewhat dissolute family; for several months my sister Olympia and I were looked after by a Fräulein from Vevey, though it is true she presently had to decamp because female contention arose between her and my mother, with my father as its object; my godfather Schimmelpreester, with whom I was on the most intimate terms, was a greatly admired artist whom everyone in our little town called "Herr Professor" though it is doubtful whether he was officially entitled to this distinction; and my father, though corpulent, possessed much personal charm and always laid great stress on the choice and lucid use of words. He had French blood on his grandmother's side, had himself spent his student years in France, and, as he assured us, knew Paris like the palm of his hand. He was fond of sprinkling his conversation with French phrases such as "*c'est ça*," "*épatant*," "*parfaitement*," and the like. To the end of his days he remained a great favourite with the ladies. This only by way of preface and out of its proper sequence. As to my natural instinct for good form, that is something I have always been able to count on all too well, as my whole career of fraud will prove, and in the present literary undertaking I believe I can rely on it implicitly. Moreover I am resolved to employ the utmost frankness in my writing, without fear of being reproached for vanity or impudence. For what moral value or significance can attach to confessions written from any point of view except that of truthfulness?

The Rhine Valley brought me forth—that richly blessed and benign region, harsh neither in its climate nor in the quality of its soil, rich in cities and villages, peopled by a merry folk—it must be among the sweetest regions of the habitable globe. Here, sheltered from rough winds by the mountains of the Rhine district and happily exposed to the southern sun, flourish those famous communities whose very names make the winebibber's heart rejoice—Rauenthal, Johannisberg, Rüdesheim—and here, too, is that favoured town in which, only a few years after the glorious founding of the German Empire, I first saw the light of day. It lies slightly to the west of the bend the river makes at Mainz. With a population of some four thousand souls, it is renowned for its sparkling wines and is one of the principal ports of call for the steamers plying up and down the Rhine. Thus the gay city of Mainz was very near, as were the Taunus Baths, patronized by high society—Homburg, Langenschwalbach, and Schlangenbad. The last could be reached in a half-hour trip by narrow-gauge railway. How many summertime excursions we made, my parents, my sister Olympia, and I, by boat, by carriage, or on the train! Enticements lay in every direction, for nature and human ingenuity had everywhere provided charms and delights for our enjoyment. I can still see my father in his comfortable, checked summer suit as we sat in the garden of some inn—a little way back from the table because his paunch prevented him from drawing up close—immersed in his enjoyment of a dish of prawns washed down by golden wine. My godfather Schimmelpreester was often with us, keenly studying people and landscape through his big artist's glasses and absorbing both great and small into his artist's soul.

My poor father owned the firm of Engelbert Krull, makers of the now discontinued brand of champagne *Loreley extra cuvée*. Their cellars lay on the bank of the Rhine not far from the landing, and often as a boy I used to linger in the cool vaults, wandering pensively along the stone-paved passages that led back and forth between the high shelves, examining the array of bottles, which lay on their sides in slanting rows. "There you lie," I thought to myself (though of course at that time I could not give such apt expression to my thoughts), "there you lie in the subterranean twilight, and within you the bubbling golden sap is clearing and maturing, the sap that will enliven so many hearts and awaken a brighter gleam in so many eyes! Now you look plain and unpromising, but one day you will rise to the upper world magnificently adorned, to take your place at feasts, at weddings, to send your corks popping to the ceilings of private dining-rooms and evoke intoxication, irresponsibility, and desire in the hearts of men." So, or approximately so, spoke the boy; and this much at least was true, the firm of Engelbert Krull paid unusual attention to the outside of their bottles, those final adornments that are technically known as the coiffure. The compressed corks were secured with silver wire and gilt cords fastened with purplish-red wax; there was, moreover, an impressive round seal—such as one sees on ecclesiastical bulls and old state documents—suspended from a gold cord; the necks of the bottles were liberally wrapped in gleaming silver foil, and their swelling bellies bore a flaring label with gold flourishes round the edges. This label had been designed for the firm by my godfather Schimmelpreester and bore a number of coats of arms and stars, my father's monogram, the brand name, *Loreley extra cuvée*, all in gold letters, and a female figure arrayed only in bangles and necklaces, sitting with legs crossed on top of a rock, her arm raised in the act of combing her flowing hair. Unfortunately it appears that the quality of the wine was not entirely commensurate with the splendor of its coiffure. "Krull," I have heard my godfather Schimmelpreester say to my father, "with all due respect to you, your champagne ought to be forbidden by law. Last week I let myself be talked into drinking half a bottle, and my system hasn't recovered from the shock yet. What sort of vinegar goes into that brew? And do you use petroleum or fusel oil to doctor it with? The stuff's simply poison. Look out for the police!" At this my poor father would be embarrassed, for he was a gentle man and unable to hold his own against harsh criticism. "It's easy enough for you to laugh, Schimmelpreester," he would reply, gently stroking his belly with his fingertips in his usual fashion, "but I have to keep the price down because there is so much prejudice against the domestic product–in short, I give the public something to increase its confidence. Besides, competition is so fierce, my friend, I'm hardly able to go on." Thus my father.

Our villa was a charming little estate on a gentle slope that commanded a view of the Rhine. The terraced garden was liberally adorned with earthenware gnomes, mushrooms, and all kinds of lifelike animals; on a pedestal stood a mirrored glass sphere, which distorted faces most comically; there were also an æolian harp, several grottoes, and a fountain whose streams made an ingenious figure in the air, while silvery goldfish swam in its basin. As for the interior decoration of our house, it was, in accordance with my father's taste, both cozy and cheerful. Pleasant nooks offered repose, and in one corner stood a real spinning-wheel; there were innumerable knickknacks and decorations–conch shells, glass boxes, and bottles of smelling-salts–which stood about on *étagères* and velvet-covered tables; countless downy cushions covered in embroidered silk were strewn everywhere on sofas and daybeds, for my father loved to have a soft place to lie down; the curtain rods were halberds, and between the rooms were those airy portieres made of bamboo tied with strings of glass beads. They look almost as solid as a door, but one can walk through them without raising a hand, and they part and fall back with a whispering click. Over the outside door was an ingenious mechanism, activated by air pressure as the door closed, which played with a pleasing tinkle the opening bars of Strauss's "*Freut euch des Lebens*."

CHAPTER II

Such was the home in which I was born one mild, rainy day in the merry month of May—a Sunday, to be exact. From now on I mean to follow the order of events conscientiously and to stop anticipating. If reports are true, the birth was slow and difficult and required the assistance of our family doctor, whose name was Mecum. It appears that I—if I may so refer to that far-away and foreign little being—was extremely inactive and made no attempt to aid my mother's efforts, showing no eagerness whatever to enter the world which later I was to love so dearly. Nevertheless, I was a healthy, well-formed child and thrived most promisingly at the breast of my excellent wet-nurse. Frequent reflection on this subject, moreover, inclines me to the belief that this reluctance to exchange the darkness of the womb for the light of day is connected with my extraordinary gift and passion for sleep, a characteristic of mine from infancy. I am told that I was a quiet child, not given to crying or trouble-making, but inclined to sleep and doze to an extent most convenient for my nurses. And despite the fact that later on I had such a longing for the world and its people that I mingled with them under a variety of names and did all I could to win them to myself, yet I feel that in night and slumber I have always been most at home. Even without being physically fatigued I have always been able to fall asleep with the greatest ease and pleasure, to lose myself in far and dreamless forgetfulness, and to awake after ten or twelve or even fourteen hours of oblivion even more refreshed and enlivened than by the successes and accomplishments of my waking hours. There might seem to be a contradiction between this love of sleep and my great impulse toward life and love, about which I intend to speak in due course. As I have already mentioned, however, I have devoted much thought to this matter and I have clearly perceived more than once that there is no contradiction but rather a hidden connection and correspondence. In fact, it is only now, when I have turned forty and have become old and weary, when I no longer feel the old irrepressible urge toward the society of men, but live in complete retirement, it is only now that my capacity for sleep is impaired so that I am in a sense a stranger to it, my slumbers being short and light and fleeting; whereas even in prison—where there was plenty of opportunity—I slept better than in the soft beds of the Palace Hotel. But I am falling again into my old fault of anticipating.

Often enough I heard from my parents' lips that I was a Sunday child, and although I was brought up to reject every form of superstition, I have always thought there was a secret significance in that fact taken in connection with my Christian name of Felix (for so I was called, after my godfather Schimmelpreester), and my physical fineness and attractiveness. Yes, I have always believed myself favoured of fortune and of Heaven, and I may say that, on the whole, experience has borne me out. Indeed, it has been peculiarly characteristic of my career that whatever misfortunes and sufferings it may have contained have always seemed an exception to the natural order, a cloud, as it were, through which the sun of my native luck continued to shine. After this digression into generalities, I shall continue to sketch in broad strokes the picture of my youth.

An imaginative child, my games of make-believe gave my family much entertainment. I have often been told, and seem still to remember, that when I was still in dresses I liked to pretend I was the Kaiser and would persist in this game for hours at a time with the greatest determination. Sitting in my little go-cart, which my nurse would push around the garden or the entrance hall of the house, I would draw down my mouth as far as I could so that my upper lip was unnaturally lengthened and would blink my eyes slowly until the strain and the strength of my emotions made them redden and fill with tears. Overwhelmed by a sense of my age and dignity, I would sit silent in my little wagon, while my nurse was instructed to inform all we met who I was, since I should have taken any disregard of my fancy much amiss. "I am taking the Kaiser for a drive," she would announce, bringing the flat of her hand to the side of her head in an awkward salute, and everyone would pay me homage. In particular, my godfather Schimmelpreester, a great joker, would encourage my pretence for all he was worth whenever we met. "Look, there he goes, the old hero!" he would say with an exaggeratedly deep bow. Then he would pretend to be the populace and, standing beside my path, would shout: "Hurray, hurray!" throwing his hat, his cane, even his eyeglasses into the air, and he would split his sides laughing when, from excess of emotion, tears would roll down my long-drawn face.

I used to play the same sort of game when I was older and could no longer demand the co-operation of grown-ups—which, however, I did not miss, glorying as I did in the independent and self-sufficient exercise of my imagination. One morning, for example, I awoke resolved to be an eighteen-year-old prince named Karl, and I clung to this fantasy all day long; indeed, for several days, for the inestimable advantage of this kind of game is that it never needs to be interrupted, not even during the almost insupportable hours spent in school. Clothed in a sort of amiable majesty, I moved about, holding lively imaginary conversations with the governor or adjutant I had in fantasy assigned to myself; and the pride and happiness I felt at my secret superiority are indescribable. What a glorious gift is imagination, and what satisfactions it affords! The other boys of the town seemed to me dull and limited indeed, since they obviously did not share my ability and were consequently ignorant of the secret joys I could derive from it by a simple act of will, effortlessly and without any outward preparation. They were common fellows, to be sure, with coarse hair and red hands, and they would have had trouble persuading themselves that they were princes—and very foolish they would have looked, too. Whereas my hair was silken soft, as it seldom is in the male sex, and it was fair; like my blue-grey eyes, it provided a fascinating contrast to the golden brown of my skin, so that I hovered on the borderline between blond and dark and might have been considered either. My hands, which I began to take care of early, were distinguished without being too narrow, never clammy, but dry and agreeably warm, with well-shaped nails that it was a pleasure to see. My voice, even before it changed, had an ingratiating tone and could fall so flatteringly upon the ear that I liked more than anything to listen to it myself, especially when I was alone and could blissfully engage in long, plausible, but quite meaningless conversations with my imaginary adjutant, accompanying them with extravagant gestures. Such personal advantages are mostly intangible and are recognizable only in their effect; they are, moreover, difficult to put into words, even for someone unusually talented. In any case, I could not conceal from myself that I was made of superior stuff, or, as people say, of finer clay, and I do not shrink from the charge of self-complacency in saying so. If someone accuses me of self-complacency, it is a matter of complete indifference to me, for I should have to be a fool or a hypocrite to pretend that I am of common stuff, and it is therefore in obedience to truth that I repeat that I am of the finest clay.

I grew up solitary, for my sister Olympia was several years older than I; I indulged in strange, introspective practices, of which I shall give two examples. First, I took it into my head to study the human will and to practise on myself its mysterious, sometimes supernatural effects. It is a well-known fact that the muscles controlling the pupils of our eyes react involuntarily to the intensity of the light falling upon them. I decided to bring this reaction under voluntary control. I would stand in front of my mirror, concentrating all my powers in a command to my pupils to contract or expand, banishing every other thought from my mind. My persistent efforts, let me assure you, were, in fact, crowned with success. At first as I stood bathed in sweat, my colour coming and going, my pupils would flicker erratically; but later I actually succeeded in contracting them to the merest points and then expanding them to great, round, mirror-like pools. The joy I felt at this success was almost terrifying and was accompanied by a shudder at the mystery of man.

There was another interior activity that often occupied me at that time and that even today has not lost its charm for me. I would ask myself: which is better, to see the world small or to see it big? The significance of the question was this: great men, I thought, field marshals, statesmen, empire-builders, and other leaders who rise through violence above the masses of mankind must be so constituted as to see the world small, like a chessboard, or they would never possess the ruthless coldness to deal so boldly and cavalierly with the weal and woe of the individual. Yet it was quite possible, on the other hand, that such a diminishing point of view, so to speak, might lead to one's doing nothing at all. For if you saw the world and the human beings in it as small and insignificant and were early persuaded that nothing was worth while, you could easily sink into indifference and indolence and contemptuously prefer your own peace of mind to any influence you might exert on the spirits of men. Added to that, your coldness and detachment would certainly give offence and cut you off from any possible success you might have achieved involuntarily. Is it preferable, then, I would ask myself, to regard the world and mankind as something great, glorious, and significant, justifying every effort to obtain some modicum of esteem and fame? Against this one might argue that with so magnifying and respectful a view one can easily fall a victim to self-depreciation and loss of confidence, so that the world passes you by as an uncertain, silly boy and gives itself to a more manly lover. On the other hand, such genuine credulity and artlessness has its advantages too, since men cannot but be flattered by the way you look up to them; and if you devote yourself to making this impression, it will give weight and seriousness to your life, lending it meaning in your own eyes and leading to your advancement. In this way I pondered, weighing the pros and cons. It has always been a part of my nature, however, to hold instinctively to the second position, considering the world a great and infinitely enticing phenomenon, offering priceless satisfactions and worthy in the highest degree of all my efforts and solicitude.

CHAPTER III

Visionary experiments and speculations of this kind served to isolate me inwardly from my contemporaries and schoolmates in the town, who spent their time in more conventional ways. But it is also true, as I was soon to learn, that these boys, the sons of winegrowers and government employees, had been warned by their parents to stay away from me. Indeed, when I experimentally invited one of them to our house, he told me to my face that he couldn't come because our family was not respectable. This pained me and made me covet an association that otherwise I should not have cared for. It must be admitted, however, that the town's opinion of our household had a certain justification.

I referred above to the disturbance in our family life caused by the presence of the Fräulein from Vevey. My poor father, in point of fact, was infatuated with the girl and pursued her until he gained his ends, or so it appeared, for quarrels arose between him and my mother and he left for Mainz, where he remained for several weeks enjoying a bachelor's life, as he had occasionally done before. My mother was entirely wrong in treating my poor father with such lack of respect. She was an unprepossessing woman and no less a prey to human weaknesses than he. My sister Olympia, a fat and inordinately sensual creature, who later had some success in comic opera, resembled her in this respect—the difference between them and my poor father being that theirs was a coarse-grained greed for pleasure, whereas his foibles were never without a certain grace. Mother and daughter lived on terms of unusual intimacy: I recall once seeing my mother measure Olympia's thigh with a tape measure, which gave me food for thought for several hours. Another time, when I was old enough to have some intuitive understanding of such matters though no words to express them, I was an unseen witness when my mother and sister together began to flirt with a young painter who was at work in the house. He was a dark-eyed youth in a white smock, and they painted a green moustache on his face with his own paint. In the end they roused him to such a pitch that he pursued them giggling up the attic stairs.

Since my parents bored each other to distraction, they often invited guests from Mainz and Wiesbaden, and then our house was the scene of merriment and uproar. It was a gaudy crowd who attended these gatherings: actors and actresses, young businessmen, a sickly young infantry lieutenant who was later engaged to my sister; a Jewish banker with a wife who awesomely overflowed her jet-embroidered dress in every direction; a journalist in velvet waistcoat with a lock of hair over his brow, who brought a new helpmeet along every time. They would usually arrive for seven-o'clock dinner and the feasting, dancing, piano-playing, rough-housing, and shrieks of laughter went on all night. The tide of pleasure rose especially high at carnival time and at the vintage season. My father, who was very expert in such matters, would set off the most splendid fireworks in the garden; the whole company would wear masks and unearthly light would play upon the earthenware dwarfs. All restraint was abandoned. It was my misfortune at that time to have to attend the local high school and many mornings when I came down to the dining-room for breakfast, face freshly washed, at seven o'clock or half past, I would find the guests still sitting over coffee and liqueurs, sallow, rumpled, and blinking in the early light. They would give me an uproarious welcome.

When I was no more than half grown I was allowed, along with my sister Olympia, to take part in these festivities. Even when we were alone we always kept a good table, and my father drank champagne mixed with soda water. But at these parties there were endless courses prepared by a chef from

Wiesbaden assisted by our own cook: the most tempting succession of sweets, savories, and ices; *Loreley extra cuvée* flowed in streams, but many good wines were served as well. There was for instance Berncasteler Doctor, whose bouquet especially appealed to me. In later life I became acquainted with still other notable brands and could, for instance, casually order *Grand Vin* Château Margaux or *Grand Cru* Château Mouton-Rothschild–two noble wines.

I love to recall the picture of my father presiding at the head of the table, with his white pointed beard, and his paunch spanned by a white silk waistcoat. His voice was weak and sometimes he would let his eyes drop in a self-conscious way, and yet enjoyment was written large on his flushed and shining face. "*C'est ça,*" he would say, "*épatant,*" "*parfaitement*"– and with his fingers, which curved backwards at the tips, he would give delicate touches to the glasses, the napkins, and the silver. My mother and sister would surrender themselves to mindless gluttony interrupted only by giggling flirtations behind their fans with their tablemates.

After dinner, when cigar smoke began to eddy around the gas chandeliers, there were dancing and games of forfeit. As the evening advanced I used to be sent to bed; but since sleep was impossible in that din, I would wrap myself in my red woollen bedspread and in this becoming costume return to the feast, where I was received by all the ladies with cries of joy. Snacks and refreshments, punch, lemonade, herring salad, and wine jellies were served in relays until the morning coffee. Dancing was unconstrained and the games of forfeit became a pretext for kissing and fondling. The ladies, décolleté, bent low over the backs of chairs to give the gentlemen exciting glimpses of their bosoms, and the high point of the evening would come when some prankster turned out the gaslight amid general uproar and confusion.

It was mostly these social affairs that provoked the town gossip that called our household disreputable, but I learned early that it was the economic aspect of the situation that was principally in question. For it was rumoured (and with only too much justification) that my poor father's business was in desperate straits, and that the expensive fireworks and dinners would inevitably furnish the *coup de grâce*. My sensitivity early made me aware of this general distrust, and it combined, as I have said, with certain peculiarities of my character to cause me first and last a good deal of pain. It was therefore all the more delightful to have the experience that I now set down with special pleasure.

The summer that I was eight years old my family and I went to spend several weeks at the famous near-by resort of Langenschwalbach. My father was taking mud baths for his gout, and my mother and sister made themselves conspicuous on the promenade by the exaggerated size of their hats. There as elsewhere our opportunities for social advancement were meagre. The natives, as usual, avoided us. Guests of the better class kept themselves very much to themselves as they usually do; and such society as we met did not have much to recommend it. Yet I liked Langenschwalbach and later on often made such resorts the scene of my activities. The tranquil, well-regulated existence and the sight of aristocratic, well-groomed people in the gardens or at sport satisfied an inner craving. But the strongest attraction of all was the daily concert given by a well-trained orchestra for the guests of the cure. Though I have never taken occasion to acquire any skill in that dreamlike art, I am a fanatical lover of music; even as a child I could not tear myself away from the pretty pavilion where a becomingly uniformed band played selections and potpourris under the direction of a leader who looked like a gypsy. For hours on end I would crouch on the steps of this little temple of art, enchanted to the marrow of my bones by the ordered succession of sweet sounds and watching with rapture every motion of the musicians as they manipulated their instruments. In particular I was thrilled by the gestures of the violinists, and when I went home I delighted my parents with an imitation performed with two sticks, one long and one short. The swinging movement of the left arm when producing a soulful tone, the soft gliding motion from one position to the next, the dexterity of the fingering in virtuoso passages and cadenzas, the fine and supple bowing of the right wrist, the cheek nestling in utter abandonment on the violin—all this I succeeded in reproducing so faithfully that the family, and especially my father, burst into enthusiastic applause. Being in high spirits because of the beneficial effects of the baths, he conceived the following little joke with the connivance of the long-haired, almost inarticulate little conductor. They bought a small, cheap violin and plentifully greased the bow with Vaseline. As a rule little attention was paid to my appearance, but now I was dressed in a pretty sailor suit complete with gold buttons and lanyard, silk stockings and shiny patent-leather shoes. And one Sunday afternoon at the hour of the promenade I took my place beside the little conductor and joined in the performance of a Hungarian dance, doing with my fiddle and Vaselined bow what I had done before with my two sticks. I make bold to say my success was complete.

The public, both distinguished and undistinguished, streamed up from all sides and crowded in front of the pavilion to look at the infant prodigy. My pale face, my complete absorption in my task, the lock of hair falling over my brow, my childish hands and wrists in the full, tapering sleeves of the becoming blue sailor suit—in short, my whole touching and astonishing little figure captivated all hearts. When I finished with the full sweep of the bow across all the fiddle strings, the garden resounded with applause and delighted cries from male and female throats. After the bandmaster had safely got my fiddle and bow out of the way, I was picked up and set down on the ground, where I was overwhelmed with praises and caresses. The most aristocratic ladies and gentlemen stroked my hair, patted my cheeks and hands, called me an angel child and an amazing little devil. An aged Russian princess, wearing enormous white side curls and dressed from head to toe in violet silk, took my head between her beringed hands and kissed my brow, beaded as it was with perspiration. Then in a burst of enthusiasm she snatched a lyre-shaped diamond brooch from her throat and pinned it on my blouse, amid a perfect torrent of ecstatic French. My family approached and my father made excuses for the defects of my playing on the score of my tender years. I was taken to the confectioner's, where at three different tables I was treated to chocolate and cream puffs. The children of the noble family of Siebenklingen, whom I had admired from a distance while they regarded me with haughty aloofness, came up and asked me to play croquet, and while our parents drank coffee together I went off with them in the seventh heaven of delight, my diamond brooch still on my blouse. That was one of the happiest days of my life, perhaps the happiest. A cry was raised that I should play again, and the management of the casino actually approached my father and asked for a repeat performance, but he refused, saying that he had only permitted me to play by way of exception and that repeated public appearances would not be consistent with my social position. Besides, our stay in Bad Langenschwalbach was drawing to a close. . . .

CHAPTER IV

I will now speak of my godfather Schimmelpreester, who was by no means an ordinary man. In build he was short and thick-set. He had thin, prematurely grey hair, which he wore parted over one ear so that almost all of it was brushed across the crown. He was clean-shaven, with a hook nose and thin, compressed lips, and he wore large round glasses in celluloid frames. His face was further remarkable for the fact that it was bare above the eyes; that is, there were no eyebrows; his whole appearance gave the impression of a sharp and bitter turn of mind; there was proof of this in the splenetic interpretation he used to give to his own name. "Nature," he would say, "is nothing but mould and corruption, and I am her high priest. The high priest of mould, that's the real meaning of Schimmelpreester. But why I am called Felix, God only knows." He came from Cologne, where he had once moved in the best circles and had served as carnival steward. But for reasons that remained obscure he had been obliged to leave the place; he had gone into retirement in our little town, where very soon—a number of years before I was born—he became a family friend of my parents. At all our evening gatherings he was a regular and indispensable guest, in high favour with young and old. When he tightened his lips and fixed the ladies with appraising eyes, through his round eyeglasses, they would scream and raise their arms for protection. "Ooh, the painter!" they would cry. "What eyes he has! Now he is looking straight through us, right into our hearts. Mercy, Professor, please take your eyes away!" But however much he was admired, he himself had no very high regard for his calling and often made highly ambiguous remarks about the nature of artists. "Phidias," he used to say, "also called Pheidias, was a man of more than ordinary gifts, as may perhaps be gathered from the fact that he was convicted and put in jail for embezzling the gold and ivory entrusted to him for his statue of Athena. Pericles, who found him out, allowed him to escape from prison, thereby proving himself not only an expert in art but, what is more important, an expert in understanding the nature of the artist, and Phidias or Pheidias went to Olympia, where he was commissioned to make the great gold-and-ivory Zeus. And what did he do? He stole again. And imprisoned in Olympia he died. A striking combination. But that is the way people are. They want talent, which is in itself something out of the ordinary. But when it comes to the other oddities that are always associated with it, and perhaps are essential to it, they will have none of them and refuse them all understanding." Thus my godfather. I have been able to recall his comments verbatim, because he repeated them so often and always with the same turns of phrase.

As I have said, we lived on terms of mutual affection; indeed, I believe that I enjoyed his special favour, and often as I grew older it was my particular delight to act as his model, dressing up in all sorts of costumes, of which he had a large and varied collection. His studio was a sort of storeroom with a large window, under the roof of a little house that stood by itself on the bank of the Rhine. He rented this house and lived in it with an old serving-woman, and there on a rude, homemade dais I would sit to him, as he called it, for hours on end while he brushed and scraped and painted away. Several times I posed in the nude for a large picture out of Greek mythology that was to adorn the dining-room of a wine-dealer in Mainz. When I did this my godfather was lavish in his praises; and indeed I was a little like a young god, slender, graceful, yet powerful in build, with a golden skin and flawless proportions. These sittings still constitute a unique memory. Yet I enjoyed even more, I think, the "dressing up" itself; and that took place not only in the studio but at our house as well. Often when my godfather was to dine with us he would send up a large bundle of costumes, wigs, and accessories and try them all on me after the meal, sketching any particularly good effect on the lid of a cardboard box. "He's a natural costume boy," he would say, meaning that everything became me, and that in each disguise I assumed I looked better and more natural than in the last. I might appear as a Roman flute-player in a short tunic, a wreath of roses twined in my curly locks; as an English page in snug-fitting satin with lace collar and plumed hat; as a Spanish bullfighter in spangled jacket and broad-brimmed hat; as a youthful abbé at the time of powdered white wigs, with cap and bands, mantle and buckled shoes; as an Austrian officer in white military tunic with sash and dagger; or as a German mountaineer in leather breeches and hobnailed boots, with a tuft of goat's hair in my green felt hat—whatever the costume, the mirror assured me that I was born to wear it, and my audience declared that I looked to the life exactly the person whom I aimed to represent. My godfather even asserted that with the aid of costume and wig I seemed not only able to put on whatever social rank or personal characteristics I chose, but could actually adapt myself to any given period or century. For each age, my godfather would say, imparts to its children its own facial stamp; whereas I, in the costume of a Florentine dandy of the late Middle Ages, would look as though I had stepped out of a contemporary portrait, and yet be no less convincing in the full-bottomed wig that was the fashionable ideal of a later century. Ah, those were glorious hours! But when they were over and I resumed my ordinary dull dress, how indescribably boring seemed all the world by contrast, in what depths of dejection did I spend the rest of the evening!

Of Schimmelpreester I shall say no more in this place. Later on, at the end of my exacting career, he was to intervene in my destiny decisively and providentially. . . .

CHAPTER V

As I search my mind for further impressions of my youth, I am at once reminded of the day when I first attended the theatre, in Wiesbaden, with my parents. I should mention here that in my description of my youth I am not adhering to strict chronological order, but am treating my younger days as a whole and moving freely from incident to incident. When I posed for my godfather as a Greek god I was between sixteen and eighteen years of age and thus no longer a child, though very backward at school. But my first visit to the theatre fell in my fourteenth year—though even so my physical and mental development, as will presently be seen, was well advanced and my receptivity to impressions of certain kinds much greater than ordinary. What I saw that evening made the strongest impression on me and gave me endless food for thought.

We first visited a Viennese café, where I drank a cup of punch and my father imbibed absinthe through a straw—this in itself was calculated to stir me to the depths. But how can one describe the fever that possessed me when we drove in a cab to the theatre and entered the lighted auditorium with its tiers of boxes? The women fanning their bosoms in the balconies, the men leaning over their chairs to chat; the hum and buzz of conversation in the orchestra, where we presently took our seats; the odours which streamed from hair and clothing to mingle with that of the illuminating-gas; the confusion of sounds as the orchestra tuned up; the voluptuous frescoes that depicted whole cascades of rosy, foreshortened nymphs—certainly all this could not but rouse my youthful senses and prepare my mind for all the extraordinary scenes to come.

Never before except in church had I seen so many people gathered together in a large and stately auditorium; and this theatre with its impressive seating-arrangements and its elevated stage where privileged personages, brilliantly costumed and accompanied by music, went through their dialogues and dances, their songs and routines—certainly all this was in my eyes a temple of pleasure, where men in need of edification gathered in darkness and gazed upward open-mouthed into a realm of brightness and perfection where they beheld their hearts' desire.

The play that was being given was unpretentious, a work of the loose-zoned muse, as people say. It was an operetta whose name I have, to my sorrow, forgotten. Its scene was Paris, which delighted my poor father's heart, and its central figure was an idle attaché, a fascinating rogue and lady-killer, played by that star of the theatre, the well-loved singer Müller-Rosé. I heard his real name from my father, who enjoyed his personal acquaintance, and the picture of this man will remain forever in my memory. He is probably old and worn-out by now, like me, but at that time his power dazzled all the world, myself included; it made so strong an impression upon me that it belongs to the decisive experiences of my life. I say dazzled, and it will be seen hereafter how much meaning I wish to convey by that word. But first I must try to set down my still vivid recollections of Müller-Rosé's effect on me.

On his first entrance he was dressed in black, and yet he radiated sheer brilliance. In the play he was supposed to be coming from some meeting-place of the gay world and to be slightly intoxicated, a state he was able to counterfeit in agreeable and sublimated fashion. He wore a black cloak with a satin lining, patent-leather shoes, evening dress, white kid gloves, and a top hat; his hair was parted all the way to the back of his head in accordance with the military fashion of the day. Every article of his attire was so well pressed, and fitted with such flawless perfection, that it could not have lasted more than a quarter-hour in real life. He seemed, indeed, not to belong to this world. In particular his top hat, which he wore nonchalantly tipped forward over his brow, was the ideal and model of what a top hat should be, without a particle of dust or roughness and with the most beautiful reflections, just as in a picture. And this higher being had a face to match, rosy, fine as wax, with almond-shaped, black-rimmed eyes, a small, short, straight nose, a perfectly clear-cut, coral-red mouth, and a little black moustache as even as if it had been drawn with a paintbrush, following the outline of his arched upper lip. Staggering with a fluid grace such as drunken men do not possess in everyday life, he handed his hat and stick to an attendant, slipped out of his cloak, and stood there in full evening dress, with diamond studs in his thickly pleated shirt front. As he drew off his gloves, laughing and chatting in a silvery voice, you could see that the backs of his hands were white as milk and adorned with diamond rings, but that the palms were as pink as his face. He stood before the footlights on one side of the stage and sang the first stanza of a song about what a wonderful life it was to be an attaché and a ladies' man. Then he spread out his arms, snapped his fingers, and drifted delightedly to the other side of the stage, where he sang the second stanza and made his exit, only to be recalled by loud applause. The third stanza he sang in midstage in front of the prompter's box. Then with careless grace he plunged into the action of the play. He was supposed to be very rich, which in itself lent his figure a magical charm. He appeared in a succession of costumes: snow-white sports clothes with a red belt; a full-dress, fancy uniform—yes, at one ticklish and sidesplitting moment in sky-blue silk drawers. The complications of the plot were audacious, adventurous, and risqué by turns. One saw him at the feet of a countess, at a champagne supper with two ambitious daughters of joy, and standing with raised pistol confronting a dull-witted rival in a duel. And not one of these elegant but strenuous exercises was able to disarrange a single fold of his shirt front, extinguish any of the reflections in his top hat, or overheat his rosy countenance. He moved so easily within the frame of the musical and dramatic conventions that they seemed, far from restricting him, to release him from the limitations of everyday life. His body seemed informed to the fingertips with a magic for which we have only the vague and inadequate word "talent," and which obviously gave him as much pleasure as it did us. To watch him take hold of the silver head of his cane or plunge both hands in his trouser pockets was a spontaneous delight; the way he rose from a chair, bowed, made his exits and entrances, possessed such delightful self-assurance that it filled one's heart with the joy of life. Yes, that was it: Müller-Rosé dispensed the joy of life—if that phrase can be used to describe the precious and painful feeling, compounded of envy, yearning, hope, and love, that the sight of beauty and lighthearted perfection kindles in the souls of men.

The audience in the orchestra was made up of middle-class citizens and their wives, clerks, one-year servicemen, and girls in blouses; and despite the rapture of my own sensations I had presence of mind and curiosity enough to look about me and interpret their feelings. The expression on their faces was both silly and blissful. They were wrapped in self-forgetful absorption, a smile played about their lips, sweeter and more lively in the little shopgirls, more brooding and thoughtful in the grown-up women, while the faces of the men expressed that benevolent admiration which plain fathers feel in the presence of sons who have exceeded them and realized the dreams of their youth. As for the clerks and the young soldiers, everything stood wide open in their upturned faces—eyes, mouths, nostrils, everything. And at the same time they were smiling. Suppose we were up there in our underdrawers, how should we be making out? And look how boldly he behaves with those ambitious tarts, as though he had been dealing with them all his life! When Müller-Rosé left the stage, shoulders slumped and virtue seemed to go out of the audience. When he strode triumphantly from backstage to footlights, on a sustained note, his arms outspread, bosoms rose as though to meet him, and satin bodices strained at the seams. Yes, this whole shadowy assembly was like an enormous swarm of nocturnal insects, silently, blindly, and blissfully rushing into a blazing fire.

My father enjoyed himself royally. He had followed the French custom and brought his hat and stick into the theatre with him. When the curtain fell he put on the one and with the other pounded long and loud on the floor. "*C'est épatant*," he repeated several times, quite weak from enthusiasm. But when it was all over and we were outside in the lobby among a crowd of exalted clerks, who were quite obviously trying to imitate their hero in the way they walked, talked, held their canes, and regarded their reddened hands, my father said to me: "Come along, let's shake hands with him. By God, weren't we on intimate terms, Müller and I! He will be *enchanté* to see me again." And after instructing the ladies to wait for us in the vestibule, we actually went off to hunt up Müller-Rosé.

Our way lay through the darkened director's box beside the stage and then through a narrow iron door into the wings. The half-darkened stage was animated by the eerie activity of scene-shifting. A girl in red livery, who had played the role of a liftboy, was leaning against the wall sunk in thought. My poor father pinched her playfully where her figure was at its broadest and asked her the way to the dressing-rooms, which she irritably pointed out. We went through a whitewashed corridor, where naked gas-jets flared in the confined air. From behind several doors came loud laughter and angry voices, and my father gestured with his thumb to call my attention to these manifestations. At the end of the narrow passage he knocked on the last door, pressing his ear to it as he did so. From within came a gruff shout: "Who's there?" or "What the devil?" I no longer remember the words spoken in that clear, rude voice. "May I come in?" asked my father, whereupon he was instructed to do something quite different, which I must not mention in these pages. My father smiled his deprecatory smile and called through the door: "Müller, it's

Krull, Engelbert Krull. I suppose I may shake your hand after all these years?" There was a laugh from inside and the voice said: "Oh, so it's you, you old rooster! Always out for a good time, eh?" And as he opened the door he went on: "I don't imagine my nakedness will do you any harm!" We went in. I shall never forget the disgusting sight that met my boyish eyes.

Müller-Rosé was seated at a grubby dressing-table in front of a dusty, speckled mirror. He had nothing on but a pair of gray cotton drawers, and a man in shirt sleeves was massaging his back, the sweat running down his own face. Meanwhile the actor was busy wiping face and neck with a towel already stiff with rouge and greasepaint. Half of his countenance still had the rosy coating that had made him radiant on the stage but now looked merely pink and silly in contrast to the cheese-like pallor of his natural complexion. He had taken off the chestnut wig and I saw that his own hair was red. One of his eyes still had deep black shadows beneath it and metallic dust clung to the lashes; the other was inflamed and watery and squinted at us impudently. All this I might have borne. But not the pustules with which Müller-Rosé's back, chest, shoulders, and upper arms were thickly covered. They were horrible pustules, red-rimmed, suppurating, some of them even bleeding; even today I cannot repress a shudder at the thought of them. Our capacity for disgust, let me observe, is in proportion to our desires; that is, in proportion to the intensity of our attachment to the things of this world. A cool indifferent nature would never have been shaken by disgust to the extent that I was then. As a final touch, the air in the room, which was overheated by an iron stove, was compounded of the smell of sweat and the exhalations from the pots and jars and sticks of greasepaint that littered the table, so that at first I thought I could not stand it for more than a minute without being sick.

However, I did stand it and looked about—but I can add nothing to this description of Müller-Rosé's dressing-room. Indeed, I should perhaps be ashamed at reporting so little and at such length about my first visit to a theatre, if I were not writing primarily for my own amusement and only secondarily for the public. It is not my intention to maintain dramatic suspense; I leave such effects to the writers of imaginative fictions, who are intent on giving their stories the beautiful and symmetrical proportions of works of art—whereas my material comes from my own experience alone and I feel I may make what use of it I think best. Thus I shall dwell on those experiences and encounters that brought me particular understanding and illumination about the world and myself, passing by more quickly what is less precious to me.

I have almost forgotten what Müller-Rosé and my poor father chatted about—no doubt because I had no time to pay attention. For it is undoubtedly true that we receive stronger impressions through the senses than through words. I recall that the singer—though surely the applause that had greeted him that evening must have reassured him about his triumph—kept asking my father whether he had made a hit and how much of a hit he had made. How well I understood his uneasiness! I even have a vague memory of some rather vulgar witticisms he injected into the conversation. To some gloating comment of my father's, for example, he replied: "Shut your trap—" adding at once: "or you'll fall through it." But I lent only half an ear, as I have said, to this and other examples of his mental accomplishments, being completely absorbed in my own sense impressions.

This, then—such was the tenor of my thoughts—this grease-smeared and pimply individual is the charmer at whom the twilight crowd was just now gazing so soulfully! This repulsive worm is the reality of the glorious butterfly in whom those deluded spectators believed they were beholding the realization of all their own secret dreams of beauty, grace, and perfection! Is he not like one of those repellent little creatures that have the power of glowing phosphorescently at night? But the grown-up people in the audience, who on the whole must know about life, and who yet were so frightfully eager to be deceived, must they not have been aware of the deception? Or did they privately not consider it one? And that is quite possible. For when you come to think of it, which is the real shape of the glowworm: the insignificant little creature crawling about on the palm of your hand, or the poetic spark that swims through the summer night? Who would presume to say? Rather recall the picture you saw before: the giant swarm of poor moths and gnats, rushing silently and madly into the enticing flame! What unanimity in agreeing to let oneself be deceived! Here quite clearly there is in operation a general human need, implanted by God Himself in human nature, which Müller-Rosé's abilities are created to satisfy. This beyond doubt is an indispensable device in life's economy, which this man is kept and paid to serve. What admiration he deserves for his success tonight and obviously every night! Restrain your disgust and consider that, in full knowledge and realization of his frightful pustules, he was yet able—with the help of greasepaint, lighting, music, and distance—to move before his audience with such assurance as to make them see in him their hearts' ideal and thereby to enliven and edify them infinitely.

Consider further and ask yourself what it was that impelled this miserable mountebank to learn the art of transfiguring himself every night. What are the secret sources of the charm that possessed him and informed him to the fingertips? To learn the answer, you have but to recall (for you know it well!) the ineffable power, which there are no words monstrously sweet enough to describe, that teaches the firefly to glow. Remind yourself how this man could not hear often enough or emphatically enough the assurance that he had truly given pleasure, pleasure altogether out of the ordinary. It was the devotion and drive of his heart toward that yearning crowd that made him skilful in his art; and if he bestows on them the joy of life and they satiate him with their applause for doing so, is not that a mutual fulfilment, a meeting and marriage of his yearning and theirs?

CHAPTER VI

The above lines indicate the general tenor of my hot and excited thoughts as I sat in Müller-Rosé's dressing-room, and again and again in the following days and weeks they returned to this subject with trance-like persistence. It was a subject that always aroused emotions so profound and shattering, such a drunkenness of yearning, hope, and joy, that even today, despite my weariness, the mere memory makes my heart beat faster. In those days my feelings were of such violence that they threatened to burst my frame; indeed, they often actually made me ill and thus served as an excuse for my staying away from school.

I consider it superfluous to dwell on the reasons for my increasing detestation of that malignant institution. I am only able to live in conditions that leave my spirit and imagination completely free; and so it is that the memory of my years in prison is actually less hateful to me than the recollection of the slavery and fear to which my sensitive boyish soul was subjected through the ostensibly honourable discipline in the small square white schoolhouse down there in the town. Add to this the feeling of isolation, the sources of which I have indicated, and it is not surprising that I soon hit on the idea of escaping from school more often than on Sundays and holidays.

In carrying out this idea I was helped a good deal by a playful diversion I had long indulged in—the imitation of my father's handwriting. A father is the natural and nearest model for the growing boy who is striving to adapt himself to the adult world. Similarity of physique and the mystery of their relationship incline the boy to admire in his parent's conduct all that he himself is still incapable of and to strive to imitate it—or rather it is, perhaps, his very admiration that unconsciously leads him to develop along the lines heredity has laid down. Even when I was still making great hens' tracks on my lined slate, I already dreamed of guiding a steel pen with my father's swiftness and sureness; and many were the pages I covered later with efforts to copy his hand from memory, my fingers grasping the pen in the same delicate fashion as his. His writing was not, in fact, hard to imitate, for my poor father wrote a childish, copybook hand, quite undeveloped, its only peculiarity being that the letters were very tiny and separated by long hairlines to an extent I have never seen anywhere else. This mannerism I quickly mastered to perfection. As for the signature "E. Krull," in contrast to the angular Gothic letters of the text, it had a Latin cast. It was surrounded by a perfect cloud of flourishes, which at first sight looked difficult to copy, but were in reality so simple in conception that with them I succeeded best of all. The lower half of the *E* made a wide sweep to the right, in whose ample lap, so to speak, the short syllable of the last name was neatly cradled. A second flourish arose from the *u*, embracing everything before it, cutting the curve of the *E* in two places and ending in an s-shaped downstroke flanked like the curve of the *E* with ornamental rows of dots. The whole signature was higher than it was long, it was naïve and baroque; thus it lent itself so well to my purpose that in the end its inventor would have certified my product as his own. But what was more obvious, once I had acquired this skill for my own entertainment, than to put it to work in the interests of my intellectual freedom? "On the 7th instant," I wrote, "my son Felix was afflicted by severe stomach cramps which compelled him to stay away from school, to the regret of yours—E. Krull." And again: "An infected gumboil, together with a sprained right arm, compelled Felix to keep his room from the 10th to the 14th of this month. Therefore, much to our regret, he was unable to attend school. Respectfully yours—E. Krull." When this succeeded, nothing prevented me from spending the school hours of one day or even of several wandering freely outside the town or lying stretched out in a green field, in the whispering shade of the leaves, dreaming the dreams of youth. Sometimes I hid in the ruins of the old episcopal palace on the Rhine; sometimes, even, in stormy winter weather, in the hospitable studio of my godfather Schimmelpreester, who rebuked me for my conduct in tones that showed he was not without a certain sympathy for my motives.

Now and again, however, I stayed at home in bed on school days—and not always, as I have explained, without justification. It is a favourite theory of mine that every deception which fails to have a higher truth at its root and is simply a barefaced lie is by that very fact so grossly palpable that nobody can fail to see through it. Only one kind of lie has a chance of being effective: that which in no way deserves to be called deceit, but is the product of a lively imagination which has not yet entered wholly into the realm of the actual and acquired those tangible signs by which alone it can be appraised at its proper worth. Although it is true that I was a sturdy boy, who, except for the usual childish ailments, never had anything serious the matter with him, it was nevertheless not a gross deception when I decided one morning to avoid the painful oppressions of school by becoming an invalid. For why should I subject myself to such treatment when I had at hand the means of neutralizing the cruel power of my intellectual lords and masters? No, the painfully intense excitement and exaltation which, as I have explained, accompanied certain states of mind used often to overwhelm me to such an extent as to produce, in combination with my abhorrence of the misunderstandings and drudgery of a day in school, a condition that created a solid basis of truth for my behaviour. I was effortlessly provided with the means of gaining the sympathy and concern of the doctor and of my family.

I did not at first produce my symptoms for an audience, but for myself alone. On a certain day when my need for freedom and the possession of my own soul had become overpowering, my decision was taken and became irrevocable through the simple passage of time. The latest possible hour for rising had been passed in brooding; downstairs breakfast had been put on the table by the maid and was growing cold; all the dull fellows in town were trudging off to school; daily life had begun, and I was irretrievably committed to a course of rebellion against my taskmasters. The audacity of my conduct made my heart flutter and my stomach turn over. I noted that my fingernails had taken on a bluish tint. The morning was cold and all I needed to do was to throw off the covers for a few moments and lie relaxed in order to bring on a most convincing attack of chills and chattering teeth. All that I am saying is, of course, highly indicative of my character. I have always been very sensitive, susceptible, and in need of care; and everything I have accomplished in my active life has been the result of self-conquest—indeed, must be regarded as a moral achievement of a high order. If it were otherwise I should never, either then or later, merely by willing my mind and body to relax, have succeeded in producing the appearance of physical illness and thus inclining those about me to tenderness and concern. To counterfeit illness effectively could never be within the powers of a coarse-grained man. But anyone of finer stuff, if I may repeat the phrase, is always, though he may never be ill in the crude sense of the word, on familiar terms with suffering and able to control its symptoms by intuition. I closed my eyes and then opened them to their widest extent, making them look appealing and plaintive. I knew without a mirror that my hair was rumpled from sleep and fell in damp strands across my brow, and that my face was pale. I made it look sunken by a device of my own, drawing in my cheeks and unobtrusively holding them in with my teeth. This made my chin appear longer, too, and gave me the appearance of having grown thin overnight. A dilation of the nostrils and an almost painful twitching of the muscles at the corners of the eyes contributed to this effect. I put my basin on a chair beside my bed, folded my blue-nailed fingers across my breast, made my teeth chatter from time to time, and thus awaited the moment when somebody would come to look for me.

That happened rather late, for my parents loved to lie abed, and so two or three school hours had passed before it was noticed that I was still in the house. Then my mother came upstairs and into the room to ask if I was ill. I looked at her wide-eyed, as though in my dazed condition it was hard for me to tell who she was. Then I said yes, I thought I must be ill. What was the trouble then, she asked. "My head . . . Pains in my bones . . . And why am I so cold!" I answered in a monotonous voice, speaking with an effort and tossing myself from side to side in the bed. My mother was sympathetic. I do not believe she took my sufferings very seriously, but her sensibilities were far in excess of her reason and she could not bring herself to spoil the game. Instead, she joined in and began to support me in my performance. "Poor child," she said, laying her forefinger on my cheek and shaking her head in pity, "don't you want something to eat?" I declined with a shudder, pressing my chin on my chest. This strict consistency in my behaviour sobered her, made her seriously concerned, and, so to speak, startled her out of her enjoyment in our joint game; that anyone should refuse food and drink for frivolous reasons went quite beyond her powers of imagination. She looked at me with a growing sense of reality. When she had got this far I helped her to a decision by a display of art as arduous as it was effective. Starting up in bed with a fitful, shuddering motion, I drew my basin toward me and bent over it with spasmodic twitchings and contortions of my whole body, such as no one could witness without profound emotion unless he had a heart of stone. "Nothing in me . . ." I gasped between my writhings, lifting my wry and wasted face from the basin. "Threw it all up in the night. . . ." And then I launched upon my main effort, a prolonged attack of cramps and retching which made it seem that I would never breathe again. My mother held my head, repeatedly calling me by name in an effort to bring me to myself. By the time my limbs finally began to relax she was quite overcome and, exclaiming: "I'll send for Düsing!" she rushed out of the room. I sank back among the pillows exhausted but full of indescribable joy and satisfaction.

How often I had imagined such a scene, how often I had practised it in my mind before I caused it to become a reality! I don't know whether people will understand if I say that I seemed to be in a happy dream when I first gave it concrete expression and achieved complete success. Not everyone can do such a thing. One may dream of it, but not do it. Suppose, a man thinks, something awful were to happen to me: suppose I were to faint or blood were to gush out of my nose, or I were to have some kind of seizure—then how quickly the world's harsh unconcern would turn into attention, sympathy, and belated remorse! But the flesh is obtusely strong and enduring, it holds out long after the mind has felt the necessity of sympathy and care; it will not manifest the alarming tangible symptoms that would make an onlooker see himself in a similar plight and would speak with stern voice to the conscience of the world. But I—I had produced these symptoms as effectively as though I had nothing to do with their appearance. I had improved upon nature, realized a dream; and only he who has succeeded in creating a compelling and effective reality out of nothing, out of sheer inward knowledge and contemplation—in short, out of nothing more than imagination and the daring exploitation of his own body—he alone understands the strange and dreamlike satisfaction with which I rested from my creative task.

An hour later Health Councillor Düsing arrived. He had been our family physician ever since the death of old Dr. Mecum, who had ushered me into the world. Dr. Düsing was tall and stooped, with bad carriage and bristling grey hair; he was either rubbing his long nose between thumb and forefinger all the time or rubbing his big bony hands. This man might have been dangerous to my enterprise. Not through his professional ability, probably, which was, I believe, of the slightest (though a true doctor devoted to science and to the pursuit of medicine for its own sake is easiest of all to deceive), but through a certain native human shrewdness, which is often the whole stock in trade of inferior characters. This unworthy disciple of Æsculapius was both stupid and ambitious and had achieved his title through personal influence, exploitation of wine-house acquaintances, and the receipt of patronage; he was always going to Wiesbaden to advance his interests with the authorities. Most indicative to me was the fact that he did not receive the patients who came to his waiting-room in the order in which they arrived, but took the more influential first, letting the humbler sit and wait. His manner toward the former class was obsequious, toward the latter harsh and cynical, indicating often that he did not believe in their complaints. I am convinced he would not have stopped at any lie, corruption, or bribery that might ingratiate him with his superiors or recommend him as a zealous party man to those in power; such behaviour was consistent with the shrewd common sense he relied on to see him through in default of higher qualifications. Although my poor father's position was already doubtful, as a businessman and a taxpayer he still belonged to the influential classes of the town, and Dr. Düsing naturally wished to stand well with him. It may even be that the wretched man willingly seized every opportunity to school himself in corruption, and may have believed for this reason that he ought to make common cause with me.

Whenever he came and sat beside my bed with the usual avuncular phrases like: "Well, well, what have we here?" or: "What seems to be wrong today?" the moment would come when a wink, a smile, or a significant little pause would encourage me to admit that we were partners in the deceptive little game of playing sick—"school sick" as he would probably have called it. Never did I make the smallest response to his advances. Not out of caution, for he would probably not have betrayed me, but out of pride and contempt. At each of his attempts I only looked all the more ailing and helpless, my cheeks grew hollower, my breathing shorter and more irregular, my mouth more lax. I was quite prepared to go through another attack of vomiting if needs must; and so persistently did I fail to understand his worldly wisdom that in the end he had to abandon this approach in favour of a more scientific one.

That was not very easy for him. First because of his stupidity; and secondly because the clinical picture I presented was very general and indefinite in character. He thumped my chest and listened to me all over, peered down my throat with the aid of a spoon handle, annoyed me by taking my temperature, and finally, for better or worse, was forced to express his opinion. "Migraine," he said. "No cause for alarm. We know our young friend's tendency in this direction. Unfortunately his stomach is involved to no small degree. I prescribe rest, no visits, little conversation, and preferably a darkened room. Besides, citric acid and caffeine have proved valuable in these cases. I'll write a prescription . . ." If, however, there had been a few cases of grippe in the town, he would say: "Grippe, dear Frau Krull, with gastric complications. Yes, that's what our friend has caught! The inflammation of the respiratory tract is as yet insignificant, but it's detectable. You do cough, don't you, dear boy? I also observe an elevation of temperature, which will no doubt increase in the course of the day. Moreover, the pulse is rapid and irregular." And, with his hopeless lack of imagination, he could think of nothing but to prescribe a certain bittersweet tonic wine from the druggist's, which, moreover, I liked very much. I found it induced a state of warm and quiet satisfaction after my victory in battle.

Indeed, the medical profession is not different from any other: its members are, for the most part, ordinary empty-headed dolts, ready to see what is not there and to deny the obvious. Any untrained person, if he is a connoisseur and lover of the body, exceeds them in his knowledge of its subtler mysteries and can easily lead them around by the nose.

The inflammation of the respiratory tract was something I had not thought of, and so had not included in my performance. But once I had forced the doctor to drop his theory of "school sickness," he had to fall back on grippe, and to that end had to assume that my throat was inflamed and my tonsils swollen, which was just as little the case. He was quite right about the fever—though the fact entirely disproved his first diagnosis by presenting a genuine clinical phenomenon. Medical science maintains that fever can be caused only by an infection of the blood through some agent or other, and that fever on other than physical grounds does not exist. That is absurd. My readers will be as convinced as I that I was not really ill when Health Councillor Düsing examined me. But I was highly excited; I had concentrated my whole being upon an act of will; I was drunk with the intensity of my own performance in my role of parodying nature—a performance that had to be masterly if it was not to be ridiculous; I was delirious with the alternate tension and relaxation necessary to give reality, in my own eyes and others', to a condition that did not exist; and all this so heightened and enhanced my organic processes that the doctor was actually able to read the result on the thermometer. The same explanation applies to the pulse. When the Councillor's head was pressed against my chest and I inhaled the animal odour of his dry, grey hair, I had it in my power to feel a violent reaction that made my heart beat fast and irregularly. And as for my stomach, Dr. Düsing always said that it too was affected, whatever other diagnosis he made; and it was true enough that it was an uncommonly sensitive organ, pulsing and contracting with every stir of emotion, so that I could properly speak of a throbbing stomach where others under stress of circumstances speak of a throbbing heart. Of this phenomenon the doctor was aware and he was not a little impressed by it.

And so he prescribed his acid tablets or his bittersweet tonic wine and stayed for a while sitting on my bed chatting and gossiping with my mother; while I lay breathing irregularly through my flaccid lips and staring vacantly at the ceiling. My father used to come in, too, and look at me self-consciously, avoiding my glance. He would take advantage of the occasion to consult the doctor about his gout. Then I was left to spend the day alone—perhaps two or three days—on short rations, to be sure, which tasted all the better for their sparseness, given over to dreams of my brilliant career in the world. When my healthy young appetite rebelled at the diet of gruel and zwieback, I would get cautiously out of bed, noiselessly open the top of my little desk, and partake of the chocolates that almost always lay there in abundant store.

CHAPTER VII

Where had I procured them? They had come into my possession in a strange, almost fantastic fashion. Down in the town on a corner of what was, comparatively speaking, our busiest street, there was a neat and attractively stocked delicatessen store, a branch, if I am not mistaken, of a Wiesbaden firm. It was patronized by the best society. My way to school led me past this shop daily and I had stopped in many times, coin in hand, to buy cheap candies, fruit drops or barley sugar. But on going in one day I found it empty not only of customers but of attendants as well. There was a little bell on a spring over the door, and this had rung as I entered; but either the inner room was empty or its occupants had not heard the bell —I was and remained alone. The glass door at the rear was covered by some pleated material. At first the emptiness surprised and startled me, it even gave me an uncanny feeling; but presently I began to look about me, for never before had I been able to contemplate undisturbed the delights of such a spot. It was a narrow room, with a rather high ceiling, and crowded from floor to ceiling with goodies. There were rows and rows of hams and sausages of all shapes and colours—white, yellow, red, and black; fat and lean and round and long —rows of canned preserves, cocoa and tea, bright translucent glass bottles of honey, marmalade, and jam; round bottles and slender bottles, filled with liqueurs and punch—all these things crowded every inch of the shelves from top to bottom. Then there were glass showcases where smoked mackerel, lampreys, flounders, and eels were displayed on platters to tempt the appetite. There were dishes of Italian salad, crayfish spreading their claws on blocks of ice, sprats pressed flat and gleaming goldenly from open boxes; choice fruits—garden strawberries and grapes as beautiful as though they had come from the Promised Land; rows of sardine tins and those fascinating little white earthenware jars of caviar and *foie gras*. Plump chickens dangled their necks from the top shelf, and there were trays of cooked meats, ham, tongue, beef, and veal, smoked salmon and breast of goose, with the slender slicing knife lying ready at hand. There were all sorts of cheeses under glass bells, brick-red, milk-white, and marbled, also the creamy ones that overflow their silver foil in golden waves. Artichokes, bundles of asparagus, truffles, little liver sausages in silver paper —all these things lay heaped in rich profusion; while on other tables stood open tin boxes full of fine biscuits, spice cakes piled in criss-cross layers, and glass urns full of dessert candies and candied fruits.

I stood enchanted, straining my ears and breathing in the delightful atmosphere and the mixed fragrance of chocolate and smoked fish and earthy truffles. My mind was filled with memories of fairytale kingdoms, of underground treasure chambers where Sunday children might fill their pockets and boots with precious stones. It was indeed either a fairytale or a dream! Everyday laws and prosaic regulations were all suspended. One might give free rein to one's desires and let imagination roam in blissful unrestraint. So great was the joy of beholding this bountiful spot completely at my disposal that I felt my limbs begin to jerk and twitch. It took great self-control not to burst into a cry of joy at so much newness and freedom. I spoke into the silence, saying: "Good day" in quite a loud voice; I can still remember how my strained, unnatural tones died away in the stillness. No one answered. And my mouth literally began to water like a spring. One quick, noiseless step and I was beside one of the laden tables. I made one rapturous grab into the nearest glass urn, filled as it chanced with chocolate creams, slipped a fistful into my coat pocket, then reached the door, and in the next second was safely round the corner.

No doubt I shall be accused of common theft. I will not deny the accusation, I will simply withdraw and refuse to contradict anyone who chooses to mouth this paltry word. But the word—the poor, cheap, shopworn word, which does violence to all the finer meanings of life—is one thing, and the primeval absolute deed forever shining with newness and originality is quite another. It is only out of habit and sheer mental indolence that we come to regard them as the same. And the truth is that the word, as used to describe or characterize a deed, is no better than one of those wire fly-swatters that always miss the fly. Moreover, whenever an act is in question, it is not the what nor the why that matters (though the second is the more important), but simply and solely the who. Whatever I have done or committed, it has always been first of all *my* deed, not Tom's or Dick's or Harry's: and though I have had to accept being labelled, especially by the law, with the same name as ten thousand others, I have always rebelled against such an unnatural identification in the unshakable belief that I am a favourite of the powers that be and actually composed of finer flesh and blood. The reader, if I ever have one, will pardon this digression into the abstract, which perhaps ill suits me, since I am not trained in abstract thought. But I regard it as my duty to reconcile him as far as I can to the eccentricities of my way of life or, if this should prove impossible, to prevent him betimes from reading further.

When I got home I went up to my room, still wearing my overcoat, spread my treasures out on the table, and examined them. I had hardly believed that they were real and would still be there; for how often do priceless things come into our possession in dreams, yet when we wake, our hands are empty. No one can share my lively joy unless he can imagine that the treasures vouchsafed him in a delightful dream are ready and waiting for him on the coverlet of his bed in the light of morning, as though left over from the dream. They were of the best quality, those candies, wrapped in silver paper, filled with sweet liqueurs and flavoured creams; but it was not alone their quality that enchanted me; even more it was the carrying over of my dream treasure into my waking life that made up the sum of my delight—a delight too great for me not to think of repeating it when occasion offered. For whatever reason—I did not consider it my duty to speculate—the delicatessen shop occasionally proved to be unattended at noon. This did not happen often nor regularly, but after a longer or shorter interval it would occur, and I could tell by strolling slowly past the glass door with my schoolbag on my shoulder. I would return and go in, having learned to open the door so gently that the little bell did not ring, the clapper simply quivering on its wire. I would say "Good morning," just in case, quickly seize whatever was available, never shamelessly, but rather choosing moderately—a handful of candies, a slice of honey cake, a bar of chocolate—so that very likely nothing was ever missed. But in the incomparable expansion of my whole being which accompanied these free and dreamlike forays upon the sweets of life, I thought I could clearly recognize anew the nameless sensation that had been so long familiar to me as the result of certain trains of thought and introspection.

CHAPTER VIII

Unknown reader! I have put aside my fluent pen for purposes of reflection and self-examination before treating a theme on which I have had earlier occasion to touch lightly in the course of my confessions. It is now my conscientious duty to dwell on it at somewhat greater length. Let me say immediately that whoever expects from me a lewd tone or scabrous anecdote will be disappointed. It is rather my intention to see that the dictates of morality and good form should be combined with the frankness which I promised at the outset of this enterprise. Pleasure in the salacious for its own sake, though an almost universal fault, has always been incomprehensible to me, and verbal excesses of this kind I have always found the most repulsive of all, since they are the cheapest and have not the excuse of passion. People laugh and joke about these matters precisely as though they were dealing with the simplest and most amusing subject in the world, whereas the exact opposite is the truth; and to talk of them in a loose and careless way is to surrender to the mouthings of the mob the most important and mysterious concern of nature and of life. But to return to my confession.

First of all I must make clear that the above-mentioned concern began very early to play a role in my life, to occupy my thoughts, to shape my fancies and form the content of my childish enterprises—long, that is, before I had any words for it or could possibly form any general ideas of its nature or significance. For a considerable time, that is, I regarded my tendency to such thoughts and the lively pleasure I had in them to be private and personal to myself. Nobody else, I thought, would understand them, and it was in fact advisable not to talk of them at all. Lacking any other means of description, I grouped all my emotions and fancies together under the heading of "The Best of All" or "The Great Joy" and guarded them as a priceless secret. And thanks to this jealous reserve, thanks also to my isolation, and a third motive to which I shall presently return, I long remained in a state of intellectual ignorance which corresponded little to the liveliness of my senses. As far back as I can remember, this "Great Joy" took up a commanding position in my inner life—indeed, it probably began further back than my conscious memory extends. For small children are ignorant and in that sense innocent; but to maintain that theirs is an angelic purity is certainly a sentimental superstition that would not stand the test of objective examination. For myself at least, I have it from an excellent authority (whom I shall shortly identify) that even at my nurse's breast I displayed the most unambiguous evidence of sensual pleasure—and this tradition has always seemed highly credible to me, as indicative of the eagerness of my nature.

In actual fact my gifts for the pleasures of love bordered on the miraculous; even today it is my conviction that they far exceeded the ordinary. I had early grounds to suspect that this was so, but my suspicions were converted to certainty by the evidence of that person who told me of my precocious behaviour at my nurse's breast. For several years I carried on a secret relationship with this person. I refer to our housemaid Genovefa, who had been with us from a tender age and was in her early thirties when I reached sixteen. She was the daughter of a sergeant major and for a long time had been engaged to the station master at a little station on the Frankfurt-Niederlahnstein line. She had a good deal of feeling for the refinements of life, and although she did all the hard work in the house, her position was halfway between a servant and a member of the family. Her marriage was—for lack of money—only a distant prospect; and the long waiting must have been a genuine hardship for the poor girl. In person she was a voluptuous blonde with exciting green eyes and a graceful way of moving. But despite the prospect of spending her best years in renunciation she never lowered herself to heeding the advances of soldiers, labourers, or such people, for she did not consider herself one of the common folk, and felt only disgust for the way they spoke and the way they smelt. It was different with the son of the house, who may well have won her favour as he developed, and she may have had the feeling that in satisfying him she was not only performing a domestic duty but advancing her social position. Thus it happened that my desires encountered no serious resistance.

I am far from inclined to go into details about an episode that is too common to be of interest to a cultivated public. In brief, then, my godfather Schimmelpreester had dined with us one evening and later we had spent the time trying on costumes. When I went up to bed it happened—not without her connivance—that I met Genovefa in the dark corridor outside the door of my attic room. We stopped to talk, by degrees drifted into the room itself, and ended by occupying it together for the night. I well remember my mood. It was one of gloom, disillusion, and boredom such as often seized me after an evening of trying on costumes—only this time it was even more severe than usual. I had resumed my ordinary dress with loathing, I had an impulse to tear it off, but no desire to forget my misery in slumber. It seemed to me that my only possible consolation lay in Genovefa's arms—yes, to tell the truth, I felt that in complete intimacy with her I should find the continuation and logical conclusion of my brilliant evening and the proper goal of my adventuring among the costumes from my godfather's wardrobe. However that may be, the soul-satisfying, unimaginable delights I experienced on Genovefa's white, well-nourished breast defy description. I cried aloud for bliss, I felt myself borne heavenwards. And my desire was not of a selfish nature, for characteristically I was truly inflamed only by the joy Genovefa evinced. Of course, every possibility of comparison is out of the question; I can neither demonstrate nor disprove, but I was then and am now convinced that with me the satisfaction of love is twice as sweet and twice as penetrating as with the average man.

But it would be unjust to conclude that because of my extraordinary endowment I became a libertine and lady-killer. My difficult and dangerous life made great demands on my powers of concentration—I had to be careful not to exhaust myself. I have observed that with some the act of love is a trifling matter, which they discharge perfunctorily, going their way as though nothing had happened. As for me, the tribute I brought was so great as to leave me for a time quite empty and deprived of the power to act. True, I have often indulged in excesses, for the flesh is weak and I found the world all too ready to satisfy my amorous requirements. But in the end and on the whole I was of too manly and serious a temper not to return from sensual relaxation to a necessary and healthful austerity. Moreover, is not purely animal satisfaction the grosser part of what as a child I had instinctively called "The Great Joy"? It enervates us by satisfying us too completely; it makes us bad lovers of the world because on the one hand it robs life of its bloom and enchantment while on the other hand it impoverishes our own capacity to charm, since only he who desires is amiable and not he who is satiated. For my part, I know many kinds of satisfaction finer and more subtle than this crude act which is after all but a limited and illusory satisfaction of appetite; and I am convinced that he has but a coarse notion of enjoyment whose activities are directed point-blank to that goal alone. Mine have always been on a broader, larger, and more general scale; they found the most piquant viands where others would not look at all; they were never precisely defined or specialized—and it was for this reason among others that despite my special aptitude I remained so long innocent and unconscious, a child and dreamer indeed, my whole life long.

CHAPTER IX

Herewith I leave a subject in the treatment of which I believe I have not for a moment transgressed the canons of propriety and good taste, and hasten forward to the tragic moment which was the turning-point in my career and which terminated my sojourn under my parents' roof. But first I must mention the betrothal of my sister Olympia to Second Lieutenant Übel of the Second Nassau Regiment, stationed in Mainz. The betrothal was celebrated on a grand scale but led to no practical consequences. It was broken off under the stress of circumstances and my sister, after the break-up of our family, went on the stage in comic opera. Übel was a sickly young man, inexperienced in life. He was a constant guest at our parties, and it was there, excited by dancing, games of forfeit, and Berncasteler Doctor, and fired by the calculated glimpses that the ladies of our household granted so freely, that he fell passionately in love with Olympia. Longing for her with the desirousness of weak-chested people and probably overestimating our position and importance, he actually went down on his knees one evening and, almost weeping with eagerness, spoke the fatal words. To this day I am amazed that Olympia had the face to accept him, for she certainly did not love him and had doubtless been informed by my mother of the true state of our affairs. But she probably thought it was high time to make sure of some refuge, however insubstantial, from the oncoming storm; and it may even have been indicated to her that her engagement to an army officer, however poor his prospects, might delay the catastrophe. My poor father was appealed to for his consent and gave it with an embarrassed air and little comment; thereupon the family event was communicated to the assembled guests, who received the news with loud huzzahs and christened it, so to speak, with rivers of *Loreley extra cuvée*. After that, Lieutenant Übel came almost daily from Mainz to visit us, and did no little damage to his health by constant attendance upon the object of his sickly desire. When I chanced to enter the room where the betrothed pair had been left alone for a little while, I found him looking so distracted and cadaverous that I am convinced the turn affairs presently took was a piece of unmixed good fortune for him.

As for me, my mind was chiefly occupied in these weeks with the fascinating subject of the change of name my sister's marriage would bring with it. I remember that I envied her almost to the point of dislike. She who for so long had been called Olympia Krull would sign herself in future Olympia Übel—and that fact alone possessed all the charm of novelty. How tiresome to sign the same name to letters and papers all one's life long! The hand grows paralyzed with irritation and disgust—what a pleasant refreshment and stimulation of the whole being comes, then, from being able to give oneself a new name and to hear oneself called by it! It seemed to me that the female sex enjoyed a great advantage over the male through being afforded at least once in life the opportunity of enjoying this restorative tonic—whereas for a man any change is practically forbidden by law. As I personally, however, was not born to lead the easy and sheltered existence of the majority, I have often disregarded a prohibition that ran counter to both my safety and my dislike of the humdrum and everyday. In doing so I have displayed a very considerable gift of invention and I mention now, by way of anticipation, the peculiar charm of that place in my notes where I first speak of the occasion on which I laid aside like a soiled and worn-out garment the name to which I was born, to assume another which for elegance and euphony far surpassed that of Lieutenant Übel.

But events had taken their course in the midst of the betrothal, and ruin—to express myself metaphorically—knocked with a bony knuckle on our door. Those malicious rumours about my poor father's business, the avoidance we suffered from all and sundry, the gossip about our domestic affairs, all these were most cruelly confirmed by the event—to the miserable satisfaction of the prophets of doom. The wine-drinking public had more and more eschewed our brand. Lowering the price (which could not, of course, improve the product) did nothing to allure the gay world nor did the enticing design produced to oblige the firm and against his better judgment by my good-natured godfather Schimmelpreester. Presently sales dropped to zero, and ruin fell upon my poor father in the spring of the year I became eighteen.

At that time I was, of course, entirely lacking in business experience—nor am I any better off in that respect now, since my own career, based on imagination and self-discipline, gave me little business training. Accordingly I refrain from exercising my pen on a subject of which I have no detailed knowledge and from burdening the reader with an account of the misfortunes of the Loreley Sparkling Wine Company. But I do wish to give expression to the warm sympathy I felt for my father in these last months. He sank more and more into a speechless melancholy and would sit about the house with head bent, the fingers of his right hand gently caressing his rounded belly, ceaselessly and rapidly blinking his eyes. He made frequent trips to Mainz, sad expeditions no doubt designed to raise cash or to find some new source of credit; he would return from these excursions greatly depressed, wiping his forehead and eyes with his batiste handkerchief. It was only at the evening parties we still held in our villa, when he sat at table with his napkin tied around his neck, his guests about him, and his glass in his hand, presiding over the feast, that anything like comfort revisited him. Yet in the course of one such evening there occurred a most unpleasant exchange between my poor father and the Jewish banker, husband of the jet-laden female. He, as I later learned, was one of the most hardhearted cutthroats who ever lured a harried and unwary businessman into his net. Very soon thereafter came that solemn and ominous day—yet for me refreshing in its novelty and excitement—when my father's factory and business premises failed to open, and a group of cold-eyed, tight-lipped gentlemen appeared at our villa to attach our possessions. My poor father had filed a petition in bankruptcy, expressed in graceful phrases and signed with that naïve, ornamental signature of his which I knew so well how to imitate, and the proceedings had solemnly begun.

On that day, because of our disgrace, I had an excuse for staying away from school—and I may say here that I was never permitted to finish my course. This was due, first, to my having never been at any pains to hide my aversion to the despotism and dullness which characterized that institution, and secondly because our domestic circumstances and ultimate downfall filled the masters with venom and contempt. At the Easter holidays after my poor father's failure they refused to give me my graduation certificate, thus presenting me with the alternatives of staying on in a class below my age or of leaving school and losing the social advantages of a certificate. In the happy consciousness that my personal abilities were adequate to make up for the loss of so trifling an asset, I chose the latter course.

Our financial collapse was complete; it became clear why my poor father had put it off so long and involved himself so deeply in the toils of the usurers, for he was aware that when the crash came, it would reduce him to total beggary. Everything went under the hammer: the warehouses (but who wanted to buy so notoriously bad a product as my father's wine?), the real estate—that is, the cellars and our villa, encumbered as they were with mortgages to two thirds of their value, mortgages on which the interest had not been paid for years—the dwarfs, the toadstools and earthenware animals in the garden—yes, even the mirrored ball and the æolian harp went the same sad way. The inside of the house was stripped of every pleasant luxury: the spinning-wheel, the downy cushions, the glass boxes and smelling-salts all went at public auction; not even the halberds over the windows or the portieres were spared; and if the little device over the entrance door that played the Strauss melody as the door closed still jingled unmindful of the desolation, it was only because it had not been noticed by its legal owners.

One could hardly say at first that my father gave the impression of a broken man. His features even expressed a certain satisfaction that his affairs, having passed beyond his own competence, now found themselves in such good hands; and since the bank that had purchased our property let us for very pity remain for the time being within its bare walls, we still had a roof over our heads. Temperamentally easy-going and good-natured, he could not believe his fellow human beings would be so pedantically cruel as to reject him utterly; he was actually naïve enough to offer himself as director to a local company that manufactured sparkling wine. Contemptuously rejected, he made other efforts to re-establish himself in life—and if he had succeeded would no doubt have resumed his old practice of feasting and fireworks. But when everything failed he at last gave up; and as he probably considered that he was only in our way and that we might get along better without him, he decided to make an end of it all.

It was five months after the opening of the bankruptcy proceedings, and autumn had begun. Since Easter I had not gone back to school and was enjoying my temporary freedom and absence of definite prospects. We had gathered in our bare dining-room, my mother, my sister Olympia, and I, to eat our meagre meal, and were waiting for the head of the house. But when we had finished our soup and he had not yet appeared, we sent Olympia, who had always been his favourite, to summon him. She had scarcely been gone three minutes when we heard her give a prolonged scream and run still screaming upstairs and down and then distractedly up again. Chilled to the marrow of my bones and prepared for the worst. I hurried to my father's room. There he lay on the floor, his clothes loosened, his hand resting on his protuberant belly, beside him the fatal shining thing with which he had shot himself through his gentle heart. Our maid Genovefa and I lifted him to the sofa, and while she ran for the doctor, and my sister Olympia still rushed screaming through the house, and my mother for very fear would not stir out of the dining-room, I stood beside the body of my sire, now growing cold, with my hand over my eyes and paid him the tribute of my flowing tears.

BOOK TWO

CHAPTER I

These papers have lain for a long time under lock and key; for at least a year now indifference toward the enterprise and doubt of my success have kept me from continuing my confessions, piling page on page in faithful sequence. For although I have often maintained that I am setting down these reminiscences principally for my own occupation and amusement, I will now honour truth in this respect, too, and admit freely that I have in secret and as it were out of the corner of my eye given some heed to the reading public as well; indeed, without the encouraging hope of their interest and approval I should hardly have had the perseverance to continue my work even this far. At this point, however, I have had to decide whether these true recollections, conforming modestly to the facts of my life, could compete with the inventions of writers, especially for the favour of a public whose satiety and insensitivity—the result of just such crass productions—cannot be exaggerated. Heaven knows, I said to myself, what excitement, what sensationalism, people will expect in a book whose title seems to place it side by side with murder mysteries and detective stories—whereas my life story, though it does indeed appear strange and often dreamlike, is totally devoid of stage effects and rousing denouements. And so I thought I must abandon hope.

Today, however, my eye chanced to fall on the composition in question; once more and not without emotion I ran through the chronicle of my childhood and early youth; aroused, I continued to spin out my reminiscences in imagination; and as certain striking moments of my career appeared vividly before me, I was quite unable to believe that incidents which exercise so enlivening an effect on me could fail to entertain the reading public as well. If I recall, for example, one of the great houses of Germany where, masquerading as a Belgian aristocrat, I sat in the midst of a distinguished company chatting over coffee and cigars with the director of police, an unusually humane man with a deep understanding of the human heart, discussing the characteristics of confidence men and their appropriate punishment; or if I recollect, just to choose a case in point, the fateful hour of my first arrest, when a young novice among the police officers who came to fetch me was so impressed by the gravity of the occasion and so confused by the magnificence of my bedchamber that he knocked at the open door, carefully wiped his shoes, and humbly murmured: "Permit me," thereby earning a glower of rage from the officer in charge: then I cannot deny myself the cheery hope that although my disclosures, in respect of vulgar excitement and the satisfaction of common curiosity, may be put in the shade by the fables of the novelists, yet to compensate, they will be all the more certain to triumph in the end through a certain refined impressiveness and fidelity to truth. Accordingly my desire has been rekindled to continue and complete these reminiscences; and it is my intention while doing so to exercise, in the matter of purity of style and propriety of expression, even greater care, if possible, than hitherto, so that my offerings may pass muster in even the best houses.

CHAPTER II

I take up the thread of my story exactly where I dropped it—that is, at the moment when my poor father, driven into a corner by the hardheartedness of his contemporaries, took his own life. To provide a proper funeral presented difficulties, for the Church averts her face from an act such as his, and even a morality independent of canonical dogma must disapprove it too. Life is by no means the highest good, so precious it must be clung to in all circumstances. Instead it seems to me we should regard it as a heavy and exacting task that has been assigned us, one which we have in some sense chosen and which we are absolutely obliged to carry through with loyal perseverance. To abandon it before our time is unquestionably an act of dereliction. In this particular case, however, my judgment was suspended and converted into wholehearted sympathy—especially since we survivors held it of great moment that the departed should not go to his grave unblessed—my mother and sister, because of what people would say and out of a tendency to bigotry (for they were zealous Catholics); I, however, because I am conservative by nature and have always had an unforced affection for traditional procedures in preference to the vulgarities of progress. Accordingly, since the women's courage failed them, I undertook to persuade the official town minister, Spiritual Counsellor Chateau, to take charge of the obsequies.

I encountered that cheerful and worldly cleric, who had only recently assumed office in our town, at his lunch, which consisted of an omelet *fines herbes* and a bottle of Liebfraumilch, and he received me kindly. For Spiritual Counsellor Chateau was an elegant priest who most convincingly personified the nobility and distinction of his Church. Although he was short and stout he possessed much grace of manner, swayed his hips expertly and attractively when he walked, and was master of the most charmingly accomplished gestures. His manner of speech was studied and impeccable, and below his silky black cassock peeped black silk socks and patent-leather shoes. Freemasons and antipapists maintained that he wore them simply because he suffered from sweaty, evil-smelling feet; but even today I consider that malicious gossip. Although I was as yet personally unknown to him, with a wave of his plump, white hand he invited me to sit down, shared his meal with me, and, in the manner of a man of the world, gave every indication of believing my report, which was to the effect that my poor father, in the process of examining a long unused gun, had been struck down by a shell that went off unexpectedly. This, then, is what he gave the appearance of believing, as a matter of policy, no doubt (for very likely in times like these the Church must rejoice when people sue for her gifts even deceitfully). He bestowed words of human comfort on me and declared himself ready to conduct the priestly rites of burial, the cost of which my godfather Schimmelpreester had nobly engaged to pay. His Reverence thereupon made some notes concerning the manner of life of the departed, which I was at pains to portray as both honourable and happy, and finally he directed to me certain questions about my own circumstances and prospects, which I answered in general and approximate terms. "My dear son," was the general tenor of his reply, "you seem hitherto to have conducted yourself somewhat carelessly. As yet, however, nothing is lost, for your personality makes a pleasing impression and I should like to praise you in particular for the agreeable quality of your voice. I should be much surprised if Fortuna did not prove gracious to you. I make it my business at all times to recognize those with bright prospects, such as have found favour in the eyes of God, for a man's destiny is written on his brow in characters that are not indecipherable to the expert." And therewith he dismissed me.

Cheered by the words of this clever man, I hastened back to my mother and sister to tell them the happy outcome of my mission. The funeral, I must, alas, admit, turned out to be less impressive than one might have hoped, for the participation of our fellow citizens was meagre in the extreme, a not surprising fact so far as our townspeople were concerned. But where were our other friends, who in his prosperous days had watched my poor father's fireworks and had done so well by his Berncasteler Doctor? They stayed away, less from ingratitude perhaps than simply because they were people who had no taste for those solemn occasions on which one's attention is directed toward the eternal, and avoided them as something upsetting, a course of action that certainly bespeaks an indifferent character. Among them all only Lieutenant Übel, of the Second Nassau Regiment in Mainz, put in an appearance, though in civilian clothes, and it was thanks to him that my godfather Schimmelpreester and I were not the only ones to follow the swaying coffin to the grave.

Nevertheless, the reverend gentleman's prophecy continued to ring in my ears, for it not only accorded completely with my own presentiments and impressions, but came from a source to which I could attribute particular authority in these arcane matters. To say why would be beyond most people's competence; I believe, however, that I can at least outline the reasons. In the first place, belonging to a venerable hierarchy like the Catholic clergy develops one's perception of the gradations of human worth to a far subtler degree than life in ordinary society can do. Now that this simple thought has been safely stated, I shall go a step further and in doing so I shall try to be consistent and logical. We are here talking about a perception and therefore about a function of our material nature. Now, the Catholic form of worship, in order to lead us to what lies beyond the world of the senses, takes special account of that world and works with it, takes it into consideration in every possible way, and more than any other explores its secrets. An ear accustomed to lofty music, to harmonies designed to arouse a presentiment of heavenly choruses—should not such an ear be sensitive enough to detect native nobility in a human voice? An eye familiar with the most gorgeous pomp of colour and form, prefiguring the majesty of the heavenly mansions—should not such an eye be especially quick to detect the signs of mysterious favour in charm and natural endowment? An organ of smell familiar with and taking pleasure in clouds of incense in houses of worship, an organ of smell that in former times would have perceived the lovely odour of sanctity—should it not be able to detect the immaterial yet nevertheless corporeal emanation of a child of fortune, a Sunday child? And one who has been ordained to preside over the loftiest secret of the Church, the mystery of Flesh and Blood—should he not be able to differentiate, thanks to his higher sensibility, between the more distinguished and the meaner forms of human clay? With these carefully chosen words I flatter myself that I have given my thoughts the completest possible expression.

In any case, the prophecy I had received told me nothing that my insight and opinion of myself did not confirm in the happiest fashion. At times, to be sure, depression weighed my spirit down, for my body, which once an artist's hand had fixed on canvas in a legendary role, was clothed in ugly and shabby garments, and my position in the small town could only be called disgraceful—indeed, suspect. Of disreputable family, son of a bankrupt and suicide, an unsuccessful student without any real prospects in life, I was the object of dark and contemptuous glances; and though the fellow townsmen from whom they came were, in my opinion, superficial and unattractive, they could not but wound painfully a nature such as mine. For as long as I was compelled to stay there, they made it distressing for me to appear in the public streets. This period reinforced the tendency to misanthropy and withdrawal from the world which had always been a part of my character, a tendency that can go so amiably hand in hand with an eager delight in the world and its people. And yet something mingled in those glances—nor was this the case simply among my townswomen—that one might have described as unwilling admiration and that in more auspicious circumstances would have promised the finest recompense for my inner distress. Today, when my face is haggard and my limbs show the marks of age, I can say without conceit that my nineteen years had fulfilled all that my tender youth had promised, and that even in my own estimation I had bloomed into a most attractive young man. Blond and brown at once, with melting blue eyes, a modest smile on my lips, a charmingly husky voice, a silken gleam in my hair, which was parted on the left and brushed back from my forehead in a decorous wave, I would have seemed as appealing to my simple fellow countrymen as later I seemed to the citizens of other parts of the world, if their sight had not been confused and clouded by their awareness of my misfortunes. My physique, which in earlier days had pleased the artistic eye of my godfather, Schimmelpreester, was by no means robust, and yet every limb and muscle was developed with a symmetry usually found only in devotees of sport and muscle-building exercises—whereas I, in dreamer's fashion, had always shunned bodily exercise and had done nothing of an outdoor kind to promote my physical development. It must further be observed that the texture of my skin was of an extraordinary delicacy, and so very sensitive that, even when I had no money, I was obliged to provide myself with soft, fine soaps, for if I used the common, cheap varieties, even for a short time, they chafed it raw.

Natural gifts and innate superiorities customarily move their possessors to a lively and respectful interest in their heredity. And so at this time one of my absorbing occupations was to search about among the likenesses of my ancestors—photographs and daguerreotypes, medallions and silhouettes, in so far as these could be helpful—trying to discover in their physiognomies some anticipation or hint of my own person in order that I might know to whom among them I might perhaps owe special thanks. My reward, however, was meagre. I found, to be sure, among my relations and forebears on my father's side much by way of feature and bearing that provided a glimpse of preparatory experiments on the part of Nature (just as I made a point of saying earlier, for example, that my poor father, despite his corpulence, was on the friendliest footing with the Graces). On the whole, however, I had to conclude that I did not owe much to heredity; and unless I was to assume that at some indefinite point in history there had been an irregularity in my family tree whereby some cavalier, some great nobleman, must be reckoned among my natural forebears, I was obliged, in order to explain the source of my superiorities, to look within myself.

What was it really about the words of the divine that had made such an extraordinary impression on me? Today I can answer precisely, just as at the time I was instantly certain about it in my own mind. He had praised me—and for what? For the agreeable tone of my voice. But that is an attribute or gift that in the common view has nothing at all to do with one's deserts and is no more considered a subject for praise than a cockeye, a goitre, or a club foot is thought blameworthy. For praise or blame, according to the opinion of our middle-class world, is applicable to the moral order only, not to the natural; to praise the latter seems on such a view unjust and frivolous. That Town Minister Chateau happened to think otherwise struck me as wholly new and daring, as the expression of a conscious and defiant independence that had a heathenish simplicity about it and at the same time stimulated me to happy reverie. Was it not difficult, I asked myself, to make a sharp distinction between natural deserts and moral? These portraits of uncles, aunts, and grandparents had taught me how few, indeed, of my assets had come to me by way of natural inheritance. Was it true that I had had so little to do, in an inner sense, with the development of those assets? Had

I not instead the assurance that they were my own work, to a significant degree, and that my voice might quite easily have turned out common, my eyes dull, and my legs crooked, had my soul been less watchful? He who really loves the world shapes himself to please it. If, furthermore, the natural is a consequence of the moral, it was less unjust and capricious than might have appeared for the reverend gentleman to praise me for the pleasing quality of my voice.

CHAPTER III

A few days after we had consigned my father's mortal remains to the earth, we survivors, together with my godfather, Schimmelpreester, assembled for a deliberation or family council, for which our good friend arranged to come out to our villa. We had been officially informed that we should have to vacate the premises by New Year's, and so it had become urgently necessary for us to make serious plans about our future residence.

In this connection I cannot praise highly enough the counsel and assistance of my godfather. Nor can I express sufficient gratitude for the plans and suggestions that extraordinary man had worked out for each of us. These proved in the sequel to be altogether happy and fruitful inspirations, especially for me.

Our former salon, once furnished with refinement and elegance and filled so often with an atmosphere of joy and festivity, now barren, pillaged, and hardly furnished at all, was the sorry scene of our conference. We sat in one corner on cane-bottomed walnut chairs, which had been part of the dining-room furniture, around a small green table that was really a nest of four or five fragile tea or serving tables.

"Krull!" my godfather began (in his comfortable, friendly way he used to call my mother simply by her last name). "Krull!" he said, turning toward her his hooked nose and those sharp eyes without brows or lashes, which were so strangely emphasized by the celluloid frames of his glasses, "you hang your head, you look limp and you're entirely wrong to act like that. The bright and cheery possibilities of life only reveal themselves after that truly cleansing catastrophe which is correctly called social ruin, and the most hopeful situation in life is when things are going so badly for us that they can't possibly go worse. Believe me, dear friend, I am thoroughly familiar with this situation, through inner experience if not in a material sense! Furthermore, you are not really in it yet and that's bound to be what's weighing down the wings of your soul. Courage, my dear! Arouse your spirit of initiative! Here the game is up, but what of it? The wide world lies before you. Your small personal account in the Bank of Commerce is not yet entirely exhausted. With that remaining nest egg you shall set yourself up to keep lodgers in some big city, Wiesbaden, Mainz, Cologne, or even Berlin. You are at home in the kitchen–forgive my inept expression–you know how to make a pudding out of crumbs and a tangy hash out of day-before-yesterday's leftovers. Furthermore, you are used to having people around you, used to feeding them and entertaining them. And so you will rent a few rooms, you will let it be known that you are ready to take in boarders and lodgers at reasonable rates, you will go on living as you have hitherto, only now you will let the consumers pay and thereby get your profit. It will simply be a matter of your patience and good humour producing an atmosphere of cheerfulness and comfort among your clients, and I shall be much surprised if your institution does not prosper and expand."

Here my godfather paused, and we had an opportunity to give heartfelt expression to our approval and thanks. Presently he took up his discourse again.

"As far as Lympchen is concerned," he continued (that was my sister's pet name), "the obvious idea would be for her to remain with her mother and follow her natural vocation of making their guests' stay agreeable, and it is undeniable that she would prove herself an admirable and attractive *filia hospitalis*. Indeed, the chance of making herself useful in this capacity will always remain open. But for a start, I have something better in mind for her. In the days of your prosperity she learned to sing a little. Not to amount to much, her voice is weak, but it has a pleasant, tender quality, and her other advantages, which spring to the eye, add to its effectiveness. Solly Meerschaum in Cologne is a friend of mine from the old days, and his principal business interest is a theatrical agency. He will have no trouble finding a place for Olympia either in a light-opera troupe, at first of the simpler sort, or in a music-hall company—and her first outfit will be paid for out of what remains of my ill-gotten gains. At the start her career will be dark and difficult. She may have to wrestle with life. But if she shows signs of character (which is more important than talent) and knows how to profit by her single gift, which consists of so many pounds, her path will swiftly lead upward from her lowly beginning—possibly to glittering heights. Of course, I, for my part, can only indicate general directions and sketch in possibilities; the rest is your affair."

Shrieking with joy, my sister flew to our counsellor and threw her arms around his neck. During his next words she kept her head hidden on his breast.

"Now," he said, and it was easy to see that what was coming lay especially close to his heart, "in the third place I come to our costume boy." (The reader will understand the reference contained in this epithet.) "I have given thought to the problem of his future and, despite considerable difficulties in the way of finding a solution, I think I have hit upon one, though it may be only of a temporary kind. I have even begun a foreign correspondence on the subject; with Paris, to be specific—I'll explain in a moment. In my opinion, the most important thing is to introduce him to that way of life to which, through a misunderstanding, the school authorities thought they ought not to grant him honourable admittance. Once we have him in the clear, the flood tide will bear him along and bring him, as I confidently hope, to happy shores. Now it seems to me that in his case a career as a hotel waiter offers the most hopeful prospects: both as a career in itself (which can lead to very lucrative positions in life) and thanks to those bypaths which open up here and there to left and right of the main thoroughfare and have provided a livelihood for many a

Sunday's child before now. The correspondence I mentioned has been with the director of the Hotel Saint James and Albany in Paris, on the rue Saint-Honoré not far from the Place Vendôme (a central location, that is; I'll show it to you on my map)—with Isaak Stürzli, an intimate friend since the days when I lived in Paris. I have put Felix's family background and personal qualities in the most favourable light and I have vouched for his polish and his adroitness. He has a smattering of French and English; he will do well in the immediate future to extend his knowledge of these languages as much as possible. In any case, as a favour to me, Stürzli is prepared to accept him on probation—at first, to be sure, without salary. Felix will have free board and lodging and he will also be given some help in acquiring his livery, which will certainly be very becoming to him. In short, here is a way, here are space and a favourable environment for the development of his gifts, and I count on our costume boy to wait upon the distinguished guests of the Saint James and Albany to their complete satisfaction."

It is easy to imagine that I showed myself no less grateful to this splendid man than the women. I laughed for joy and embraced him in complete ecstasy. My cramped and odious native place disappeared at once, and the great world opened before me; Paris, that city whose very memory had made my poor father weak with joy throughout his life, arose in brightest majesty before my inner eye. However, the matter was not so simple, there was indeed a difficulty, or, as people say, a hitch; for I could not and might not go in search of the wide world until the matter of my military service was attended to; until my papers were in order, the borders of the Empire were insuperable barriers, and the question presented all the more disquieting an aspect since, as the reader knows, I had not succeeded in gaining the prerogatives of the educated class and would have to enter the barracks as a common recruit if I was found fit for service. This circumstance, this difficulty which I had hitherto put out of mind so lightly, weighed heavy on my heart at this moment when I was so elated by hope; and when I hesitantly mentioned the matter, it transpired that neither my mother and sister nor even Schimmelpreester had been aware of it: the former out of womanly ignorance and the latter because, as an artist, he was accustomed to pay scant attention to political and official affairs. Furthermore, he confessed to complete helplessness in this case; for, as he irritably explained, he did not have any sort of connection with army doctors and there was therefore no chance of exerting personal influence on the authorities; I could just see about getting my head out of this noose myself.

Thus I turned out to be entirely dependent on my own resources in this very ticklish matter, and the reader will judge whether I rose to the occasion. In the meanwhile, however, my youthful and volatile spirits were diverted and distracted in a variety of ways by the prospect of leaving, the imminent change of scene, and our preparations. My mother hoped to be taking in lodgers and boarders by New Year's, and so the move was to be made before the Christmas holiday. We had finally fixed on Frankfurt am Main as our goal because of the greater opportunities afforded by so large a city.

How lightly, how impatiently does youth, bent on taking the wide world by storm, turn its back, contemptuous and unfeeling, on its little homeland, without once looking round at the towers and vineyard-covered hills! And yet, however much a man may have outgrown it and may continue to outgrow it, its ridiculous, too familiar image still remains in the background of his consciousness, or emerges from it strangely after years of complete forgetfulness: what was absurd becomes estimable; among the actions, impressions, successes of one's life abroad, at every juncture, one takes secret thought for that small world, at every increase in one's fortunes one asks inwardly what it may be saying or what it might say, and this is true especially when one's homeland has behaved unkindly, unjustly, and obtusely toward one. While he is dependent on it, the youth defies it; but when it has released him and may long since have forgotten him, of his own free will he gives it the authority to pass judgment on his life. Yes, some day, after many years rich in excitement and in change, he will probably be drawn back to his birthplace, he will yield to the temptation, conscious or unconscious, to show himself to its narrow view in all the glitter he has gained abroad, and with mixed anxiety and derision in his heart he will feast upon its astonishment—just as, in due course, I shall report of myself.

I wrote a polite letter to the aforementioned Stürzli in Paris, asking him to be patient on my account since I was not free to cross the border right away but must wait until the question of my fitness for military service had been decided—a decision, I ventured to add, that would probably prove favourable for reasons in no way affecting my future calling. Our remaining possessions were quickly transferred to packing-cases and hand luggage. Among them were six magnificent starched shirts that my godfather had given me as a parting gift and that were to stand me in good stead in Paris. And one gloomy winter day we three, leaning out to wave from the window of the departing train, saw the fluttering red handkerchief of our good friend disappear in the fog. I only saw that splendid man once again.

CHAPTER IV

I shall pass quickly over the first confused days following our arrival in Frankfurt, for it pains me to recall the distressing role we were obliged to play in that rich and resplendent centre of commerce, and I should be afraid of earning the reader's displeasure by a circumstantial account of our situation. I say nothing of the dingy hostelry or rooming-house, unworthy of the name of hotel which it arrogated to itself, where, for reasons of economy, my mother and I spent several nights, my sister Olympia having parted company with us at the junction in Wiesbaden in order to seek her fortune in Cologne with Meerschaum, the agent. For my own part, I spent those nights on a sofa teeming with vermin that both stung and bit. I say nothing of our painful wanderings through that great, cold-hearted city, so unfriendly to poverty, in search of an abode we could afford, until, in a mean section, we finally came on one that had just been vacated and that corresponded fairly well to my mother's idea of a starting-place. It consisted of four small, sunless rooms and an even smaller kitchen, and was situated on the ground floor of a rear building, with a view of ugly courtyards. As, however, it cost only forty marks a month, and as it ill became us to be fastidious, we rented it on the spot and moved in the same day.

Whatever is new holds infinite charm for the young, and although this gloomy domicile could not be compared even faintly with our cheerful villa at home, I nevertheless felt cheered by the unfamiliar surroundings and satisfied to the point of boisterousness. With rough and ready helpfulness I joined my mother in the necessary preliminaries, moving furniture, unpacking cups and plates from protective wood-shavings, stocking shelves and cupboards with pots and pans; I also undertook to negotiate with our landlord, a repulsively fat man with vulgar manners, about the necessary alterations in our quarters. Fatbelly, however, obstinately refused to pay for them, and in the end my mother had to dip into her own pocketbook so that the rooms we hoped to rent would not look completely dilapidated. This came hard, for the costs of moving and settling in had been high, and if our paying guests did not put in an appearance, our establishment would be threatened with bankruptcy before it was properly started.

On the very first evening, as we were standing in the kitchen eating our supper of fried eggs, we decided, for reasons of pious and happy memory, to call our establishment "Pension Loreley," and we immediately communicated this decision to my godfather, Schimmelpreester, on a postcard we jointly composed; next day I hurried to the office of Frankfurt's leading newspaper with an advertisement couched in modest yet enticing terms and designed, by the use of boldface type, to impress that poetic name on the public consciousness. Because of the expense, we were unable for several days to put up a sign on the house facing the street that would attract the attention of passers-by to our establishment. How describe our jubilation when, on the sixth or seventh day after our arrival, the mail from home brought a package of mysterious shape with my godfather Schimmelpreester's name on it? It contained a metal sign, one end of which was bent at a right angle and pierced by four holes. It bore, painted by the artist's own hand, that female figure clothed only in jewelry which had adorned our bottle labels, with the inscription: "Pension Loreley" emblazoned in gold letters beneath it. When this had been fastened to the corner of the house facing the street in such a way that the fairy of the rock pointed with outstretched, ring-bedecked hand across the courtyard to our establishment, it produced the most beautiful effect.

As it turned out, we did get customers: first of all in the person of a young technician or mechanical engineer, a solemn, quiet, even morose man, clearly discontented with his lot, who nevertheless paid punctually and led a discreet and orderly life. He had been with us barely a week when two other guests arrived together: members of the theatrical profession—a comic bass, unemployed because of having lost his voice completely, heavy and jolly in appearance but in a furious temper as a result of his misfortune and determined to restore his organ through persistent and futile exercises which sounded as though someone were drowning inside a hogshead and shouting for help; and with him his female supplement, a red-haired chorus girl with long, rose-coloured fingernails, who wore a dirty dressing-gown—a pathetic, frail creature who seemed to have chest trouble, but whom the singer, either on account of her shortcomings or simply to give vent to his general bitterness, beat frequently and severely with his braces, without, however, making her at all dubious about him or his affection for her.

These two, then, occupied a room together, the machinist another; the third served as a dining-room, where we all consumed the meals my mother skilfully concocted out of very little. As I did not wish to share a room with my mother, for obvious reasons of propriety, I slept on a kitchen bench with bedding spread over it, and washed myself at the kitchen sink, mindful that this state of affairs could not last and that, in one way or another, my road would soon have a turning.

The Pension Loreley began to flourish; the guests, as I have indicated, drove us into a corner, and my mother could properly look forward to an enlargement of the enterprise and the acquisition of a maid. In any case, the business was on its feet, my assistance was no longer required, and, left to myself, I saw that until I departed for Paris or was compelled to put on a uniform, there would be a prolonged period of leisurely waiting of the sort that is so welcome to a high-minded youth—indeed, so necessary for his inner development. Education is not won in dull toil and labour; rather it is the fruit of freedom and apparent idleness; one does not achieve it by exertion, one breathes it in; some secret machinery is at work to that end; a hidden industry of the senses and the spirit, consonant with an appearance of complete vagabondage, is hourly active to promote it, and you could go so far as to say that one who is chosen learns even in his sleep. For one must after all be of educable stuff in order to be educated. No one grasps what he has not possessed from birth, and you can never yearn for what is alien. He who is made of common clay will never acquire education; he who does acquire it was never crude. And here once again it is very hard to draw a just and clear distinction between personal desert and what are called favourable circumstances; if, on the one hand, beneficent fortune had placed me in a big city at the right moment and granted me time in abundance, on the other hand it must be said that I was entirely deprived of the means which alone throw open the many places of entertainment and education such a city contains. And in my studies I had, as it were, to be content with pressing my face against the magnificent gates of a pleasure garden.

At this time I devoted myself to sleep almost to excess, usually sleeping until lunchtime, often until much later, eating a warmed-over meal in the kitchen or even a cold one, and afterward lighting a cigarette, a gift from our machinist (who knew how greedy I was for this pleasure and how unable I was to provide it for myself out of my own funds). I did not leave the Pension Loreley until late in the afternoon, four or five o'clock. At that hour the fashionable life of the city reached its height, rich ladies rode out in their carriages to pay calls or go shopping, the coffee houses were filling, and the store windows began to come magnificently alight. Then it was that I betook myself to the centre of town, embarking on a journey of pleasure and entertainment through the populous streets of the famous city, from which I would not return to my mother's house until the grey of dawn, though usually with much profit.

Now observe this youth in ragged clothes, alone, friendless, and lost in the crowd, wandering through this bright and alien world. He has no money with which to take any real part in the joys of civilization. He sees them proclaimed and touted on the placards stuck on advertising pillars, so excitingly that they would arouse curiosity and desire in even the dullest (whereas he is especially impressionable)—and he must content himself with reading their names and being aware of their existence. He sees the portals of the theatres festively open and dares not join the crowd that goes streaming in; he stands dazzled in the unearthly light that spills across the sidewalk from music halls and vaudeville houses, in front of which, perhaps, some gigantic Negro, his countenance and purple costume blanched by the white brilliance, towers fabulously in tricorn hat, waving his staff—and he cannot accept the flashing-toothed invitation and the enticements of the spiel. But his senses are lively, his mind attentive and alert; he sees, he enjoys, he assimilates; and if at first the rush of noise and faces confuses this son of a sleepy country town, bewilders him, frightens him indeed, nevertheless he possesses mother wit and strength of mind enough slowly to become master of his inner turmoil and turn it to good purpose for his education, his enthusiastic researches.

And what a happy institution the shop window is! How lucky that stores, bazaars, salons, that market places and emporia of luxury do not stingily hide their treasures indoors, but shower them forth in glittering profusion, in inexhaustible variety, spreading them out like a splendid offering behind shining plate glass. Brighter than day on a winter's afternoon is the illumination of these displays; rows of little gas flames at the bottoms of the windows keep the panes from frosting over. And there stood I, protected from the cold only by a woollen scarf wrapped around my neck (for my overcoat, inherited from my poor father, had long since gone to the pawnshop for a paltry sum), devouring with my eyes these wares, these precious and splendid wares, and paying no attention to the cold and damp that worked their way up from my feet to my thighs.

Whole suites were arranged in the windows of the furniture stores: drawing-rooms of stately luxury, bedchambers that acquainted one with every intimate refinement of cultivated life; inviting little dining-rooms, where the damask-covered, flower-bedecked tables, surrounded by comfortable chairs, shimmered enchantingly with silver, fine porcelain, and fragile glassware; princely salons in formal style with candelabra, fireplaces, and brocaded armchairs; and I never tired of observing how firmly and splendidly the legs of that noble furniture rested on the colourful, softly glowing Persian carpets. Farther on, the windows of a haberdasher and a fashion shop drew my attention. Here I saw the wardrobes of the rich and great, from satin dressing-gowns and silk-lined smoking-jackets to the evening severity of the tail-coat, from the alabaster collar in the latest, most favoured style to the delicate spat and the mirror-bright patent-leather shoe, from the pin-striped or dotted shirt with French cuffs to the costly fur jacket; here their hand luggage was displayed before me, those knapsacks of luxury, of pliant calfskin or expensive alligator, which looks as though it were made out of little squares; and I learned to know the appurtenances of a high and discriminating way of life, the bottles, the hairbrushes, the dressing-cases, the boxes with plates and cutlery and collapsible alcohol stoves of finest nickel; fancy waistcoats, magnificent ties, sybaritic underclothes, morocco slippers, silk-lined hats, deerskin gloves, and socks of gauzy silk were strewn in seductive display; the youth could fix in his memory the wardrobe requirements of a man of fashion down to the last, sturdy, convenient button. But perhaps I needed only to slip across the street, carefully and adroitly dodging between carriages and honking buses, to arrive at the windows of an art gallery. There I saw the treasures of the decorative industry, such objects of a high and cultivated visual lust as oil paintings by the hands of masters, gleaming porcelain figures of animals of various sorts, beautifully shaped earthenware vessels, small bronze statues, and dearly would I have liked to pick up and fondle those poised and noble bodies.

But what sort of splendour was it a few steps farther on that held me rooted to the spot in amazement? It was the window display of a big jeweller and goldsmith—and here nothing but a fragile pane of glass divided the covetousness of a freezing boy from all the treasures of fairyland. Here, more than anywhere else, my first dazzled enchantment was combined with the eagerest desire to learn. Pearl necklaces, palely shimmering on lace runners, arranged one above another, big as cherries in the middle and decreasing symmetrically toward the sides, ending in diamond clasps, and worth whole fortunes; diamond jewelry bedded on satin, sharply glittering with all the colours of the rainbow and worthy to adorn the neck, the bosom, the head of queens; smooth golden cigarette cases and cane heads, seductively displayed on glass shelves; and everywhere, carelessly strewn, polished precious stones of magnificent colour: blood-red rubies; grass-green, glossy emeralds; transparent blue sapphires that held a star-shaped light; amethysts whose precious violet shade is said to be due to organic content; mother-of-pearl opals whose colour changed as I shifted my position; single topazes; fanciful arrangements of gems in all the shadings of the spectrum—all this was not only a joy to the senses, I studied it, I immersed myself completely in it, I tried to decipher the few price tags that were visible, I compared, I weighed by eye, for the first time I became aware of my love for the precious stones of the earth, those essentially quite worthless crystals whose elements through a playful whim of Nature have combined to form these precious structures. It was at this time that I laid the groundwork for my later reliable connoisseurship in this magical domain.

Shall I speak too of the flower shops out of whose doors, when they were opened, gushed the moist, warm perfumes of paradise, and behind whose windows I saw those sumptuous flower baskets, adorned with gigantic silk bows, that one sends to women as evidence of one's attention? Or of the stationery stores whose displays taught me what sort of notepaper a cavalier uses for his correspondence, and how the initials of one's name are engraved on it with crest and coat of arms? Or the windows of the perfumers and hairdressers, where in glittering, elegant rows shone the many different scents and essences that come from France, and the delicate instruments used for the manicure and the care of the face were displayed in richly lined cases? The gift of seeing had been granted me and it was my be-all and end-all at this time—an instructive gift, to be sure, when material things, the enticing, educational aspects of the world, are its object. But how much more profoundly does the gift of perception engage one's feelings! Perception, that visual feasting on the human spectacle as it unfolds in the fashionable districts of a great city—whither I went by preference—how very different from the attraction of inanimate objects must be the pull it exerts on the longings and curiosity of a passionately ambitious youth!

O scenes of the beautiful world! Never have you presented yourselves to more appreciative eyes. Heaven knows why one in particular among the nostalgic pictures I stored up at that time has sunk so deeply into me and clings so persistently in my memory that despite its unimportance, its insignificance indeed, it fills me with delight even today. I shall not resist the temptation to record it here, though I know very well that a story-teller—and it is as a story-teller that I present myself in these pages—ought not to encumber the reader with incidents of which "nothing comes," to put the matter bluntly, since they in no way advance what is called "the action." But perhaps it is in some measure permissible, in the description of one's own life, to follow not the laws of art but the dictates of one's heart.

Once more, it was nothing, it was only charming. The stage was above my head—an open balcony of the *bel étage* of the great Hotel Zum Frankfurter Hof. Onto it stepped one afternoon—it was so simple that I apologize—two young people, as young as myself, obviously a brother and sister, possibly twins—they looked very much alike—a young man and a young woman moving out together into the wintry weather. They did so out of pure high spirits, hatless, without protection of any kind. Slightly foreign in appearance, dark-haired, they might have been Spanish, Portuguese, South American, Argentinian, Brazilian—I am simply guessing—but perhaps, on the other hand, they were Jews—I could not swear they were not and I would not on that account be shaken in my enthusiasm, for gently reared children of that race can be most attractive. Both were pretty as pictures—the youth not a whit less than the girl. In evening dress, both of them, the youth with a pearl in his shirt front, the girl wearing one diamond clip in her rich, dark, attractively dressed hair and another at her breast, where the flesh-coloured silk of her princess gown met the transparent lace of the yoke and sleeves.

I trembled for the safety of their attire, for a few damp snowflakes were falling and some of them came to rest on their wavy black hair. But they carried on their childish family prank for only two minutes at most, only long enough to point out to each other, as they leaned laughing over the railing, some incident in the street. Then they pretended to shiver with cold, knocked one or two snowflakes from their clothes, and withdrew into their room, where the light was at once turned on. They were gone, the enchanting phantasmagoria of an instant, vanished never to be seen again. But for a long time I continued to lean against the lamppost, staring up at their balcony, while I tried in imagination to force my way into their existence; and not on that night only but on many following nights, when I lay down on my kitchen bench exhausted from wandering and watching, my dreams were of them.

Dreams of love, dreams of delight and a longing for union—I cannot name them otherwise, though they concerned not a single image but a double creature, a pair fleetingly but profoundly glimpsed, a brother and sister—a representative of my own sex and of the other, the fair one. But the beauty here lay in the duality, in the charming doubleness, and if it seems more than doubtful that the appearance of the youth alone on the balcony would have inflamed me in the slightest, apart perhaps from the pearl in his shirt, I am almost equally sure that the image of the girl alone, without her fraternal complement, would never have lapped my spirit in such sweet dreams. Dreams of love, dreams that I loved precisely because—I firmly believe—they were of primal indivisibility and indeterminateness, double; which really means that only then is there a significant whole blessedly embracing what is beguilingly human in both sexes.

Dreamer and idler! I hear the reader addressing me. Where are your adventures? Do you propose to entertain me throughout your whole book with such fine-spun quiddities, the so-called experiences of your covetous idleness? No doubt, until the policeman drove you away, you pressed your forehead and nose against the big glass panes and peered into the interior of elegant restaurants through the openings in the cream-coloured curtains—stood in the mixed, spicy odours that drifted up from the kitchen through cellar gratings and saw Frankfurt's high society, served by attentive waiters, dining at little tables on which stood shaded candles and candelabra and crystal vases with rare flowers? So I did—and I am astounded at how accurately the reader is able to report the visual joys I purloined from the beau monde, just exactly as though he had had his own nose pressed against that pane. So far as "idleness" is concerned, he will very soon see the inaccuracy of any such description and will, like a gentleman, withdraw it and apologize. Let it be said right now, however, that, divorcing myself from the spectator's role, I sought and found a personal relationship with that world to which I was drawn by nature. I would, to wit, linger around the entrances of the theatres at closing-time and, like an active and obliging lad, make myself useful to the exalted public that streamed chattering out of the lobbies, stimulated by the delights of art. I would do this by hailing droshkies and summoning waiting carriages. I would rush out in front of a droshky to stop it in front of the marquee for my patron, or I would run some distance up the street to catch one and then drive back, sitting beside the coachman. Swinging down like a lackey, I would open the door for the people who were waiting with a bow so perfect as to startle them. To summon the private coupés and coaches, I would inquire in flattering fashion the names of their fortunate owners and I took no small delight in shouting those names and titles down the street in a clear, strong voice—Privy Councillor Streisand! Consul General Ackerbloom! Lieutenant-Colonel von Stralenheim or Adelebsen! And then the horses would drive up. Many names were quite difficult and their owners hesitated to tell them to me, doubtful of my ability to pronounce them. A dignified married couple, for example, with an obviously unmarried daughter, was named Crequis de Mont-en-fleur, and what pleased surprise all three showed at the correctness and elegance with which that name rang out when they finally entrusted it to me, that name compounded, as it were, of sneezes and giggles terminating in a nasal but flowery poesy! It came to the ears of their fairly far-off and aged family coachman like the clarion morning call of chanticleer, so that there was no delay in bringing up the old-fashioned but well-washed carriage and the plump, dun-coloured pair.

Many a welcome coin, often enough a silver one, was slipped into my hand for these services tendered to Society. But more precious to my heart, a dearer, more reassuring reward was mine as well—an intercepted look of astonishment, of attentive kindliness on the part of the world, a glance that measured me with pleased surprise, a smile that dwelt on my person with amazement and curiosity; and so carefully did I treasure up these secret triumphs that I could today report them more easily than almost anything else, however significant and profound.

What a wonderful phenomenon it is, carefully considered, when the human eye, that jewel of organic structures, concentrates its moist brilliance on another human creature! This precious jelly, made up of just such ordinary elements as the rest of creation, affirming, like a precious stone, that the elements count for nothing, but their imaginative and happy combination counts for everything—this bit of slime embedded in a bony hole, destined some day to moulder lifeless in the grave, to dissolve back into watery refuse, is able, so long as the spark of life remains alert there, to throw such beautiful, airy bridges across all the chasms of strangeness that lie between man and man!

Of delicate and subtle matters one should speak delicately and subtly, and so a supplementary observation will be cautiously inserted here. Only at the two opposite poles of human contact, where there are no words or at least no more words, in the glance and in the embrace, is happiness really to be found, for there alone are unconditional freedom, secrecy, and profound ruthlessness. Everything by way of human contact and exchange that lies between is lukewarm and insipid; it is determined, conditioned, and limited by manners and social convention. Here the word is master—that cool, prosaic device, that first begetter of tame, mediocre morality, so essentially alien to the hot, inarticulate realm of nature that one might say every word exists in and for itself and is therefore no better than claptrap. I say this, I, who am engaged in the labour of describing my life and am exerting every conceivable effort to give it a belletristic form. And yet verbal communication is not my element; my truest interest does not lie there. It lies rather in the extreme, silent regions of human intercourse—that one, first of all, where strangeness and social rootlessness still maintain a free, primordial condition and glances meet and marry irresponsibly in dreamlike wantonness; but then, too, the other in which the greatest possible closeness, intimacy, and commingling re-establish completely that wordless primordial condition.

CHAPTER V

But I am conscious of a look of concern on the reader's face lest as a result of all these tokens of kindliness I may have forgotten, frivolously and completely, the matter of my military obligations, and so I hasten to assure him that this was by no means the case; I had instead kept my eye fixed constantly and uneasily on that fatal question. It is true that after I had reached a decision about handling this unpleasant problem, my uneasiness turned, to a certain extent, into the kind of happy nervousness we feel when we are about to test our abilities in a great, indeed excessive, enterprise and—here I must curb my pen and, out of calculation, resist in some measure the temptation to blurt out everything in advance. For since my intention has steadily strengthened to give this little composition to the press, if I ever get to the end of it, and thus present it to the public, I should be much in the wrong if I did not obey those general rules and maxims professional writers use to maintain interest and tension, against which I should be sinning grossly if I yielded to my inclination to blurt out the best at once and, so to speak, burn up all my powder in advance.

Let just this much be said: I went to work with great thoroughness, with scientific precision, in fact, and took good care not to underestimate the difficulties in my path, for plunging ahead was never my way of undertaking a serious enterprise; instead I have always felt that precisely those actions of extreme daring which are most incredible to the common crowd require the coolest consideration and the most delicate foresight, if their result is not to be defeat, shame, and ridicule—and I have not fared badly. Not content with informing myself exactly as to the methods and practices of the recruiting-office and the nature of the regulations on which it acted (which I accomplished partly through conversations with our machinist boarder who had seen military service, and partly with the help of a general reference work in several volumes which another boarder, hopeful of improving himself, had installed in his room), once my plan was sketched in general outline I saved up one and a half marks from my tips for fetching carriages to buy a publication I had discovered in a bookstore window, a publication of clinical character, in the reading of which I immersed myself with both enthusiasm and profit.

Just as a ship requires ballast, so talent requires knowledge, but it is equally certain that we can really assimilate, indeed have a real right to, only just so much knowledge as our talent demands and hungrily draws to itself in each urgent, individual instance, in order to acquire the requisite substance and solidity. I devoured with the greatest joy the instructive content of that little book, and translated what I had acquired into certain practical exercises carried out by candlelight in front of a mirror in the nightly privacy of my kitchen, exercises that would have looked foolish to a secret observer but with which I was pursuing a clear and reasoned goal. Not a word more about it here! The reader will be compensated shortly for this momentary deprivation.

Before the end of January, in compliance with official regulations, I had reported in writing to the military authorities, enclosing my birth certificate, which was in perfect order, as well as the necessary certificate of good behaviour from the Police Bureau, the reticent and negative form of which (to wit, that concerning my way of life nothing reprehensible was known to the authorities) made me childishly angry and uncomfortable. At the beginning of March, just as twittering birds and sweet breezes were charmingly heralding the advent of spring, I was obliged by statute to present myself at the recruiting-centre for an initial interview and, summoned to Wiesbaden, I travelled thither by train, fourth class, in a fairly relaxed state of mind, for I knew that the die could hardly be cast that day and that almost everyone comes up before the final authority, which is known as the Superior Draft Commission on the Fitness and Recruitment of Youth. My expectations proved correct. The episode was brief, hurried, unimportant, and my memories of it have faded. I was measured up and down, tapped and questioned, and received no information in return. Dismissed and, for the time being, free, as though on the end of a long tether, I went for a walk in the splendid parks that adorn the spa, amused myself by training my eye in the fine stores in the casino colonnade, and returned to Frankfurt the same day.

But when two more months had passed (half of May was over and a premature midsummer heat hung over the district), the day arrived when my respite ended, the long tether I spoke of figuratively was hauled in, and I had to present myself for recruitment. My heart beat hard when I found myself seated once more on the narrow bench of a fourth-class compartment in the Wiesbaden train, surrounded by characters of the lower sort, and borne on wings of steam toward the moment of decision. The prevailing closeness lulled my travelling-companions into a nodding doze, but could not be allowed to enervate me; awake and alert I sat there, automatically on guard against leaning back, while I tried to picture the circumstances in which I should have to prove myself, and which, to judge by experience, would turn out to be quite different from any I could prefigure. If my feelings were apprehensive as well as happy, it was not because I had any serious doubts about the outcome. That was quite definite in my mind. I was completely determined to go all the way, yes, even if it proved necessary to put all the latent powers of body and soul into the game (in my opinion, it is silly to undertake any great enterprise without being prepared to do this), and I did not for an instant doubt that I was bound to succeed. What made me apprehensive was simply my being uncertain how much of myself I should have to give, what sort of sacrifice in enthusiasm and energy I should have to make to gain my ends—in other words, a sort of tenderness toward myself which had been part of my character from of old and could quite easily have turned into softness and cowardice had not more manly qualities evened the balance and held it steady.

I can still see before my eyes the low, large room, with wooden beams, into which I was roughly herded by the guard and which I found, on entering, filled with a great crowd of young men. Located on the second floor of a dilapidated and abandoned barracks on the outer edge of the city, this cheerless room offered through four bare windows a view of suburban fields disfigured by all sorts of refuse, tin cans, rubbish, and waste. Seated behind an ordinary kitchen table, papers and writing-materials spread out before him, a harsh-voiced sergeant called out names. Those summoned had to pass through a doorless entry into a passage where they stripped to a state of nature and then entered an adjoining room, the real scene of the examination. The behaviour of the man in charge was brutal and deliberately frightening. Frequently he thrust out his fists and legs, yawning like an animal, or made merry, as he ran through the roster, over the impressive degrees of those who appeared before him, headed for that decisive corridor. "Doctor of philosophy!" he shouted, laughing derisively as though he meant to say: "We'll beat it out of you, my young friend!" All this aroused fear and revulsion in my heart.

The business of conscription was in full swing, but it advanced slowly, and as it proceeded in alphabetical order, those whose names began with letters well along in the alphabet had to resign themselves to a long wait. An oppressive silence hung over the assembly, which consisted of young men from the most varied walks of life. You saw helpless country bumpkins and unruly young representatives of the urban proletariat; semi-refined shop employees and simple sons of toil; there was even a member of the theatrical profession, who aroused much covert merriment by his plump, dark appearance; hollow-eyed youths of uncertain profession, without collars and with cracked patent-leather shoes; mothers' darlings just out of Latin school, and gentlemen of more advanced years with pointed beards, pallid faces, and the cultivated deportment of scholars, pacing through the room, restless and painfully intent, conscious of their undignified position. Three or four of the potential recruits whose names would soon be called stood barefooted near the door, stripped to their undershirts, their clothes over their arms, hat and shoes in their hands. Others were sitting on the narrow benches that ran around the room or, perched on one thigh on the window-sills, were making friends and exchanging subdued comments on one another's physical peculiarities and the vicissitudes of conscription. Once in a while, no one knew how, rumours circulated from the room where the board was sitting that the number of those already accepted for service was very large and so the chances of escaping, for those who had not yet been examined, were improving, rumours no one was in a position to verify. Here and there in the crowd jokes and coarse comments broke out about the men already called up, who had to stand about almost entirely naked, and they were laughed at with increasing openness until the biting voice of the uniformed man at the table restored a respectful silence.

I for my part remained aloof as always, took no part in the idle chatter or the coarse jokes, and replied in chilly and evasive fashion when I was spoken to. Standing at an open window (for the human smell in the room had become distressing), I glanced from the desolate landscape outside to the mixed gathering in the room, and let the hours run by. I should have liked to get a glimpse of the neighbouring room where the commission sat, so as to form an impression of the examining doctor; but this was impossible and I kept emphasizing to myself that nothing depended on that particular individual and that my fate rested not in his hands but in mine alone. Boredom weighed heavily on the spirits of those around me. I, however, did not suffer from it, first because I have always been patient by nature, can endure long periods unoccupied, and love the free time those addicted to mindless activity either squander or obliterate; moreover, I was in no hurry to engage in the daring and difficult feat that awaited me, but was instead grateful for the prolonged leisure in which to collect, accustom, and prepare myself.

Noon was already approaching when names beginning with the letter *K* came to my ears. But, as though fate were bent on teasing me, there were a great many, and the list of Kammachers, Kellermanns, and Kilians, as well as Knolls and Krolls, seemed to have no end, so that when my name was finally pronounced by the man at the table, I set about the prescribed toilet rather unnerved and weary. I can declare, however, that my weariness not only failed to detract from my resolution but actually strengthened it.

For that particular day I had put on one of those starched white shirts my godfather had given me at parting, which until now I had conscientiously saved; I had realized in advance that here one's linen would be of special importance and so I now stood at the entrance to the passage, between two fellows in checked, faded cotton shirts, conscious that I could afford to be seen. To the best of my knowledge, no word of ridicule was directed at me from the room, and even the sergeant at the table looked at me with the sort of respect that underlings, used to being subordinate, never deny to elegance of manner and attire. I was quick to notice how curiously he compared the information on his list with my appearance; indeed, he was so engrossed in this study that for a moment he neglected to call my name again at the appropriate time, and I had to ask him whether I was to step inside. He said yes. I crossed the threshold on bare soles and, alone in the passage, placed my clothes on the bench beside those of my predecessor, put my shoes underneath, and took off my starched shirt as well; I folded it neatly and added it to the rest of my outfit. Then I waited alertly for further instructions.

My feeling of tension was painful, my heart hammered irregularly, and I incline to believe that the blood left my face. But with this agitation there was mixed another, happier feeling, to describe which there are no words readily available. Somewhere or other—perhaps in an aphorism or *aperçu* that I came on while reading in prison or glancing through the daily paper—this notion has come to my attention: that nakedness, the condition in which Nature brought us forth, is levelling and that no sort of injustice or order of precedence can obtain between naked creatures. This statement, which immediately aroused my anger and resistance, may seem flatteringly self-evident to the crowd, but it is not true in the least, and one might almost say by way of correction that the true and actual order of precedence is established only in that original state, and that nakedness can only be called just in so far as it proclaims the naturally unjust constitution of the human race, unjust in that it is aristocratic. I had perceived this long ago, when my godfather Schimmelpreester's artistry had conjured up my likeness on canvas in its higher significance, and on all those other occasions, as in public baths, where men are freed of their accidental trappings and step forth in and for themselves. So, too, from that moment on, I was filled with joy and lively pride that I was to present myself before a high commission not in the misleading garb of a beggar but in my own free form.

The end of the passage adjoining the committee room was open, and although a wooden partition blocked my view of the examination scene, I was able to follow its course very accurately by ear. I heard the words of command with which the staff doctor directed the recruit to bend this way and that, to show himself from all sides, heard the short questions and the answers, rambling accounts of an inflammation of the lung, which obviously failed of their transparent purpose, for they were presently cut short by a declaration of unconditional fitness for service. This verdict was repeated by other voices, further instructions followed, the order to withdraw was given, pattering steps approached, and presently the conscript joined me: a poor specimen, I saw, with a brown streak around his neck, plump shoulders, yellow spots on his upper arms, coarse knees, and big, red feet. In the narrow space I was careful to avoid contact with him. At that moment my name was called in a sharp and nasal voice and simultaneously the assisting noncom appeared in front of the cabinet and motioned to me; I stepped out from behind the partition, turned to the left, and strode with dignified but modest bearing to the place where the doctor and the commission awaited me.

At such moments one is blind, and it was only in blurred outline that the scene penetrated to my at once excited and bemused consciousness: obliquely to my right a longish table cut off one corner of the room, and at this the gentlemen sat in a row, some bending forward, some leaning back, some in uniform, some in civilian clothes. To the left of the table stood the doctor, he too very shadowy in my eyes, especially since he had the window at his back. I, however, inwardly repelled by so many importunate glances turned on me, bemused by the dreamlike sensation of being in a highly vulnerable and defenceless position, seemed to myself to be alone, cut off from every relationship, nameless, ageless, floating free and pure in empty space, a sensation I have preserved in memory as not only not disagreeable but actually precious. The fibres of my body might continue to quiver, my pulse go on beating wildly and irregularly; nevertheless, from then on, my spirit, if not sober, was yet completely calm, and what I said and did in the sequel happened as though without my co-operation and in the most natural fashion—indeed, to my own momentary amazement. Here exactly lies the value of long advance preparation and conscientious immersion in what is to come: at the critical moment something somnambulistic occurs, halfway between action and accident, doing and being dealt with, which scarcely requires our attention, all the less so because the demands actuality makes on us are usually lighter than we expected, and we find ourselves, so to speak, in the situation of a man who goes into battle armed to the teeth only to discover that the adroit use of a single weapon is all he needs for victory. To protect himself the more readily in minor contingencies the prudent man practises what is most difficult, and he is happy if he needs only the most delicate and subtle weapons in order to triumph, for he is naturally averse to anything gross and crude and accommodates himself to their use only in cases of necessity.

" That's a one-year man," I heard a deep, benevolent voice say from the commission table, as though in explanation, but immediately thereafter I was disgusted to hear another, that sharp and nasal voice, declare by way of correction that I was only a recruit.

"Step up," said the staff doctor. His voice was a rather weak tremolo. I obeyed with alacrity and, standing close in front of him, I made this statement with an absurd but not unpleasant assurance.

"I am entirely fit for service."

"That's not for you to judge," he broke in angrily, thrusting his head forward and shaking it violently. "Answer what I ask you and refrain from such remarks!"

"Certainly, Surgeon General," I said softly, although I knew very well that he was nothing but a senior staff doctor, and I looked at him with startled eyes. I could now make him out a little better. He was lean of build, and his uniform blouse hung on him in loose folds. His sleeves, their facings reaching almost to the elbows, were so long that half of each hand was covered and only the thin fingers stuck out. A full beard, sparse and narrow, of a neutral dark shade like the wiry hair on his head, lengthened his face, and this effect was the more pronounced because of his hollow cheeks and his habit of letting his lower jaw sag with his mouth half open. A pince-nez in a silver frame that was bent out of shape sat in front of his narrowed, reddened eyelids in such a way that one lens rested awkwardly against the lid while the other stood far out.

This was the external appearance of my partner. He smiled

woodenly at my manner of address and glanced out of the corner of his eye at the table where the commission sat.

"Lift your arms. State your position in civil life," he said, and at the same time, like a tailor, put a green tape measure with white figures on it around my chest.

"It is my intention," I replied, "to devote myself to hotel service."

"Hotel service? So, it is your intention. When do you intend to do this?"

"I and mine have reached an understanding that I am to begin this career after I have finished my military service."

"Hm. I did not ask about your people. Who are your people?"

"Professor Schimmelpreester, my godfather, and my mother, the widow of a champagne-manufacturer."

"So, so, the widow of a champagne-manufacturer. And what are you doing at present? Are you nervous? Why are your shoulders jerking and twitching that way?"

I had in fact begun, since I had been standing there, half unconsciously and entirely spontaneously, an oddly contrived twisting of the shoulders, an action by no means obtrusive but recurring frequently, which had somehow seemed appropriate. I replied thoughtfully:

"No. It has never for an instant crossed my mind that I might be nervous."

"Then stop that jerking!"

"Yes, Surgeon General," I said shamefacedly, and yet at the same instant I jerked again, a fact he appeared to overlook.

"I am not the Surgeon General," he bleated at me sharply, and shook his outstretched head so violently that the pince-nez threatened to drop off and he was forced to push it back in place with all five fingers of his right hand, an action that could do nothing to remedy the root of the trouble, the fact that it was bent.

"Then I beg your pardon," I replied very softly and penitently.

"Just answer my question!"

Confused, without comprehension, I looked around me, glanced, too, as though in entreaty at the row of commissioners, in whose deportment I thought I had detected a certain sympathy and interest. Finally I sighed without speaking.

"I have asked about your present occupation."

"I assist my mother," I replied with restrained enthusiasm, "in the operation of a quite large boarding-house or rooming-house in Frankfurt am Main."

"My compliments," he said ironically. "Cough!" he then commanded immediately, for he had placed a black stethoscope against my chest and was bending over to listen to my heart.

I had to cough again and again while he poked about on my body with his instrument. Thereupon he exchanged the stethoscope for a little hammer that he picked up from a nearby table, and he began to tap.

"Have you had any serious illnesses?" he asked.

I replied: "No, colonel! Never serious ones! To the best of my knowledge I am entirely healthy and have always been so, if I may pass over certain insignificant fluctuations in my health, and I feel myself qualified in the highest degree for any form of military service "

"Silence!" he said, suddenly interrupting his auscultation and glancing angrily up into my face from his stooping position. "Leave the question of your military fitness to me and don't make so many irrelevant observations! You continually talk irrelevancies!" he repeated as though distracted, and, interrupting his examination, he straightened up and stepped back from me a little. "Your manner of speech is lacking in restraint. That struck me some time ago. What is your position anyway? What schools have you attended?"

"I went through six grades at high school," I replied softly, feigning distress at having alienated and offended him.

"And why not the seventh?"

I let my head hang and threw him an upward glance that

may well have spoken for me and struck the recipient to the heart. "Why do you torment me?" I asked with this look. "Why do you force me to speak? Don't you hear, don't you feel, don't you see that I am a refined and remarkable youth who, beneath an agreeable and conventional exterior, hides deep wounds that life has cruelly inflicted on him? Is it delicate of you to force me to reveal my shame before so many respectable gentlemen?" Thus my glance; and, discriminating reader, it was by no means a lie, even though its piteous plaint at this particular instant was the product of calculation and design. For lies and hypocrisy refer properly to a sensation that is illegitimately produced because its outward expression corresponds to no true and deep experience, a state of affairs that can only result in pathetic, bungling apishness. Should we not, however, be able to command the timely and useful manifestation of our own precious experiences? Briefly, sadly, and reproachfully my glance spoke of early acquaintance with the injustices and misfortunes of life. Then I sighed deeply.

"Answer," said the senior staff doctor in a milder tone.

Struggling with myself, I replied hesitantly: "I was passed over at school and did not complete the course because of a recurrent indisposition that on several occasions confined me to my bed and frequently prevented me from attending class. Also, the teachers thought it their duty to reproach me with lack of attention and diligence, which depressed me very much and disheartened me, since I was not aware of any failure or carelessness in this respect. And yet it so happened that at times a good deal escaped me, I did not hear it or absorb it, whether a classroom exercise was in question or the prescribed homework, whose completion I neglected because I knew nothing about it, not because I entertained other and unsuitable thoughts but because it was exactly as though I had not been present, had not been there in the classroom when the assignments were given out, and this led to reprimands and severe disciplinary measures on the part of the authorities, and on my own part to great–"

Here I could no longer find words, grew confused, fell silent, with my shoulders twitching strangely.

"Stop!" he said. "Do you have trouble hearing? Step farther back there! Repeat what I say." And now with laughable distortions of his thin lips and sparse beard, he began to whisper cautiously: "Nineteen, twenty-seven," and other figures, which I took pains to say after him promptly and exactly; for like all my faculties my hearing was not simply normal but of a special acuity and fineness, and I saw no reason to hide this fact. And so I understood and repeated compound numbers that he only breathed out, and my unusual talent seemed to fascinate him, for he pressed on with the experiment further and further, sending me into the remotest corner of the room in order to hide rather than communicate numbers of four figures at a distance of six or seven yards, and then with pursed mouth he directed significant glances at the commissioners' table when I, half-guessing, understood and repeated what he believed he had barely let slip across his lips.

"Well," he said finally with pretended indifference, "you hear very well. Step up here again and tell us precisely how this indisposition that occasionally kept you from school manifested itself."

Obediently I approached.

"Our family doctor," I replied, "Health Councillor Düsing, used to explain it as a kind of migraine."

"So, you had a family doctor. Health Councillor, was he? And he explained it as migraine! Well, how did it show itself, this migraine? Describe an attack for us. Did you have headaches?"

"Headaches, too!" I replied in surprise, looking at him with respect. "A kind of roaring in both ears and especially a great feeling of distress and fear or rather a timorousness of the whole body, which finally turns into a spasm of choking so violent that it almost hurls me out of bed."

"Spasms of choking?" he said. "Any other spasms?"

"No, certainly no others," I assured him with great earnestness.

"But roaring in the ears."

"A roaring in the ears did certainly often accompany it."

"And when did the attacks occur? Possibly when there had been preceding excitement of some sort? Some specific cause?"

"If I am right," I replied hesitantly and with a questioning glance, "during my school days they often ensued upon just such an incident—that is, a difficulty of the sort I told—"

"When you failed to hear certain things just as though you had not been there?"

"Yes, Surgeon-in-Chief."

"Hm," he said. "And now just think back and tell us carefully whether you noticed any signs that regularly preceded and heralded this condition when it seemed to you that you weren't present. Don't be hesitant. Overcome your natural embarrassment and tell us frankly whether you noticed anything of the sort at such times."

I looked at him, looked him resolutely in the eye for a considerable time, while I nodded my head, heavily, slowly, and as it were in bitter reflection.

"Yes, I often feel strange; strange, alas, was and is very often my state of mind," I finally said softly and reflectively. "Often it seems as though I have suddenly come close to an oven or a fire, so hot do my limbs feel, first my legs, then the upper parts, and this is accompanied by a kind of tickling or prickling that astonishes me, all the more so because at the same time I have before my eyes a play of colour that is really beautiful but that nevertheless terrifies me; and if I may come back to the prickling for a moment, one might describe it as ants running over one."

"Hm. And after this you fail to hear certain things?"

"Yes, that is so, superintendent, sir! There is a great deal I don't understand about my nature, and even at home it has caused me embarrassment, for at times I know I have involuntarily dropped my spoon at the table and stained the tablecloth with soup, and afterward my mother scolds me because I, a full-grown man, behave so boorishly in the presence of our guests—theatrical artists and scholars they are, for the most part."

"So, you drop your spoon? And only notice it a bit later? Tell me, did you ever tell your family doctor, this Health Councillor or whatever that civilian title is, about these little irregularities?"

Softly and dejectedly I replied that I had not.

"And why not?" the other persisted.

"Because I was ashamed," I replied falteringly, "and did not want to tell anyone; it seemed to me that I must keep it secret. And then, too, I hoped secretly that in time it would go away. And I would never have thought I could have enough confidence in anyone to confess to him what very strange experiences I sometimes have."

"Hm," he said, twitching his sparse beard derisively, "because you probably thought they would simply explain it all as migraine. Didn't you say," he went on, "that your father was a distiller?"

"Yes—that is, he owned a sparkling-wine establishment on the Rhine," I said, politely confirming his words and at the same time correcting them.

"Right, a sparkling-wine establishment! And so your father was probably a distinguished connoisseur of wine, was he not?"

"He was indeed, superintendent, sir!" I said happily, while a wave of amusement visibly swept the commission table. "Yes, he was indeed."

"And no hypocrite about himself either, rather a man who loved a good drop, was he not, and, as the saying goes, a mighty drinker before the Lord?"

"My father," I replied evasively, as though withdrawing my levity, "was love of life itself. That much I can agree to."

"So, so, love of life. And what did he die of?"

I was silent. I glanced at him, then bowed my head. And in an altered voice I replied:

"May I most humbly request the battalion surgeon to be so kind as not to insist on an answer?"

"You are not permitted to refuse any information whatsoever!" he replied in a shrill bleat. "What I ask you is asked with deliberation, and your answers are important. In your own interest I warn you to tell us truthfully the manner of your father's death."

"He received a church funeral," I said with heaving breast, and my excitement was too great for me to report things in their proper order. "I can bring you papers to prove that he was buried from a church, and inquiries will show that a number of officers and Professor Schimmelpreester walked behind the coffin. Spiritual Counsellor Chateau himself said in his funeral oration," I went on with increasing vehemence, "that the gun went off accidentally as my father was examining it, and if his hand shook and he was not completely master of himself, that was because we had been visited by a great calamity."

I said "great calamity" and made use of other extravagant and figurative expressions. "Ruin had knocked at our door with her bony knuckle," I said, beside myself, knocking in the air with my own bent index finger by way of illustration, "for my father had fallen into the toils of evil men, bloodsuckers, who cut his throat, and everything was sold and squandered–the glass–harp," I stammered foolishly, and felt myself change colour, for now something altogether astounding was about to happen to me, "the æolian–wheel–" and at that instant this is what occurred.

My face became contorted–but that tells very little. In my opinion, it was contorted in an entirely new and terrifying fashion, such as no human passion could produce, but only a satanic influence and impulse. My features were literally thrust apart in all directions, upward and downward, right and left, only to be violently contracted toward the centre immediately thereafter; a horrible, one-sided grin tore at my left, then at my right cheek, compressing each eye in turn with frightful force while the other became so enormously enlarged that I had the distinct and frightful feeling that the eyeball must pop out—and it could have done so for all of me—let it happen! Whether or not it popped out was hardly the important question, and in any case this was not the moment for tender solicitude about my eye. If, however, so unnatural a play of expression might well have aroused in those present that extreme distaste which we call horror, it was nevertheless only the introduction and prelude to a real witches' Sabbath of face-making, a whole battle of grimaces, fought out during the following seconds on my youthful countenance. To recount in detail the distortions of my features, to describe completely the horrible positions in which mouth, nose, brows, and cheeks—in short, all the muscles of my face—were involved, changing constantly, moreover, so that not a single one of these facial deformities repeated itself—such a description would be far too great an undertaking. Let just this much be said, that the emotional experiences which might correspond to these physiognomical phenomena, the sensations of mindless cheerfulness, blank astonishment, wild lust, inhuman torment, and tooth-grinding rage, simply could not be of this world, but must rather belong to an infernal region where our earthly passions, magnified to monstrous proportions, would find themselves horribly reproduced. But is it not true that those emotions whose expressions we assume really do reproduce themselves in premonitory and shadowy fashion in our souls? Meanwhile, the rest of my body was not still, though I remained standing in one spot. My head lolled and several times it twisted almost entirely around just as if Old Nick were in the act of breaking my neck; my shoulders and arms seemed on the point of being wrenched out of their sockets, my hips were bowed, my knees turned inward, my belly was hollowed, while my ribs seemed to burst the skin over them; my teeth were clamped together; not a single finger but was fantastically bent into a claw. And so, as though stretched on a hellish engine of torture, I remained for perhaps two thirds of a minute.

I was not conscious during this most difficult and consequently lengthy period, at least I was not aware of my surroundings and audience, for to keep them in mind was rendered wholly impossible by the rigours of my condition. Rough shouts reached my ears as though from a great distance without my being able to understand them. Coming to myself on a chair, which the army doctor had hurriedly pushed under me, I choked violently on some stale, warmish tap water which this scholar in uniform had been at pains to pour down my throat. Several of the gentlemen of the commission had sprung up and were bending forward over the green table with expressions of consternation, indignation, and even disgust. Others revealed more sympathetically their amazement at the impressions they had received. I saw one who was holding both fists against his ears; probably through some kind of contagion he had twisted his own face into a grimace; another had two fingers of his right hand pressed against his lips and was blinking his eyelids with extraordinary rapidity. As far as I myself was concerned, I had no sooner looked about me with a restored but naturally shocked expression than I hastened to put an end to a scene that could only appear unseemly to me. I rose from my chair quickly and bewilderedly and took up a military posture beside it, which, to be sure, ill suited my naked human state.

The doctor had stepped back, with the glass still in his hand.

"Have you come to your senses?" he asked with a mixture of anger and sympathy.

"At your service, sir," I replied in a zealous tone.

"And do you retain any recollection of what you have just gone through?"

"I humbly beg your pardon," I replied. "For a moment I was a little distraught."

Short, rather harsh laughter answered me from the commission table. There was repeated murmuring of the word "distraught."

"You certainly didn't seem to be paying very close attention," the doctor said dryly. "Did you come here in a state of excitement? Were you especially anxious about the decision on your fitness for service?"

"I must admit," I replied, "that it would have been a great disappointment to be turned down, and I hardly know how I could have broken such news to my mother. In earlier days she was used to having many members of the officers' corps in her home, and she regards the Army with the greatest admiration. For this reason it is especially important to her for me to be taken into the service, and she not only looks forward to conspicuous advantages in respect of my education but also, and particularly, to a desirable strengthening of my health, which occasionally leaves something to be desired."

He seemed to regard my words with contempt and as worthy of no further consideration.

"Rejected," he said, putting down the glass on the little table where lay the instruments of his profession, the measuring-tape, stethoscope, and little hammer. "The barracks are not a health resort," he snapped at me over his shoulder, turning to the gentlemen at the commission table.

"This individual called up for service," he explained in a thin bleat, "suffers from epileptoid attacks, the so-called equivalents, which are sufficient to negate absolutely his fitness for service. My examination shows that there is obviously a hereditary taint from his alcoholic father, who, after his business failure, ended his life by suicide. The appearance of the so-called aura was unmistakable in the patient's obviously embarrassed descriptions. Furthermore, the feeling of severe distress which, as we heard, at times confined him to bed and which my colleague in civil life" (here a wooden derision appeared once more on his thin lips) "attempted to diagnose as so-called migraine, is to be scientifically designated as a depressed condition following a precedent attack. Especially significant for the nature of the illness is the secrecy the patient observed in regard to his symptoms; for though he is obviously of a communicative character, he kept them secret from everyone, as we heard. It is worth noting that even today there persists in the consciousness of many epileptics something of that mystical, religious attitude which the ancient world adopted toward this nervous disorder. This individual came here in a tense and excited emotional state. Indeed, his exalted way of speaking made me suspicious. Furthermore there were indications of a nervous disorder in the extremely irregular though organically sound beat of his heart and the habitual twitching of the shoulders, which he appeared unable to control. As an especially fascinating symptom I should like to draw your attention to the really astounding hyperacuity of hearing which the patient manifested upon further examination. I have no hesitation in connecting this supernormal sensory sharpness with the rather severe attack we have witnessed, which had perhaps been latent for hours and was instantly precipitated by the excitement I induced in the patient through my unwelcome questions. I recommend to you"—he concluded his clear and learned survey and turned condescendingly to me—"that you put yourself in the hands of a competent doctor. You are rejected."

"Rejected," repeated the sharp, nasal voice that I knew.

Aghast I stood there, not moving from the spot.

"You are exempt from service and may go." These words were spoken, not without some traces of sympathy and kindliness, by that bass voice whose possessor had discriminatingly taken me for a one-year serviceman.

Then I rose on tiptoe and said with beseechingly raised brows: "Would it not be possible to try? Is it not conceivable that a soldier's life would improve my health?"

Some of the gentlemen at the commission table laughed so that their shoulders shook, but the doctor remained harsh and truculent.

"I repeat," he said, rudely throwing the words at my feet,

"that the barracks are not a health resort. Dismissed!" he bleated.

"Dismissed!" repeated the sharp, nasal voice, and a new name was called. "Latte" it was, if I remember correctly, for it was now the turn of the letter *L*, and a tramp with shaggy chest appeared on the scene. I, however, bowed and withdrew to the passage. While I put on my clothes the assisting noncom kept me company.

Happy of course and yet serious in mood; wearied by experiences so extreme as hardly to lie within the human range, experiences to which I had yielded myself, acting and being acted upon; still preoccupied in particular by the significant comments the army doctor had made about the esteem formerly attached to the mysterious sickness from which he believed I was suffering, I paid hardly any attention to the intimate chatter of the underling, with his inadequate stripes, watered hair, and waxed moustaches; it was only later that I remembered his simple words.

"Too bad," he said, looking at me, "too bad about you, Krull, or whatever your name is! You're a promising fellow, you might have amounted to something in the Army. One can see right away whether a man is going to get anywhere with us. Too bad about you; you have what it takes, that's certain, you would certainly have made a first-rate soldier. Who knows if you mightn't have made sergeant major if you'd only given in!"

It was only afterward, as I have said, that this confidential speech reached my consciousness. While hurrying wheels bore me homeward, I thought to myself that the fellow might well have been right; yes, when I pictured how admirably, how naturally and convincingly a uniform would have become me, what a satisfying effect my figure would have made in it, I almost regretted that I had had to dismiss on principle this way of attaining a form of existence that would so well become me and a world where a sense for the natural hierarchy is obviously so highly developed.

More mature consideration, however, compelled me to realize that my entering that world would have been a gross mistake and error. I had not, after all, been born under the sign of Mars—at least not in the specific and actual sense! For although martial severity, self-discipline, and danger have been the conspicuous characteristics of my strange life, its primary prerequisite and basis has been freedom, a necessity completely irreconcilable with any kind of commitment to a grossly factual situation. Accordingly, if I lived *like* a soldier, it would have been a silly misapprehension to believe that I should therefore live *as* a soldier; yes, if it is permissible to describe and define intellectually an emotional treasure as noble as freedom, then it may be said that to live like a soldier but not as a soldier, figuratively but not literally, to be allowed in short to live symbolically, spells true freedom.

CHAPTER VI

After this victory (a real victory of David over Goliath, if I may say so), the moment not having yet arrived for my induction into the Paris hotel, I returned for the nonce to that existence on the streets of Frankfurt which I have already sketched in broad outline—an existence of sensitive loneliness amid the tumult of the world. As I drifted foot-loose through the bustle of the great city, I could have found, had I desired it, abundant opportunity for conversation and companionship with a variety of individuals who might outwardly have seemed to be living lives very like my own. This, however, was by no means my intention; I either avoided such contacts entirely or took care that they never became intimate; for in early youth an inner voice had warned me that close association, friendship, and companionship were not to be my lot, but that I should instead be inescapably compelled to follow my strange path alone, dependent entirely upon myself, rigorously self-sufficient. Furthermore, it seemed to me that if I made myself common in the least, fraternized with acquaintances or, as my poor father would have said, put myself on a *frère-et-cochon* footing—if, in short, I spent myself in a loose sociability—I should literally do violence to some secret part of my nature, should, so to speak, thin the vital sap and disastrously weaken and reduce the tension of my being.

When therefore I had to deal with inquisitiveness and importunity—as would happen, for instance, in the café where I would sit late beside a sticky little marble-topped table—I would behave with that courtesy which better befits my taste and character than rudeness and is, moreover, incomparably better protection. For rudeness makes one common; it is courtesy that creates distinctions. And so I summoned courtesy to my aid on those occasions when unwelcome proposals (I assume that the reader schooled in the multifarious world of the emotions will not be astounded) were made to me from time to time in more or less veiled and diplomatic language by men of a certain sort. It is small wonder, considering the appealing face Nature granted me and the altogether winning appearance that my miserable clothing could not conceal—the scarf around my neck, my mended coat, and broken shoes. For the petitioners of whom I speak and who, of course, belonged to the higher levels of society this mean exterior served as an incitement to desire and an encouragement as well; it was, on the other hand, a barrier between me and the world of fashionable women. I do not mean that there was any lack of attention from that quarter, or of involuntary interest in my naturally favoured person, indications I joyfully noted and remembered. How often have I seen the egotistical, absent-minded smile fade at sight of me from some pure white face scented with eau-de-lis and the face assume an expression of almost suffering tenderness! Your black eyes, precious creature in the brocade evening wrap, grew attentive, wide, almost afraid, they penetrated my rags till I felt their searching touch on my bare body, they returned inquiringly to my clothes, your glance met mine, absorbed it deep within, while your little head tilted a trifle backward as though you were drinking, you returned my glance, plunged deep into my eyes with a sweet, uneasy, importunate attempt to understand. Then, of course, you had to turn away "indifferently," had to enter your wheeled home, and yet when you were already halfway into your silken cage and your servant, with an air of fatherly benevolence, was handing me a coin, the charms of your person seen from behind, tightly spanned by figured cloth of gold, illuminated by the moonlight of the great lamps in the lobby of the opera house, still seemed to hesitate irresolutely in the narrow frame of the carriage door.

No indeed, there was no lack of silent encounters, one of

which I have just summoned up—with emotion. On the whole, however, what good was I to women in gold evening gowns? A penniless youth, I could hardly expect more from them than a shrug of the shoulders. The beggarliness of my appearance, the absence of everything that constitutes the cavalier, wholly devalued me in their eyes and altogether banished me from the radius of their attention. Women only notice "gentlemen"—and I was not one. Matters stood quite otherwise with certain vagrant gentlemen, eccentrics who were seeking neither a woman nor a man, but some extraordinary being in between. And I was that extraordinary being. That is why I needed so much evasive courtesy to calm their importunate enthusiasm; at times, indeed, I found myself compelled to reason with and soothe some beseeching and inconsolable individual.

I refrain from pronouncing moral judgment on a craving which, when I was the object of it, seemed not incomprehensible. Rather I may say with the Roman that I regard nothing human as alien to me. In the story of my personal education in love, however, the following incident must be recorded.

Of all the varieties of humankind which the great city presented to view, one was especially strange—whose very existence in our workaday world afforded no little food for the imagination—one that must needs attract the particular attention of a youth bent on self-education. It was that variety of female known as public persons, daughters of joy, or simply creatures or, more genteelly, priestesses of Venus, nymphs and Phrynes. They either stay together in licensed houses or at night wander the streets in certain sections, holding themselves, with official sanction or toleration, at the disposal of a world of men at once needy and able to pay. It always seemed to me that this arrangement, seen, if I am right, as one should see everything—that is, with a fresh eye undimmed by habit—that this phenomenon, I say, intrudes on our dull-mannered age like a colourful and romantic survival from a gaudier epoch. Its very existence always produced an enlivening and pleasurable effect on me. To visit those particular houses was beyond my means. On the streets and in the cafés, however, I had plenty of opportunity to study these enticing creatures. Nor did this interest remain one-sided; indeed, if I could congratulate myself on sympathetic attention from any quarter, it was from these flitting nightbirds, and before long, despite my habitual attitude of aloofness, I had established personal relations with some of them.

Birds of death is the popular name for the small owls or hawks which, it is said, fly at night against the windows of those who are sick unto death and lure their fearful souls into the open with the cry: "Come with me!" Is it not strange that this same formula is used by the disreputable sisterhood when its members, strolling beneath the street lights, boldly yet covertly summon men to debauchery? Some are corpulent as sultanas, tightly encased in black satin, against which the powdered whiteness of their faces glares in ghostly contrast; others in turn are of a sickly emaciation. Their make-up is crass, designed for effectiveness in the blaze and shadow of nocturnal streets. Raspberry lips glow in chalk-white faces; others have put rosy powder on their cheeks. Their brows are sharply and clearly arched, their eyes, lengthened at the corners by the use of eyebrow pencil and darkened at the edge of the lower lid, often show an unnatural brilliance induced by drugs. Imitation diamonds blaze in their ears; large feather hats nod on their heads; and in their hands all carry little bags, known as reticules or pompadours, in which are hidden toilet articles, lipstick, powder, and certain preventive devices. Thus they stroll past you on the sidewalk, touching your arm with theirs; their eyes, agleam in the street light, are directed sidewise at you, their lips are twisted in a hot, provocative smile, and hastily, furtively whispering the enticing cry of the bird of death, they gesture with a short, sidewise motion of the head toward some undefined promise, as though for the man of courage who follows their invitation and summons there awaited somewhere a wonderful, never tasted, illimitable joy.

As I repeatedly observed this secret scene from a distance

and with rapt attention, I saw too how the well-dressed gentlemen either remained unmoved or entered into negotiations and, if these proved satisfactory, went off with buoyant step in company with their lascivious guides. The creatures did not approach me for this purpose, for my poor attire promised no pecuniary gain from my patronage. Soon, however, I was to rejoice in their private and unprofessional favour. If, mindful of my economic impotence, I did not dare approach them, it not infrequently happened that after a curious and approving examination of my person they would begin a conversation with me in the most cordial manner, inquiring in a comradely way about my occupation and interests—to which I would lightly reply that I was staying in Frankfurt for purposes of amusement. In the conversations that took place in entries and archways between me and members of this gaudy sisterhood they expressed their interest in me in the most various ways in their coarse, outspoken vocabulary. Such persons, let me say parenthetically, ought not to talk. Silently smiling, glancing, gesturing, they are significant; but once they open their mouths they run the risk of sobering us and losing their own halo. For speech is the foe of mystery and the pitiless betrayer of the commonplace.

My friendly association with them was not devoid of a certain attractive tinge of danger, for the following reason. Whoever makes a career of catering to desire and earns a living by so doing is not in consequence by any means exempt from that particular human weakness; he would not otherwise devote himself so completely to its cultivation, stimulation, and satisfaction. He would understand it less thoroughly if it were not especially alive in him, yes, if he were not in his own person a true child of desire. So it happens, as we well know, that these girls usually have a bosom friend, a private lover, besides the many lovers to whom they give themselves professionally. Coming from the same lowly world, he calculatingly bases his way of life on their dream of bliss just as they do theirs on the dreams of others. These fellows are rash and violent characters for the most part, and though they lavish on their girls the joys of nonprofessional tenderness, supervise and regulate their work, and provide them with a certain knightly protection, they make themselves absolute lords and masters, confiscate most of the earnings, and if the returns are unsatisfactory, beat the girls unmercifully, a chastisement they bear willingly and happily. The authorities are hostile to this profession and persecute it constantly. Therefore in these flirtations I was exposing myself to a double danger: first, that I might be mistaken by the police for one of these rude cavaliers and picked up, and, on the other hand, that I might arouse the jealousy of these tyrants and have a taste of the knives with which they make so free. Thus caution was enjoined from both directions, and if more than one of the sisterhood let me see clearly that she would not be averse for once to neglecting her tedious profession in favour of my company, for a long time this double consideration stood firmly in the way—until in one particular case it was, in its graver aspect at least, happily suspended.

One evening, then—I had been applying myself with particular pleasure and persistence to my study of city life, and the night was far advanced—I was resting in a medium-grade café, at once weary and excited from my wanderings, a glass of punch in front of me. A wicked wind was sweeping the streets, and the snowy rain that fell unremittingly made me reluctant to go in search of my distant lodgings; but my present refuge, too, was in an inhospitable state; some of the chairs had already been piled on the tables, scrubwomen were at work with wet rags on the dirty floor, the waiters were lolling about, disgruntled and half asleep, and if despite all this I still lingered, it was principally because I was finding it harder than usual to abandon the sights of the world for sleep.

Desolation reigned in the room. Next to one wall slept a man who looked like a cattle-dealer, leaning forward with his cheek on his leather money-belt. Opposite him two aged men with pince-nez, no doubt incapable of sleep, played dominoes in complete silence. But not far from me, only two tables away, with a little glass of green liqueur in front of her, sat a stranger, a girl easily recognizable as one of Them, but someone I had never seen before. We examined each other with mutual approval.

She was marvellously foreign in appearance; straight, glossy black hair fell in a pageboy bob from beneath the red wool cap perched on one side of her head, half covering cheeks that looked slightly concave beneath the prominent cheekbones. Her nose was blunt, her mouth wide and painted red, and her eyes, which slanted up at the outer corners, shimmered with an indeterminate colour, the direction of their gaze indeterminate, too, in a way altogether her own and unlike other people's. With her red cap she wore a canary-yellow jacket under which the delicate contours of her body revealed themselves as spare but rounded. Nor did I fail to notice that she was long-legged after the fashion of a filly, something that always appealed strongly to my taste. When she lifted the green liqueur to her lips, the fingers of her hand were spread outward and upward, and for some reason, I do not know why, that hand looked hot—perhaps because the veins on the back stood out so prominently. She had, too, the strange habit of pushing her underlip forward and up, rubbing it against the other.

And so I exchanged glances with her, though her slanting, shimmering eyes never clearly betrayed in what direction she was looking, and finally, after we had thus taken each other's measure for a while, I noticed not without youthful confusion that she had favoured me with the signal, that sidewise nod toward the wanton and unknown, with which her guild accompany the enticing call of the bird of death. In pantomime I turned one of my pockets inside out; but, replying with a shake of her head to indicate I need not worry about money, she repeated the signal and, counting out the coins for her green liqueur on the marble tabletop, got up and moved smoothly to the door.

I followed her without delay. Dirty slush lay on the sidewalk, rain drove down at an angle, and the big, misshapen flakes that accompanied it settled on our shoulders, face, and arms like soft, wet animals. I was therefore well content when my unknown bride signalled a cab that was wobbling by. In broken German she gave the driver her address, which was in a street unknown to me, slipped in, and I, drawing the rattling door shut behind me, sank down on the shabby cushions beside her.

Only after the nocturnal vehicle had again set itself into jogging motion did our conversation begin. I scruple to set it down, for I am sensible enough to see that its freedom lies beyond the compass of my voluble and chatty pen. It was without introduction, this conversation, it was without polite conventions of any sort; from the very beginning it had the free, exalted irresponsibility that is usually a characteristic only of dreams, where our "I" associates with shadows that have no independent life, with creations of its own, in a way that is after all impossible in waking life where one flesh-and-blood being exists in actual separation from another. Here it happened, and I happily admit that I was moved to the depths of my soul by the intoxicating strangeness of the experience. We were not alone and even less were we as two; for duality ordinarily creates an inhibiting social situation—and there could be no talk of that here. My darling had a way of putting her leg over mine as though she were simply crossing her own; everything she said and did was marvellously unconstrained, bold and free as lonely thoughts are, and I was joyously ready to follow her lead.

In brief, this exchange consisted in the expression of the lively attraction we had immediately felt for each other, in the exploration, explanation, analysis of this attraction, as well as in an agreement to cultivate it in every way, augment it, and turn it to account. My companion for her part lavished on me many words of praise that reminded me distantly of certain expressions of that wise cleric, the Spiritual Counsellor at home, except that hers were at once more inclusive and more emphatic. For at first glance, so she assured me, anyone who knew anything about such matters could see that I had been created and predestined for the service of love, that I would indeed provide the world and myself with much pleasure and much joy if I hearkened to this special calling and arranged my life entirely to that end. Moreover, she wished to be my instructress and to put me through a thorough schooling, for it was obvious that my gifts still required the direction of an expert hand. . . . This I understood from what she said, but only approximately, for just as her appearance was foreign, her speech was broken and ungrammatical; indeed, she really did not know German at all, so that her words and expressions were often completely absurd and verged strangely upon the irrational—a fact that increased the dreamlike quality of her company. It must be especially and specifically noted, however, that her behaviour was devoid of any frivolity or light-mindedness; instead she maintained in all circumstances—and how strange the circumstances sometimes were!—a severe, almost fierce seriousness, both then and during the whole time of our association.

After prolonged jolting and rattling the carriage finally stopped, we got out, and my friend paid the driver. Then we went upward through a dark, cold stairwell which smelled of dead lampwicks, and my guide opened the door to her room, just opposite the stairs. Here it was suddenly very warm: the smell of a greatly overheated iron stove mingled with the heavy, flowery scent of cosmetics, and when the hanging lamp was lighted, a deep-red glow suffused the room. Comparative luxury surrounded me; on little velvet-topped tables stood colourful vases with dried sheaves of palm leaves, paper flowers, and peacocks' feathers; soft, furry hides lay about; a canopy bed with hangings of red wool adorned with gold braid dominated the room, and there was a great abundance of mirrors, even in places where one does not ordinarily expect them—as, for instance, in the canopy of the bed and in the wall at its side. But since we were filled with longing to know each other completely, we set to work at once, and I stayed with her until the following morning.

Rozsa (this was my antagonist's name) had been born in Hungary, but of the most doubtful antecedents; her mother had been employed in a travelling circus to leap through tissue-paper-covered hoops, and who her father had been remained wholly obscure. She had early shown a very marked inclination to unlimited *galanterie*, and while she was still young she had been placed, by no means against her will, in a house of ill fame in Budapest, where she had spent a number of years as the establishment's chief attraction. But a businessman from Vienna, who believed he could not live without her, had extracted her from this den of iniquity by dint of great cunning plus the active co-operation of a society for the suppression of the white-slave trade and had installed her in his home. No longer young, and prone to apoplexy, he had been excessive in expressing his joy at possessing her and had unexpectedly passed away in her arms. Thus Rozsa had found herself left to her own devices. Living by her arts, she had moved from city to city and had only recently settled in Frankfurt. Unsatiated and unsatisfied by her purely professional activities, she had entered into a permanent relationship with a man who had originally been a butcher's assistant. His fierce energy and wild virility, however, had led him to choose pimping, extortion, and other kinds of blackmail as his calling. This fellow had made himself Rozsa's master and had derived the best part of his income from her amorous activities. But on account of some bloody deed he had been picked up by the police and had been forced to leave her unattended for a protracted period. As she was by no means inclined to give up her private pleasures, she had turned her eyes toward me and had chosen the quiet, still-untrained youth as her bosom companion.

She told me this simple tale in a relaxed hour, and I reciprocated with a condensed version of my own earlier life. For the rest, however, both then and in the future, conversation played a very minor role in our association, for Rozsa restricted herself to simple, practical directions and commands, accompanied by short, exciting cries, which were survivals from her earliest youth—that is, from the circus ring. But on those occasions when our conversation took a broader turn, it was devoted to mutual admiration and praise, for the promise that we had held for each other at our first encounter was richly confirmed, and my mistress, for her part, gave me repeated and unsolicited assurance that my adroitness and prowess in love exceeded her fondest expectations.

Here, earnest reader, I am in the same position as once before in these pages when I was relating certain early and happy experiences with the sweets of life and I added a warning not to confuse an act with the name it goes by, or to make the elementary mistake of dismissing something living and specific with a general term. For if I now set down the fact that for a number of months, until my departure from Frankfurt, I was on intimate terms with Rozsa, often stayed with her, secretly superintended the conquests she made on the street with those slanted, shimmering eyes and the gliding play of her underlip, sometimes, even, was there in hiding when she received her paying customers (occasions that gave me small grounds for jealousy) and did not disdain to accept a reasonable share of the proceeds, one might well be tempted to apply a short, ugly word to my way of life at that time and to lump me summarily with those dark gallants about whom I was talking above. Whoever thinks that actions make people equal may go ahead and take refuge in this simple procedure. For my own part, I am in agreement with folk wisdom which holds that when two persons do the same thing it is no longer the same; yes, I go further and maintain that labels such as "drunkard," "gambler," or even "wastrel" not only do not embrace and define the actual living case, but in some instances do not even touch it. This is my point of view; others may judge differently about this confidence—in respect to which it should be remembered that I am making it of my own free will and could quite easily have passed over it in silence.

If, however, I have treated the present interlude in as much detail as good taste will permit, it is because in my view it was of the most crucial importance for my education: not in the sense that it especially advanced my knowledge of the world or in itself refined my social manners—for that purpose my wild Eastern blossom was by no means the right person. And yet the word "refine" can claim a place here, which I withhold only in order to clarify my meaning. For our vocabulary offers no other term for the profit I derived, in person and character, from my association with this exacting and beloved mistress, whose demands coincided so precisely with my gifts. Moreover, here one must think not only of a refinement *in* love but also *through* love. These italics must be understood aright, for they point to a distinction between, and at the same time an amalgamation of, means and ends, in which the former take on a narrower and more specific meaning and the latter a far more general one. Somewhere in these pages I have already remarked that because of the extraordinary demands life imposed on my energies it was not permissible for me to squander myself in enervating passion. Now, however, during the six-month period that is signalized by the name of the inarticulate but audacious Rozsa I did just that—except that the censorious word "enervating" comes from the vocabulary of hygiene, and its appropriateness in certain important instances is very doubtful. For it is the enervating that benerves us—if certain vital prerequisites are met—and makes us capable of performances and enjoyments in the world that are beyond the compass of the un-benerved. I take no little pride in my invention of this word "benerved" with which I have quite spontaneously enriched our vocabulary; it is intended to serve as the scientific antonym to the virtuously deprecatory word "enervate." For I know from the very bottom of my being that I could never have borne myself with so much subtlety and elegance in the many vicissitudes of my life if I had not passed through Rozsa's naughty school of love.

CHAPTER VII

With the coming of Michaelmas the leaves began to fall from the trees that bordered our streets, and the moment arrived for me to take up the position my godfather Schimmelpreester had secured for me through his international connections. One cheery morning, after a tender farewell from my mother—the pension had acquired a maid and was enjoying a modest success—with my few possessions packed in one small suitcase, hurrying wheels bore me toward my new goal in life—no less than the capital city of France.

They hurried, rattled, and jolted, those wheels, beneath the communicating compartments of a third-class carriage. On the yellow wooden benches a mixed lot of depressingly insignificant travellers of the poorer sort went on with their miserable existence throughout the day, snoring, smacking their lips, gossiping, and playing cards. My own interest was mainly attracted by some children between two and four years of age Although they were blubbering and roaring intermittently, I gave them some chocolate creams out of a bag my mother had included among my supplies; for I have always liked to share. Later I did a great deal of good with the treasures that passed from the hands of the rich into mine. The little ones came tripping up to me, repeatedly touching me with their sticky hands and speaking to me in lisps and gurgles. They were delighted when I replied in exactly the same fashion. Now and again this intercourse earned me a benevolent glance from the grown-ups, despite their schooling in reserve—not that I had any such purpose in view. On the contrary, this day's journey taught me afresh that the more receptive one's mind and soul to human charm, the more abysmally depressing one finds the sight of human ragtag and bobtail. I know very well these people can do nothing about their ugliness; they have their little joys and no doubt their heavy sorrows; in short, like other creatures they love, suffer, and endure life. From a moral point of view, every one of them very likely has a claim to our sympathy. But the alert and sensitive æsthetic perception that Nature has endowed me with compels me to avert my eyes. Only at the tenderest age are they tolerable, like these waifs to whom I gave chocolates and whom I set roaring with laughter by using their own language, thus paying sociability its due.

Moreover, I shall now take occasion to say for the reader's reassurance that this was the last time I ever travelled third class, companioned by misery. What is called fate, and is actually ourselves, working through unknown but infallible laws, soon found ways and means of keeping this from ever happening again.

My ticket, of course, was in perfect order, and in my own fashion I relished the fact that it was so irreproachable—that consequently I myself was irreproachable, and when, in the course of the day, the honest conductors in their smart uniforms visited me in my wooden carriage to examine and punch my ticket, they returned it each time with silent official approval. Silent of course and expressionless: that is, with an expression of indifference that was barely animate and bordered on affectation. This prompted me to reflect on the aloofness, the standoffishness, amounting almost to lack of interest, which one human being, especially an official, feels compelled to manifest toward his fellows. This honest man who punched my valid ticket earned his livelihood thereby; somewhere a home awaited him—there was a wedding ring on his finger—he had a wife and children. But I had to behave as though the thought of his human associations could never occur to me, and any question about them, revealing that I did not regard him simply as a convenient marionette, would have been completely out of order. On the other hand, I had my own particular human background about which he might have inquired. But this, for one thing, was not his privilege and, for another, was beneath his dignity. He was concerned only with the validity of the ticket held by a passenger who was no less a marionette than he. What became of me once the ticket had been used was something he must coldly disregard.

There is something strangely unnatural and downright artificial in this behaviour, though one must admit that to abandon it would be going too far for various reasons—indeed, even slight departures usually result in embarrassment. This time, in fact, toward evening, when the conductor, lantern at waist, returned my ticket, he accompanied it with a prolonged glance and a smile that was obviously inspired by my youth.

"You're going to Paris?" he asked, though my destination was clear to see.

"Yes, inspector," I replied, nodding cordially. "That's where I'm bound."

"What are you planning to do there?" he took the further liberty of asking.

"Just imagine!" I replied. "Thanks to a recommendation, I am going into the hotel business."

"Think of that!" he said. "Well, lots of luck!"

"Good luck to you, too, chief inspector," I replied. "Please give my regards to your wife and the children."

"Yes, thanks—well, what do you know!" He laughed in embarrassment, mixing his words up oddly, and hastened to leave. But on his way out he tripped over a nonexistent obstacle, so completely had this human touch upset him.

I felt very cheerful at the border station, too, where we all had to get out with our luggage for the customs inspection. My heart was light and pure, for my small bag actually did not contain anything I had to hide from the eyes of the inspectors. Even the necessity of a very long wait (since the officials understandably gave distinguished travellers precedence over those of the meaner sort, whose possessions they then all the more thoroughly mussed and mauled) was not able to cloud my sunny mood. When the man before whom I was finally permitted to spread out my meagre belongings at first seemed bent on shaking every shirt and sock to see whether some contraband might not fall out, I immediately engaged him in a conversation I had composed in advance and thus quickly won him over and kept him from hauling everything out. Frenchmen naturally love and honour conversation—and quite rightly! That, after all, is what distinguishes human beings from animals, and it is certainly not unreasonable to assume that a human being distinguishes himself the more from animals, the better he speaks—especially in French. For France regards its language as the language of mankind, exactly, I imagine, as those happy tribes of ancient Greeks took their idiom for the only human mode of expression, holding everything else for barbaric barking and quacking—an opinion the rest of mankind involuntarily subscribed to, more or less, inasmuch as it regarded Greek, as we today do French, as the finest.

"*Bonsoir, monsieur le commissaire!*" I greeted the inspector, dwelling with a kind of muted hum on the third syllable of the word "*commissaire.*" "*Je suis tout à fait à votre disposition avec tout ce que je possède. Voyez en moi un jeune homme très honnête, profondément dévoué à la loi et qui n'a absolument rien à déclarer. Je vous assure que vous n'avez jamais examiné une pièce de bagage plus innocente.*"

"*Tiens!*" he said, looking at me more closely. "*Vous semblez être un drôle de petit bonhomme. Mais vous parlez assez bien. Êtes-vous Français?*"

"*Oui et non,*" I replied. "*A peu près. A moitié—à demi, vous savez. En tout cas, moi, je suis un admirateur passionné de la France et un adversaire irréconciliable de l'annexion de l'Alsace-Lorraine!*"

His face took on an expression that I might describe as deeply moved.

"*Monsieur*," he said decisively, "*je ne vous gêne plus longtemps. Fermez votre malle et continuez votre voyage à la capitale du monde avec les bons vœux d'un patriote français!*"

And while I was stuffing back my odds and ends of linen, still expressing my thanks, he was already putting his chalk mark on the top of my open bag. In the course of my hasty repacking, however, chance decreed that this piece of luggage should lose some of the innocence I had quite honestly ascribed to it, for an additional small item slipped into it that had not been there before. To be specific: beside me at the tin-roofed luggage counter, behind which the inspectors carried on their activities, a middle-aged lady, wearing a mink coat and a velvet cloche adorned with heron feathers, was engaged in a heated altercation with the official in charge, who obviously held a different view from hers about the value of some of her possessions, certain pieces of lace which he held in his hand. Her handsome luggage, from which he had plucked forth the lace in question, was strewn about, several pieces of it so close to my own possessions as to be mixed up with them; nearest of all was a very costly small morocco case, almost square in shape, and it was this that had unexpectedly slipped into my little bag along with the other things while my friend was inscribing his chalk mark on top. This was an occurrence rather than an action, and it happened quite secretly; the case simply smuggled itself in, so to speak, as a by-product of the good humour that my friendly relations with the authorities of this country had produced in me. Actually during the rest of my trip I hardly thought about my accidental acquisition and I only fleetingly considered the possibility that the lady might have missed her jewel case while repacking. Eventually I was to find out more about that.

And so at the end of a trip that, with interruptions, had lasted twelve hours, the train rolled slowly into the North Station. While porters busily and loquaciously helped the wealthy travellers with their numerous pieces of baggage, while some of the latter were exchanging embraces and kisses with friends who had come to meet them, while even the conductors condescended to receive handbags and blanket rolls handed to them out of doors and windows, the lonely youth descended into this tumult from his refuge for third-class members of society. Observed by no one, his small suitcase in his hand, he departed from the noisy, rather unattractive hall. Outside on the dirty street (a shower was falling) the driver of a fiacre saw I was carrying a suitcase, and lifted his whip invitingly in my direction, calling to me: "Eh! Shall we drive, *mon petit*?" or "*mon vieux*" or something of the sort. And yet how was I to pay for the ride? I had almost no money, and if that little case foreshadowed an improvement in my financial position, its contents could certainly not be put to immediate use. Besides, it would hardly have been proper to arrive at my future place of employment in a fiacre. It was my intention to make my way there on foot, even though it might be a considerable distance, and I politely inquired from passers-by the direction I must take to reach the Place Vendôme—for reasons of discretion I mentioned neither the hotel nor even the rue Saint-Honoré. I did this several times, but no one I asked so much as slowed his step to give ear to my inquiry. And yet I did not look like a beggar, for my mother had in the end disgorged a few talers to spruce me up a bit for my journey. My shoes had been newly soled and mended, and I wore a warm, short jacket with patch pockets, and a becoming sports cap to match, below which my blond hair showed attractively. But a young fellow who does not hire a porter and carries his possessions through the street without engaging a fiacre is a stepson of our civilization, not worthy of a single glance. To be more precise, a feeling of anxiety warns others against having anything whatever to do with him. He is suspected of a disquieting attribute: to wit, poverty; and he is therefore suspected of even worse things as well. It thus seems wisest to society simply to avert her eyes from this damaged product of her order. "Poverty," it is said, "is no sin," but that is just talk. To its possessor it is highly sinister—half defect, half undefined reproach; it is in every way extremely repulsive, and any association with it may lead to unpleasant consequences.

This attitude toward poverty has often been painfully brought home to me, and it was so on this occasion. Finally I stopped a little old woman, who, for what reason I do not know, was pushing ahead of her a child's cart filled with all sorts of pots and pans; and it was she who not only pointed out the direction in which I must go, but also described the place where I could get a bus that would take me to the famous square. I could at least spare the few sous this form of transportation would cost and so I was happy to have this information. Moreover, the longer the good old woman looked at me in giving these directions, the wider her toothless mouth stretched in the friendliest of smiles. Finally she patted me on the cheek with her hard hand, saying: "*Dieu vous bénisse, mon enfant!*" This caress made me happier than many another I was to receive in future from fairer hands.

For the traveller who enters the streets of Paris from that particular station, the first impression of the city is not by any means enchanting; but splendour and magnificence increase apace as he nears the glittering centre. If in manly fashion I repressed the timidity I felt, it was yet with astonishment and delighted reverence that, from my narrow seat in the omnibus, my little suitcase on my knee, I looked out upon the flaming magnificence of those avenues and squares, at the confusion of carriages, crowds of pedestrians, the sparkling stores that proffered everything, the inviting cafés and restaurants, and the blinding theatre façades with their white arc lights or hanging gaslights. Meanwhile, the conductor pronounced names I had often heard lovingly uttered by my poor father: "Place de la Bourse," "rue du Quatre Septembre," "boulevard des Capucines," "Place de l'Opéra," and many others.

The uproar, pierced by the shrill cries of newsboys, was deafening, and the lights made one's head swim. In front of the cafés, sheltered by the marquees, men in hats and coats sat at little tables, their canes between their knees, and looked out as though from a loge at the crowds hurrying by. Meanwhile, dark figures stooped to snatch cigarette butts from between their feet. To them the gentlemen paid no heed nor did they seem distressed by this creeping occupation. They obviously considered it a persistent and accepted feature of that civilization whose happy tumult they were in a secure position to enjoy.

It is the proud rue de la Paix that connects the Place de l'Opéra with the Place Vendôme. Here, then, beside the pillar surmounted by the statue of the mighty Emperor, I left the bus and went afoot in search of my real goal, the rue Saint-Honoré, which, as travellers know, runs parallel to the rue de Rivoli. It proved easy to find, and from a distance, in letters of impressive size and brilliance, the name of the Hotel Saint James and Albany sprang to my eyes.

There people were arriving and departing. Gentlemen, about to get into carriages already loaded with their luggage, were handing tips to the servants who had looked after them; porters were carrying into the building the bags of new arrivals. I know the reader will smile when I admit that I was almost overcome by timidity at the thought of boldly entering this imposing, expensive, fashionably located edifice. But did not right and duty combine to encourage me? Had I not been directed and engaged to come here, and was not my godfather Schimmelpreester on intimate terms with the general manager of the establishment? Nevertheless, modesty bade me choose, not one of the two revolving glass doors through which the guests were entering, but rather the side entrance through which the porters passed. The latter, however, whatever they may have taken me for, motioned me back; I was not one of them. Nothing remained for me but to go in through one of those magnificent revolving doors, my little bag in my hand. In the process of negotiating it, I had, to my shame, to be helped by a pageboy in a diminutive red tail-coat who was posted there. "*Dieu vous bénisse, mon enfant!*" I said to him, automatically using the words of that good old woman—at which he burst into as hearty a roar of laughter as the children with whom I had been playing on the train.

I found myself in a stately lobby with porphyry columns and a gallery circling it at the height of the entresol. Crowds surged back and forth, and people dressed for travel sat in the deep armchairs arranged on the carpeted floor beneath the columns. Among them were several ladies who held tiny, shivering dogs in their laps. A boy in livery officiously tried to take my bag out of my hand, but I resisted and turned to the right toward the easily identifiable concierge's desk. There a gentleman with cold unfriendly eyes, dressed in a gold-braided frock coat and obviously accustomed to large tips, was dispensing information in three or four languages to the crowd clustered around his desk. From time to time, smiling benignly, he would hand room keys to such of the hotel's guests as asked for them. I had to stand there a long time before I had an opportunity to ask him whether he thought the general manager, Monsieur Stürzli, was in, and where I might perhaps have the opportunity of presenting myself to him.

"You wish to speak to Monsieur Stürzli?" he asked with insolent surprise. "And who are you?"

"A new employee of the *établissement*," I replied. "With the highest personal recommendations to *monsieur le directeur*."

"*Étonnant!*" replied this benighted man, and added with a disdain that cut me to the quick: "No doubt Monsieur Stürzli has been awaiting your visit with painful impatience for hours. Perhaps you would be so good as to take yourself a few steps farther on to the reception desk."

"A thousand thanks, *monsieur le concierge*," I replied. "And may large tips come your way from every side, so that you will soon be able to retire to private life!"

"Idiot!" I heard him call after me. But that neither concerned nor disturbed me. I carried my suitcase over to the reception desk, which was indeed only a few steps away, on the same side of the lobby. It was even more densely beleaguered. Numerous travellers vied for the attention of the two gentlemen in severe morning coats who were in charge, inquiring for their reservations, learning the numbers of the rooms assigned to them, signing the register. To work my way forward to the desk cost me much patience; finally I stood face to face with one of the gentlemen, a still young man with a small waxed moustache, a pince-nez, and a sallow, indoor complexion.

"You wish a room?" he asked, since I had deferentially waited to be spoken to.

"Oh, no indeed—not that, *monsieur le directeur*," I answered smiling. "I am a member of the staff, if I may already say so. My name is Krull, first name Felix, and I am reporting here by arrangement between Monsieur Stürzli and his friend, my godfather Professor Schimmelpreester. I am to be employed as an assistant in this hotel. That is—"

"Step back!" he commanded hastily in a low voice. "Wait! Step all the *way* back!" And at this a faint flush tinged his sallow cheeks. He glanced about uneasily, as though the fact of a new employee, not yet in uniform, appearing before the hotel guests as if he were a human being, had caused him the most acute embarrassment. Some of those busy at the desk were, indeed, glancing at me curiously. They interrupted their filling out of forms to look round at me.

"*Certainement, monsieur le directeur!*" I answered in subdued tones, and withdrew well behind those who had come after me. There were not many of them, however, and after a few minutes the reception desk was entirely clear, though it would not be for long.

"Well, now what about you?" The gentleman of the indoor complexion was finally forced to turn to where I was standing some way off.

"*L'employé-volontaire Félix Kroull*," I replied without moving from the spot, for I wanted to force him to invite me to approach.

"Well, come here!" he said nervously. "Do you think I want to keep shouting at you at this distance?"

"I withdrew on your orders, *monsieur le directeur*," I replied, approaching eagerly, "and I was just waiting for you to countermand them."

"My orders," he interposed, "were only too necessary. What are you doing here? What possessed you to march into the lobby like one of our guests and mix willy-nilly with the clientele?"

"I beg a thousand pardons," I said contritely, "if that was a mistake. I knew of no other way to reach you except by frontal attack through the revolving door and the lobby. But I assure you I would not have hesitated to take the dirtiest, darkest, most secret way if that had been necessary to gain your presence."

"What kind of talk is that?" he replied, and once more a faint flush tinged his sallow cheeks. This tendency of his to blush pleased me.

"You seem," he added, "either a fool or possibly a little too intelligent."

"I hope," I replied, "to prove quickly enough to my superiors that my intelligence functions within precisely the right limits."

"It seems to me very doubtful," he said, "whether you will have the chance. I don't know at the moment of any vacancy in our staff."

"Nevertheless, I take the liberty of pointing out," I reminded him, "that we are dealing with a firm agreement between *monsieur le directeur général* and a boyhood friend of his, who held me at the baptismal font. I have intentionally refrained from asking for Monsieur Stürzli, for I know very well that he is not dying of impatience to see me and I am under no illusions that I will see that gentleman soon or perhaps ever. But that is of minor importance. Instead, all my desires and efforts have been directed toward paying my respects to you, *monsieur le directeur*, and learning from you, and from you alone, where, how, and in what manner of service I can prove myself useful to the *établissement*."

"*Mon Dieu, mon Dieu!*" I heard him murmur. Nevertheless, he took down a bulky volume from a shelf on the wall and searched angrily through it, repeatedly licking the two middle fingers of his right hand. Presently he stopped at an entry and said to me:

"At least get away from here as fast as you can and go some place where you belong! Your employment has been provided for, that much is correct–"

"But that's the important point," I remarked.

"*Mais oui, mais oui!* Bob"–he turned to one of the half-grown bellboys sitting on a bench at the back of the office, hands on knees, waiting for errands–"show this individual to the *dortoir des employés* number four on the top floor. Use the service elevator! You will hear from us early tomorrow," he added sharply to me. "Go!"

The freckled boy, obviously English, went with me.

"Why don't you carry my bag a little way?" I said to him. "I can tell you both my arms are lame from lugging it."

"What will you give me?" he asked in broadly accented French.

"I have nothing."

"Well, I'll do it anyway. Don't feel pleased about *dortoir* number four! It is very bad. We are all very badly housed. Also the food is bad and the pay too. But a strike is out of the question. Too many are ready to take our places. That whole crowd of pirates ought to be exterminated. I am an anarchist, you must know, *voilà ce que je suis*."

He was a very nice, childish youngster. We rode up together in the service lift to the fifth floor, the garret, and there he let me pick up my bag again, pointed to a door in the ill-lit, carpetless corridor, and said: "*Bonne chance*."

The plate on the door showed it was the right one. As a precaution I knocked, but there was no answer. Although it was already after ten o'clock, the dormitory was still completely dark and empty. Its appearance, when I turned on the electric light bulb that hung unshielded from the ceiling, was indeed far from attractive. Eight beds, with grey flannel blankets and flat, obviously long-unwashed pillows, were arranged like bunks, two and two, one above the other along the side walls. Between them open shelves were set against the walls to the height of the upper bunk, and on these the occupants had placed their bags. The room, whose single window seemed to open on an air shaft, offered no further conveniences, nor was there any space for them, since its width was considerably less than its length, leaving very little room in the middle. At night, obviously, one would have to put one's clothes at the bottom of one's bed or in a bag on the shelf.

Well, I thought, you need not have gone to so much trouble to escape the barracks, for it could not have been more Spartan there than in this room—probably somewhat cosier. A bed of roses, however, was something I had not been accustomed to for a long time—not since the break-up of my happy home. Moreover, I knew that a man and his circumstances usually come to a tolerable adjustment; indeed, that the latter, however difficult they may appear at the start, show, if not for everyone, then at least for the more fortunate, a certain flexibility that is not altogether a question of habit. The same situations are not the same for everyone, and general conditions, so I would maintain, are subject to extensive personal modification.

Let the reader forgive this digression on the part of a spirit that is by nature philosophically inclined and is devoted to observing life less for its ugly and brutal aspects than for its delicate and amiable qualities.

One of the shelves was empty, from which I deduced that one of the eight beds must also be vacant; only I did not know which—to my regret, for I was weary from my journey, and my youth demanded sleep. I had no choice, however, but to await the arrival of my roommates. For a while I entertained myself by inspecting the washroom, a side door to which stood open. There were five washstands of the commonest sort, with squares of linoleum in front of them, washbowls and pitchers, with slop jars beside them, and hand towels hanging on a rack. Mirrors were entirely lacking. In place of them, thumbtacked on door and wall—and in the bedroom, too, so far as space permitted—were all sorts of enticing pictures of women cut out of magazines. Not much comforted, I returned to the bedroom and in order to have something to do I prudently decided to get my nightshirt out of my suitcase. In doing so, however, I came upon the little morocco case that had slipped in so unobtrusively during the customs inspection; happy at seeing it again, I set about investigating it.

Whether curiosity about its contents may not all the time have been at work in the secret recesses of my soul and the notion of getting out my nightshirt had been only an excuse to acquaint myself with the jewel case—on this subject I offer no opinion. Sitting on one of the lower beds, I took it on my knees and began to examine it with the prayerful hope of remaining undisturbed. Its light lock was not fastened, and it was kept shut only by a small hook and eye. I found no fairy-tale treasure inside, but what it did contain was very charming and in part truly remarkable. Right at the top, in a tray that divided the satin-lined interior into two compartments, lay a necklace of several strands of large, graduated, golden topazes in a carved setting, such as I had never seen in any shop window and hardly could have, since it was obviously not of modern design but came from a past century. I may say it was the essence of magnificence, and the sweet, transparent, shimmering honey-gold of the stones enchanted me so completely that for a long time I could not take my eyes off them; it was with considerable reluctance that I lifted the tray to look into the bottom. This was deeper than the upper compartment and less completely filled than the latter had been by the topaz necklace. Nevertheless, charming items laughed up at me, each one of which I retain clearly in memory. A long string of little diamonds set in platinum lay there piled in a glittering heap. There were in addition: a very handsome tortoise-shell comb, ornamented with silver vines set with numerous diamonds, though these, too, were small; a gold double-bar brooch with platinum clasps, ornamented on top with a sapphire the size of a pea surrounded by ten diamonds; a dull-gold brooch delicately formed to represent a little basket filled with grapes; a bracelet in the shape of a bugle, tapering toward the end, with a platinum safety catch, the value of which was enhanced by a noble white pearl, surrounded by diamonds in an *à jour* setting, which was set in the bell; in addition, three or four very attractive rings, one of which contained a grey pearl with two large and two small diamonds, another a dark triangular ruby also set off by diamonds.

I took these precious objects in my hand and let their noble rays flash in the vulgar light of the naked electric bulb. But who can describe the confusion I felt when, plunged in this amusing occupation, I suddenly heard a voice above my head say dryly:

"You have some quite pretty things there."

Although there is always something disconcerting about believing oneself alone and unobserved and suddenly discovering that this is not so, the present situation redoubled that unpleasantness. No doubt I failed to hide a slight start; nevertheless, I compelled myself to be completely calm, closed the little case without haste, casually put it back in my suitcase, and then and only then got up so that by stepping back a little I could look in the direction from which the voice had come. There, indeed, on the bed above the one I had been sitting on, someone was lying propped up on an elbow looking down at me. My earlier inspection had not been thorough enough to reveal this fellow's presence. Perhaps he had been lying up there with a blanket over his head. He was a young man who could have used a shave, so dark was his chin. His hair was mussed from lying in bed, he had sideburns, and eyes of a Slavic cast. His face was feverishly red, but although I saw he must be sick, dismay and confusion prompted me to say awkwardly:

"What are you doing up there?"

"I?" he answered. "It's my privilege to inquire what interesting job you're engaged in down there."

"Don't speak familiarly to me, please," I said irritably. "I am not aware that we are relatives or on terms of intimacy."

He laughed and replied not altogether unreasonably: "Well, what I saw in your hands is likely to create a certain bond between us. Your dear mother surely did not pack that in your grip for you. Just show me your little hands—what long fingers you have, or how long you can make them!"

"Don't talk nonsense!" I said. "Do I owe you an explanation of my property simply because you were so rude as to watch me without letting me know you were there? That's very bad form—"

"Yes, you're a fine one to complain about me," he interrupted. "Drop the high-flown nonsense, I'm no wild man. Moreover, I can tell you that I was asleep until just a little while ago. I have been lying here with influenza for two days and I have a filthy headache. When I woke up I said to myself quietly: 'What's the pretty boy playing with down there?' For you are pretty; even envy must admit that. Where wouldn't I be today with a phiz like yours!"

"My phiz is no excuse for you to go on saying *tu* to me. I'll not speak another word till you stop."

"By God, prince, I can call you 'Your Highness' if you like. But we're colleagues, as I understand it. You're a newcomer?"

"The management had me shown up here," I replied, "so that I could choose a free bed. Tomorrow I am to begin my duties in this establishment."

"As what?"

"That has not yet been decided."

"Very odd. I work in the kitchen—that is, in the *garde-manger* where the cold dishes are. The bed you were sitting on is taken. The second one above it is free. What's your nationality?"

"I arrived this evening from Frankfurt."

"I'm a Croat," he said in German. "From Agram. I worked in a restaurant kitchen there, too. But I've been in Paris for three years. Do you know your way around in Paris?"

"What do you mean, 'know my way around'?"

"You understand very well. I mean, have you any idea where you can sell that stuff of yours at a decent price?"

"Something will turn up."

"Not by itself. And it's not smart to carry a find like that around with you for long. If I give you a safe address, shall we split fifty-fifty?"

"What are you talking about, fifty-fifty? And for nothing but an address!"

"Something that a greenhorn like you needs just as much as food. I will tell you that the string of diamonds–"

Here we were interrupted. The door opened and a number of young people came in whose working-hours were over: a liftboy in red-braided grey livery; two messengers in high-necked blue jackets with two rows of gold buttons and gold stripes on their trousers; a half-grown youngster in a blue-striped jacket, who was carrying an apron over his arm and was probably employed in the lower kitchen as pot-washer or something of the sort. Before long they were followed by another bellboy of Bob's class and a youth whose white jacket and black trousers showed he might be a busboy or assistant waiter. They said: "*Merde!*" and as there were Germans among them: "Damnation!" and "Devil take it!"–imprecations that probably had to do with their day's work, now over. They called up to the man in bed: "Hello, Stanko, how bad do you feel?" They yawned noisily and at once began to undress. To me they paid very little attention, only saying in jest as though they had expected me: "*Ah, te voilà. Comme nous étions impatients que la boutique deviendrait complète!*"

One of them confirmed the fact that the upper bunk that Stanko had pointed out was free. I climbed up, put my bag on the appropriate shelf, undressed sitting on the bed, and almost before my head touched the pillow fell into the deep, sweet sleep of youth.

CHAPTER VIII

At almost the same instant several alarm clocks shrilled and rattled; it was six o'clock and still dark; those who were out of bed first turned on the ceiling light. Only Stanko paid no attention to this reveille and stayed where he was. As I felt greatly refreshed and much cheered by my sleep, I was not unduly upset by the annoying crowd of untidy young men yawning, stretching, and pulling their nightshirts over their heads in the narrow space between the bunks. Even the battle for the five washstands—five for seven youths much in need of a wash—was something I did not allow to dim my cheerfulness, despite the fact that the water in the jugs was insufficient and we had to rush out naked into the corridor, one after another, to fetch more from the faucet. After I had followed the others in soaping and rinsing, I got only a very wet hand towel that was no longer much use for drying. By way of compensation, however, I was allowed to share the hot water that the liftboy and busboy had warmed over an alcohol stove, and while I guided my razor with practised strokes over my cheeks and chin, I was allowed to join them in peering into a fragment of mirror they had succeeded in fastening to the window catch.

"*Hé, beauté*," Stanko called to me as I came back into the bedroom, hair brushed and face washed, to finish dressing and, like everyone else, to make my bed. "Hans or Fritz, what's your name?"

"Felix, if that's all right with you," I replied.

"First-rate. Will you be so kind, Felix, as to bring me a cup of *café au lait* from the *cantine* when you're through with breakfast? Otherwise I'll probably get nothing till they bring the gruel up at noon."

"With pleasure," I replied. "I will do it gladly. First I will bring you a cup of coffee and then I will come back in a very short time."

I said this for two reasons. First, because of the disquieting fact that although my suitcase had a lock I did not have the key, and I was far from happy about leaving Stanko alone with it. Secondly, because I wished to reopen my conversation of yesterday and get, on more reasonable terms, the address he had mentioned.

The spacious *cantine des employés* opened off the end of the corridor; it was warm there and smelt agreeably of coffee, which the man in charge and his fat and motherly wife were dispensing from two shiny machines behind the buffet. The sugar was set out ready in bowls, and the woman poured in milk and gave each of us a brioche as well. There was a great horde of all kinds of hotel people from the various dormitories, including waiters from the main dining-room in blue tail-coats with gold buttons. For the most part they ate and drank standing up, but a few sat at small tables. In accordance with my promise I asked the motherly lady for a cup "*pour le pauvre malade de numéro quatre*," and she handed me one, giving me at the same time the glance and smile I had come to expect. "*Pas encore équipé?*" she asked, and I explained my present situation. Then I hurried back to Stanko with the coffee and told him again that I would drop in to talk with him very shortly. He gave an amused snort as I turned away, for he thoroughly understood both of my reasons.

Back in the cantine, I served myself, drank my *café au lait*, which tasted extremely good, for I had had nothing warm in a long time, and ate my brioche. The room began to empty, for it was getting on toward seven o'clock, and presently I was able to make myself comfortable at one of the little oilcloth-covered tables in the company of an elderly, frock-coated *commis-de-salle*. When he took out a pack of Caporals and lighted one, all I had to do was smile and give the hint of a wink for him to offer them to me. Moreover, when he got up to go—after a short conversation in which I told him about my still uncertain position—he left the still half-filled pack behind as a present.

The after-breakfast taste of the black, aromatic tobacco was most agreeable, but I dared not linger long over it. Instead, I hurried back to my patient. He received me in a bad temper, which I easily recognized as feigned.

"Here again?" he asked crossly. "What do you want? I have no need of your company. I have a headache and a sore throat and no inclination whatever for chitchat."

"So you're not feeling any better?" I said. "I'm sorry. I was just about to inquire whether you weren't somewhat cheered by the coffee I brought you out of a natural desire to be of service."

"I know very well why you brought the coffee. I'm not going to get mixed up in your miserable affairs. A simpleton like you will just make a mess of things."

"It was you," I replied, "who started the talk about business. I don't see why I shouldn't keep you company, and leave business out of it. They're not going to pay any attention to me right away and I have more time than I know what to do with. Just accept the idea that I'd like to share some of it with you."

I sat down on the bed under his, but this had the disadvantage of preventing me from seeing him. That was no way to talk, I found, and I was compelled to get up again.

He said: "It's some progress that you realize you need me and not the other way about."

"If I understand you aright," I replied, "you are referring to an offer you made yesterday. It's very friendly of you to come back to it. That reveals, however, that you, too, have a certain interest in it."

"Damn little. A ninny like you will get done out of his loot. How did you get hold of it anyway?"

"By accident. Actually because a happy moment so decreed."

"That happens. Besides, you may have been born lucky; there's something about you. But show me your trinkets again so I can make a guess at their value."

Pleased though I was to find him so much softened, I replied: "I'd rather not, Stanko. If someone came in, it could easily lead to a misunderstanding."

"Well, it's not really necessary," he said. "I saw it all pretty clearly yesterday. Don't get any mistaken ideas about that topaz necklace. It is–"

There was instant proof of how right I had been to anticipate interruptions. A scrubwoman with pail, rags, and broom came in to mop up the puddles of water in the washroom and to put things straight. As long as she was there, I sat on the lower bed and we did not say a word. Only after she had gone lumbering off in her clattering clogs did I ask him what he had been about to say.

"I, say?" He started to dissemble again. "You wanted to hear something, but there wasn't anything I wanted to say. At most I was going to advise you not to put your hopes in that topaz necklace you looked at so long and so lovingly yesterday. Stuff like that costs a lot if you buy it at Falize's or Tiffany's, but what you get for it is a laugh."

"What do you call a laugh?"

"A couple of hundred francs."

"Well, nevertheless."

"A nincompoop like you says 'nevertheless' to everything! That's what makes me sick. If I could only go with you or take charge of this myself!"

"No, Stanko. How could I take the responsibility for that! You have a temperature, after all, and have to stay in bed."

"Oh, all right. Besides, even I couldn't get a knight's estate for the comb and brooch. Or even the breast pin, in spite of the sapphire. The best is still the necklace; it's easily worth ten thousand francs. And I wouldn't turn up my nose at one or two of the rings, especially when I remember the ruby and the grey pearl. In short, at a quick guess, the whole lot should be worth eighteen thousand francs."

"That was just about my own estimate."

"Imagine that! Have you any idea at all about such things?"

"Yes, I have. The jewellers' windows back home in Frankfurt were always my favourite study. But you probably don't mean that I will get the full eighteen thousand?"

"No, my pet, I don't. But if you knew how to look out for your interests a bit and didn't say 'nevertheless' to everything and everybody, you should be able to get a good half of it."

"Nine thousand francs, then."

"Ten thousand. As much as the string of diamonds is worth by itself. If you're halfway a man, you won't let it go for less."

"And where do you advise me to take it?"

"Aha! Now my beautiful friend wants me to make him a present. Now I'm to tie my information to the ninny's nose gratis out of pure affection."

"Who's talking about gratis, Stanko? Naturally I'm prepared to show my appreciation. Only I consider what you said yesterday about fifty-fifty somewhat extreme."

"Extreme? In such joint enterprises fifty-fifty is the most natural division in the world, the division by the book. You forget that without me you're as helpless as a fish out of water, and besides that I can always tip off the management."

"Shame on you, Stanko! One doesn't say things like that, let alone do them. You wouldn't dream of doing it either. I am convinced you would prefer a couple of thousand francs to a tip-off from which you would get nothing."

"You think you can take care of me with a couple of thousand francs?"

"That's what it comes to in round figures if I generously concede you one third of the ten thousand francs which, in your opinion, I will get. Besides, you ought to be proud of me for looking out for my own interests a bit, and that ought to give you confidence in my ability to stand up to the cut-throat."

"Come here," he said, and when I approached he said, softly and clearly:

"*Quatre-vingt-douze, rue de l'Échelle au Ciel.*"

"*Quatre-vingt-douze, rue de–*"

"*Échelle au Ciel.* Can't you hear?"

"What an auspicious name!"

"Even though it's been called that for hundreds of years? Go ahead and take it as a good omen! It's a very quiet little street, only it's a long way off, out beyond the Cimetière de Montmartre. Your best way is up to the Sacré-Cœur, which is easy to see, then go through the Jardin between the church and the cemetery and follow the rue Damrémont in the direction of the boulevard Ney. Before Damrémont runs into Championnet, a little street goes off to the left, rue des Vierges Prudentes, and from it your Échelle branches off. You really can't miss it."

"What's the man's name?"

"It doesn't matter. He calls himself a clockmaker and he is that, too, among other things. Try not to act too much like a sheep. I only told you the address to get rid of you so I could get some rest. As for my money, just remember I can report you any time."

He turned his back to me.

"I am really grateful to you, Stanko," I said, "and you can be sure you will have no reason to complain of me to the management."

Thereupon I left, silently repeating the address to myself. I went back to the now completely deserted *cantine*, for where else was I to spend my time? I had to wait until the people downstairs remembered me. For a good two hours I sat at one of the little tables without permitting myself the slightest impatience, smoked some more of my Caporals, and devoted myself to thought. It was ten by the wall clock in the *cantine* when I heard a harsh voice in the corridor shouting my name. Before I could get to the door a bellboy appeared there and shouted:

"*L'employé Félix Kroull*—report to the general manager!"

"That's me, dear friend. Take me with you. Even if it were the President of the Republic, I am quite prepared to appear before him."

"All the better, dear friend," he answered my genial speech rather pertly, measuring me with his eyes. "Be so kind as to follow me."

We walked down a flight of stairs to the fourth floor, where the corridors were much wider and had red carpets. There he rang for one of the guest elevators that came up that high. We had a while to wait.

"How come the Rhinoceros wants to speak to you himself?" he asked.

"You mean Monsieur Stürzli? Connections. Personal connections," I added. "Tell me, what makes you call him the Rhinoceros?"

"*C'est son sobriquet*. Pardon, I didn't invent it."

"Not at all, I am grateful for any information," I replied.

The elevator had handsome wainscoting, an electric light, and a red satin banquette. At the controls stood a youth in that sand-coloured livery with red braid. He stopped first too high, then much too low, and let us clamber up over the resulting high step.

"*Tu n'apprendras jamais, Eustache*," said my guide, "*de manier cette gondole*."

"*Pour toi je m'échaufferais!*" the other replied rudely.

This displeased me and I could not refrain from saying: "Those who are weak ought not to show their contempt for one another. That does nothing to improve their position in the eyes of the strong."

"*Tiens*," said the man I had reprimanded. "*Un philosophe!*"

Now we were down, and as we walked from the lift at one side of the lobby past the reception desk, I could not fail to notice how the bellboy glanced at me repeatedly and curiously out of the corner of his eye. I was always pleased when I made an impression not simply by my attractive appearance but by my intellectual gifts as well.

The private office of the general manager was beyond the reception desk on a corridor that also led, as I saw, to billiard rooms and reading-rooms. My guide knocked cautiously, was answered by a grunt from inside, and opened the door. With a bow he ushered me in, his cap at his thigh.

Herr Stürzli was a very fat man with a pointed grey beard for which there hardly seemed room on his bulging double chin. He was seated at his desk looking through papers and at first he paid no attention to me. His appearance immediately explained his nickname among the staff, for not only was his back massively rounded and his neck larded in fatty folds, but from the end of his nose there actually protruded a horny wart that confirmed his right to the appellation. By contrast, his hands, with which he was sorting the papers into orderly piles of equal size, were astonishingly small and delicate in proportion to his over-all bulk. Despite his size there was nothing awkward about him; on the contrary, as sometimes happens with corpulent people, he possessed a certain elegance of movement.

"So you are the young man," he said in German with a slight Swiss accent, still busily sorting his papers, "who was recommended to me by a friend—Krull, if I am not mistaken—*c'est ça*—the young man who wishes to work for us?"

"Exactly as you say, *Herr Generaldirektor*," I replied, discreetly drawing somewhat closer—and as I did so I observed, not for the first time nor the last, a strange phenomenon. When he looked me in the eye his face was contorted by an expression of revulsion which, as I understood perfectly well, was simply a consequence of my youthful beauty. By this I mean that those men whose interest is wholly concentrated on women, as was no doubt Monsieur Stürzli's case, what with his enterprising imperial and his gallant *embonpoint*, when they encounter what is sensually attractive in a person of their own sex are often curiously embarrassed by their own impulses. This is due to the fact that the boundary line between the sensual in its most general and in its more specific sense is not easy to draw; constitutionally, however, these men are revolted at any hint of correspondence between this specific sense and their own desires; the result is just this reaction, this grimace of revulsion. Any sort of serious consequence is, of course, out of the question, for the person involved will politely assume the blame for the wavering of this sensual boundary rather than hold it against the innocent who made him conscious of it. He will therefore not attempt to avenge his embarrassment. Nor did Monsieur Stürzli do so in this instance, especially since, confronted by his confusion, I lowered my eyelashes in sincere and decorous modesty. On the contrary, he became very sociable and inquired:

"Well, how are things with my old friend, your uncle Schimmelpreester?"

"Pardon me, *Herr Generaldirektor*," I replied, "he is not my uncle, but my godfather, which is perhaps even closer. Thank you for inquiring, everything is going very well with my godfather so far as I know. He enjoys the highest reputation as an artist in the whole Rhineland and even beyond."

"Yes, yes, a gay old dog, a sly fellow," he said. "Really? Is he successful? *Eh bien*, all the better. A gay dog. We had good times together here in the old days."

"I don't need to say," I continued, "how thankful I am to Professor Schimmelpreester for putting in a good word for me with you, *Herr Generaldirektor*."

"Yes, he did that. What, is he Professor too? How is that? *Mais passons*. He wrote me about you and I did not disregard the matter, because in the old days we had so many larks together. But I must tell you, my friend, there are difficulties. What are we to do with you? You obviously have not the slightest experience in hotel work. You are as yet entirely untrained—"

"Without presumption I think I can say in advance," I replied, "that a certain natural adroitness will very quickly make up for my lack of training."

"Well," he remarked in a teasing tone, "your adroitness no doubt shows itself mainly with pretty women."

In my opinion he said this for three reasons. First of all, the Frenchman—and Herr Stürzli had long been that—loves to pronounce the phrase "pretty women" for his own gratification as well as that of others. "*Une jolie femme*" is the most popular raillery in that country; with it one can be sure of a gay and sympathetic response. It is much the same as mentioning beer in Munich. There one has only to pronounce the word to produce general high spirits. This in the first place. Secondly, and looking more deeply, in talking about pretty women and joking about my presumed skill with them, Stürzli wanted to subdue the confusion of his instincts, be rid of me in a certain sense, and, as it were, push me toward the female side. This I understood perfectly well. In the third place, however—in opposition, it must be admitted, to the above effort—it was his intention to make me smile, which could only lead to his experiencing that same confusion again. Obviously, in a muddled way, that was just what he wanted. The smile, however restrained, was something I could not refuse him and I accompanied it with the following words:

"Assuredly in this domain, as in every other, I stand far behind you, *Herr Generaldirektor*."

My pretty speech was wasted. He did not hear it at all, but simply looked at my smile, and his face once more bore a look of revulsion. This is what he had wanted, and there was nothing for me to do but to lower my eyes once more in decorous modesty. And once again he did not make me pay for it.

"That's all very well, young man," he said, "the question is what about your rudimentary information? You drop in like this on Paris—do you even know how to speak French?"

This was grist to my mill. I was filled with elation, for now the conversation had taken a turn in my favour. This is the place to insert an observation about my general gift for languages, a gift that was always amazing and mysterious. Universal in my endowments and possessed of every possible potentiality, I did not really need to learn a foreign language, once I had acquired a smattering of it, to give the impression, for a short time at least, of fluent mastery. This was accompanied with such an exaggerated but precise imitation of the characteristic national gestures as bordered on the comic. The imitative, parody element in my performance did not lessen its credibility but actually enhanced it, and with it came a pleasant, almost ecstatic feeling of being possessed by a foreign spirit. Plunged in this or rather taken captive by it, I was in a state of inspiration, in which, to my astonishment (and this in turn increased the daring of my performance) the vocabulary simply flashed into my head, God knows from where.

In the first case, however, my glibness in French had no such supernatural background.

"*Ah, voyons, monsieur le directeur général,*" I gushed with extreme affectation. "*Vous me demandez sérieusement si je parle français? Mille fois pardon, mais cela m'amuse! De fait, c'est plus ou moins ma langue maternelle—ou plutôt paternelle, parce que mon pauvre père—qu'il repose en paix!—nourrissait dans son tendre cœur un amour presque passionné pour Paris et profitait de toute occasion pour s'arrêter dans cette ville magnifique dont les recoins les plus intimes lui étaient familiers. Je vous assure: il connaissait des ruelles aussi perdues comme, disons, la rue de l'Échelle au Ciel, bref, il se sentait chez soi à Paris comme nulle part au monde. La conséquence? Voilà la conséquence. Ma propre éducation fut de bonne part française, et l'idée de la conversation, je l'ai toujours conçue comme l'idée de la conversation française. Causer, c'était pour moi causer en français et la langue française—ah, monsieur, cette langue de l'élégance, de la civilisation, de l'esprit, elle est la langue de la conversation, la conversation elle-même. . . . Pendant toute mon enfance heureuse j'ai causé avec une charmante demoiselle de Vevey—Vevey en Suisse—qui prenait soin du petit gars de bonne famille, et c'est elle qui m'a enseigné des vers français, vers exquis que je me répète dès que j'en ai le temps et qui littéralement fondent sur ma langue—*

> *Hirondelles de ma patrie,*
> *De mes amours ne me parlez-vous pas?"*

"Stop!" he interrupted the cascade of my chatter. "Stop that poetry at once! I can't stand poetry, it upsets my stomach. Here in the lobby at five o'clock in the afternoon we sometimes let French poets appear, if they have anything decent to wear, and recite their verses. The ladies like it, but I keep as far away as possible, it makes the cold sweat break out on me."

"*Je suis désolé, monsieur le directeur général. Je suis violemment tenté de maudir la poésie—*"

"All right. Do you speak English?"

Yes, did I? I did not, or at most I could act for three minutes or so as though I did—that is, just so long as I could manage with what I had once heard of the accent of the language in Langenschwalbach and in Frankfurt and the bits of vocabulary I had picked up here and there in books. The important thing was to construct out of a total lack of materials something that would be at least momentarily dazzling. And so I said—not in the broad, flat accents that the ignorant tend to associate with English, but pointing my lips instead and whispering, with my nose arrogantly raised in the air:

"I certainly do, sir. Of course, sir, quite naturally I do. Why shouldn't I? I love to, sir. It's a very nice and comfortable language, very much so indeed, sir, very. In my opinion, English is the language of the future, sir. I'll bet you what you like, sir, that in fifty years from now it will be at least the second language of every human being. . . ."

"Why do you wave your nose around in the air like that? It's not necessary. Also, your theories are superfluous. I simply asked what you knew. *Parla italiano?*"

Instantly I was an Italian; in place of soft-voiced refinement I became possessed by the fieriest of temperaments.

There happily rose up in me all the Italian sounds I had ever heard from my godfather Schimmelpreester, who had enjoyed frequent sojourns in that sunny land. Moving my hand with fingers pressed together in front of my face, I suddenly spread all five fingers wide and carolled and sang:

"*Ma, signore, che cosa mi domanda? Son veramente innamorato di questa bellissima lingua, la più bella del mondo. Ho bisogno soltanto d'aprire la mia bocca e involontariamente diventa il fonte di tutta l'armonia di quest' idioma celeste. Sì, caro signore, per me non c'è dubbio che gli angeli nel cielo parlano italiano. Impossibile d'immaginare che queste beate creature si servano d'una lingua meno musicale–*"

"Stop!" he commanded. "You're slipping into poetry again and you know that makes me ill. Can't you leave it alone? It's not fitting for a hotel employee. But your accent is not bad, and you have a certain knowledge of languages, as I see. That is more than I had expected. We will try you out, Knoll–"

"Krull, *Herr Generaldirektor.*"

"*Ne me corrigez pas!* So far as I am concerned, you could be called Knall. What's your first name?"

"Felix, *Herr Generaldirektor.*"

"That doesn't suit me at all. Felix–Felix, there's something private and presumptuous about it. You will be called Armand."

"It gives me the greatest joy, *Herr Generaldirektor*, to change my name."

"Joy or not, Armand is the name of the liftboy who is quitting his job tonight. You can take his place tomorrow. We will try you out as a liftboy."

"I venture to promise, *Herr Generaldirektor*, that I will prove quick to learn and that I will do my job even better than Eustache."

"What's this about Eustache?"

"He stops too high or too low and it makes an awkward step, *Herr Generaldirektor*. Only, of course, when he is carrying his equals. With hotel guests, if I understood him properly, he is more careful. This lack of consistency in carrying out his duties seems to me less than praiseworthy."

"What business is it of yours to praise things around here? Besides, are you a Socialist?"

"No, indeed, *Herr Generaldirektor!* I find society enchanting just as it is and I am on fire to earn its good opinion. I only meant that when a man knows his business he should never permit himself to make a botch of it even when nothing much is at stake."

"Socialists are something we have no place whatever for in our business."

"*Ça va sans dire, monsieur le—*"

"Go on now, Knull! Have them give you the proper livery in the storeroom down in the basement. This is supplied by us, but the appropriate shoes are not, and I must call your attention to the fact that yours—"

"That is simply a temporary error, *Herr Generaldirektor*. By tomorrow it will be rectified to your complete satisfaction. I know what I owe the *établissement* and I assure you that my appearance will leave nothing whatever to be desired. I am enormously pleased about the livery, if I may say so. My godfather Schimmelpreester loved to dress me up in the most varied costumes and always praised me for looking so much at home in each of them, although inborn talent is not really a cause for praise. But I have never yet tried on a liftboy's uniform."

"It will be no misfortune," he said, "if in it you please the pretty women. *Adieu*, your services will not be required here today. Take a look at Paris this afternoon. Tomorrow morning ride up and down a few times with Eustache or one of the others and see how the mechanism works; it's simple and will not exceed your competence."

"It will be handled with love," was my reply. "I will not rest until I no longer make the smallest step. *Du reste, monsieur le directeur général,*" I added and let my eyes melt, "*les paroles me manquent pour exprimer—*"

"*C'est bien, c'est bien,* I've got things to do," he said and turned away, his face twisting once more in that grimace of distaste. This did not disturb me. Posthaste—for it was important for me to find that clockmaker before noon—I went downstairs to the basement, found the door marked "Storeroom" without difficulty, and knocked. A little old man with eyeglasses was reading the newspaper in a room that looked like a secondhand store or the costume room of a theatre, so crowded was it with colourful servants' liveries. I mentioned my needs, which were promptly met.

"*Et comme ça,*" said the old man, "*tu voudrais t'apprêter, mon petit, pour promener les jolies femmes en haut et en bas?*"

This nation cannot stop doing it. I winked and agreed that this was my wish and duty.

Very briefly he measured me with his eyes, took a sand-coloured livery with red piping, jacket and trousers, from the hanger, and quite simply folded it over my arm.

"Wouldn't it be better for me to try it on?" I asked.

"Not necessary, not necessary. What I give you will fit. *Dans cet emballage la marchandise attirera l'attention des jolies femmes.*"

The wizened old man was very likely thinking of something else. He spoke quite mechanically, and just as mechanically I winked back at him, called him "*mon oncle*" at parting, and assured him I would owe my *carrière* to him alone.

I took the basement elevator to the fifth floor. I was in a hurry, for I was still a little worried as to whether Stanko would leave my suitcase alone in my absence. On the way, the elevator made several stops. Guests demanded the services of the lift; as they came in I modestly flattened myself against the wall. A lady entered from the lobby and asked to be taken to the second floor. An English-speaking bride and groom got in at the first floor and asked for the third. The single lady, who had entered first, excited my attention—and here, to be sure, the word "excited" is appropriate. I observed her with a rapid beating of the heart that was not without sweetness.

I knew the lady although she was not wearing a cloche with heron feathers, but another hat instead, a broad-brimmed creation trimmed in satin, over which she had put a white scarf that was tied under her chin and lay on her coat in long streamers. And although this coat was a different one from the one she had worn yesterday, a lighter, brighter one, with big cloth-covered buttons, there could not be the slightest doubt that I had before me my neighbour of the customs shed, the lady with whom I was connected through the possession of the jewel case. I recognized her first of all by a widening of the eyes that she had practised constantly during her argument with the inspector, but that was obviously a habit, for now she kept doing it constantly without cause. There were further signs of nervous tension in her not unlovely face. Otherwise, so far as I could see, there was nothing in the appearance of this forty-year-old brunette that could mar the tender relationship in which I stood to her. A little downy moustache lay not unbecomingly on her upper lip. Moreover, her eyes had the golden-brown colour that always pleases me in women. If only she would not keep widening them in such a disturbing way! I had a feeling I ought to talk her out of that compulsive habit.

So we had really alighted here simultaneously—if the word "alight" can be used in my case. It was only by chance that I had not met her again in front of the blushing gentleman at the reception desk. Her presence in the narrow space of the elevator produced a strange effect on me. Without knowing about me, without ever having seen me, without being aware of me now, she had been carrying me, featureless, in her thoughts ever since the moment yesterday evening or this morning when in unpacking her suitcase she had discovered that the jewel case was missing. I could not bring myself to attribute a hostile intent to her interest, however much this may surprise the solicitous reader. That her concern about me and her questions might have resulted in steps being taken against me (perhaps she was even now returning from taking such steps), these obvious possibilities flitted through my mind, without producing any real conviction; they had small weight against the enchantment of a situation in which the seeker was unwittingly so close to the object of her search. How I regretted, for her as well as for myself, that this proximity was of such short duration, lasting only to the second floor!

As she in whose thoughts I lay stepped out she said to the red-haired liftboy: "*Merci, Armand.*"

It was remarkable, and a proof of her sociability as well, that she, who had so recently arrived, already knew this fellow's name. Perhaps she had been a frequent guest at the Saint James and Albany and had known him for some time. I was even more struck by the name and by the fact that it was Armand who was running the elevator. The meeting had been rich in associations.

"Who was that lady?" I asked as we went on.

Like an ignorant boor, the redhead made no reply. Nevertheless, as I got out on the fifth floor I added this question:

"Are you the Armand who is quitting this evening?"

"That's none of your damn business," he said hoarsely.

"You're wrong," I replied. "It is my business. As a matter of fact, I'm Armand now. I'm following in your footsteps. I'm your successor and I'm going to try to cut a less boorish figure than you."

"*Imbécile!*" he shouted, slamming the elevator gate in my face.

Stanko was asleep when I entered *dortoir* number four. Hastily I proceeded as follows: I removed my suitcase from the shelf, carried it into the washroom, took out the little case that the honest Stanko, thank God, had left untouched, and, after removing my jacket and vest, put the charming topaz necklace around my neck and with some difficulty made sure the safety catch was closed behind. I then put my clothing back on, and crammed the rest of the jewelry, which was less bulky, into my right- and left-hand pockets. This done, I put my suitcase back in its place, hung up my livery in the wardrobe beside the hall door, put on my outdoors jacket and cap, and—I think through being disinclined to ride with Armand again—ran down all five flights and was on my way to the rue de l'Échelle au Ciel.

With my pockets full of treasure I still did not have the few sous necessary for a bus. I had to go on foot, and with difficulty, for I had to ask my way and, besides, my pace soon suffered from the weariness of going uphill. It took me a good three quarters of an hour to reach the Montmartre Cemetery, for which I had been inquiring. From there on, to be sure, Stanko's directions proved completely reliable, and I quickly made my way through the rue Damrémont to the sidestreet of the Wise Virgins. Once there, I was within a few strides of my goal.

A mammoth settlement like Paris consists of many quarters and communities, and very few of these give any hint of the majesty of the whole to which they belong. Behind the magnificent façade the metropolis exhibits to the stranger is hidden the middle-class small town that carries on an independent existence within it. Many of the inhabitants of the street called "Ladder to Heaven" had probably not seen for years the glitter of the avenue de l'Opéra or the cosmopolitan hubbub of the boulevard des Italiens. An idyllic provincial scene surrounded me. Children played on the narrow cobbled street. Along the quiet sidewalks were rows of simple houses, with here and there a store on the ground floor—a grocer's, a butcher's, a baker's, a saddler's—modestly displaying its wares. There must be a clockmaker here, too. I soon found number 92. "*Pierre Jean-Pierre, Horloger*" was inscribed on the door of the shop beside the show window, which contained all kinds of timepieces—pocket watches for ladies and gentlemen, tin alarm clocks, and cheap pendulum clocks.

I pressed the latch and stepped in to the accompaniment of a tinkling bell that was set in motion by the opening of the door. The owner, a jeweller's loupe clamped in his eye, sat behind the counter, which was arranged as a showcase and also contained within its glass walls all sorts of watches and chains. He was examining the works of a pocket watch whose owner obviously had reason for complaint. The many voiced tick-tock of table clocks and grandfather clocks filled the store.

"Good day, master," I said. "Would it surprise you to know that I would like to buy a pocket watch and perhaps a handsome chain to go with it?"

"No one will stop you, my boy," he replied, taking the lens from his eye. "Presumably it's not to be a gold one?"

"Not necessarily," I replied. "I don't care anything about glitter and show. The inner quality, the precision, that's what I'm interested in."

"Sound principles. A silver one, then," he said, opening the inner side of the showcase and taking from among his wares several objects which he laid before me.

He was a haggard little man with stubbly yellow-grey hair and the sort of cheeks that start much too high, directly under the eyes, and hang sallowly where they ought to curve out. A cheerless, depressing picture.

With the silver stem-winder he had recommended in my hand, I asked the price. It was twenty-five francs.

"Incidentally, master," I said, "it is not my intention to pay cash for this watch, which I like very much. I prefer to go back to the older way of doing business—barter. Look at this ring!" And I got out the circlet with the grey pearl, which I had kept separate, for just this moment, in the change pocket inside the right-hand pocket of my jacket. "My idea," I explained, "is to sell you this pretty item and to receive from you the difference between its worth and the price of this watch—in other words, to pay you for the watch out of my receipts for the ring—or, to put it in still another way, to ask you simply to deduct the price of the watch, to which I entirely agree, from the sum of two thousand francs, let us say, which you will no doubt offer me for the ring. What do you think of that little transaction?"

Sharply, with narrowed eyes, he examined the ring in my hand and then stared in the same fashion into my face, while a slight quiver became noticeable in his malformed cheeks.

"Who are you, and where did you get this ring?" he asked in a tight voice. "What do you take me for and what kind of deal are you proposing? Get out of here at once! This store belongs to an honest man!"

Dejectedly I hung my head, but after a short pause said with warmth: "Master Jean-Pierre, you are making a mistake. The mistake of distrust–something I had to reckon with, to be sure, but from which your knowledge of people should have saved you. Look me in the eye. . . . Well? Do I look like a–like the sort of person you thought I might be? I don't blame you for your first idea, it is understandable. But your second–I shall be much disappointed if that is not corrected by your personal impressions."

He continued to peer at the ring and at my face with an abrupt up-and-down motion of his head.

"Where did you hear about my business?" he inquired.

"From a fellow worker and roommate," I replied. "He is not altogether well at the moment; if you like, I will take him your good wishes for a speedy recovery. His name is Stanko."

He still hesitated, peering up and down at me, his cheeks quivering. But I clearly saw that desire for the ring was gaining the upper hand over his timidity. With a glance at the door he took it out of my hand and quickly seated himself behind the counter to examine it through his watchmaker's loupe.

"It has a flaw," he said, referring to the pearl.

"Nothing could surprise me more," I replied.

"I can easily believe that. Only an expert would see it."

"Well, so well hidden a flaw can't affect the value. And the diamonds, if I may ask?"

"Trash, splinters, roses, chipped-off stuff and simple decoration. A hundred francs," he said, tossing the ring down between us on the glass top but closer to me.

"I must have misunderstood you!"

"If you think you misunderstood me, my boy, take your loot and be on your way."

"But then I can't buy the watch."

"*Je m'en fiche*," he said. "*Adieu*."

"Listen to me, Master Jean-Pierre," I began again. "With all due regard for your feelings, I can't spare you the reproach of negligence in the way you conduct your business. Through extreme miserliness you are endangering negotiations that have hardly yet begun. You overlook the possibility that this ring, valuable though it is, may not be the hundredth part of what I have to offer. This possibility is, nevertheless, a fact, and you would do well to alter your attitude toward me accordingly."

He looked at me wide-eyed and the quivering in his misshapen cheeks increased remarkably. Once more he glanced at the door and then, motioning with his head, he muttered between his teeth: "Come back here."

He took the ring, led me around the counter, and opened the door to an unaired, windowless back room; there he lighted a brilliant white gas flame in the lamp hanging above a round table with a velvet cover and crocheted doilies. A safe and a small desk gave the place an appearance halfway between middle-class living-room and business office.

"Come on! What have you got?" the clockmaker demanded.

"Allow me to remove this," I replied, taking off my outer jacket. "There, that's better." And one by one I took out of my pockets the tortoise-shell comb, the breastpin with the sapphire, the brooch in the form of a little fruit basket, the bracelet with the white pearl, the ruby ring, and, as climax, the string of diamonds, and laid them all, well separated, on the crocheted table cover. Finally, requesting permission, I unbuttoned my vest, took the topaz jewelry from around my neck, and added it to the display on the table.

"What do you think of that?" I asked with quiet pride.

I saw he could not quite conceal a glitter in his eye and a smacking of his lips. But he gave the appearance of waiting for more and finally inquired in a dry voice: "Well? Is that all?"

"All?" I repeated. "Master, you mustn't pretend a collection like this comes your way every day."

"You'd be happy to get rid of your collection, wouldn't you?"

"Don't overestimate my eagerness," I replied. "If you are asking whether I would like to dispose of it at a reasonable price, I can say yes."

"Quite so," he returned. "Reasonableness is just what you need, my fine fellow."

Thereupon he drew up one of the plush-covered armchairs that stood around the table and sat down to examine the objects. Without invitation I took a chair, crossed my legs, and watched him. I clearly saw his hands shaking as he took up one piece after another, appraised it, and then abruptly tossed it back onto the table. That was probably to cover up the quiver of greed, as was the repeated shrugging of his shoulders, especially when—this happened twice—he held the string of diamonds in his hands and, blowing on the stones, let them slowly slide between his fingers. And so it sounded all the more ridiculous when he finally said, gesturing at the whole collection:

"Five hundred francs."

"What for, may I ask?"

"For the whole thing."

"You're joking."

"My boy, there's no occasion for either of us to joke. Do you want to leave your loot here for five hundred? Yes or no?"

"No," I said and got up. "Very far from it. With your permission I'll take my keepsakes, as I see I am being taken advantage of disgracefully."

"Dignity," he said jokingly, "becomes you. And your strength of character is remarkable, too, for your years. As a tribute to it I'll say six hundred."

"That's a step that doesn't get you out of the realm of the ridiculous. I look younger, dear sir, than I am, and it won't help at all to treat me as a child. I know the real worth of these things, and although I am not simple-minded enough to think I can insist on getting it, I will not permit the payment to differ to an immoral degree. Finally, I know that in this field of business there are competitors, and I'll be able to find them."

"You have an oily tongue—along with your other talents. But the idea hasn't occurred to you that the competitors with whom you threaten me are very well organized and may have agreed upon common terms."

"The question is simply this, Master Jean-Pierre, whether *you* want to buy my things, or whether someone else is to buy them."

"I am inclined to take them and, as we agreed in advance, at a reasonable price."

"And what's that?"

"Seven hundred francs—my last word."

Silently I began to stow the jewelry in my pockets, first of all the string of diamonds.

With trembling cheeks he watched me.

"Blockhead," he said, "you don't know your own good luck. Think what a quantity of money that is, seven or eight hundred francs—for me who has to lay it out and for you who will pocket it! What a lot of things you can buy yourself for, let us say, eight hundred and fifty francs—pretty women, clothes, theatre tickets, good dinners. Instead of that, like a fool, you want to go on carrying the stuff around with you in your pockets. How do you know the police aren't waiting for you outside? And don't you take my own risk into account?"

"Have you," I said at a venture, "read about these objects anywhere in the newspapers?"

"Not yet."

"You see? Despite the fact that we are dealing with a total real value of not less than eighteen thousand francs. Your risk is absolutely theoretical. Nevertheless, I will take it into account, as though it were real, since in point of fact I find myself momentarily short of cash. Give me half their worth, nine thousand francs, and it's a deal."

He pretended to roar with laughter, unpleasantly revealing the stumps of decayed teeth. Squeakingly he repeated over and over the figure I had named. Finally he said solemnly: "You're crazy."

"I take that," I said, "as the first thing you've said since the last thing you said. And you will change that, too."

"Listen, my young greenhorn, this is certainly the very first transaction of this sort you have ever tried to carry on?"

"And suppose that were so?" I replied. "Pay attention to the advent of a new talent that has just appeared on the scene. Don't reject it through stupid miserliness. Try rather to win it over to your side through openhandedness, since it may yet bring you large profits, instead of steering it to another purchaser with a better nose for luck and more taste for the youthful and promising!"

Taken aback, he looked at me. Doubtless he was weighing my reasonable words in his shrivelled heart while studying the lips with which I had spoken them.

Taking advantage of his hesitation, I added: "There's no point, Master Jean-Pierre, in our going on with these offers and counter-offers in lump sums. The collection ought to be examined and evaluated piece by piece. We must take our time about it."

"That's all right with me," he said. "Let's reckon it up."

That's where I made a stupid blunder. Of course if we had kept to lump sums I should never in the world have been able to stick to nine thousand francs, but the arguing and haggling that now ensued over the price of each piece, while we sat at the table and the clockmaker noted down on his pad the miserable valuations he forced on me, beat me down too heartbreakingly. It lasted a long time, probably three quarters of an hour or more. In the midst of it the shop bell rang, and Jean-Pierre went out after commanding in a whisper: "Hush! Don't move!"

He came back again, and the haggling continued. I got the string of diamonds up to two thousand francs, but if that was a victory it was my only one. In vain I called upon the heavens to witness the beauty of the topaz jewelry, the rarity of the sapphire that adorned the breastpin, of the white pearl in the armband, of the ruby and the grey pearl. The rings together produced fifteen hundred; all the other items except the string of diamonds were in the range of fifty to three hundred. The sum total was forty-four hundred and fifty francs, and this villain of mine acted as though he were horrified by it and were ruining himself and his whole fraternity. He declared, moreover, that in these circumstances the silver watch that I had to buy would come to fifty francs instead of twenty-five—as much, that is, as he was going to pay for the enchanting gold brooch with the grapes. The final result was, accordingly, forty-four hundred. And Stanko? I thought. Here was a heavy charge against my receipts. Nevertheless, there was nothing for me to do but to say "*Entendu.*" Jean-Pierre opened the iron door of his safe, bestowed his purchases there under my regretful leave-taking gaze, and laid four thousand-franc notes and four hundred-franc notes before me on the table.

I shook my head.

"Please make these a little smaller," I said, pushing the thousand-franc notes back to him, and he replied:

"Well, bravo! I was just giving you a little test in discretion. I see that you don't intend to make too much of a splash when you make your purchases. I like that. I like you altogether," he went on as he changed the thousand-franc notes into hundreds and some gold and silver as well, "and I should never have made so inexcusably generous a deal if you had not really inspired me with confidence. Look, I would like to continue this connection of ours. There may really be something special about you. You have a kind of sunny manner. What's your name anyway?"

"Armand."

"Well, Armand, prove yourself grateful by coming back! Here's your watch. I'll make you a present of this chain to go with it." (It was absolutely worthless.) "*Adieu*, my boy! Come again! I have fallen a little in love with you in the course of our business."

"You certainly controlled your emotions well."

"Badly, very badly!"

Joking thus, we parted. I took an omnibus to the boulevard Haussmann and found a shoe store in a neighbouring sidestreet where I had myself fitted with a pair of handsome button shoes, at once solid and flexible. These I kept on, explaining that I had no further use for the old ones. After that, in the Printemps department store near by I wandered from department to department, acquiring first certain useful minor items: three or four collars, a tie, a silk shirt, a soft hat in place of my cap, which I hid in the inside pocket of my jacket, an umbrella that fitted inside the shaft of a cane and pleased me enormously, deerskin gloves, and a lizard-skin wallet. After that I asked my way to the ready-made department, where I bought straight off the hanger an attractive suit of light, warm grey wool that fitted me as though made to order and, with my turn-down collar and the blue-and-white dotted tie, was extremely becoming. This, too, I kept on, and asked them to deliver the clothes I had come in, giving, as a joke, the name: "*Pierre Jean-Pierre, quatre-vingt-douze, rue de l'Échelle au Ciel.*"

I was well content as, thus brightened in appearance, I left the Printemps, my umbrella-cane hooked over my arm and in my gloved fingers the convenient little wooden handle that was hooked to the red ribbon of my package. Well content, too, when I thought of the woman who bore my featureless image in her mind and, so I believed, was even now searching for a figure more worthy of her and her interest than heretofore. She would certainly have rejoiced with me that I had brought my outer appearance to a polish more in keeping with our relationship. The afternoon was well advanced after these accomplishments and I felt hungry. In a *brasserie* I ordered a strengthening but by no means gluttonous meal, consisting of a fish soup, a good steak with vegetables, cheese, and fruit, and I drank two glasses of beer. Well fed, I decided to allow myself the diversion for which I had envied those engaged in it when I had ridden by the day before—that is, to sit in front of one of the cafés in the boulevard des Italiens and observe the passing crowd. This I did. Taking a seat at a little table near a warming brazier, I drank my *double* and smoked, glancing alternately at the colourful and noisy stream of life flowing in front of me and down at my handsome buttoned shoes; I had crossed my legs in order to swing one of them in the air. I must have sat there for an hour, so pleased was I, and I should probably have stayed longer if the creatures creeping around and under my table in search of unregarded trifles had not by degrees become too numerous. I had, to be sure, discreetly slipped a present to a ragged old man and to an equally shabby boy who were picking up my cigarette butts—a franc to the former and ten sous to the latter, to their unspeakable delight—and this had caused an additional contingent of their fellows to come crowding up, before whom I had to flee since I could not possibly succour all the misery in the world. Nevertheless, I have to admit that the impulse to make a gift of this kind, an impulse I had been aware of on the previous evening, had played its part in my desire to visit the café.

It was, incidentally, a financial problem that had occupied me while I sat there, and continued to do so during my further diversions. What about Stanko? In respect to him, I was faced with a difficult choice. I could either admit to him that I had been too maladroit and childish to come anywhere near getting the price for my wares he had so confidently set; in proportion to this shameful failure, I could then settle with him for fifteen hundred francs at most. Or, to my honour and his advantage, I could deceive him and pretend I had at least achieved approximately the stipulated price. In that case I should have to pay out twice as much, and there would remain as my share of all that magnificence a tiny sum, miserably close to Master Jean-Pierre's original shameless offer. Which way would I decide? From the first I suspected that my pride or my vanity would prove stronger than my greed.

As for the diversions after the coffee hour, I entertained myself, for a trivial entrance fee, in looking at a magnificent panorama representing the Battle of Austerlitz with a full sweep of landscape, including burning villages, and teeming with Russian, Austrian, and French troops. It was so admirably executed that one could hardly perceive the division between what was only painted and the actual objects in the foreground, discarded weapons and knapsacks and the puppet figures of fallen warriors. On a hill, surrounded by his staff, the Emperor Napoleon was observing the strategic situation through a spyglass. Exalted by this sight, I visited still another spectacle, a panopticon, where to your terrified delight you encounter at every turn potentates, famous swindlers, artists crowned by fame, and notorious murderers of women, and expect at every instant to hear them call you by name. The Abbé Liszt, with long white hair and the most natural-looking wart on his face, was sitting at a grand piano, his foot on the pedals, his eyes directed toward Heaven, reaching for the keys with waxen fingers, while near by General Bazaine held a revolver to his temple but did not fire. These were exciting impressions for a young mind, but, despite Liszt and Bazaine, my powers of assimilation were not exhausted. Evening had fallen during my adventures; as she had done the day before, Paris adorned herself with light, with colourful flashing signs, and after a little wandering about I spent an hour and a half in a variety theatre, where sea lions balanced lighted oil lamps on their noses, a magician ground up someone's gold watch in a mortar only to produce it in perfect condition from the back trouser pocket of a completely disinterested spectator sitting well toward the rear of the orchestra, a pale diseuse in long black gloves scattered shady improprieties in a graveyard voice, and a gentleman gave a masterful performance as a ventriloquist. I could not stay for the end of this wonderful program, for I wanted to get a cup of chocolate and hurry back before the dormitory filled.

By way of the avenue de l'Opéra and the rue des Pyramides I returned to home territory in the rue Saint-Honoré. Before entering the hotel I removed my gloves, for, taken with the various other improvements in my toilet, they seemed to me possibly a trifle provocative. Nobody paid any attention to me, however, as I rode up to the fourth floor in the elevator along with a number of guests. When I entered the room one flight higher, Stanko showed his surprise as he examined me in the light of the hanging bulb.

"*Nom d'un chien!*" he said. "He has adorned himself. And so the affair went well?"

"Tolerably," I replied, while I took off my jacket and stepped in front of his bed. "Quite tolerably, Stanko, I might venture to say, even though all our hopes were not fulfilled. That fellow is by no means the worst of his kind; he's really quite affable if you know how to handle him and if you keep your guard up. I forced him up to nine thousand. Now permit me to pay my debt." And climbing onto the edge of the lower bed in my button shoes, I counted three thousand francs from my overflowing lizard-skin wallet onto the flannel blanket.

"You swindler!" he said. "You got twelve thousand."

"Stanko, I swear to you—"

He burst into laughter.

"My pet, don't excite yourself!" he said. "I don't believe you got twelve thousand or even nine. At the very most, you got five thousand. Look, I am lying here and my fever has gone down. A fellow gets weak and sentimental from exhaustion after a bout like that. And so I'll admit to you that I myself couldn't have squeezed out more than four or five thousand. Here's a thousand back. We're both honest fellows, aren't we? I'm enchanted by us. *Embrassons-nous! Et bonne nuit!*"

CHAPTER IX

There is really nothing easier than running an elevator; it can be mastered in almost no time. As I was very pleased with myself in my handsome livery and as many a glance from those members of the beau monde who rode up and down with me showed they were pleased too; as, moreover, I took genuine pleasure in my new name, the work at first was decidedly fun. But, child's play though it was in itself, when one had been at it with only short interruptions from seven in the morning until nearly midnight it could become decidedly fatiguing. After such a day one clambered into one's upper bunk rather broken in body and spirit. Sixteen hours at a stretch, it lasted, with time out only during the brief intervals when the staff went to be fed in relays in a room between kitchen and dining-hall. Wretched meals they were, too—little Bob had been only too right about that; stewed up out of all kinds of unappetizing leftovers, they were a constant cause of grumbling. I found these dubious ragouts, hashes, and fricassees, stingily accompanied by a sour *petit vin du pays*, most offensive; in actual fact I have never been so disgustingly fed except in jail. One stood, then, for all that time, without being able to sit down, in an enclosed space, heavy with the perfume of the guests, manipulating the controls, glancing at the indicator, stopping where directed, taking in guests, letting them off again, and being amazed by the brainless impatience of the ladies and gentlemen who would stand in the lobby ringing incessantly when anyone ought to know that you could not instantly dash down for them from the fourth floor, but first had to get out, there and on the lower floors, and with a polite bow and your best smile admit those wishing to descend.

I smiled a great deal and said: "*M'sieur et dame*—" and "Watch your step," which was quite unnecessary, for it was only on the first day that I was occasionally guilty of a slightly uneven landing; after that I was never again responsible for a step that required a warning, or if I was, I immediately rectified it. I gently supported the elbows of elderly women, as though they might have difficulty in getting out, and received in return the slightly bewildered glances of thanks, tinged sometimes with a melancholy coquetry, with which the aged repay the gallantry of youth. Others, to be sure, repressed any sign of pleasure, or had no need to since their hearts were cold and empty of everything except class pride. Moreover, I was equally helpful to young women, and in these cases there was many a delicate blush accompanied by a murmured "*Merci*" for my attentiveness. This sweetened my monotonous day's work, for I really intended these courtesies only for One, and in a sense was simply practising them for her. I was waiting for her who bore me, featureless, in her mind and whom I bore most distinctly in mine, the mistress of the jewel case, the provider of my button shoes, my umbrella-cane, and my Sunday outfit—the woman with whom I lived in sweet secrecy and for whom, unless she had suddenly departed, I should not have long to wait.

It was on the second day toward five in the afternoon—Eustache, too, had just brought his car down—when she appeared in front of the elevator bank in the lobby, wearing a scarf over her hat as she had done before. My hopelessly commonplace colleague and I were standing in front of the open gates, and she stopped midway between us, looking at me; she widened her eyes briefly and smiled, swaying slightly, undecided which car to choose. There was no doubt she was drawn to mine, but as Eustache had already stepped aside and invited her into his with a wave of his hand, she probably thought it was his turn. Into his car she stepped and was borne away, but not without an undissembled glance at me over her shoulder and a renewed widening of her eyes.

That was all, for the time being, except that at my next meeting with Eustache downstairs I learned her name. She was Mme Houpflé and came from Strassburg. "*Impudemment riche, tu sais*," Eustache added, whereupon I answered him with a cool "*Tant mieux pour elle.*"

On the following day at the same hour, when the two other lifts were under way and I was standing alone in front of mine, she appeared again, this time in a very beautiful long-waisted mink jacket and a beret of the same fur. She had been shopping, for she was carrying in her arms several fairly large, elegantly wrapped packages. She nodded in satisfaction at seeing me, smiled at my bow which, accompanied by a deferential "madame," had some of the quality of an invitation to dance, and let herself be enclosed with me in the bright, suspended room. Meanwhile there was a ring from the fourth floor.

"*Deuxième, n'est-ce pas, madame?*" I asked, as she had given me no directions.

She had not stepped to the back of the car nor was she standing behind me, but at my side, looking alternately at my hand on the control lever and at my face.

"*Mais oui, deuxième*," she said. "*Comment savez-vous?*"

"*Je le sais, tout simplement.*"

"Ah? The new Armand, if I am not mistaken?"

"At your service, madame."

"One might say," she replied, "that this change represents an improvement in the personnel."

"*Trop aimable, madame.*"

Her voice was a very pleasant, nervously vibrant alto. While I was thinking of this she spoke of my own voice.

"I should like to commend you," she said, "for your agreeable voice." The very words of Spiritual Counsellor Chateau!

"*Je serais infiniment content, madame*," I replied, "*si ma voix n'offenserait pas votre oreille!*"

There was insistent ringing from above. We had arrived at the second floor. She remarked:

"C'est en effet une oreille musicale et sensible. Du reste, l'ouïe n'est pas le seul de mes sens qui est susceptible."

She was astounding! I tenderly held her elbow as she got out, as though there had been any need for that, and said:

"Permit me at last, madame, to relieve you of your burdens and carry them to your room."

Thereupon I took her packages from her one by one and followed her down the corridor, simply abandoning my lift. It was only twenty paces. She opened number 23 on the left and preceded me into her bedroom, from which a door opened into the salon. A luxurious bedroom it was, with a hardwood floor, on which lay a large Persian rug, cherrywood furniture, a glittering array of articles on the toilet table, a wide brass bedstead with satin coverlet, and a grey silk chaise-longue. On this and on the glass-topped tables I deposited the packages while Madame took off her beret and opened her fur jacket.

"My maid is not here," she said. "Her room is on the floor above. Would you make your kindness complete by helping me out of this thing?"

"With great pleasure," I replied, starting to work. While I was engaged in removing the silk-lined fur, warm from her shoulders, she turned her head. One ringlet of her thick brown hair, whitened before its time, stood out impudently over her forehead; widening her eyes briefly and then narrowing them in a dreamy, swimming look, she spoke these words:

"You are undressing me, daring menial?"

An incredible woman and very articulate!

Taken aback, but full of determination, I managed to reply: "Would God, madame, that time permitted me to accept that interpretation and go on as long as I liked with this enchanting occupation!"

"You have no time for me?"

"Unhappily not at this moment, madame. My elevator is waiting. It stands open while people upstairs and down are ringing for it, and perhaps there's a crowd standing in front of it on this floor. I shall lose my job if I neglect it any longer."

"But you would have time for me—if you had time for me?"

"An endless amount, madame!"

"*When* will you have time for me?" she asked, alternating the sudden widening of her eyes and the swimming look, and she moved close to me in her blue-grey tailored suit.

"At eleven o'clock I shall be off duty," I replied softly.

"I shall wait for you then," she said in the same tone. "Here is my pledge!" And before I knew what she was about, my head was between her hands and her mouth on mine in a kiss that went quite far—far enough to make it an unusually binding pledge.

I must certainly have been somewhat pale as I put her fur jacket, which I still had in my hand, on the chaise-longue and withdrew. Three persons were in fact waiting bewilderedly in front of the open lift. I had to make my apologies to them not only for my absence, due to an important errand, but also because, before taking them down, I first had to go to the fourth floor, whence there had been a summons but where now there was no one. Downstairs I had to listen to abuse for interrupting traffic. Against this I defended myself by explaining that I had been compelled to accompany to her room a lady suddenly overcome by faintness.

Mme Houpflé faint! A woman of such boldness! That quality, I reflected, came more easily to her than to me because of her greater age and also because of my subordinate position, to which she had given so oddly lofty a name. "Daring menial" she had called me—a women of poetry! "You are undressing me, daring menial?" This exciting phrase lay in my mind all evening, the entire six hours that had to be endured until I should have time for her. It wounded me a little, her phrase, and yet at the same time filled me with pride—even for the daring which I had not in the least possessed but which she had simply imputed to me. In any case, I now possessed it in plenty. She had inspired it in me—particularly by that very binding pledge.

At seven o'clock I took her down to dinner: when she entered my car there were other guests already in it. She wore a wonderful white silk dress with a short train, lace, and an embroidered tunic; around her waist was a black satin belt, and around her neck a string of flawless, shimmering, milky pearls which, to her good fortune—and the misfortune of Master Jean-Pierre—had not been in the jewel case. The thoroughness with which she disregarded me—and this after so far-reaching a kiss!—nettled me, but I revenged myself, as they got out, by putting my hand not under her elbow but under that of a bedizened, ghostlike old woman. It seemed to me I saw her smile at this charitable gallantry.

At what hour she returned to her room I did not learn. Some time, however, it would have to be eleven, and at that hour service was maintained by one lift only, while the operators of the other two had the rest of the evening off. Tonight I was one of them. To freshen up after my day's labours for the tenderest of rendezvous, I first made my way up to our washroom and then descended afoot to the second floor. The corridor with its red carpet that silenced all footsteps lay already in undisturbed peace. I considered it discreet to knock on the door of Mme Houpflé's salon, number 25, but received no answer. I opened the outside door of number 23, her bedroom, and, inclining my ear, knocked discreetly on the inner one.

An inquiring "*Entrez?*" in a slightly surprised tone answered me. I obeyed, for I felt entitled to disregard the surprise. The room lay in the reddish twilight thrown by a silk-shaded night lamp, which was the only illumination. The daring occupant—it is with justification and pleasure that I return to her the epithet she had bestowed on me—was discovered by my rapid, inquiring survey in bed under the purple satin cover—in the splendid brass bed that stood with its head against the wall and the chaise-longue at its feet close to the heavily curtained window. My fair traveller lay there, her arms crossed behind her head, in a cambric nightgown with short sleeves and billowing lace-edged décolletage. She had undone the knot of her hair for the night and had wound the braids around her head in a very becoming, loose, tiara-like fashion. Twisted into a curl, the white strand lay back from her brow, which was no longer unfurrowed. Hardly had I shut the door when I heard the bolt—which was controlled from the bed by a wire—fall into place.

She widened her golden eyes for just an instant, as usual, but her face remained slightly disturbed in a kind of nervous deceitfulness as she said:

"Why, what's this? A hotel employee, a domestic, a young man of the people comes into my room at this hour when I have already retired?"

"You expressed the wish, madame," I replied, approaching the bed.

"The wish? Did I so? You say 'the wish' and behave as though you meant the order a lady gives some minor servant, an elevator boy perhaps, but what you really mean in your unheard-of pertness, yes, shamelessness, is the longing, the hot, yearning desire, you mean it quite simply and straightforwardly because you are young and beautiful, so beautiful, so young, so insolent. . . . 'The wish'! Tell me at least, you answer to wishes, dream of my senses, *mignon* in livery, sweet helot, whether you insolently dare to share this wish a little!"

Thereupon she took me by the hand and drew me down to an unsteady perch on the edge of her bed. To keep my balance I had to stretch my arm across her and brace myself against the head of the bed, so that I was bent over her nakedness, so lightly veiled in linen and lace, and enveloped in its fragrant warmth. Slightly offended, I admit, by her repeated insistence on my humble state—what did she expect to gain by that?—instead of answering I bent all the way down to her and pressed my lips against hers. She not only carried this kiss to even greater lengths than the one that afternoon—with no lack of co-operation from me—she also took my hand from its support and guided it inside her décolletage to her breasts, which were very nicely fitted to the hand, moving it about by the wrist in such a way that my manhood, as she could not fail to notice, was most urgently aroused. Touched by this observation, she cooed softly with compassion and delight: "O lovely youth, far fairer than this body that has the power to inflame you!"

Then she began to tug at the collar of my jacket with both hands, unhooked it, and with incredible speed proceeded to undo the buttons.

"Off, off, away with that and away with that, too," her words tumbled out. "Off and away, so that I can see you, can catch sight of the god! Quick, help! *Comment, à ce propos, quand l'heure nous appelle, n'êtes-vous pas encore prêt pour la chapelle? Déshabillez-vous vite! Je compte les instants! La parure de noce!* So I call your divine limbs that I have been thirsting to behold since I first saw you. Ah so, ah there! The holy breast, the shoulders, the sweet arms! Away then finally with this too—oh, la, la, that's what I call gallantry! Come to me, then, *bien-aimé!* To me, to me . . ."

Never was there a more articulate woman! It was poetry she uttered, nothing less. And she continued to express herself when I was with her; it was her habit to put everything into words. In her arms she held the pupil and initiate of that exacting teacher, Rozsa. He made her very happy and was privileged to hear about it as he did so:

"Oh, sweetheart! Oh, you angel of love, offspring of desire! Ah, ah, you young devil, naked boy, how you can do it! My husband can do nothing at all, absolutely nothing, you must know. Oh, blessed one, you are killing me! Ecstasy robs me of breath, breaks my heart, I will die of your love!" She bit my lip, my neck. "Call me *tu!*" she groaned suddenly, near the climax. "Be familiar with me, degrade me! *J'adore d'être humiliée! Je t'adore! Oh, je t'adore, petit esclave stupide qui me déshonore. . . .*"

She came. We came. I had given my best, had in my enjoyment made proper recompense. But how could I fail to be annoyed that at the very climax she had been stammering about degradation and had called me a stupid little slave? We rested, still united, still in close embrace, but through annoyance at this "*qui me déshonore*" I did not return her thankful kisses. With her mouth on my body she breathed again:

"Quick call me *tu!* I have not yet heard this *tu* from you to me. I lie here and make love with a divine and yet quite common servant boy. How delightfully that degrades me! My name is Diane. But you, with your lips, call me whore, explicitly 'You sweet whore!' "

"Sweet Diane!"

"No, say 'You whore!' Let me fully savour my degradation in words. . . ."

I freed myself from her. We lay side by side, our hearts still beating high. I said:

"No, Diane, you will hear no such word from me. I refuse. And I must admit I find it very bitter that you think my love degrading."

"Not yours," she said, drawing me to her. "Mine! My love for you, you insignificant boy! Oh, you lovely fool, you don't understand!" Whereupon she took my head and knocked it several times against her own in a kind of tender exasperation. "I am an author, you must know, a woman of the intellect. Diane Philibert—my husband, his name is Houpflé, *c'est du dernier ridicule*—I write under my maiden name. Diane Philibert, *sous ce nom de plume*. Naturally you have never heard the name—how should you, indeed?—which is on so many books, they are novels, you understand, full of psychological insight, *pleins d'esprit, et des volumes de vers passionnés. . . .* Yes, my poor darling, your Diane, she is *d'une intelligence extrême*. And yet the intellect—oh!"—and once more she knocked our heads together, somewhat harder than before—"how could you understand that? The intellect longs for the delights of the non-intellect, that which is alive and beautiful *dans sa stupidité*, in love with it, oh, in love with it to the point of idiocy, to the ultimate self-betrayal and self-denial, in love with the beautiful and the divinely stupid, it kneels before it, it prays to it in an ecstasy of self-abnegation, self-degradation, and finds it intoxicating to be degraded by it—"

"Well now, dear child," thus I finally interrupted her. "Beauty apart—and if Nature made a good job of me, so much the better—you mustn't think me as stupid as all that, even if I haven't read your novels and poems—"

She did not let me go on. I had enchanted her in a quite unintentional way.

"You call me 'dear child'?" she cried, embracing me stormily and burying her mouth in my neck. "Oh, that's delicious! That's much better than 'sweet whore'! That's a much deeper delight than anything you've done, you artist in love! A little naked liftboy lies beside me and calls me 'dear child,' me, Diane Philibert! *C'est exquis, ça me transporte! Armand, chéri*, I didn't mean to offend you. I didn't mean to say that you're especially stupid. All beauty is stupid because it simply exists as an object for glorification by the spirit. Let me see you, see you completely—heaven help me, how beautiful you are! The breast so sweet in its smooth, clear strength, the slim arms, the noble ribs, the narrow hips, and, oh, the Hermes legs—"

"Stop it, Diane, this isn't right. It is I who should be praising you."

"Nonsense! That's just a male convention. We women are lucky that our curves please you. But the divine, the masterpiece of creation, the model of beauty, that's you, you young, very young men with Hermes legs. Do you know who Hermes is?"

"I must admit at the moment—"

"*Céleste!* Diane Philibert is making love with someone who has never heard of Hermes! What a delicious degradation of the spirit! I will tell you, sweet fool, who Hermes is. He is the suave god of thieves."

I was taken aback and blushed. I looked at her closely, was suspicious, and then let the suspicion drop. An idea came to me, but I pushed it aside; besides, it was soon drowned in the flood of avowals she was pouring forth, now whispering them into my arm, now lifting her voice, warm and chanting.

"Would you believe, beloved, that I have loved only you, always only you since I was able to feel? That means, of course, not you but the idea of you, the lovely instant you incarnate. Call it perversion if you will, but I detest the grown man full-bearded and woolly-chested, the mature and significant man—*affreux*, dreadful! I am significant myself—that's just what I would consider perverse: *de me coucher avec un homme penseur*. It's only you boys I have loved from the beginning—as a girl of thirteen I was crazy about a boy of fourteen or fifteen. The ideal grew a little as I grew, but it never went above eighteen; my taste, the yearning of my senses never reached beyond that. . . . How old are you?"

"Twenty," I replied.

"You look younger, you are practically too old for me."

"I, too old for you?"

"Come, come! The way you are is right for me, right to the point of heavenly bliss. I will tell you: perhaps my passion is connected with the fact that I was never a mother, never bore a son. I would have loved him with idolatry if he had been only halfway beautiful, which, to be sure, would have been very unlikely if I had got him from Houpflé. Perhaps, I say, this love for you is transferred mother-love, the yearning for a son. . . . Perversity, do you say? And all of you? What do you want with our breasts that gave you suck, our womb that bore you? Isn't it your wish simply to go back to them, to become sucklings again? Isn't it the mother you illicitly love in the wife? Perversion! Love is perversion through and through, it can't be anything else. Probe it where you will, you will find perversion. . . . But it's admittedly sad and painful for a woman to be able to love a man only when he is quite, quite young, when he is a boy. *C'est un amour tragique*, inadmissible, not practical, not for life, not for marriage. I, I married Houpflé, a rich businessman, so that in the shelter of his riches I could write my books, *qui sont énormément intelligents*. My husband can do nothing, as I told you, at least with me. *Il me trompe*, as they say, with a theatrical demoiselle. Perhaps he is some good with her—I should rather doubt it. It's a matter of indifference to me—this whole world of men and women and marriage and betrayal is a matter of indifference. I live in my so-called perversion, in the love of my life that lies at the bottom of everything I am, in the happiness and misery of this enthusiasm with its heavy curse that nothing, nothing in the whole visible world equals the enchantment of the youthful male. I live in my love for all of you, you, you image of desire, whose beauty I kiss in complete abnegation of spirit. I kiss your presumptuous lips over the white teeth you show when you smile. I kiss the tender stars of your breast, the little golden hairs on the dark skin of your armpits. And how does that happen? With your blue eyes and blond hair, where do you get this colouring, this tint of light bronze? You are baffling. How baffling! *La fleur de ta jeunesse remplit mon cœur âgé d'une éternelle ivresse.* This intoxication will never end, I shall die of it, but my spirit will woo you forever with its wiles. You, too, *bien-aimé*, will all too soon grow old and approach the grave, but here are comfort and balm for my heart: ye will endure forever, brief joy of beauty, gracious inconstancy, eternal instant!"

"How strangely you speak!"

"How so? You are surprised that one praises in verse what one so ardently admires? *Tu ne connais pas donc le vers alexandrin—ni le dieu voleur, toi-même si divin?*"

Abashed, like a small boy, I shook my head. She did not on that account cease her endearments, and I must admit that so much praise and adulation, finally even expressed in poetry, had greatly excited me. Although my offering in our first embrace had, as was usual with me, been my utmost—she found me once more in manly state—found me so with that combination of compassion and delight that I had noted in her before. We were united again. But did she on that account desist from what she called the self-abnegation of the spirit, from this nonsense about degradation? She did not.

"Armand," she whispered in my ear, "be rough with me! I am entirely yours, I am your slave! Treat me as you would the lowest wench! I don't deserve anything else, and it would be heaven for me!"

I paid no attention to this. We expired again. In the ensuing lassitude, however, she brooded and suddenly said:

"Listen, Armand."

"What is it?"

"How would it be if you beat me? Beat me hard, I mean. Me, Diane Philibert? It would serve me right, I would be thankful to you. There are your braces, take them, beloved, turn me over and whip me till I bleed!"

"I wouldn't think of it, Diane. What do you take me for? I'm not that kind of lover."

"Oh, what a shame! You have too much respect for this fine lady."

At that the thought that had slipped away from me returned. I said: "Listen to me, Diane. I will confess something to you that perhaps will make up in a way for what I have had to refuse you on grounds of good taste. Tell me this, when you were unpacking your bag, the big one, or having it unpacked, was there perhaps something missing?"

"Missing? No. But yes! How did you know?"

"A little case?"

"A little case, yes! With jewelry. How do you know about that?"

"I took it."

"Took it? When?"

"At the customs we were standing side by side. You were busy. I took it then."

"You stole it? You are a thief? *Mais ça c'est suprême!* I am lying in bed with a thief! *C'est une humiliation merveilleuse, tout à fait excitante, un rêve d'humiliation!* Not only a domestic—a common, ordinary thief!"

"I knew it would give you pleasure. But at that time I did not know, and so I must ask your pardon. I could not foresee that we would love each other. Otherwise I would not have inflicted on you the distress and shock of having to get along without your wonderfully beautiful topaz jewelry, the diamonds and all the rest."

"Distress? Shock? Get along without? Beloved, Juliette, my maid, searched for a while. As for me, I didn't worry about the stuff for two seconds. What does it matter to me? You stole it, sweetheart—so it is yours. Keep it. What are you going to do with it, by the way? Never mind. My husband, who is coming tomorrow to take me away, is so rich! He makes bathroom toilets, I must tell you. Everyone needs them, as you can understand. Strassburg toilets by Houpflé, they are much in demand, they are shipped to the four corners of the earth. He bedecks me with too much jewelry out of sheer bad conscience. He'll present me with things three times as pretty as the ones you stole. Oh, how much more precious to me is the thief than what he took! Hermes! He does not know who it is—and it is he! Hermes, Hermes! . . . Armand?"

"What is it?"

"I have a wonderful idea."

"What's that?"

"Armand, you shall steal from me. Here under my very eyes. That is, I'll shut my eyes and pretend to both of us that I am asleep. But secretly I'll watch you steal. Get up, as you are, thievish god, and steal! You haven't by any means stolen all the things I have with me; I did not deposit anything at the office for these few days before my husband arrives. In the upper right-hand drawer of the cupboard is the key to my bureau. You will find all sorts of things under the lingerie. There's cash there, too. Prowl around my room on cat feet and catch the mice! You will do this favour for your Diane, won't you?"

"But, dear child—I call you that because you like to hear me say it—dear child, that would not be nice or at all gentlemanly after what we have been to each other."

"Fool! It would be the most enchanting fulfilment of our love!"

"And tomorrow Monsieur Houpflé comes. What will he—"

"My husband? What has he to say? I'll explain to him, casually and with an expression of complete indifference, that I was robbed on my journey. That happens when rich women are a trifle careless. Gone is gone, and the robber has long ago disappeared. No, just leave my husband to me!"

"But, sweet Diane, under your eyes—"

"Oh, to think that you have no feeling for the charm of my idea! All right, I will not see you. I'll put out the light." And in fact she turned off the little red-shaded lamp on the night table so that darkness shrouded us. "I will not see you. I will only listen to the parquet softly creaking under your thief's tread, only hear your breathing as you steal, and the soft clink of the thief's booty in your hands. Go on, steal away from my side, prowl, find and take! It is my dearest wish."

And so I obeyed her. Cautiously I left her and took what the room offered—too easy a theft, for right on the night table in a little dish were her rings, and the pearl necklace she had worn to dinner lay on top of the table around which the easy chairs were grouped. Despite the complete darkness I had no trouble in finding the key to the bureau in the corner cupboard. I opened the top drawer almost noiselessly and had only to take out a few items of lingerie to come upon the jewelry, pendants, bracelets, brooches, in addition to some encouragingly large-sized notes. All this I brought to her in the bed, for reasons of propriety, as though I had got it together for her. But she whispered:

"Little fool, what are you doing? This is your booty of love and theft. Put it in your pockets, get dressed and vanish, as is proper! Hurry and flee! I heard it all, I heard you breathing as you stole. And now I am going to telephone the police. Or would it be better for me not to? What do you think? How far along are you? Through soon? Have you your livery on again with all your booty of love and theft in it? Surely you didn't steal my button-hook, here it is. . . . *Adieu*, Armand! Farewell, farewell forever, my idol! Do not forget your Diane, for in her you will survive. After years and years when—*le temps t'a détruit, ce cœur te gardera dans ton moment béni.* Yes, when the grave covers us, me and you too, Armand, *tu vivras dans mes vers et dans mes beaux romans*, every one of which—never breathe this to the world!—has been kissed by your lips. *Adieu, adieu, chéri* . . ."

BOOK THREE

CHAPTER I

The fact that I have devoted a whole chapter to the foregoing extraordinary episode and have used it as a festive ending to the second book of my confessions will, I trust, seem understandable and even commendable. It was, I can say with assurance, the experience of a lifetime, and its heroine's earnest pleas not to forget her were entirely unnecessary. A woman so singular as Diane Houpflé, in every sense of the word, and the amazing circumstances of my meeting with her are not likely to be forgotten ever. This does not mean that the situation in which the reader was privileged to overhear us, considered simply as situation, stands by itself in my career. Horror is not always the only reaction of ladies travelling alone, particularly older ladies, who discover that a young man has found something in their bedrooms to interest him; if their first impulse is to raise an alarm, it is an impulse they sometimes succeed in suppressing. But if I have had such experiences (and I have), they fell far short of that significant and unique night, and at the risk of blunting my reader's interest in the further course of my confessions, I must announce that in the sequel, however high I rose in society, I never again had the experience of being addressed in alexandrines.

For the treasure trove of love and theft which the poetess's bizarre idea had left in my hands I received from Master Pierre Jean-Pierre six thousand francs and innumerable pats on the shoulder. Moreover, as Diane's bureau drawer had provided the thieving god with cash as well—four thousand-franc notes hidden under the lingerie, to be exact—I was now the possessor, all told, of twelve thousand three hundred and fifty francs. Naturally enough, I did not wish to carry such a sum around with me any longer than necessary, and at the first opportunity I deposited it in a checking-account at the Crédit Lyonnais under the name of Armand Kroull, retaining only a couple of hundred francs for pocket money on my afternoons off.

The reader will learn of this step with approval and a feeling of relief. It would be easy to picture a young fop, endowed with such means through the tempting favour of fortune, immediately abandoning his unpaid position, setting himself up in attractive bachelor quarters, and indulging in all the delights that Paris has to offer—until the easily foreseeable day when his treasure was exhausted. I did not think of such a thing, or if I thought of it, I banished the idea with proper decisiveness as soon as it occurred. What could I expect if I acted on it? Where would I be when sooner or later, depending on the liveliness of my dissipations, my windfall was used up? The temptation was easily overcome when I recalled the words of my godfather Schimmelpreester (with whom, now and then, I exchanged short messages on picture postcards)—the words in which he described to me the splendid goals of a hotel career, goals that might be reached by straightforward advancement but also by one or another of the bypaths. I could not show myself ungrateful to him by throwing away the opportunity he had secured for me through his world-wide connections. To be sure, in holding on to my first position with characteristic tenacity, I gave little or no thought to the "straightforward advancement" he had mentioned and I did not picture myself as headwaiter, concierge, or even manager. The bypaths were all the more vivid in my mind and I had only to guard against mistaking the first cul-de-sac, such as was offered me now, for a reliable shortcut to happiness.

And so, possessor of a checkbook though I was, I remained a liftboy at the Hotel Saint James and Albany. There was a certain charm in playing this role against a background of secret wealth, thanks to which my becoming livery took on the quality of a costume my godfather might have had me try on. My secret wealth—or this is how my dream-acquired riches seemed to me—transformed my uniform and my job into a role, a simple extension of my talent for "dressing up." Although later on I achieved dazzling success in passing myself off for more than I was, for the time being I passed myself off for less, and it is an open question which deception gave me the greater inner amusement, the greater delight in this fairy-tale magic.

It is true I was ill fed and ill housed in that luxurious and expensive hotel; but in both respects I was at least put to no expense, and if, moreover, I got no salary, I not only could husband my own resources but could increase them modestly through the *pourboires*, or, as I preferred to call them, *douceurs*, which regularly came my way from the travelling public—just as they fell to my colleagues in the elevators. Rather, to be quite accurate, they fell to me in somewhat larger quantities and more readily, a preference revealing people's recognition of finer clay which my more common companions, perceptively enough, never really begrudged me. One franc, two or three, even five, as much as ten francs in special cases of reckless generosity, would be tucked into my never importunate hand by departing guests or, at intervals of a week or fortnight, by grateful permanent residents. They would come from ladies with averted faces or smiling glances—sometimes also from gentlemen who, to be sure, often had to be prompted to it by their ladies. I remember many a little scene between husband and wife, which I was not supposed to see and which I appeared not to; a poke in the ribs accompanied by a murmur: "*Mais donnez donc quelque chose à ce garçon.* Give him something, he is nice." Whereupon the husband would draw out his wallet murmuring something in reply, only to be rebuked: "*Non, c'est ridicule.* That's not enough, don't be so stingy!" Twelve to fifteen francs per week is what it always amounted to—an agreeable addition to my pocket money on the half-day off that the establishment, in its miserly way, granted us every two weeks.

It sometimes happened that I spent those afternoons and evenings with Stanko, who had long ago recovered from his illness and was back at work in the *garde-manger*, preparing his cold dishes and other delicacies for the big buffet. He was fond of me; I liked him well enough and was glad of his company in cafés and places of entertainment, though his presence was hardly distinguished. In ordinary clothes he had a comical, ambiguously exotic appearance, for his taste ran to large checks and bright colours, and no doubt he looked far better in the white apron and high white linen chef's hat of his calling. It is a common mistake: the working-class ought never to attempt to be fashionable, at least by bourgeois standards. They do it awkwardly and it damages them in the eyes of the public. More than once I have heard my godfather Schimmelpreester express himself on this subject, and Stanko's appearance reminded me of his words. The abasement of the people, he said, through their acceptance of fashion, which was a result of the standardization of the world through bourgeois taste, was much to be regretted. The holiday attire of the peasantry and the former pomp and circumstance of the artisans' guilds had been far finer spectacles than some plump maid trying to play the lady on Sunday in feathered hat and train, not to mention the party clothes of the factory worker awkwardly striving to be fashionable. Since, however, the time was over and done when the classes were distinguished from one another by mutual respect, he was for a society in which there were no more classes at all, neither maid nor lady, neither fine gentleman nor commoner, and all wore the same thing. Golden words, spoken as though out of my own soul. What, I thought, would I have against shirt, breeches, belt, and nothing more? It would become me, and Stanko too would look better thus than in his clumsy approximation of fashion. Almost anything is becoming to a human being except the perverse, the stupid, and the half-baked.

So much by way of marginal comment. It was with Stanko, then, that I visited for a time the cabarets and terrace cafés, including the Café de Madrid, where a colourful and instructive society gathered after the theatres closed. But one special gala evening we spent at the Stoudebecker Circus, which had just opened in Paris for a few weeks' run. A word or two about that—or perhaps more! I should never forgive myself if I passed over such an experience without imparting to it some of the colour it so richly possessed.

This famous institution had pitched its vast round tent on the Square Saint-Jacques near the Théâtre Sarah Bernhardt and the Seine. The attendance was tremendous, since the performance obviously equalled or perhaps excelled the best in this field that had ever been offered the knowledgeable and highly exacting taste of the Parisian public. What an attack on the senses and nerves, what sensuous delight, in fact, lies in the uninterrupted succession of scenes as the fantastic program unrolls! Exploits that lie at the extreme limits of human prowess are achieved with bright smiles and lightly thrown kisses; their basic pattern is the *salto mortale*, for they all involve the fatal risk of a broken neck. Schooled to grace at moments of utmost daring, the performers are accompanied by the flourishes of a music appropriate enough in its commonplaceness to the physical character of the performance but not to the extreme heights to which it is raised; it is this that furnishes the breath-taking build-up for the last not-to-be-accomplished act—which nevertheless is accomplished.

With a brief nod (for the circus has no use for bows) the artist acknowledges the ecstatic applause of the massed onlookers. This is a unique audience, confusingly and excitingly compounded of the sensation-seeking crowd and the rude elegance of the horsy world. Cavalry officers in the loges, their caps at an angle; young rakes, freshly shaved, wearing monocles, a carnation or a chrysanthemum in the buttonholes of their loose yellow topcoats; cocottes, mingling with inquisitive ladies from the fashionable faubourgs, accompanied by knowledgeable cavaliers in grey frock coats and grey top hats, their field glasses slung in sporting fashion around their necks as though at a race at Longchamp. Add to this the excitement of the animals' physical presence, the magnificent, colourful costumes, the glittering spangles, the stable smell extending everywhere, the naked limbs of men and women. Breasts, throats, beauty in its most instantly appreciated form, the savage charm of dangerous deeds performed for the pleasure of the bloodthirsty crowd cater to every taste and enflame every desire. Women riders from the Hungarian steppe spring as though possessed onto wild-eyed, saddleless horses, roused to berserk frenzy by harsh cries. Gymnasts in tight-fitting, flesh-coloured tights; the hairless, bulging arms of athletes, stared at by the ladies with a strange, cold fixity; and charming boys. How forcibly I was struck by a troupe of tumblers and tightrope-walkers distinguished from the fantastic crowd not only by their simple sport clothes, but also by their agreeable trick of consulting briefly before each of their hair-raising performances, as though they first had to come to an agreement. Their star, who was obviously a favourite with everyone, was a boy of fifteen who bounded from a springboard, turned two and a half somersaults in the air, and then landed without so much as a wobble on the shoulders of the man behind him, apparently his elder brother. He was, to be sure, successful in doing this only on his third attempt. Twice he failed, missing his brother's shoulders and falling; his laughter and the way he shook his head at this failure were just as enchanting as the ironic gallantry of the gesture with which his senior summoned him back to the springboard. Possibly it was all intentional, for naturally enough the applause and *bravo*'s of the multitude were all the more tumultuous when on the third attempt he not only completed his *salto mortale* and landed without a quiver, but managed to heighten the storm of applause by a gesture of his outspread hands which seemed to say: "*Me voilà!*" It is certain, however, that his calculated or half-intended failures had taken him closer to a broken spine than his triumphant success.

What fabulous creatures these artists are! Are they really human at all? Take the clowns, for example, those basically alien beings, funmakers, with little red hands, little thin-shod feet, red wigs under conical felt hats, their impossible lingo, their handstands, their stumbling and falling over everything, their mindless running to and fro and unserviceable attempts to help, their hideously unsuccessful efforts to imitate their serious colleagues—in tightrope-walking, for instance—which bring the crowd to a pitch of mad merriment. Are these ageless, half-grown sons of absurdity, at whom Stanko and I laughed so heartily (I, however, with a thoughtful fellow-feeling), are they human at all? With their chalk-white faces and utterly preposterous painted expressions—triangular eyebrows and deep perpendicular grooves in their cheeks under the reddened eyes, impossible noses, mouths twisted up at the corners into insane smiles—masks, that is, which stand in inconceivable contrast to the splendour of their costumes—black satin, for example, embroidered with silver butterflies, a child's dream—are they, I repeat, human beings, men that could conceivably find a place in everyday daily life? In my opinion it is pure sentimentality to say that they are "human too," with the sensibilities of human beings and perhaps even with wives and children. I honour them and defend them against ordinary bad taste when I say no, they are not, they are exceptions, side-splitting monsters of preposterousness, glittering, world-renouncing monks of unreason, cavorting hybrids, part human and part insane art.

Everything must be "human" for the man in the street, and he thinks himself amazingly tender-hearted and perceptive when he penetrates appearances and finds the human beneath the surface. What about Andromache—"*La Fille de l'aire*," as she was called on the lengthy program? Was she, by chance, human? I still dream of her, and though her person was as far as possible from the sphere of the absurd, it was really she whom I had in mind when I let myself run on about the clowns. She was the star of the circus, the main attraction, and she did an act on the high trapeze that was incomparable. She did it—and this was the sensational novelty, something unique in circus history—without a safety net below her. Her partner, a man of considerable ability who was, nevertheless, not to be compared to her, performed with personal restraint, only extending his hand to her at the end of her foolhardy, amazingly executed evolutions in space between the two rapidly swinging trapezes; he really served only to set off her feats. Was she twenty years old, or less, or more? Who can say? Her features were severe and noble. Strangely enough, they were not disfigured but made clearer and more attractive by the elastic cap she pulled on when she set to work, without which her heavy, tightly braided brown hair would have whipped about during her wild, head-over-heels flight. She was more than average size for a woman. Her short pliant silver breastplate was edged with swansdown, and attached to her shoulder-blades, as though to confirm her title of "daughter of the air," she wore a small pair of white wings. As if they could help her to fly! Her breasts were meagre, her hips narrow, the muscles of her arms, naturally enough, more developed than in other women, and her amazing hands, though not so big as a man's, were nevertheless not so small as to rule out the question whether she might not, Heaven forfend, be a boy in disguise. No, the female conformation of her breasts was unmistakable, and so too, despite her slimness, was the form of her thighs. She barely smiled. Her beautiful lips, far from being compressed, were usually slightly parted, and the nostrils of her pure Grecian nose were dilated. She disdained all flirtatiousness toward the crowd. Pausing after a tour de force on the crossbar, one hand resting against the rope, she would just perceptibly stretch out the other in greeting. But her serious eyes, staring straight ahead under even, unruffled, motionless brows, did not join in the greeting.

I worshipped her. She would stand up, set the trapeze in violent motion, leap off and fly past her partner, who would be coming toward her from the opposite trapeze; seize the crossbar with her hands, which were neither male nor female, execute, with body fully extended, a complete giant swing—which few gymnasts can perform—and utilize the tremendous impetus thus attained to fly back, once more passing her partner, and execute another *salto mortale* in mid-career; seize the bar of the swinging trapeze, draw herself up with a barely visible contraction of her arm muscles, and, impassively raising her hand, seat herself on it.

It was incredible, impossible, and nevertheless she did it. A shudder of enthusiasm shook anyone witnessing it and his heart grew cold. The crowd repaid her with awe rather than acclaim; they worshipped her, as I did, in the deathly stillness that followed the cutting off of the music during her daredevil feats. That the most precise calculation was a vital condition of everything she did goes without saying. At exactly the right instant, figured to the fraction of a second, just as she was ready to alight after her giant swing on the opposite trapeze and her *salto* on the way back, the flying trapeze her partner had abandoned must swing toward her, and not on any account start its back swing. If the bar was not there, those magnificent hands would close on emptiness and she would pitch headlong from the element of her art, the air, down to the common ground, which was death. The extreme accuracy these calculations called for made one shudder.

But I repeat my question: was Andromache really human? Was she a human being outside the ring, apart from her professional accomplishments, her almost unnatural—indeed, for a woman, wholly unnatural—achievements? To imagine her as wife and mother was simply stupid; a wife and mother, or even anyone who could possibly be thought of as one, does not hang head-down from a trapeze, swinging so violently that it almost turns all the way over. She does not let go and fly through the air to her partner, who seizes her by her hands, executes a pendulum motion back and forth, and releases her at the top of the swing so that she returns to her own trapeze to the accompaniment of the famous mid-air *salto*. This was Andromache's way of consorting with a man; any other was unthinkable, for one recognized too well that this disciplined body lavished upon the adventurous accomplishments of her art what others devote to love. She was not a woman; but she was not a man either and therefore not a human being. A solemn angel of daring with parted lips and dilated nostrils, that is what she was, an unapproachable Amazon of the realms of space beneath the canvas, high above the crowd, whose lust for her was transformed into awe.

Andromache! Her vision, painful and uplifting at once, lingered in my mind long after her act was over and others had replaced it. The ringmasters and their attendants formed an avenue through which Director Stoudebecker entered with his twelve black stallions. He was a middle-aged sporting gentleman with a grey moustache, in evening clothes, the ribbon of the Legion of Honour in his buttonhole. In one hand he held a riding-crop and a long whip with an inlaid handle—a gift from the Shah of Persia, as he was careful to explain—which he could crack explosively. Standing in the sand of the ring in his gleaming patent-leather shoes, he addressed quiet, personal directions to one or another of his magnificent pupils, their proud heads decked in white bridles. At his command they went through their paces, knelt and turned and, finally, confronted by his raised crop, executed a magnificent circle of the ring on their hind feet. An impressive sight, but I was thinking of Andromache. Magnificent animal bodies; and it is between animal and angel, so I reflected, that man takes his stand. His place is closer to the animals, that we must admit. But she, my adored one, though all body, was a chaster body, untainted by humanity, and stood much closer to the angels.

Then iron bars were put around the ring and the lion cage was rolled in to offer a spice of danger to the unheroic, gaping crowd. The trainer, Monsieur Mustafa, had gold rings in his ears, was naked to the waist, and wore wide red trousers and a red hat. He entered through a small door, which was quickly opened for him and closed behind him just as fast. Five beasts awaited him inside, their sharp, carnivorous scent mingling with the smell of the stables. They retreated before him and at his command, one after another crouched reluctantly on the five stools arranged around the cage. They snarled with hideously contorted faces and struck at him with their paws—possibly half in play but with a large element of rage as well, for they knew that entirely against their inclination and nature they were going to be forced to leap through hoops, and ultimately through fiery ones. A couple of them shook the air with the thunderous roar that had once terrified and scattered the small creatures of the forest. He retorted by shooting his revolver into the air. At this they cringed, snarling, for they realized their nature-given roar was out-trumped by his deafening report. Thereupon Mustafa swaggeringly lighted a cigarette, an action they observed with deep resentment. Then softly but firmly he pronounced a name, Achille or Nero, and with the utmost decisiveness summoned the first of them to his performance. One after another the kingly cats had unwillingly to leave their stools and spring back and forth through hoops held high in the air and finally, as I have said, through a hoop smeared with blazing pitch. Well or ill, they leaped through the flames; it was not hard for them to do, but it was an indignity. Growling, they returned to their stools, which were in themselves an insult, and stared fascinated at the man in red trousers. He kept moving his head lightly and quickly, fixing his dark eyes on the green eyes of each beast in turn—eyes narrowed by fear and by a certain hate and affection. At the slightest sound of disturbance he would swing round instantly and impose quiet with a glance of amazement and a name spoken softly but firmly.

Everyone felt the uncanny and cruel fellowship in which he moved, and this was exactly the titillation for which the rabble sitting in safety had paid. It was perfectly clear that his revolver would be of no use if the five mighty beasts awoke from their illusion of helplessness and decided to tear him to pieces. It was my impression that if he had injured himself in any way and they had seen his blood, it would have been all over with him. I realized, too, that if he went into the cage half naked it was as a boon to the crowd, so that their craven joy might be enhanced by the sight of flesh, the flesh into which the great cats—who knows, perhaps it will happen tonight!—might set their terrible claws. Since I, however, continued to think of Andromache, I felt tempted to picture her as Mustafa's beloved; at any rate, there was a kind of appropriateness in that. At the mere thought, jealousy pierced my heart like a knife and I actually lost my breath; hastily I banished the image. Comrades in the face of death they might well be, but not a pair of lovers, no, no; besides, it would bode ill to both of them! If he were involved in an affair, the lions would know and would refuse him obedience. And she, the angel of daring, would miss the flying bar, I was sure of it, if she abased herself and became a woman; she would pitch headlong toward the ground into disgrace and death. . . .

What more was there, early and late, in the Stoudebecker Circus? A great variety of things, a superfluity of disciplined marvels. There is little to be gained by recalling them all. I do remember that from time to time I glanced sidewise at my friend Stanko, who, like all the people round about, was sunk in passive, blank enjoyment of this never-ending stream of dazzling skill, this colourful cascade of confusing, intoxicating feats and sights. This was not my style at all nor my way of meeting experience. Nothing, to be sure, escaped me; I seized on every detail with passionate attention. This was surrender, but in it there was—how shall I say?—an element of rebellion; I stiffened my back; my soul—how in the world can I express it?—exerted a kind of counter-pressure against the overwhelming flood of impressions. For all my admiration, there was a certain distrust—I am not putting this accurately but only approximately—in my penetrating observation of the tricks and arts and their effects. The crowd around me seethed with joy and merriment—I, however, in some measure shut myself off from their seething and yearning, coolly, like someone who was a member of the profession, who "belonged" to the performers. Not as a member of the circus profession or a performer of the *salto mortale*, of course; I could not feel myself that, but as a member of a more general profession, as an entertainer and illusionist. That is why I inwardly withdrew from the crowd, which was only the passive victim of entertainment, revelling in self-forgetfulness, and repudiated any idea that I was one of them. They merely enjoyed, and enjoyment is a passive condition that will never satisfy one who feels himself born to act and to achieve.

My neighbour, honest Stanko, had no share in any such thoughts, and so we were dissimilar companions whose friendship could not possibly amount to much. On our walks my delighted attention was held by the spaciousness and splendour of the Parisian scenes; certain glorious perspectives of incredible distinction and magnificence always reminded me of my poor father and the way in which, almost fainting at the memory, he would exclaim "*Magnifique! Magnifique!*" But as I made no ado about my admiration and amazement, my companion hardly noticed any difference in the responsiveness of our souls. On the other hand, he was slowly forced to notice that in some mysterious way our friendship failed to advance, that no real intimacy sprang up between us. This was simply due to my natural inclination toward taciturnity and reserve, to my insistence upon privacy and separateness. I have already mentioned this characteristic, which I consider one of the basic elements of my character, one which I could not have altered even had I wished to.

It is always thus with men who feel, not so much with pride as with acquiescence, that fate has something special in store for them. This feeling creates around them an atmosphere or emanation of coolness which, almost to their own regret, foils and repels all honest offers of friendliness and companionship. Thus it was with Stanko and me. He went to great lengths to confide in me and saw that I was patient rather than receptive. One afternoon, for example, as we were drinking wine in a bistro, he told me that before coming to Paris he had spent a year in jail because of a robbery he had been caught at not through any fault of his own but through the stupidity of his accomplice. I received this less than startling news with cheerful sympathy, and in itself it would have done nothing to injure our friendship. Next time, however, he went further and let me see that his confidences had been based on calculation, and this displeased me. He saw in me someone naturally lucky and possessed of childish cunning and skilful fingers, with whom, therefore, it would be useful to work, and as he was obtuse enough not to realize that I was not born to be anyone's accomplice he made me a proposal. He had ferreted out a villa in Neuilly where he said a pretty haul could be made quite easily and almost without risk. When I declined with indifference, he became angry and asked me what made me think I was too good for it, adding that he knew all about me. As I have always despised people who thought they knew all about me, I simply shrugged my shoulders and replied that that might well be but I was not interested. Whereupon he shouted "Fool!" or perhaps "*Imbécile!*" and stalked out.

Even this disappointment which I had caused him did not lead to an immediate break in our relations, but they grew less and less close until finally, without actually becoming enemies, we ceased to go out together.

CHAPTER II

I continued to be an elevator boy all winter, and in spite of the signs of favour that came my way from the transient public, I soon became bored. I had reason to fear it would go on forever and I would, so to speak, be forgotten there and grow old and grey in the job. What I heard from Stanko increased my concern. He, for his part, wished to be transferred to the main kitchen, with its two big ranges, four roasting-ovens, grill, and singeing-grate, so that in time he might become, if not actually a chef, then perhaps assistant kitchen-manager, whose duty it is to take the orders from the waiters and divide them among the company of cooks. But in his opinion his chances of such advancement were slight; there was too strong an inclination to keep a man where he happened to be, and he darkly predicted that I would stay tied to the lift forever, though perhaps not permanently without pay, and would never come to know our cosmopolitan establishment from any point of view other than my narrow and limited one.

It was just this that worried me. I felt imprisoned in my elevator cage and in the shaft up and down which it moved at my direction. There was no chance, or at best only a fleeting one, for a glance at the scenes of high life in the lobby at five-o'clock teatime, when subdued music filled the air and girls in Greek attire danced for the entertainment of the guests who sat in wicker chairs at their usual small tables, consuming *petits fours* and delicate little sandwiches with their golden drink, and getting rid of the crumbs afterward by a kind of fluttering of their fingers in the air. The grand staircase swept between rows of palms in sculptured urns up to a gallery adorned with potted plants; here, on the carpeted steps, they would pause to chat; their expressions and the movement of their heads betokened wit; they exchanged jokes and indulged in the light laughter of men of the world. How fine it would be to move among them, waiting on them or on the ladies in the card rooms or, at evening, to attend them in the dining-room, whither I saw tail-coated gentlemen proceeding, and ladies blazing with jewels. In short, I was restless, longing for my existence to expand, for richer possibilities of contact with the world; and in actual fact kind fortune brought this to pass. My desire to get away from the elevator, put on a new uniform, and embark on a new occupation with wider horizons was fulfilled: at Easter I became a waiter. This is how it happened.

The maître d'hôtel, Monsieur Machatschek by name, was a man of great consequence; clad daily in fresh linen, he moved his expansive belly around the dining-room with a vast authority. His clean-shaven moon face beamed. He commanded to perfection those lofty gestures of the lifted arm by which the master of the tables from afar directs the entering guests to their places. His way of dealing with any mistake or awkwardness on the part of the staff—in passing, and out of the corner of his mouth—was both discreet and biting. It was he who summoned me one morning, I must assume on the suggestion of the management, and received me in a small office opening off the magnificent *salle-à-manger*.

"Kroull?" he said. "Called Armand? *Voyons, voyons. Eh bien,* I have heard of you—not exactly to your discredit and not altogether inaccurately, as would appear at first glance. That may be deceptive, *pourtant*. You realize, of course, that the services you have so far rendered this establishment are child's play and represent a very meagre use of your gifts? *Vous consentez?* It is our intention to make something out of you if possible, here in the restaurant—*si c'est faisable*. Do you feel a certain vocation for the profession of waiter, some *degree* of talent, I say—nothing exceptional and brilliant as you seem to be assuring me, that would mean carrying self-confidence too far, although of course courage doesn't hurt—a certain talent for elegant service and all the subtle attentions that go with it? For a decently skilful attendance on a public like ours? Innate? Of course something of this sort is innate, but the things you seem to consider innate in you would make one's head whirl. However, I can only repeat that healthy self-confidence is no drawback. You have some knowledge of languages? I did not say a comprehensive knowledge, as you claim, but only the most basic. *Bon.* These, of course, are all questions for a later day. In the nature of things, you can hardly expect to start anywhere except at the bottom. First of all, your job will be to scrape food off the plates that come from the dining-room before they go on to the scullery to be washed. You will receive forty francs a month for this employment—an almost exaggeratedly high salary, as your expression seems to indicate. Moreover, it's not customary when conversing with me to smile before I myself smile. I am the one who gives the signal to smile. *Bon.* We will provide the white jacket for your job as scraper. Are you in a position to acquire a waiter's uniform in case we should need you some day to carry dishes out of the dining-room? You no doubt know this must be done at your own expense. You are *entirely* in a position to do it? Splendid. I see that we will have no difficulties with you. You are also provided with the necessary linen, decent evening shirts? Tell me: have you means of your own, money from your family? Some means? *A la bonne heure.* I believe, Kroull, within the foreseeable future we will be able to increase your salary to fifty or sixty francs. You can get the address of the tailor who makes our uniforms at the office. You may join us whenever you like. We need an assistant, and there are hundreds of applicants for the job of liftboy. *A bientôt, mon garçon.* We are getting close to the middle of the month, and so you will be paid twenty-five francs this month, for I propose to start you at a salary of six hundred a year. This time your smile is permissible, for I set the example. That is all. You may go."

Thus Machatschek in his conversation with me. That this momentous interview led at first to a come-down in my status and in what I represented is not to be denied. I had to turn in my liftboy's uniform at the store and receive a white jacket in exchange. I promptly had to acquire a usable pair of trousers to go with it, since it was out of the question to work in the ones belonging to my Sunday suit. This job of scraping scraps from the dishes into the garbage pail was somewhat degrading in comparison with my former occupation, which had been at any rate loftier, and at first it was not a little repulsive. Moreover, my chores extended into the scullery, where the china passed from hand to hand through a series of washings and ended up with the driers; from time to time I found myself among them attired in a white apron. Thus, in a sense, I stood at the beginning and at the end of this process of restoration.

To submit cheerfully to a position that is beneath one and to remain on cordial terms with those to whom such a situation is appropriate, is not difficult if one can only keep the word "temporary" in mind. Despite people's insistence on equality, I felt complete confidence in the instinct for what is naturally pre-eminent and the impulse to recognize it. I was therefore convinced that I should not be kept in this position long; indeed, that I had only been put there as a matter of form. And so as soon after my conversation with Monsieur Machatschek as I had the opportunity, I ordered a waiter's dress suit *à la* Saint James and Albany at the shop in the rue des Innocents, not far from the hotel, that specialized in uniforms and livery. It meant an investment of seventy-five francs, a special price agreed upon between the firm and the hotel. Employees without means had to pay it out of their wages, in instalments, but I of course paid cash. The livery was extremely pretty, especially if one knew how to wear it. The trousers were black, the tail-coat dark blue with gold buttons and velvet trimming at the collar; there were gold buttons, too, smaller ones, on the deep-cut waistcoat. I was thoroughly delighted by this acquisition, which I hung up beside my Sunday clothes in the wardrobe outside the dormitory. I then procured the appropriate white tie and enameled studs and cufflinks. Thus it came about that I was ready when, after five weeks in the scullery, one of the two tuxedo-clad head-waiters who assisted Monsieur Machatschek told me I would be needed in the dining-room. He instructed me to make the necessary preparations and I was able to inform him that I was completely prepared and could appear at any moment.

Thus at lunchtime the next day I made my debut in the dining-room in full glory. It is a magnificent hall, as spacious as a cathedral, with fluted columns whose gilded capitals support the white stucco ceiling. There are wall lights with red shades, billowing draperies at the windows, and countless tables, large and small, covered with white damask and adorned with orchids. Around them stand white lacquer chairs with red upholstered seats, and on the tables rest napkins folded like fans or pyramids, shining silver, delicate glasses, and bottles of wine in gleaming coolers or light wicker baskets—the responsibility of the wine steward, who is identifiable by his chain and cellarman's apron. Long before the first guests appeared I had been on hand, helping to set places and distribute menus at the tables to which I had been assigned as an assistant. I missed no opportunity, when my superior was busy elsewhere, to greet the entering guests with every sign of delight, to push in the ladies' chairs, hand them menus, fill their glasses—in short, to make my presence agreeable to our charges equally without respect to their unequal charms.

At first I had scant right or chance to do this. It was not my place to take orders or serve the courses, but simply to carry out the dishes and silverware after each course and, after the *entremets* and before the dessert was brought in, to remove the crumbs with a brush and flat scoop. The higher duties were the prerogative of my superior, Hector, a rather elderly man with a sleepy expression, whom I instantly recognized as the *commis-de-salle* with whom I had sat in the canteen on my first morning and who had given me his cigarettes. He too remembered me with a "*Mais oui, c'est toi,*" accompanied by a weary gesture of resignation, which was to characterize his attitude toward me—an attitude, from the very beginning, of acceptance rather than command or reproof. He saw, of course, that the clientele, especially the ladies old and young, were interested in me, motioned to me when they wished some special item—English mustard, Worcestershire sauce, tomato catsup—wishes that in many cases I recognized as simple pretexts for calling me to the table in order to hear my "*Parfaitement, madame,*" "*Tout de suite, madame.*" They would murmur: "*Merci, Armand*" and accompany the words with a dazzling upward glance, hardly justified by the nature of my service. After a few days, while I was at the serving-table helping Hector remove the bones from a sole, he said to me:

"They would much rather be served by you, *au lieu de moi*—they are all crazy about you, *toute la canaille friande!* You'll soon squeeze me out and have these tables to yourself. You're an attraction—*et tu n'as pas l'air de l'ignorer*. The management knows it, too, and they push you ahead. You heard—of course you heard—what Monsieur Cordonnier" (that was the assistant headwaiter who had come to get me) "said awhile ago to the Swedish couple with whom you were chatting so prettily: '*Joli petit charmeur, n'est-ce-pas?*' *Tu iras loin, mon cher—mes meilleurs vœux, ma bénédiction.*"

"You exaggerate, Hector," I replied. "I would still have to learn a great deal from you before I could think of ousting you—even if I had that in mind."

This was not exactly my real thought on the matter. On one of the following days at dinnertime Monsieur Machatschek himself, propelling his belly toward my section and standing beside me so that we faced in opposite directions, murmured to me out of the corner of his mouth: "Not bad, Armand. You don't work too badly. I recommend that you pay close attention to Hector when he is serving—that is, if you are interested in doing the same some time."

I replied, also sotto voce: "A thousand thanks, maître, but

I know all that already, better than he does. I know, if you will pardon me, by instinct. I will not hurry you into putting me to the proof, but as soon as you decide to do so you will find my words are true."

"*Blagueur!*" he said and gave a jerk to his stomach and a quick, amused laugh. At the same time, observing that a lady in green with a high, artificially blond coiffure had observed this little exchange, he winked at her and motioned toward me with his head, before moving on with his remarkably elastic step. As he did so he jerked his stomach again in amusement.

I soon received the additional assignment of serving coffee in the lobby twice a day with a few of my colleagues. This duty was presently extended to include serving tea there in the afternoons. In the meantime Hector had been moved to another part of the dining-room and the group of tables I had first served as an assistant was assigned to me. Thus, I had almost too much to do, and in the evening, toward the end of my varied day's work, I began to feel symptoms of exhaustion. As I handed around coffee and liqueurs, whisky and soda, and *infusion de tilleul* in the lobby after dinner, I felt that the current of sympathy between me and the world was losing vitality, that my zeal to be of service was weakening and my smile had a tendency to stiffen into a mask of pain.

By morning, however, my resilient nature would regain its freshness and gaiety; I could be seen again hurrying between breakfast room, coffee kitchen, and main kitchen, serving such guests as failed to take advantage of room service and have their breakfasts in bed, with tea, oatmeal, toast, preserves, baked fish, and pancakes with maple syrup; immediately afterward I could be seen in the dining-hall, assisted by an imbecile of a second, preparing for luncheon, spreading damask cloths over the soft base pads, setting places, and from twelve o'clock on, pencil in hand, taking down the orders of those who had come in. How well I knew how to counsel the indecisive, employing the soft, discreetly reserved tone appropriate to a waiter, and how to avoid any appearance of indifference in arranging and serving the dishes, giving each motion the quality of loving personal service. Bowing, one hand behind my back in the best waiter's tradition, I would proffer the dishes; now and then I would practise the fine art of manipulating fork and spoon with my right hand alone to serve those who preferred me to do it for them. Meanwhile, the object of this attention—whether he or she, but especially if it was she—might take notice with agreeable surprise of my busy hand, which was the hand of no ordinary man.

No wonder, then, considering all this, that they pushed me ahead, that, as Hector had said, exploiting the favour I found in the eyes of the overfed guests of this luxury hotel, they handed me over to the gale of favouritism that beat about me and left it to my ingenuity to whip it up by my melting attentiveness and yet keep it within bounds by the propriety of my conduct.

To keep clear the picture of my character which these memoirs are designed to sketch for the reader, this much must be said to my credit. I have never taken vain or cruel pleasure in the sufferings of those fellow mortals in whom my person has aroused desires that my prudence has forbidden me to gratify. Passions of which one is the unmoved object may fill natures unlike mine with a cold and unlovely vanity or inspire a contemptuous distaste that leads them to trample pitilessly on the feelings of others. How different it is with me! I have always felt compassion for such feelings, have spared them to the best of my ability out of a kind of guilt, and have tried through an attitude of understanding to persuade the victims to a sensible renunciation. As proof I shall cite here, from this period of my life, the double example of little Eleanor Twentyman from Birmingham and Lord Strathbogie, an important member of the Scottish nobility. These simultaneous incidents represented in their different ways temptations to depart prematurely from my chosen career, temptations, in fact, to hasten down one of those bypaths of which my godfather had spoken, and which one cannot too carefully examine in respect to their direction and length.

The Twentymans, father, mother, and daughter, together with a maid, had occupied a suite in the Saint James and Albany for a number of weeks, a fact which in itself indicated a gratifying degree of wealth. This was confirmed and made conspicuous by the magnificent jewelry Mrs. Twentyman wore to dinner, which, one must admit, was wasted. For Mrs. Twentyman was a joyless woman–joyless for those around her and, probably, for herself as well. Her husband's successful business activities in Birmingham had obviously raised her from some lower-middle-class sphere to a social plane that made her stiff and uncomfortable. Mr. Twentyman, his face flushed by his liberal consumption of port, radiated more human kindliness; his joviality, however, was greatly dampened by the hardness of hearing which produced an empty, strained expression in his watery blue eyes. He used a black ear trumpet, into which his wife had to speak when, as was seldom the case, she had something to say to him. He extended it to me, too, when I advised him what to order. Eleanor, his daughter, a girl of seventeen or eighteen, sat opposite him at table number eighteen. From time to time he would summon her by a gesture to come and sit beside him for a short conversation through the trumpet.

His fondness for the child was obvious and winning. As to Mrs. Twentyman, I will not contest her motherly affection, but instead of expressing it in loving words and glances she concentrated it in a critical supervision of Eleanor's conduct. Each time she raised her tortoise-shell lorgnette to her eyes, Mrs. Twentyman would find something to correct in her daughter's coiffure or deportment; she would forbid her to roll bread crumbs into little balls, lift a chicken bone in her fingers, or peer inquisitively around the dining-room–and so on. All this supervision indicated a parent's uneasiness and concern and may well have been annoying to Miss Twentyman;

the equally annoying experiences I had with her, however, forced me to admit that they were not unjustified.

She was a blonde creature, pretty in the fashion of a young chamois, and when she wore her little silk evening dress with its modest décolletage her collarbones were the most touching sight in the world. Since I have always had a weakness for the Anglo-Saxon type, of which she was a very notable example, I enjoyed seeing her. Moreover, I saw her constantly, at meal-times, after meals, and at the teatime musicales where I served and where the Twentymans, at least at first, used to appear. I was kind to my little chamois, surrounded her with the attentions of a devoted brother, set her food before her, passed her the dessert twice, provided her with grenadine, which she loved to drink, and gently draped her embroidered shawl around her thin, snow-white shoulders when she got up from the table. All in all, I did decidedly too much, I thoughtlessly sinned against this too responsive soul by not sufficiently taking into account the magnetism my being exerts, whether I will or no, on all my fellow creatures who are not completely insensitive. The effect would have been the same, I venture to believe, even if my mortal dress, as it is called at the end—my appearance, that is—had been less attractive; for that was only an external symbol of a deeper power—sympathy.

In short, I was very soon forced to realize that the little one had fallen head over heels in love with me, and this realization, naturally, was not mine alone. Peering worriedly through her tortoise-shell lorgnette, Mrs. Twentyman had made the same discovery, as I learned at lunch one day from her hisses and whispers behind my back:

"Eleanor! If you don't stop staring at that boy, I'll send you up to your room and you'll have to eat alone till we leave!"

But, alas, the little chamois was lacking in self-control; it never occurred to her to obey or to make the slightest attempt to conceal that she had fallen in love. Her blue eyes clung to me constantly in a dreamy ecstasy; when they met mine she lowered them to her plate and flushed scarlet, but she immediately raised them again, as though under some compulsion, in a glance of complete and glowing surrender. One could understand her mother's watchfulness; no doubt she had been warned by earlier indications that this child of Birmingham respectability was inclined to be irresponsible, inclined, in fact, to an innocent and fierce belief in her right and even her duty to surrender openly to passion. Certainly I did nothing to encourage this; my considerateness bordered on severity, and in my attitude toward her I never went beyond the attentiveness that was part of my duty. I approved the decision, which no doubt was made by her mother and must certainly have seemed cruel to her, when the Twentymans at the beginning of the second week gave up their table with me and moved to the distant part of the hall where Hector served.

But my wild chamois was not without resources. Suddenly at eight o'clock one morning she appeared in the breakfast room for *petit déjeuner*, whereas her practice hitherto, like her parents', had been to have breakfast in her room. She changed colour on entering and searched for me with reddened eyes. There was no trouble in finding a table in my section, for at that hour the room was almost empty.

"Good morning, Miss Twentyman. Did you rest well?"

"Very little rest, Armand, very little," she murmured.

I indicated I was sorry to hear it. "But then," I said, "perhaps it would have been wiser to stay in bed awhile longer and have your tea and porridge there. I'll get them for you right away, but I can't help thinking you would have enjoyed them more comfortably there. It's so calm and peaceful in the room, in bed. . . ."

What did the child reply? "No, I prefer to suffer."

"But you are making me suffer, too," I replied softly, indicating to her on the menu the kind of marmalade to order.

"Oh, Armand, then we suffer together!" she said and looked up at me with her tired, tearstained eyes.

What was to come of it? I wished heartily for their departure, but it was delayed; it was understandable enough that

Mr. Twentyman was reluctant to have his stay in Paris cut short by his daughter's emotional whims, of which he had no doubt heard through his black trumpet. Miss Twentyman, however, came down every morning while her parents still slept—they used to sleep until ten o'clock, so that Eleanor could pretend, if her mother looked in to see her, that the breakfast dishes had already been taken down by room service—and I had the devil's own time to protect her reputation in the eyes of those around, and conceal her unhappy state, her attempts to press my hand, and other infatuated nonsense. She remained deaf to my warnings that her parents must some day discover the trick she was playing on them, her breakfast secret. No, she replied, Mrs. Twentyman slept most soundly in the mornings, and how much better she liked her when she was asleep than when she was supervising her! Mummy did not love her, she was only interested in keeping a sharp eye on her through her lorgnette. Daddy loved her, but did not take her heart seriously; this was something that Mummy did, if only in the worst sense, and Eleanor was inclined to put that down to her credit. "For I love you!"

For the moment I pretended not to hear her. But when I came back to serve her I said softly and persuasively:

"Miss Eleanor, the words you let fall just now about 'love' are pure imagination and simple nonsense. Your Daddy is perfectly right not to take them seriously—although your mother is right too, in her way, to take them seriously—that is, as nonsense—and to forbid you to indulge in this sort of thing. Please don't take yourself quite so seriously, to your distress and mine, but try instead to see the funny side of this—something I certainly won't do, far from it, but you must try to. For what good is all this? You must see that it is unnatural. Here you are, the daughter of a man like Mr. Twentyman, who has reached a pinnacle of wealth and who has brought you with him for a few weeks' stay at the Saint James and Albany, where I am employed as a waiter. For that's all I am, Miss Eleanor, a waiter, a lowly member of our social order, which

I regard with reverence, but toward which you behave rebelliously. It's abnormal, too, for you not to ignore me, as would be natural and as your Mummy quite properly demands, but instead to come down secretly to breakfast and talk to me about 'love' while your parents are prevented by their peaceful slumbers from coming to the defence of the social order. This 'love' of yours is a forbidden love which I cannot approve, and I am forced to reject any pleasure of my own in the fact that you like to see me. It's all right for me to like to see you, if I keep it to myself, that's quite true. But for you, Mr. and Mrs. Twentyman's daughter, to like to see me, that's impossible, that's contrary to nature. Besides, it's nothing but an optical illusion arising principally from this tail-coat *à la* Saint James and Albany with its velvet trim and gold buttons, which is only an adornment concealing my lowly state; without it I would look like nothing at all, I assure you! What you call 'love' is something that happens to people on trips and at the sight of tail-coats like mine. When you have left, as you will very soon, you'll forget it before you get to the next station. Leave the memory of our encounter behind you, leave it to me; then it will be preserved without encumbering you!"

Was that not kindly said? What more could I do for her? But she only wept, so that I was glad the near-by tables were empty; sobbing, she chided me for my cruelty and would hear nothing about the natural social order and the unnaturalness of her infatuation, but every morning insisted that if only we could be entirely alone and undisturbed, untrammelled in word and deed, then everything would work out happily—provided only that I was a little fond of her, a fact I did not dispute, at least to the extent of my being grateful for her partiality. But how were we to contrive a rendezvous where we would be alone and untrammelled in word and deed? She had no more idea than I, but did not on that account cease her pleading; she imposed on me the duty of finding such an opportunity.

In short, I had the very devil of a time with her. And this

would have been bad enough if it had happened by itself and not at exactly the same time as the even more serious incident with Lord Strathbogie! No small trial this, since what was at stake was not an infatuated young girl but a personality of great importance whose sensibilities counted for something in the world, so that one could neither invite him to see the funny aspect of the affair nor find anything funny in it oneself. At any rate, I was not the man to do so.

His lordship, who had been staying with us for two weeks and who ate at one of my small single tables, was a man of obvious distinction, about fifty years of age, of moderate height, slender, elegantly dressed; his still thick, carefully brushed hair was iron grey, like the clipped moustache which did not conceal the almost feminine delicacy of his lips. There was nothing delicate or aristocratic about the cut of his too large, almost blocklike nose, which jutted straight out of his face to form a high ridge between the somewhat slanting brows beetling above the green-grey eyes. These eyes seemed to meet one as though with a great effort of self-discipline. If his nose was deplorable, his cheeks and chin were quite the reverse, clean-shaven to the ultimate degree of smoothness and well massaged. He used some kind of violet water on his handkerchief, whose perfume had a natural and springlike scent such as I have never encountered since.

There was always a kind of embarrassment in his way of entering the dining-hall, which might have seemed puzzling in so important a gentleman, but which, in my eyes at least, did nothing to detract from his impressiveness. It was completely compensated for by his extreme dignity, and it simply led one to imagine that there was something remarkable about him and that he therefore felt himself singled out and observed. His voice was soft, and I replied to it even more softly, only to discover too late that this was not good for him. His manner was friendly but tinged with melancholy, like that of a man who has suffered a great deal; what person of good will would not have reacted to it as I did by a responsive attentiveness in serving him? However, it was not good for him. To be sure, he seldom looked at me during the brief exchanges about the weather or the menu to which our conversation was at first restricted—just as in general he employed his eyes very little, keeping them in reserve and making sparing use of them, as though he were afraid their play might produce unpleasant consequences. It was a week before our relationship became somewhat freer and ceased to be bound completely by the formal and conventional; then I observed with pleasure, which was not unmixed with anxiety, the signs of his personal interest in me. A week—that is probably the minimum time required by a person in daily association with an unfamiliar being to become aware of certain changes, especially when the eyes are so little used.

It was then that he asked me how long I had been in service, where I came from, how old I was, hearing the number of my years with an emotional shrug of the shoulders and the exclamation "*Mon Dieu!*" or "*Good Heavens!*"—he spoke English and French interchangeably. Why, he inquired, if I was German by birth did I have the French name of Armand. It was not mine, I replied, I simply answered to it in obedience to instructions from my superiors. My real name was Felix. "Ah, pretty," he said. "If it were within my power, I would give you back your real name." He added the information that his own Christian name was Nectan, which had been the name of a king of the Picts, the original inhabitants of Scotland. There was something, it seemed to me, inconsistent with his exalted position, something that impressed me as unstable in his saying this. I replied, to be sure, with a show of attentive interest, but I couldn't help wondering what use I was to make of the information that his name was Nectan. It was of no good to me, for I had to call him milord and not Nectan.

Bit by bit I learned that he owned a castle not far from Aberdeen, where he lived alone with an elderly sister, who was unfortunately in delicate health; and he had a summer estate as well on one of the highland lakes in a region where the people still talked Gaelic (he spoke a little himself), a place that was very beautiful and romantic, with rugged and precipitous cliffs and air perfumed by the wildflowers of the heath. Near Aberdeen, too, it was very beautiful, the city afforded every kind of entertainment for those interested in that sort of thing, the air blew in from the North Sea strong and clean. I was further given to understand that he loved music and played the organ. In his country house on the mountain lake it was, to be sure, only a harmonium.

These confidences, which were not made in a single conversation but dropped casually and fragmentarily now and then, could not, with the possible exception of "Nectan," be considered as evidences of excessive communicativeness on the part of a man travelling alone who had no one to chat with but the waiter. The most favourable opportunity came after lunch, when his lordship, as was his custom at noon, instead of taking his coffee in the lobby, remained at his small table in the almost deserted dining-hall smoking Egyptian cigarettes. He always took several cups of coffee. Before that he would not have drunk anything or eaten much of anything. Indeed, he ate very little, and one was forced to wonder how he could exist on the nourishment he consumed. He made a good start, to be sure, with a soup; strong consommé, mock turtle, or oxtail soup disappeared completely from his plate. After that, however, whatever delicacies I placed before him were only tasted; he would light another cigarette immediately and let course after course be carried out almost untouched. After a while I could not refrain from commenting on this.

"*Mais vous ne mangez rien, milord,*" I said in distress. "*Le chef se formalisera, si vous dédaignez tous ses plats.*"

"What can I do, I have no appetite," he replied. "I never have. The business of nourishment—I have a decided dislike for it. Perhaps it's a symptom of a certain self-repudiation."

The phrase, which I had never heard before, startled me and called forth my politeness.

"Self-repudiation?" I exclaimed softly. "Milord, no one

can follow you there or agree with you. You will meet with the strongest opposition!"

"Really?" he asked and slowly raised his eyes from his plate to my face. His glance still seemed an act of self-discipline. But this time his eyes showed that the effort was gladly made. His lips smiled with a delicate melancholy. But over them his oversized nose jutted toward me straight and massive.

How can one, I thought, have so delicate a mouth and such a block of a nose?

"Really!" I assured him in some confusion.

"Perhaps, *mon enfant*," he said, "self-repudiation helps one to appreciate someone else."

At this he got up and went out of the hall. I stayed behind, occupied with a variety of thoughts, while I cleared and reset the small table.

There was little doubt that contact with me several times a day was not good for his lordship. But I could neither put an end to it nor could I render it harmless even by excluding all sensitive responsiveness from my conduct and keeping it so stiff and formal that I wounded the very feelings I had inspired. To make merry over them was even more impossible than in the case of little Eleanor. It was equally out of the question to fall in with their intention. This resulted in a difficult conflict, which was to turn into a temptation through the unexpected proposal he made to me—unexpected in its form, though not at all in essence.

It happened toward the end of the second week, while I was serving coffee in the lobby after dinner. The small orchestra was playing behind a hedge of plants near the entrance to the dining-room. At some distance from it, at the other end of the room, his lordship had chosen a small, isolated table which he had used several times before, and it was here that I served his coffee. As I passed him a second time he asked for a cigar. I brought him two boxes of imported cigars, one with bands, the other without. He looked at them and said:

"Well, then, which shall I take?"

"The dealer," I replied, "recommends these," and I pointed to the banded ones. "Personally, if I may, I recommend the others."

I could not resist giving him this chance for a display of courtesy.

He took it. "I will follow your advice," he said, but let me stand there holding both boxes while he stared first down at them and then up at me.

"Armand?" he asked softly beneath the music.

"Milord?"

He changed his manner of address. "Felix?"

"Milord wishes?" I asked, smiling.

"You wouldn't like, would you," he said without raising his eyes from the cigars, "to exchange hotel work for a position as a valet?"

There I had it.

"How so, milord?" I asked in apparent incomprehension.

He pretended I had asked "With whom?" and answered with a slight shrug of the shoulders: "With me, that's very simple. You will accompany me to Aberdeen and Nectan Hall Castle. You will take off this livery and exchange it for ordinary clothes, distinguished clothes that will indicate your position and set you off from the other servants. There are all sorts of servants there. Your duties would be confined entirely to personal attendance on me. You would be with me all the time, at the castle and at the summer estate in the mountains. Your salary," he added, "will be, assuredly, two or three times what you make here."

I was silent, and he did not prompt me to speak by glancing at me. Instead, he took one the boxes from my hand and compared that brand with the other.

"This requires careful consideration, milord," I replied finally. "I need not say that I am greatly honoured by your offer. But it comes so unexpectedly. . . . I must take time for consideration."

"There is very little time for consideration," he replied.

"Today is Friday, I leave on Monday. Come with me! It is my wish."

He took one of the cigars I had recommended, regarded it thoughtfully from all sides, and passed it under his nose. No observer could have guessed what he was saying as he did so. What he said softly was: "It is the wish of a lonely heart."

Who so inhuman as to reproach me for feeling moved? Yet I knew at once I would not choose this bypath.

"I promise your lordship," I murmured, "that I will make good use of this period of reflection." And I withdrew.

He has, I thought, a good cigar to go with his coffee. That combination is highly enjoyable, and enjoyment is, after all, a minor form of happiness. There are circumstances in which one must content oneself with it.

This thought was a tacit temptation to try to help him to help himself. But there now ensued trying days when, at each meal and after tea as well, his lordship would glance at me once and say: "Well?" I either lowered my eyes and raised my shoulders as though they were heavy-laden, or I replied anxiously: "I have not yet been able to reach a decision."

His sensitive mouth became steadily more bitter. But although his ailing sister might have eyes for his happiness alone, had he considered the painful role I would have to play among the numerous servants of whom he had spoken and even among the Gaelic mountaineers? Their contempt, I said to myself, would strike not the great lord but the plaything of his whim. Secretly, despite all my sympathy, I considered him guilty of egotism. If only in addition to this I had not had to keep a close rein on Eleanor Twentyman's demands for untrammelled speech and action!

At dinner on Sunday a lot of champagne was drunk. His lordship, to be sure, drank none, but at the Twentymans' table corks were popping and I thought to myself that this was not good for Eleanor. My concern proved to be justified.

After dinner I served coffee in the lobby as usual. A glass door covered with green silk led from the lobby into a library with leather armchairs and a long table for newspapers. This room was little used; at most, a few people sat there in the morning and read the newly laid-out papers. Guests were really not supposed to remove them from the library, but someone had taken the *Journal des Débats* into the lobby and had left it on the chair beside one of the little tables. In my orderly fashion I rolled it around its staff and carried it back into the empty reading-room. I had just arranged it in its proper place on the long table when Eleanor came in, and it was clear to see that a few glasses of Moët-Chandon had been too much for her. She came straight up to me, quivering and trembling, threw her thin, bare arms around my neck, and stammered:

"Armand, I love you so desperately and helplessly, I don't know what to do, I am so deeply, so utterly in love with you that I am lost, lost, lost. . . . Speak, tell me, do you love me a little bit, too?"

"For heaven's sake, Miss Eleanor, be careful. Somebody might come in. Your mother, for instance. How on earth did you manage to get away from her? Of course I love you, sweet little Eleanor! You have such touching collarbones, you are such a lovely child in every way. . . . But now take your arms from around my neck and watch out. . . . This is extremely dangerous."

"What do I care about danger? I love you, I love you, Armand, let's run away together, let's die together, but first of all kiss me. Your lips, your lips, I am dying for your lips!"

"No, dear Eleanor," I said, gently attempting to loosen her embrace, "we won't begin that. You have been drinking champagne, several glasses, I think, and if I kiss you now, it will be all up, you will be inaccessible to any sensible idea. I have, after all, candidly explained to you how unnatural it is for the daughter of parents like Mr. and Mrs. Twentyman, raised to a pinnacle of wealth, to become infatuated with the first young waiter who comes along. It is simply an aberration, and even if it corresponded to your nature and temperament, you would nevertheless have to triumph over it out of respect for propriety and the natural laws of society. Now you'll be a good, sensible child, won't you? Let me go, and return to Mummy."

"Oh, Armand, how can you be so cold and cruel when you have said, after all, that you do love me a little? Go back to Mummy? I hate Mummy and she hates me, but Daddy loves me and will become reconciled to everything if we simply confront him with an accomplished fact. We just have to flee—let's flee tonight on the express, to Spain, for example, to Morocco, that's what I came to propose to you. We will go into hiding there and I will present you with a child that will be the accomplished fact, and Daddy will be reconciled when we throw ourselves at his feet with the child, and he'll give us his money so that we will be rich and happy. . . . Your lips!"

And the mad child actually behaved as though she wanted to conceive a child by me on the spot.

"That's enough, decidedly enough, dear little Eleanor," I said finally, removing her arms from about my neck with gentle considerateness. "These are all preposterous dreams, and I do not intend on their account to abandon my course in life or take this bypath. It's not at all right and doesn't agree with your protestations of love for you to assail me this way with your proposals and try to lead me astray at a time when I have heavy cares of another sort and am faced by a dilemma from a quite different quarter. You're very egotistical, do you know that? But that's the way you all are, and I am not angry at you. Instead, I thank you, and I will never forget little Eleanor. But now let me go about my duties in the lobby."

She burst into tears. "No kiss! No child! Poor, unhappy me! Poor little Eleanor, so miserable and disdained!" And with her tiny hands in front of her face she threw herself into one of the leather chairs, sobbing as though her heart would break. I was about to step up to her and pat her comfortingly before leaving. This, however, was reserved for someone else. At that moment a man entered—not just a man, it was Lord Strathbogie of Nectan Hall. In his faultless evening dress, his feet shod not in patent leather but in dull, flexible lambskin, his freshly shaved cheeks gleaming with cream, he advanced, his jutting nose thrust forward. With his head inclined a little toward one shoulder, he stood looking thoughtfully at the weeping girl from under his slanting brows; he approached her chair and sympathetically stroked her cheek with the back of his fingers. With swimming eyes and open mouth she looked up, startled, at the stranger, leaped from her chair, and ran out of the room like a weasel through the door opposite the glass one.

He stared after her thoughtfully as before. Then he turned to me calmly and with a regal demeanour.

"Felix," he said, "the last moment has come for your decision. I leave early tomorrow morning. You will have to pack your things tonight if you are going to accompany me to Scotland. What have you decided?"

"Milord," I replied, "I thank you most humbly and I beg your indulgence. I do not feel equal to the position you have so kindly offered me and I have come to the conclusion that I had better give up any idea of pursuing this bypath."

"It's impossible for me," he said in reply, "to take seriously your plea of inadequacy. Moreover," he added, glancing at the door, "I have the impression that your affairs here have been concluded."

At this I pulled myself together and replied: "I must conclude this one as well, and I take the liberty of wishing your lordship a very pleasant journey."

He bowed his head, and raised it only slowly to look at me in his peculiar fashion, his eyes revealing the effort it cost him.

"Felix!" he said, "aren't you afraid of making the greatest mistake of your life?"

"That's just what I fear, milord, and hence my decision."

"Because you don't feel equal to the position I am offering you? I should be much surprised if you do not concur in my feeling that you were born for positions of a quite different kind. My interest in you opens possibilities you do not take into account with your refusal. I am childless and master of my own affairs. There have been cases of adoption. . . . You might wake up one day as Lord Strathbogie and heir to my possessions."

That was strong. Indeed, he certainly sprang all his mines at once. Ideas swirled through my mind, but they did not incline me to alter my decision. That would be a suspect lordship, the one he dangled before me because of his interest. Suspect in the eyes of the people and lacking the proper authority. But that was not the main thing. The main thing was that a confident instinct within me rebelled against a form of reality that was simply handed to me and was in addition sloppy—rebelled in favour of free play and dreams, self-created and self-sufficient, dependent, that is, only on imagination. When as a child I had waked up determined to be an eighteen-year-old prince named Karl and had then freely maintained this pure and enchanting conceit for as long as I wished—that had been the right thing for me, not what this man with his jutting nose offered me because of his interest.

I have set down in hasty and condensed form what then flashed through my mind. I said firmly: "Forgive me, milord, if I confine my answer to a repetition of my best wishes for your journey."

At this he blanched, and suddenly I saw his chin begin to quiver.

Who would be so inhuman as to blame me for the fact that at this sight my eyes reddened, perhaps even filled—but no, probably they simply reddened? Sympathy is sympathy, only a knave would fail to be grateful for it. I said:

"But, milord, don't take this so much to heart! You met me and have seen me regularly and you took an interest in my youth. I am sincerely grateful for that, but this interest was a matter of accident; it might equally well have fastened upon somebody else. Please—I don't want to wound you or minimize the honour you have paid me, but if someone precisely like me occurs only once—each of us, of course, occurs only once—there are nevertheless millions of young men of my age and general physique, and except for the tiny bit of uniqueness, one is made very much like another. I knew a woman who declared that she was interested in the whole genre without exception—it must be essentially that way with you, too. The genre is present always and everywhere. You are returning to Scotland now—as though it weren't charmingly represented there, and as though you needed me to awaken your interest! There they wear checked jackets and, I understand, go bare-legged, which must be a pleasure to see! So there you can select a brilliant valet from the genre and you can chat with him in Gaelic and even, in the end, adopt him. Perhaps the transfer of a lordship is not so easy as all that, but ways can be found and at least he will be a countryman of yours. I can see him as so attractive that I am convinced he will drive our accidental encounter completely out of your mind. Leave the remembrance of it to me, I will treasure it. For I promise you that these days during which I have been privileged to serve you and to advise you in the selection of your cigars, these days of your assuredly fleeting interest in me, will be remembered forever with the warmest reverence. And eat more, milord, if I may take the liberty of urging it! As for self-repudiation, no man of heart and intelligence can agree with you there."

Thus I spoke, and it did him some good despite the fact that he shook his head at my mention of the Highland jackets. He smiled with just the same sensitive and melancholy expression he had worn on the occasion when he had first mentioned self-repudiation. As he did so, he took a very handsome emerald from his finger; I had often admired it on his hand, and I am wearing it now as I write these lines. Not that he put it on my finger, he did not do that, but simply handed it to me and said softly and brokenly:

"Take this ring. It is my wish. I thank you. Farewell."

Then he turned and left. I cannot too strongly commend to the approval of the public the behaviour of this man.

So much, then, for Eleanor Twentyman and Nectan Lord Strathbogie.

CHAPTER III

My basic attitude toward the world and society can only be called inconsistent. For all my eagerness to be on affectionate terms with them, I was frequently aware of a considered coolness, a tendency to critical reflection, which astonished me. There was, for example, an idea that occasionally preoccupied me when for a few leisure moments I stood in the lobby or dining-hall, clasping a napkin behind my back and watching the hotel guests being waited and fawned upon by blue-liveried minions. It was the idea of *interchangeability*. With a change of clothes and make-up, the servitors might often just as well have been the masters, and many of those who lounged in the deep wicker chairs, smoking their cigarettes, might have played the waiter. It was pure accident that the reverse was the fact, an accident of wealth; for an aristocracy of money is an accidental and interchangeable aristocracy.

Therefore, my imaginary transpositions sometimes succeeded very well, but not always. For, in the first place, the habit of wealth does, after all, produce at least superficial refinement, which complicated my game, and, in the second place, among the polished riff-raff of hotel society there are always a few persons whose distinction is independent of money, though naturally always accompanied by it. At times I had to select myself—no one else in the corps of waiters would do—if the imaginary substitution was to succeed. This was true in the case of a very engaging young cavalier of airy and carefree manner who did not live in the hotel but made a habit of dining with us once or twice a week, always in my section. On these occasions he would reserve a single table by telephoning to Machatschek, whose good graces he had obviously taken the trouble to acquire. The latter would notify me, his sharp eye on the table setting:

"*Le Marquis de Venosta. Attention!*"

Venosta, who was about my own age, treated me in a cordial, unconstrained, almost friendly fashion. I liked to see him enter in his easy, careless way. I would push in his chair unless Maître Machatschek had done so himself, and would answer his questions about my health with an appropriate tinge of deference.

"*Et vous, monsieur le marquis?*"

"*Comme ci, comme ça.* Is the food any good tonight?"

"*Comme ci, comme ça*—that is, excellent, exactly the way you feel, *monsieur le marquis.*"

"*Farceur!*" he would laugh. "Much you know about how I feel!"

He was not really handsome, but made an elegant appearance with his fine hands and neat, curly brown hair. His cheeks, however, were fat, red, and childish beneath small, roguish eyes. The eyes, however, pleased me and certainly gave the lie to the melancholy he sometimes liked to assume.

"Much you know about how I feel, *mon cher Armand*, and it's easy for you to talk. Obviously you have a talent for your métier and so you are happy, whereas it seems very doubtful to me that I have any talent at all for mine."

He was, in fact, a painter, studying at the Académie des Beaux Arts and sketching from the nude in his teacher's studio. This and other facts I learned in the course of the fragmentary conversations we carried on while I served him his dinner, conversation that had begun with a friendly inquiry on his part about my home and my circumstances. These questions indicated that I had impressed him as being out of the ordinary, and in answering them I avoided any particulars that might have weakened this impression. During these sporadic exchanges he spoke German and French interchangeably. He knew the former very well because his mother, "*ma pauvre mère*," belonged to the German nobility. His home was in Luxemburg, where his parents, "*mes pauvres parents*," lived not far from the capital in a seventeenth-century family castle surrounded by a park. This, he assured me, looked exactly like the English castles depicted on the plates on which I served him his roast beef and *bombe glacée*. His father was chamberlain to the Grand Duke, "and all that." Incidentally, or really not incidentally at all, he had a hand in the steel industry and so was "pretty rich," as his son Louis naïvely added, with a gesture that seemed to say: "What do you expect him to be? Naturally he is pretty rich." As though his own way of life, the thick, gold chain he wore around his wrist, the precious stones in his cufflinks, and the pearl in the bosom of his shirt did not clearly reveal it.

Thus when he spoke of his parents as "*mes pauvres parents*" it was a fond affectation, but there was also an overtone of true sympathy, for in his opinion they had a real good-for-nothing for a son. He was supposed to have studied law at the Sorbonne, but had very quickly dropped it out of sheer boredom and, with the pained and grudging acquiescence of his parents, had turned his attention to the arts—not without serious doubts, however, about his gifts in that direction. From his words, it was clear that he regarded himself with a kind of self-complacent concern as a spoiled child, and, without being willing or able to do anything about it, admitted his parents were right in fearing he had no goal in life beyond loafing and leading a footless bohemian existence. As to the second point, it was soon clear to me that it was not simply a question of his spiritless pursuit of an artistic career but of an unsuitable love affair as well.

From time to time the marquis would come to dinner not alone but in the most charming company. On these occasions he would order a larger table, and Machatschek would see that the flowers on it were especially gay. He would appear about seven o'clock, accompanied by a person who was really extraordinarily pretty—I could not question his taste, although it was a taste for *le beauté de diable* and for what was obviously perishable. Just then, however, in the bloom of youth, Zaza—so he called her—was the most enchanting creature in the world. She was a shapely brunette, Parisienne by birth, type grisette, but dignified by evening dresses from expensive establishments, which he, of course, ordered for her, and by the rare antique jewelry which was, of course, his gift. Her arms, which were always bare, were remarkably beautiful; her hair was done low on her neck in a bizarre, fluffy coiffure surmounted sometimes by a very becoming turban with silver fringe at the sides and a feather that swept over her forehead; she had a snub nose and her flirtatious glances were accompanied by continual chatter.

They drank the champagne which was always substituted, when Zaza came, for the half-bottle of Bordeaux Venosta drank when he dined alone, and it was a pleasure to wait on the pair, they took such joy in each other's company. There was no doubt that he was head over heels in love with her—and no wonder—to the point of being completely indifferent to all appearances, captivated by the glimpses of her enticing décolletage, her chatter, the witchery of her black eyes. And she, I can well believe, was delighted by his tenderness and happy to respond to it, and tried in every way to inflame it; to her it meant nothing less than first prize in the grand lottery, the basis of her hopes for a glowing future. I was accustomed to address her as "madame," but once, after her fourth or fifth visit, I ventured to say "*madame la marquise*," which produced a great effect. She blushed in happy terror and threw her friend a questioning and loving glance. He met this with merry eyes, while she, in some embarrassment, lowered her own to the table.

Naturally she flirted with me, too, and the marquis pretended to be jealous, although he certainly could be sure of her faithfulness.

"Zaza, you'll drive me crazy—*tu me feras voir rouge*—if you don't stop ogling Armand. You don't really want to be responsible for a double murder and a suicide, do you? . . . Come now, admit you wouldn't mind a bit if he were in a dinner jacket sitting at the table with you and I were serving you in a blue tail-coat."

How strange that he should have put into words the preoccupation of my leisure moments, my silent game of exchanging roles! While I held the menu for them both so that they could choose dessert, I was bold enough to answer in Zaza's stead:

"Then you would have the more difficult role, *monsieur le marquis*, for waiting is a trade, but to be a marquis is existence pure and simple."

"Excellent!' she cried, laughing with the delight of her kind at a well-turned phrase.

"And are you sure," he inquired, "that you are more capable of existence pure and simple than I am of a trade?"

"I believe it would be neither courteous nor accurate," I replied, "to ascribe to you a special talent as a waiter, *monsieur le marquis*."

She was much amused. "*Mais il est incomparable, ce gaillard!*"

"Your admiration for him is killing me," he said with theatrical despair. "And, besides, he only evaded me."

I let it go at that and withdrew. The evening dress in which he had pictured me as taking his place actually existed, however; I had acquired it a short time before and kept it, together with some other things, in a little room I had rented in a quiet corner of the central section of the city, not far from the hotel. My purpose was not to sleep there—that seldom happened—but to have a place to keep my personal wardrobe and to change unobserved when I wanted to spend my free evenings in somewhat higher circles than those I had frequented in Stanko's company. The room was in a house in a little *cité*, a covey of old houses enclosed by iron fences and reached through the quiet rue Boissy d'Anglas. There were neither stores nor restaurants there; only a few small hotels and private houses of the sort one can look into from the street through the open door of the porter's loge and see the concierge at her housework and her husband sitting with his bottle of wine, the cat beside him. It was in a house of this sort that I had a short time before become the sub-tenant of a kindly middle-aged widow who occupied a four-room apartment on the third floor. For a moderate monthly rental she turned one of her rooms over to me—a kind of small bed-sitting-room with a cot and a marble fireplace surmounted by a mirror, a pendulum clock on the mantelpiece, rickety upholstered furniture, and sooty silk curtains at the French windows, from which one had a view of a narrow court with glass-roofed kitchens below. Beyond this one looked out on the back windows of the elegant houses of the faubourg Saint-Honoré, where in the evenings one could see the cooks and maids wandering through the service quarters and bedrooms. Moreover, somewhere over there lived the Prince of Monaco, and to him belonged this whole peaceful little *cité*, for which he could receive, any time he wanted it, forty-five million francs. Then it would be torn down. But he seemed not to need the money, and so, subject to cancellation, I remained the guest of this monarch and grand croupier, a thought to whose odd charm I was by no means insensible.

The good suit I had bought at the Printemps had its place in the wardrobe outside dormitory number four. My new acquisitions, however—a tuxedo, a silk-lined evening cape, in the selection of which I had been unconsciously influenced by my still vivid recollection of Müller-Rosé as attaché and woman-killer, a silk hat, and a pair of patent-leather shoes—I had not dared exhibit in the hotel; I kept them ready for use in the "*cabinet de toilette*" in my rented room. This was a kind of wallpapered closet where a cretonne curtain protected my clothes. Dress shirts, black silk socks, and bow ties were in the Louis Seize bureau in the room. My tuxedo with its satin lapels had not actually been made to order; I had bought it off the hanger and only had it altered a little, but it fitted my figure so perfectly that I would like to have seen the connoisseur who would not have sworn it had been made to measure by an expensive tailor. For what purpose did I keep these and other fineries stored in my quiet private dwelling?

But I have already divulged the answer: from time to time, by way of experiment and practice in living the higher life, I would dine in some elegant restaurant on the rue de Rivoli or the avenue des Champs-Élysées or in some hotel of the same quality as my own, or finer if possible, the Ritz, the Bristol, the Meurice, and would afterward take a loge seat in some good theatre devoted to the spoken drama or comic opera or even grand opera. This amounted, as one can see, to a kind of dual existence, whose charm lay in the ambiguity as to which figure was the real I and which the masquerade: was I the liveried *commis-de-salle* who waited on and flattered the guests in the Saint James and Albany, or was I the unknown man of distinction who looked as though he must keep a riding-horse and who would certainly, once he had finished dinner, call in at various exclusive salons but was meanwhile graciously permitting himself to be served by waiters among whom I found none equal to me in my other role? Thus I masqueraded in both capacities, and the undisguised reality behind the two appearances, the real I, could not be identified because it actually did not exist. Nor am I willing to say that I gave my role as a man of distinction any definite preference over the other. I was too good and successful a waiter to feel appreciably happier when I was the one who was waited on—a part, by the way, that requires as much natural talent as the other. An evening was to come, however, that committed me to this talent, this theatrical gift for playing the master, in a decisive and gratifying, indeed almost intoxicating, manner.

CHAPTER IV

It was a July evening shortly before the national holiday that brings the theatre season to a close, and I was enjoying one of the free nights my employers granted me every fortnight. I had decided to dine, as I had done a few times before, in the attractive roof garden of the Grand Hotel des Ambassadeurs on the boulevard Saint-Germain. From its lofty heights one has a sweeping view over the flower boxes and across the city in the direction of the Seine, on one side toward the Place de la Concorde and the Madeleine, on the other toward that masterpiece of the World Exposition of 1889, the Eiffel Tower. An elevator takes you up five or six stories and you find yourself in a refreshing atmosphere, surrounded by the subdued conversation of high society, whose manners forbid curiosity. I fitted in easily and faultlessly. Brightly clad ladies, their hats wide and daring, sat in their wicker chairs at tables lighted by little shaded lamps. The moustached gentlemen escorting them wore correct evening attire, as did I. Some even had on tails. These I did not possess, but my own elegance was more than sufficient, and I felt completely at ease as I took my place at the empty table to which the headwaiter escorted me while his assistant removed the second *couvert.* I was looking forward to a delightful evening after an agreeable meal, for I had in my pocket a ticket to the Opéra Comique, where *Faust* was to be given that night, my favourite opera, the melodious masterpiece of the late Gounod. I had heard it once before and was looking forward to renewing the charming impressions of that first occasion.

That, however, was not to be. Fate had something quite different and far more significant in store for me that evening.

I had communicated my wishes to the waiter bending over me, menu in hand, and had asked for the wine card; I was allowing my eyes to wander over the assembled company with a casual and purposely weary gaze when they encountered another pair of eyes, merry and alert, the eyes of the young Marquis de Venosta, who, appareled like me, was sitting at a single table some distance away. Understandably enough, I recognized him before he recognized me. It was obviously easier for me to trust my eyes than for him to believe what he saw. After a brief wrinkling of the brow, a look of merry astonishment appeared on his face; for, though I had hesitated to greet him (I was not sure it would be tactful), the involuntary smile with which I had met his glance assured him of my identity—the identity, that is, of the cavalier and the waiter. With a toss of his head and a brief spreading of his hands he indicated his amazement and pleasure, and, laying aside his napkin, made his way over to me between the tables.

"*Mon cher Armand*, is it you or is it not? But forgive my momentary doubt. And forgive me for using your first name out of habit—unfortunately, your family name is unknown to me, or it has escaped my mind. For us you were always just Armand."

I had risen and was shaking his hand, which of course he had never offered me before.

"Not even the first name," I said, laughing, "is exactly right, marquis. Armand is only a *nom de guerre* or *d'affaires*. Actually, my name is Félix—Félix Kroull—enchanted to see you."

"*Mon cher Kroull*, of course, how could it have slipped my mind? It is I who am enchanted, I assure you! *Comment allez-vous?* Very well indeed, to judge by your appearance, although appearances . . . I, too, look well, and yet things are going ill with me. Yes, yes, ill. But none of that. And you—am I to understand that you have quit your delightful activities at the Saint James and Albany?"

"No, indeed, marquis. They go on concurrently. Or this goes on concurrently. I am both here and there."

"*Très amusant*. You are a magician. But I am inconveniencing you. I shall leave you to– But no, let us join forces. I cannot invite you to my table, it's too small. But I see you have room. I have had my dessert, but if it is agreeable to you, I'll have my coffee here. Or do you yearn for solitude?"

"Not a bit. You are welcome here, marquis," I replied casually. And, turning to the waiter: "A chair for this gentleman!" I was at pains not to show that I was flattered or to say anything about the honour he was doing me, but contented myself with calling his proposal a good one. He sat down opposite me and while I finished ordering my dinner and he was served with coffee and a *fine*, he continued to watch me earnestly, bending slightly forward across the table. Obviously my double life fascinated him and he was eager to understand it better.

"My presence doesn't disturb you while you're eating?" he asked. "I should hate to be a bother. Least of all do I want to appear importunate, which is always a sign of bad upbringing. A cultivated man passes lightly over everything, accepts events without asking questions. That marks a man of the world, such as I ostensibly am. All right, then, such as I am. But on many occasions–the present one, for example–I realize that I am a man of the world without knowledge of the world, without that experience of life which alone justifies us in accepting events of all kinds with the worldly man's light touch. There is no pleasure in playing that role if you are really ignorant. . . . You will understand that our meeting here strikes me as remarkable as well as pleasant and it makes me eager to understand. Admit that your phrases about 'going on concurrently' and 'here and there' contain something intriguing–to one who is inexperienced. For God's sake, go on eating and don't say a word! Let me do the talking while I try experimentally to picture the way of life of a contemporary who is obviously far more a man of the world than I am. *Voyons!* You come, as one now sees not for the first time but really always has seen, of a good family–with us members of the nobility, forgive the hard word, one simply says 'of family'; only the bourgeois can come of a *good* family. Comical world! A good family, then–and you have chosen a career which will doubtless lead to a goal appropriate to your origin, to attain which it is important that you work your way up from the ranks and temporarily occupy positions which might deceive someone of less penetration into thinking that he was dealing with a person of the lower classes instead, so to speak, of a gentleman in disguise. Am I right? *A propos:* it is nice of the English to have spread the word 'gentleman' around the world. Thanks to them, we have a designation for a man who is not a nobleman, to be sure, but deserves to be, deserves it more than many a one who is styled '*Hochgeboren*,' whereas the gentleman is only called '*Hochwohlgeboren*'–'only'–and has a '*wohl*' to make it more explicit. . . . To *your* '*Wohl*'! I'll order something to drink at once; that is, if you have emptied your half-bottle, we'll order a whole one together. . . . The '*Hochgeboren*' and '*Hochwohlgeboren*' make an exact analogy to 'family' and '*good* family.' . . . My, how I chatter! It's just so you may eat in peace and not bother about me. Don't take the goose, it's not well roasted. Take the leg of mutton; my experience confirms what the maître assured me of–it has been soaked in milk for the right length of time. . . . *Enfin!* What was I saying about you? While your service in the ranks makes you appear to be a member of the lower classes–this must afford you a good deal of amusement, I imagine–you naturally keep a firm inner hold on your position as a gentleman and from time to time return to it outwardly, as you are doing tonight. Very, very nice. But completely new to me and startling–which shows you how little one knows about human life even when one is a man of the world. Technically, if you'll pardon my asking, the 'here and there' cannot be entirely easy. You have money of your own, I assume–observe I do not ask, I assume what is perfectly clear. So you are in a position to keep up your wardrobe as a gentleman in addition to your working-livery, and the interesting thing about it is that you appear as much at home in the one as in the other."

"Clothes make the man, marquis—or perhaps the other way around: the man makes the clothes."

"And I have sketched your way of life with approximate truth?"

"Very accurately." And I told him that I did indeed possess some means—oh, very modest ones—and that I kept a small apartment in the city, where I accomplished those changes in my appearance which I now had the pleasure of permitting him to observe.

I was well aware that he was observing my table manners and, without affectation, I preserved a certain well-bred formality, sitting upright with my elbows close to my sides. That my behaviour interested him was betrayed by his casual observations about foreign eating-habits. In America, he remarked, Europeans were recognized by the fact that they raised their forks with their left hands. The American cut his food first, then laid his knife aside and ate with his right hand. "There's something childish about it, isn't there?" However, he knew this only by hearsay. He had never been over there, nor had he any desire at all to travel—none whatever—not the slightest. Had I seen something of the world?

"My God, no, marquis—and yet in another sense, yes! Nothing except a few attractive Taunus spas and Frankfurt on the Main. But then Paris. And Paris is a great deal."

"Paris is everything!" he said with emphasis. "To me it is everything, and I would rather die than leave it, but I shall have to, nevertheless. I shall have to travel, more's the pity, entirely against my wishes and inclinations. The son of the house, dear Kroull. I don't know to what extent you still are that and tied to the apron strings—after all, you only come of a good family, but I, *hélas*, of family. . . ."

Almost before I had finished my *Pèche Melba* he had ordered the bottle of Lafite that was meant for both of us.

"I'll just begin on this," he said. "When you're through

with your coffee, join me. If I have too much of a start, we'll order another."

"Well, marquis, you already have a good start. When you were in my hands at the Saint James and Albany you used to be moderate."

"Care, sorrow, a breaking heart, dear Kroull! What can you do, there's nothing left but the solace of wine, and you learn to appreciate the gifts of Bacchus. That's his name, isn't it? 'Bacchus,' not 'Bachus,' as people usually say for convenience. I call it convenience not to use a harsher word. Are you strong on mythology?"

"Not very, marquis. There is, for instance, the god Hermes. But aside from him I know very little."

"Why do you need to? Learning, especially conspicuous learning, is not a gentleman's affair. That's a legacy from the days when a nobleman only needed to have a decent seat on a horse and was taught nothing else, not even reading and writing. The books he left to the priests. There's still a strong tendency in that direction among my fellows. Most of them are elegant loafers, and not even charming. Do you ride? Permit me to fill your glass with this care-killer! Your good fortune again! Oh, my good fortune? There's no point in drinking to that. It's not so easily mended. So you don't ride? I'm convinced you're perfectly suited to it, born for it, in fact; you would put all the cavaliers in the Bois to shame."

"I admit to you, marquis, I almost think so myself."

"That's no more than healthy self-confidence, dear Kroull. I call it healthy because I share it, because I myself have confidence in you and not on that point alone. . . . Let me be frank. I have the impression that you are not really a confiding man or one who opens his heart. You always hold something back. Somehow or other, there's a mystery about you. *Pardon*, I am being indiscreet. My talking this way simply demonstrates my own carefree garrulousness—that is, my confidence in you."

"For which I am sincerely grateful, dear marquis. May I take the liberty of inquiring after Mademoiselle Zaza's health? I was really surprised to find you here without her."

"How nice of you to ask after her! You do find her charming, don't you? How could you fail to? I permit you to. I permit the whole world to find her charming. And yet I should really like to withdraw her from the world and have her entirely to myself. The dear child is busy this evening at her little theatre, the Folies Musicales. She is a soubrette; didn't you know? At present she is appearing in *Le Don de la Fée*. But I've seen the thing so often I can't stand being there for every performance. Besides, it makes me a little nervous to see her wearing so little when she sings—the little is becoming, but it is very little indeed, and now I suffer because of it, although at the start that was just what made me fall so madly in love with her. Have you ever been passionately in love?"

"I'm in a very good position to follow you, marquis."

"I can readily believe you know all about matters of the heart. And yet you seem to me the type who is more loved than loving. Am I wrong? All right, let's put that question aside. Zaza still has to sing in the third act. After that I will take her home and we will have tea together in the little apartment I have furnished for her."

"My congratulations! But that means we'll have to hurry with our Lafite and end this pleasant meeting before long. For my own part, I have a ticket for the Opéra Comique."

"Really, I don't like to hurry. Besides, I can telephone the little one to look for me at home a bit later. Would you mind if you didn't get to your box until the second act?"

"Not much. *Faust* is a charming opera, but how could it attract me more than Mademoiselle Zaza attracts you?"

"The thing is, I would like to talk to you more specifically about my problems. You must have realized from a number of things I have said that I am in a dilemma, a serious and painful dilemma of the heart."

"I did realize it, dear marquis, and I have only been waiting for a signal from you to inquire sympathetically about the nature of your embarrassment. It concerns Mademoiselle Zaza?"

"Whom else? You have heard that I am to take a trip? That I am to be away for a year?"

"A whole year! Why?"

"My dear friend, this is how it is. My poor parents–I have talked to you about them once or twice–know that my liaison with Zaza has been going on for a year or more. There was no need for gossip or an anonymous letter; I myself was childish and trusting enough to let my happiness and my plans appear unmistakably in my letters to them. I wear my heart on my tongue, as you know, and from my tongue to my pen the route is short and easy. The dear old people were quite right in thinking I was serious about the affair and intended to marry the girl–or the 'person,' as they naturally say–and they have been, as might have been expected, beside themselves. They were here until day before yesterday–I've had some bad times, a week of uninterrupted argument. My father talked in a very deep voice and my mother in a very high one, vibrating with tears–he in French and she in German. Don't misunderstand me, there were no hard words except the repetition of the word 'person,' which, to be sure, hurt me more than if they had called me an irresponsible fool and a disgrace to the family. They did not do that; they simply kept on imploring me not to give them or society any grounds for such a description. I assured them in a voice that was both deep and vibrant that I was sincerely sorry to be a source of concern to them. For they really love me and want what is best for me, only they don't understand what that is–in fact, they understand so little that they actually spoke of disinheriting me in case I should carry out my scandalous intentions. They did not use the word, either in French or in German; I have already said that out of love for me they refrained from harsh words. But they indicated the possibility clearly enough–as a consequence and a threat. Now I have always thought, because of my father's position and the hand he has in the Luxemburg steel industry, that at the very least I could count on living decently. But being disinherited would be of no help whatever either to me or to Zaza. It wouldn't be much fun for her to marry someone who had been disinherited, you can understand that."

"I pretty well can. At least, I can put myself in Mademoiselle Zaza's place. But now, about the trip?"

"The story about the damned trip is this: my parents want to pry me loose—'You must be pried loose,' my father said, using the German word in the midst of his French discourse—an entirely inappropriate word, whatever they think they have to pry me loose from. For I'm neither stuck fast in the ice like an arctic explorer—the warmth of Zaza's bed and her sweet body makes that comparison wholly ridiculous—nor am I held by iron chains, but rather by the most delightful chain of roses, whose strength, however, I do not deny. However, I am to break it, at least experimentally, that's the idea, and that's the purpose of the world tour which my parents are generously prepared to finance—their intentions are so good! I am to leave—what's more, for a long time, leave Paris, the Théâtre des Folies Musicales, and Zaza. I am to see foreign lands and people and thereby acquire new ideas and get 'these whims out of my head'—'whims,' they call it—and return a different person, a different person! Can one wish to be a different person from the one he is? You look uncertain, but I, I do not want it in the least. I want to remain who I am and not to let my heart and head be turned topsy-turvy by this travel cure they prescribe and so become alien to myself and forget Zaza. Of course, that is possible. Long absence, a complete change of scene, and a thousand new experiences might accomplish it. But it's exactly because I consider it theoretically possible that I so thoroughly detest this experiment."

"Consider, nevertheless," I said, "that if you should become another person, you would not feel the lack of your present self or regret it, simply because it would no longer be you."

"What sort of comfort is that to me now? Who could wish to forget? Forgetting is the most distressing and disagreeable thing in the world."

"And yet you really know that your dread of the experiment is no proof that it will not succeed."

"Yes, theoretically. Practically, it's out of the question. For all their love and care, my parents are attempting to murder love. They will be unsuccessful, I am as sure of it as I am of myself."

"That means something. And may I ask whether your parents are ready to accept this experiment as an experiment, and if the result is negative, accommodate themselves to the proven strength of your desires?"

"I asked them that, too. But I could not get a simple yes. They were concerned with 'prying me loose,' and they did not think beyond that. That's what's so unfair about it. I had to give them my promise without getting one in return."

"So you agreed to the trip?"

"What else could I do? After all, I can't expose Zaza to the loss of my inheritance. I told her I had promised to go on the trip and she wept a great deal, partly because of the long separation, partly through her natural fear that the cure my parents propose may work and that I may return a changed man. I understand her fear. At times, after all, I feel it myself. Oh, my dear friend, what a dilemma! I have to travel and I do not want to; I have obligated myself to travel—and cannot do it. What shall I do? Who can help me out of this?"

"Indeed, dear marquis, you are to be pitied," I said. "I feel the greatest sympathy for you, but no one can release you from the obligation you have taken upon yourself."

"No, no one."

"No one."

The conversation died away for a few moments. He twisted his glass in his fingers. Suddenly he got up and said: "I had almost forgotten—I must telephone my little friend. If you will wait a moment . . ."

He left. The roof garden was almost empty. Only two other tables were still being served. Most of the waiters were standing idle. I smoked a cigarette to pass the time. When Venosta returned he ordered another bottle of Château Lafite and began again:

"Dear Kroull, I have told you about the conflict with my parents, very painful on both sides. I hope I did not fail in reverence and respect in what I said, or in expressing my gratitude for their loving care—not least for the generous offer which their concern has inspired, even though it may have the appearance of an injunction or even a command. It is only my peculiar situation that makes this invitation to take a trip around the world in total luxury such an unbearable imposition that I scarcely understand how I came to agree to it. For any other man, whether of family or of good family, such an invitation would be a gift from Heaven wrapped in the rainbow hues of novelty and adventure. Even I, in my present situation, sometimes catch myself—it is a kind of disloyalty to Zaza and to our love—picturing in imagination the manifold charms of such a year of travel, the variety of scenes, encounters, experiences, enjoyments that would certainly come with it, if only one were responsive to such things. Just consider—the wide world, the Orient, North and South America, the Far East. In China there are said to be servants in plenty. A European bachelor would have a dozen of them. He would have one to carry his visiting-cards—to run ahead with them. I have heard of a tropical sultan who was thrown from his horse and lost all his teeth; he had new ones made of gold in Paris, with a diamond in the middle of each. His beloved wears the national costume, a precious cloth wrapped around her thighs and tied in front beneath her supple hips, for she is as beautiful as a dream. Around her neck she wears three or four ropes of pearls and below them three or four strands of diamonds of fabulous size."

"Was it your revered parents who described all this to you?"

"It wasn't exactly my parents. They haven't been there. But

isn't it altogether likely and the way you would picture it, especially the hips? What's more, the sultan is said occasionally to relinquish his beloved to favoured guests, guests of distinction. Naturally, I didn't hear that from them either–they have no idea what they are offering me in this trip around the world. But however unresponsive I am, do I not theoretically owe them gratitude for their handsome offer?"

"Unquestionably, marquis. But you are taking over my role. You are, so to speak, talking with my voice. It should be up to me to reconcile you as far as possible to the idea of this trip which you hate so much, especially by pointing out to you the advantages it would offer–it will offer–and while you were telephoning I decided to make exactly that attempt."

"You would be preaching to deaf ears, even if you were to protest a hundred times how much you envied me–if only on account of the hips."

"Envy? No, marquis, that's not exactly right. It would not have been envy that inspired me in my well-meant efforts. I am not especially eager to travel. Why does a Parisian need to go abroad in the world? It comes to him. It comes to us here in the hotel, and when I sit on the terrace of the Café de Madrid about the time the theatres close, it is conveniently present right before my eyes. I don't have to tell you about that."

"No, but in your airy way you have undertaken too much if you think you can make the trip palatable to me."

"Dear marquis, I shall try, nevertheless. How could I not try to show myself grateful for your confidence? I have already thought of proposing that you take Mademoiselle Zaza with you."

"Impossible, Kroull. What are you thinking of? You mean well, but what are you thinking of? I won't mention Zaza's contract with the Folies Musicales. Contracts can be broken. But I cannot travel with Zaza and at the same time keep her hidden. In any case, there are difficulties in taking a woman who is not your wife around the world with you. And I should be seen, my parents have contacts here and there, some of them official, and they would inevitably find out if I defeated the whole purpose of the trip by taking Zaza with me. They would be beside themselves! They would cancel my letter of credit. For instance, I am to make a longish visit at the Argentinian *estancia* of a family whose acquaintance my parents once made at a French watering-place. Shall I leave Zaza alone for weeks at a time in Buenos Aires, exposed to all the dangers of that city? Your proposal is unthinkable."

"I was afraid of that when I made it. I withdraw it."

"That means you leave me in the lurch. You resign yourself to the fact that I have to travel alone. It's easy enough for you to resign yourself! But I can't. I have to travel and I want to stay here. That means I must attempt the impossible: to travel and to stay here at the same time. That, in turn, means I must become two people, must divide myself in two; one part of Louis Venosta must travel, while the other stays in Paris with his Zaza. It's important to me that the latter should be the real me. In short, the trip must go on concurrently. Louis Venosta must be here and there. Do you follow the convolutions of my thought?"

"I am trying to, marquis. In other words, it must *look* as though you were travelling, but in reality you will stay at home."

"Damnably right!"

"Damnably only because no one looks like you."

"In Argentina no one knows how I look. I have nothing against looking different in different places. As a matter of fact, I'd like it very much if I looked better there than here."

"So then your name must travel attached to a person who is not you."

"But who cannot be just anyone."

"I should think not. One can't be particular enough about that."

He filled his glass, emptied it in big gulps, and banged it down on the table.

"Kroull," he said, "as far as I'm concerned, my choice is made."

"So soon? With so little consideration?"

"We've been sitting here facing one another for quite a while."

"We? What are you thinking of?"

"Kroull," he repeated, "I call you by your name, the name of a man of good family, a name, naturally, that one would not want to relinquish even temporarily although by doing so one might appear to be a man of family. Would you be willing to help a friend in dire need? You said you were not anxious to travel. But what is the lack of a strong desire to travel compared to my horror at leaving Paris! You said, too—in fact, we agreed about it—that no one could release me from my promise to my parents. How would it be if you released me from it?"

"It seems to me, dear marquis, that you are losing yourself in fantasies."

"Why? And why do you speak of fantasies as of a realm to which you are a complete stranger? After all, there is something singular about you, Kroull! I called this quality intriguing, I finally even called it mysterious. If I had used the word 'fantastic' instead, would you have been angry?"

"No indeed, since you would not have meant it ill."

"Certainly not! And therefore you can't be angry with me because your appearance suggested the idea to me, because during this meeting my choice—my very particular choice—has fallen on you!"

"On me as the person to bear your name out in the world, represent you, *be* you in people's eyes, your parents' son, not just a member of your family but you yourself? Have you given this the consideration it requires?"

"I shall remain who I am where I really am."

"But out in the world you will be another—to wit, me. People will see you in me. In the eyes of the world you will relinquish your personality to me. 'Where I really am,' you say, but where would you really be? Would that not be a little uncertain, for you as well as for me? And if this uncertainty was all right with me, would it be all right with you, too? Would it not be unpleasant to be yourself only very locally, and in the rest of the world—that is, predominantly—to exist as me, through me, in me?"

"No, Kroull," he said, warmly extending his hand to me across the table. "It would not—you would not be—unpleasant to me. It would not be bad at all for Louis Venosta if you changed selves with him and he went about the world in your person; that is, if his name were attached to your person as now, in the world outside, it will be—provided you agree. I have an uncomfortable suspicion that it would not be at all displeasing to certain others if that were the way nature had arranged things. They will just have to put up with reality, about whose vagaries I am not in the least concerned. For I really am where Zaza is. And it is perfectly all right with me for you to be Louis Venosta elsewhere. I should take the greatest pleasure in appearing to people in your person. You are an elegant fellow both here and there, in both roles, as gentleman and as *commis-de-salle*. I could wish many of my fellow noblemen your manners. You know foreign languages, and if the conversation should turn to mythology, which hardly ever happens, you will make out well enough with Hermes. No one demands more from a nobleman—one might even say that you as a bourgeois are obliged to know more. You must take this simplification into account in making your decision. Well, then, is it agreed? You will undertake this great act of friendship?"

"My dear marquis," I said, "do you realize that so far we have been moving in mid-air and have not discussed any of the facts or the hundred difficulties that would have to be reckoned with?"

"You're right," he replied. "Above all, you're right to remind me that I have to telephone again. I must explain to Zaza that I can't come home right away because I'm involved in a conversation that is vital to our happiness. Excuse me."

And he left again—to remain away longer than before. Darkness had fallen over Paris, and for some time now the roof garden had been bathed in the white light of the arc lamps. It was completely empty at this hour and would probably not come to life again until the theatres closed. In my pocket I felt the unused opera ticket, without paying much attention to it, although at another time the incident would have pained me. Thoughts whirled through my mind, but reason, I may say, held them in check, imposing a kind of caution and forbidding them to indulge in drunken riot. I was happy to be left alone for a while so that I could appraise the situation and consider in advance a number of points that still had to be discussed. This bypath, this happy digression from the thoroughfare my godfather had opened for me—while pointing out just such a possibility—presented itself so startlingly and in so enticing a form that reason found it tedious to examine it and determine whether it might not be a cul-de-sac that was tempting me. Reason insisted I would be setting forth on a dangerous road, a road that would require cautious treading. Reason repeated this with emphasis and only succeeded in enhancing the charm of the adventure in my eyes, an adventure that would call upon all my talents. It is useless to warn the courageous against some action on the ground that it requires courage. I do not hesitate to admit that long before my companion returned I had decided to embark on the adventure, had indeed so decided at the moment when I told him that *no one* could release him from his promise. And I was less concerned about the practical difficulties we would have to face than about the danger of appearing to him in an ambiguous light because of the skill with which I could meet those difficulties.

Yet he already saw me in a sufficiently ambiguous light; the words he had used to describe my way of life—"intriguing," "mysterious," "fantastic"—proved that. I was under no illusion that he would have made his proposal to any cavalier, and the fact that he had made it to me, though it was an honour, was nevertheless an ambiguous one. And yet I could not forget the warmth of the handclasp with which he had assured me that it would be "not unpleasant" to wander up and down the world in my person; and I said to myself that if we were about to engage in a schoolboy prank, it was he, with his eagerness to deceive his parents, who had the greater stake in it, though I was to play the more active part. As he returned from his telephone conversation I could see quite clearly that he was to a considerable extent excited and enthusiastic about the idea for its own sake—that is, simply as a prank. The colour in his boyish cheeks was high and not from wine alone; there was a sly glitter in his little eyes. No doubt he still heard Zaza's silvery laughter as he outlined our plans to her.

"My dear Kroull," he said, sitting down again at my table, "we have always been on good terms, but who would have thought a short while ago that we would come so close—to the point of interchangeability! We have thought out something so amusing now—or, if we haven't quite thought it out, we have at least outlined it—that my heart laughs in my breast. And you? Don't look so solemn! I appeal to your sense of humour, to your taste for a good joke—for a joke so good that it would repay every effort to work it out for its own sake, quite apart from its importance to a pair of lovers. And you, the third person, will you deny that there is profit in it for you, too? There is a lot of profit, the whole joke is profitable to you. Do you deny it?"

"It's not my custom, my dear marquis, to take life as a joke. Frivolity is not my style, especially in the matter of jokes; for certain jokes are pointless if they are not taken seriously. A good joke does not come off unless one approaches it with complete seriousness."

"Very good. That's what we'll do. You spoke of problems, difficulties. What are the ones you see first off?"

"It would be better, marquis, if you let me put a few questions to you. Where is this prescribed tour of yours to take you?"

"Ah, my good Papa in his concern for me has laid out a very nice itinerary, most attractive for anyone but me: both Americas, the islands of the South Seas and Japan, followed by an interesting voyage to Egypt, Constantinople, Greece, Italy, and so forth. An educational journey by the book; I could not wish anything better for myself if it weren't for Zaza. Now it is you I must congratulate on the trip."

"Your Papa will pay the expenses?"

"Of course. In his desire for me to travel in proper style he has set aside no less than twenty thousand francs—not including the fare to Lisbon and my ticket to Argentina, where I am to go first. Papa bought those himself and reserved a cabin for me on the *Cap Arcona*. He deposited the twenty thousand francs in the Banque de France, and they are now mine in the form of a so-called circular letter of credit on banks in the principal ports of call on my route."

I waited.

"I shall, of course, turn the letter of credit over to you," he added.

I remained silent.

He went on: "As well as the tickets that have already been bought."

"And what," I asked, "will you live on while I am spending your money in your name?"

"What will I—oh, yes! You put me in a quandary. But you don't ask the question as though it were your intention to leave me in perplexity. Yes, dear Kroull, what shall we do about that? I am really not at all used to thinking about what I shall live on during the coming year."

"I just wanted to call your attention to the fact that it's not so simple to lend one's personality to someone else. But let's postpone that problem. I don't want to be hurried into solving it, for that would mean presupposing something like cunning in me, and where cunning is concerned, I am quite useless. Cunning is not gentlemanly."

"I thought it just possible, dear friend, that you might have succeeded in transferring a certain amount of cunning from your other existence into your life as a gentleman."

"Something much more respectable links my two existences. It is some little bourgeois savings, a small bank account—"

"Which I can in no circumstances touch!"

"Nevertheless, we'll have to include it in our calculations somehow. By the way, have you anything to write with?"

He quickly felt his pockets. "Yes, my fountain pen. But no paper."

"Here's some." And I tore a page from my notebook. "It would interest me to see your signature."

"Why? . . . As you like." With the pen inclined steeply to the left, he wrote his signature and pushed it across to me. Even seen upside down, it was very droll-looking. Dispensing with a flourish at the end, it began with one instead. The artistically elaborated *L* swept off to the right in a wide loop which returned and crossed the stem of the initial from the left; it proceeded from there in a tight backhand script within the oval thus described as *ouis Marquis de Venosta.* I could not repress a smile, but nodded to him approvingly.

"Inherited or invented?" I asked, taking the fountain pen.

"Inherited," he said. "Papa does it just that way. Only not so well," he added.

"And so you have overreached him." I spoke mechanically, for I was engaged in my first attempted imitation, which turned out very well. "Thank goodness I don't have to do it better than you. As a matter of fact, that would be a mistake." Meanwhile I had finished the second copy, less satisfactory than the first. The third, however, was flawless. I struck out the first two and handed the paper to him. He was astounded.

"Incredible!" he cried. "My writing as though it were photographed! And you pretend to know nothing about cunning! But I am not so lacking in cunning as you think, and

I understand perfectly well why you are practising. You will need my signature to draw against the letter of credit."

"How do you sign yourself when you write to your parents?"

He was taken aback and exclaimed: "Of course, I'll at least have to send the old folk a few postcards from some of the places where I stay. My friend, you think of everything! I am called Loulou at home because that was what I used to call myself as a child. This is how I do it."

He did it in the same way as his full name; he drew an ornate *L*, extended it into an oval, crossed the arabesque from the left, and then continued in a stiff backhand within the loop as *oulou.*

"All right," I said, "we can do that. Have you a page of your handwriting with you?

He said he was sorry he had none.

"Then write this, if you please." I handed him a fresh piece of paper. "Write: '*Mon cher Papa*, dearest Mama, from this fascinating city, one of the high points of my journey, I send you my thanks and best wishes. I am brimming with new impressions which drive from my mind much that seemed essential before. Your Loulou.' Something like that."

"No, exactly like that! That's marvellous. Kroull, *vous êtes admirable!* The way you shake these things out of your sleeve—" And he wrote my sentences with his hand twisted to the left, in stiff letters that were just as jammed together as my late father's had been widely spaced, but were not a bit harder to imitate. I put this model in my pocket and inquired about the names of the servants in his castle—the cook, who was called Ferblantier, and the coachman, who was called Klosmann, and the marquis's valet, a shaky man in his late sixties called Radicule, and the marquise's maid, named Adelaide. I even inquired in detail about the domestic animals, the riding-horses, Fripon the wolfhound, the marquise's Maltese lapdog, Minime, a creature who suffered a great deal from diarrhœa. Our hilarity increased the longer the meeting lasted, but Loulou's acuity of mind and powers of discrimination seemed to diminish with the passage of time. I expressed surprise that he was not going to England, to London. The reason was that he already knew the country, had actually spent two years there in a public school. "Nevertheless," he said, "it would be a very good thing if London were included in the itinerary. How easy it would be for me to trick the old folk and hurry back here to Paris and Zaza in the middle of my tour!"

"But you will be with Zaza all the time!"

"Right you are!" he cried. "That's the real trick. I was thinking of a false trick that won't compare with the real one. *Pardon.* I hope you will excuse me. The trick is that I shall be brimming with new impressions while I stay with Zaza. You know, I shall have to be on my guard not to inquire about Radicule, Fripon, and Minime when I am writing from here and you are perhaps doing the same from Zanzibar? Those are things, of course, that can't coincide, although a coincidence of persons—even though at a great distance—must take place. . . . Listen, this situation requires that we stop speaking formally to one another! Do you object? When I speak to myself I don't use a formal manner of address. Is that agreed? Let's drink to it! To your health, Armand—I mean Félix—I mean Loulou. Remember that you must not inquire about Klosmann and Adelaide from Paris, but only from Zanzibar. Besides, so far as I know, I am not going to Zanzibar and neither are you. But no matter—wherever I happen to be, during the time I stay here I must in any case vanish from Paris. There, you see how clever I am! Zaza and I have to make ourselves scarce, to use a schoolboy's expression. Don't schoolboys say 'make yourself scarce'? But how should you, a gentleman and now a young man of family, know about that? I must give notice that I am going to give up my apartment and so must Zaza. We will move together into a suburb, a pretty suburb, either Boulogne or Sèvres, and what's left of me—it will be enough, for it will be with Zaza—would do well perhaps to assume another name—logic seems to me to demand that I should call myself Kroull—to be sure, I would have to learn to imitate your signature, but I hope my cunning is sufficient for that. So there in Versailles or farther out—while I'm on my travels—I'll provide a love nest for Zaza and me. . . . But, Armand, I mean *cher Louis*," and he opened his little eyes as wide as he could, "answer me this if you can: what are we going to live on?"

I replied that we had solved that problem as soon as it arose. I possessed a bank account of twelve thousand francs, which would stand at his disposal in return for his letter of credit.

He was touched to the point of tears. "A gentleman!" he exclaimed. "A nobleman from top to toe! If you do not have the right to send greetings to Minime and Radicule, who should have? Our parents will send back the warmest greetings in their name. A last glass to the gentleman who is us!"

Our meeting had lasted through the quiet theatre hours; as we left, the roof garden was beginning to fill again in the mild night. Over my protest he paid for both dinners and the four bottles of Lafite. He was much confused both by joy and by wine. "All of it, all of it together!" he instructed the headwaiter, who brought the check. "We are one and the same. Armand de Kroullosta is our name."

"Very good," the latter replied with a patient smile, which must have come easily to him, for his tip was enormous.

Venosta took me back to my place in a fiacre and let me out there. On the way we agreed to another meeting at which I would transfer my bank account to him and he would give me his letter of credit and the tickets.

"*Bonne nuit, à tantôt, monsieur le marquis*," he said with drunken grandezza as he shook my hand. I heard this style of address for the first time from his lips, and I shivered with joy at the thought of the equality of seeming and being which life was granting me, of the appearance it was now appropriately adding to the substance.

CHAPTER V

How inventive life is! Lending substance to airy nothings, it brings our childhood dreams to pass. Had not I in boyhood tasted in imagination those delights of incognito I fully savoured now, as I continued to go about my menial occupations for a while, keeping my new estate as secret as my princedom once had been? Then it had been a merry and delightful game, now it had become reality—at least to this extent: for the space of a year, beyond which period I did not care to look, I had, as it were, a margrave's patent of nobility in my pocket. Awareness of this delicious fact filled my mind from the moment of waking, just as it had before, and companioned me all day long in the establishment where I played my liveried role, without my associates being a scrap the wiser.

Sympathetic reader! I was very happy. In my own eyes I was priceless, and I loved myself—in the way that is really socially useful, self-love turned outward as amiability. A fool might have been tempted by the secret I possessed into a show of arrogance, into effrontery and disobedience toward those above and uncomradely disdain toward those below. Not I; my courtesy toward the guests in the dining-room had never been more winning, the voice in which I addressed them had never held a gentler deference, my attitude toward those who thought themselves my equals, my fellow waiters and my roommates in the garret, had never been merrier or more cordial than during those days. My secret was perhaps reflected in the hint of a smile, but this served to hide rather than reveal. Concealment was wise, at any rate at first, for I could not be absolutely sure that the bearer of what was now my real name might not, on the very morning after our meeting, have had sober second thoughts and be preparing to rescind our agreement. I was prudent enough not to resign my livelihood overnight; essentially, however, I was sure of my man. Venosta had been too overjoyed at the solution (which I had hit on before he did), and Zaza's magnetism stood surety for his good faith.

I had not deceived myself. Our great compact had been reached on the evening of July 10, and I would not be free for the next and conclusive meeting until the 24th. On the 17th or 18th, however, I saw him again, for on one of those evenings he dined with us in company with his *petite amie* and on this occasion revealed his own constancy by appealing to mine. "*Nous persistons, n'est-ce pas?*" he whispered to me as I was serving him. To which I replied with a decisive and discreet "*C'est entendu.*" I served him with a deference that was really deference toward myself, and more than once I addressed Zaza, who was indulging in roguish winks and covert glances, as "*madame la marquise*"—a simple tribute of gratitude.

After this there was nothing frivolous in informing Monsieur Machatschek that family circumstances would compel me to leave my post in the Saint James and Albany on August 1. He would not hear of it, he said I had not given the required notice, that I was indispensable, that after this desertion I would never find another job, that he would withhold my salary for the current month, and so forth. He accomplished nothing by this. I simply bowed in pretended compliance and determined to leave the place before the 1st—in fact, at once. For if the time seemed long before I might enter on my new and higher existence, in reality it was all too short to prepare for my travels and to assemble the wardrobe I owed my new position in life. I knew that my ship, the *Cap Arcona,* was to leave Lisbon on August 15 and I thought I ought to be there a week ahead. And so one can see how little time there was for the necessary arrangements and purchases.

I discussed this matter with the stay-at-home traveller on

the occasion when I left my private refuge to call on him in his attractive three-room apartment in the rue Croix des Petits Champs, after having withdrawn my funds—that is, after transferring them to him. I had left the hotel silently in the early morning, disdainfully leaving my livery behind and relinquishing my month's salary with indifference. It cost me some effort to give my old, shopworn, and already odious name to the servant who opened the door for me at Venosta's, and I only succeeded by reflecting that I was using it for the last time. Louis received me with excited cordiality and could hardly wait to hand over to me the all-important letter of credit for our journey. It was a double document, one part of it containing the bank's authorization for the traveller to make withdrawals up to the total amount, and the other a list of the correspondent banks in the cities where stopovers were planned. On the inside of this booklet was a place for the owner's signature as a means of identification, and Loulou had inscribed his there in the manner already so familiar to me. After this he not only handed over the railroad ticket to the Portuguese capital and the steamship ticket to Buenos Aires, but the kind young man presented me with a number of very attractive going-away presents: a flat gold monogrammed watch, a fine platinum chain, a black silk chatelaine for evening wear, also bearing the initials L. d. V. in gold, one of those gold chains which run under the waistcoat to the back trouser pocket and on which in those days men liked to carry their lighters, knives, and pencils, and a thin gold cigarette case. All this was delightful enough, but there was a certain solemnity in the moment when he put on my finger an exact copy of his seal ring which he had wisely had made, a ring with the family coat of arms in malachite—a castle gate flanked by towers and guarded by griffins. This action, which was accompanied by a pantomimed "Be as I," awakened so many memories of stories heard in childhood, tales of disguise and recognition, that I was filled with strange and profound emotions. Loulou's little laughing eyes, however, were more roguish than ever and clearly revealed that he was determined not to neglect any detail of the hoax and that, quite apart from its purpose, it gave him enormous fun.

We discussed a number of other matters as we sat drinking Benedictine and smoking excellent Egyptian cigarettes. He no longer had the slightest misgivings on the score of my handwriting, but he approved my proposal to send him at his new address (Sèvres, Seine-et-Oise, rue Brancas) the letters I would receive from our parents, so that with his help I could comment, if only belatedly and by way of afterthought, on unforeseeable family or social incidents that would be sure to arise. Something else occurred to him: as he was devoting himself to art, I in his place would, at least on occasion, have to show some competence in that field. *Nom d'un nom*, how was I to manage that! We must not, I said, lose heart about it. And I asked for his sketchbook, which contained some blurred landscapes drawn on rough paper with very soft pencil or chalk, in addition to a number of female portraits and half- and whole-figure studies for which Zaza had obviously sat—or rather lain—as model. The heads were sketched, I may say, with an unjustifiable boldness, but one had to admit a certain resemblance—not much, but some. As for the landscape sketches, they had been lent a shadowy vagueness by the simple process of almost completely obliterating the lines with a stump and blurring them into misty indistinctness. Whether this procedure was artistic or fraudulent I was not called upon to say, but I decided at once that, cheating or not, it was something I could do. I asked for one of his soft pencils and one of the felt-tipped stumps, blackened by much use, with which he bestowed on his productions the consecration of vagueness. After glancing briefly into the air, I drew awkwardly enough a church steeple with storm-tossed trees beside it, meanwhile transmuting the childishness of my work into pure genius by aid of the stump. Louis seemed a little taken aback when I showed him the picture, but he was reassured as well and declared I need have no hesitation in showing my work.

He lamented, if only in the interest of his own reputation, that I should not have time to go to London and order the necessary suits from Paul, a famous tailor whom he patronized. I would require, he pointed out, tails, a frock coat, a cutaway with pin-striped trousers, as well as light, dark, and dark-blue lounge suits. He was all the more pleasantly surprised to discover my exact knowledge of the proper accessories in the way of linen and silk underclothing and various sorts of shoes, hats, and gloves. I still had time to get much of this in Paris—indeed, I would have been able to have some suits made to order—but I abandoned this formality upon reflecting that any halfway decent suit, when I wore it, would look like the most expensive custom work.

The procuring of some things I needed, especially my white tropical wardrobe, was postponed until Lisbon. For my Paris purchases Venosta gave me some hundreds of francs which his parents had presented to him in preparation for the trip, and added to them a few hundred more from the capital I had made over to him. I volunteered to return this money from savings I would make during the trip. He gave me his sketchbook as well, together with some pencils and the helpful stump. Also a box of visiting-cards with our name and his address engraved at the top; he embraced me, laughing uproariously and pounding me on the back, hoped that I would soon be brimming with a flood of new impressions, and thus sent me forth into the wide world.

It was toward that wide world, kind reader, that I was borne, two weeks and a few days later, properly ensconced in a first-class compartment of the Nord-Sud Express. I sat by the window on the grey plush sofa, my arm on the folding armrest, my head reclining against the lace runner, my legs crossed; I was wearing a well-pressed suit of English flannel, and light spats over my patent-leather boots. My well-filled steamer trunk had been checked through; my calfskin and alligator hand luggage, all stamped with the monogram L. d. V. and the nine-pointed coronet, reposed in the luggage net.

I felt no need for occupation and no desire to read. To sit and be what I was—what better entertainment could there be? My soul was filled with a dreamlike ease, but it would be a mistake to think that my satisfaction sprang solely or even predominantly from the fact that I was now so very distinguished a person. No, it was the change and renewal of my worn-out self, the fact that I had been able to put off the old Adam and slip on a new, that gave me such a sense of fulfilment and happiness. I was struck, though, by the fact that in this change of existence there was not simply delightful refreshment but also a sort of emptying out of my inmost being —that is, I had to banish from my soul all memories that belonged to my no longer valid past. As I sat there, I had ceased to have any right to them—which was certainly no loss. My memories! It was no loss whatever that they were no longer mine. Only it was not altogether easy to put others, to which I was now entitled, in their place with any degree of precision. It gave me a strange feeling of faulty memory, of emptiness of memory rather, as I sat there in my luxurious compartment. I became aware that I knew nothing about myself except that I had spent my childhood and early youth on a nobleman's estate in Luxemburg; there were only a few names like Radicule and Minime to give any degree of precision to my new past. Yes, if I so much as wanted to picture the castle within whose walls I had grown up, I had to call to my aid the representations of English castles on the china from which, in my former lowly existence, I had had to scrape remnants of food—and this, of course, amounted to mixing inadmissible memories with those that alone were appropriate to me now.

Such were the reflections that drifted through my dreaming mind to the rhythmic jolting and hurrying of the train. I do not say for a moment that they were distressing. On the contrary, that inner emptiness, that vagueness and confusion of memory, seemed to me in a kind of melancholy way appropriate to my distinguished position, and I was glad to let my face assume, as I stared straight ahead, a look of quiet, dreamy melancholy combined with a nobleman's helplessness.

The train had left Paris at six o'clock. Twilight fell, the lights went on, and my private abode seemed even more elegant than before. The conductor, a man well advanced in years, knocked softly on the door and raised his hand to the visor of his cap as he entered; returning my ticket, he repeated the salutation. Loyalty and conservatism were to be read in that honest man's face; as he went through the train in the course of his lawful occasions, he came in contact with all strata of society, including the questionable elements, and it was a visible pleasure for him to behold in me wealth and distinction, the fine flower of the social order whose very sight raised and refreshed his spirits. About my well-being, once I had ceased to be his passenger, he assuredly need have no concern. For my part, in place of any kindly questions about his family life, I gave him a gracious smile and a nod *de haut en bas* that assuredly confirmed him in his conservative principles to the point where he would gladly have fought and bled for them.

The man from the dining-car who was handing out reservations for dinner also knocked tentatively at my door. I accepted a number from him; and when, a short time later, the ringing of a gong in the corridor announced the meal, I got out my fitted travelling-case, adjusted my tie in front of the mirror, and then betook myself to the diner a few cars forward. The steward directed me to my place with hospitable gestures and pushed in my chair.

A middle-aged gentleman of fragile appearance was already seated at the little table, busying himself with the hors d'œuvres. His dress was somewhat old-fashioned—I can still see his very high stock. He had a small grey beard, and as I greeted him politely he looked up at me with starlike eyes. I am unable to say in what the starlike quality of his glance consisted. Were the pupils of his eyes especially bright, soft, beaming? They were that, to be sure—but are eyes on that account starlike? "The light in his eyes" is a common expression, but it refers to something purely physical; it by no means connotes the description that forced itself upon me; something specifically moral has to be involved for bright eyes to be starlike eyes.

They remained fixed on me as I sat down, and only very slowly was the accompanying expression of earnest attentiveness replaced by an assenting, or shall I say approving, smile. Only very tardily, after I was seated and was reaching for the menu, did he answer my greeting. It was exactly as though I had omitted that courtesy myself and the starry-eyed one was setting me an edifying example. And so involuntarily I repeated my "*Bonsoir, monsieur.*"

He, however, went on: "I wish you *bon appetit, monsieur.*" Adding: "Your youth, I feel sure, will guarantee that."

Reflecting that a man with starlike eyes was privileged to indulge in unconventional behaviour, I replied with a smile and a bow, already occupied with the plate of sardines, vegetable salad, and celery that the waiter was offering me. As I was thirsty I ordered a bottle of ale, a choice which my grey-bearded companion approved with no sign of fearing that he might be considered guilty of meddling.

"Very sensible," he said. "Very sensible to order a strong beer with your evening meal. It is calming and induces sleep, whereas wine usually has a stimulating effect and is prejudicial to sleep, except of course when taken in great quantity."

"Which would be entirely contrary to my taste."

"So I assumed. Besides, there is nothing to keep us from sleeping late tomorrow. We will not be in Lisboa until noon. Or is your destination closer?"

"No, I am going to Lisbon. A long trip."

"No doubt the longest you've ever taken?"

"But a trivial distance," I said, not answering his question directly, "in comparison with all that lies before me."

"Think of that!" he exclaimed, raising his eyebrows and throwing back his head in a gesture of mock astonishment. "You are off on a serious tour of inspection of this star and its present inhabitants."

His description of the earth as a star combined with the quality of his eyes made a strange impression on me. Besides, the adjective "present" which he had applied to the earth's inhabitants immediately aroused in me a feeling of significance and vastness. And yet his manner of speech and the expressions he used were very much like those one uses with a child, a favoured child, to be sure; they held a touch of affectionate teasing. In the consciousness of looking even younger than I was, I took this in good part.

He had refused soup and sat opposite me idle except that from time to time he poured Vichy water into his glass, an action that had to be accomplished with care, for the car was swaying violently. I had simply glanced up from my food in some bewilderment at his words and had not replied. He, however, clearly did not wish the conversation to die, for he went on:

"Well, however long your journey may be, you ought not to neglect its beginning simply because it is a beginning. You are entering a very interesting country of great antiquity, one to which every eager voyager owes a debt of gratitude, since in earlier centuries it opened up so many travel routes. Lisbon, which I hope you will have time enough to see properly, was once the richest city in the world, thanks to the voyages of discovery. Too bad you did not turn up there five hundred years ago—at that time you would have found it wrapped in the rich scent of Eastern spices and you would have seen gold by the bushel. History has brought about a sorry diminution in those fine foreign possessions. But, as you will see, the country and people are still charming. I mention the people because a good part of all longing to travel consists in a yearning for people one has never seen, a lust for the new—to look into strange eyes, strange faces, to rejoice in unknown human types and manners. Or what do you think?"

What was I to think? Probably he was right in attributing part of the love of travel to curiosity, or "lust for the new."

"Thus you will find," he continued, "in the country you are approaching, a racial mixture that is highly entertaining because of its variety and confusion. The original inhabitants were mixed—Iberians, as of course you know, with a Celtic element. But in the course of two thousand years Venetians, Carthaginians, Romans, Vandals, Suevians, West Goths, and especially the Arabs, the Moors, have co-operated to produce the type that awaits you—not to forget a sizable admixture of Negro blood from the many dark-skinned slaves that were brought in at the time when Portugal owned the whole African coast. You must not be surprised at a certain quality of the hair, certain lips, a certain melancholy animal look in the eye that appear from time to time. But the Moorish-Berber racial element, as you will find, is clearly predominant—from the long period of Arab domination. The net result is a not exactly heroic but decidedly amiable type: dark-haired, somewhat yellowish in complexion, and of delicate build, with handsome, intelligent brown eyes."

"I eagerly look forward to making its acquaintance," I said, adding: "May I ask, sir, whether you yourself are Portuguese?"

"Why, no," he replied. "But I have lived in Portugal for a long time. I was in Paris this time only on a brief visit—on business. Official business. I was about to say, if you look about a bit you will find the Arabic-Moorish influence everywhere in the architecture of the country. As far as Lisbon is concerned, I must warn you about the poverty of its historical buildings. The city, you know, lies on an earthquake fault, and the great quake of the last century laid two thirds of it in rubble. However, it has become a very handsome place again with many sights worth seeing which I can't too strongly recommend to you. Our botanical garden on the western heights ought to be your first goal. There is nothing like it in all Europe, thanks to a climate in which a tropical flora flourishes side by side with that of the temperate zone. The gardens are crowded with araucaria, bamboo, papyrus, yucca, and every kind of palm tree. And there you will see with your own eyes plants that really do not belong to the present-day vegetation of our planet, but to an earlier one—I mean the tree ferns. Go without delay and look at the tree ferns of the Carboniferous period. That's more than short-winded cultural history. That is geological time."

Again I had the feeling of undefined vastness that his words had aroused in me before.

"I shall certainly not miss them," I assured him.

"You must forgive me," he felt obliged to add, "for giving you directions in this way and trying to guide your steps. But do you know what you remind me of?"

"Please tell me," I replied, smiling.

"A sea lily."

"That sounds decidedly flattering."

"Only because it sounds to you like a flower. The sea lily, however, is not a flower but a sessile small animal of the deep sea, belonging to the order of echinoderms and constituting probably its oldest species. We have a quantity of fossils. Such non-mobile animals tend to take on flowerlike forms—that is to say, circular symmetry like that of a star or a blossom. The present-day descendant of the sea lily, the lily-star, is attached to the ground by a stem only during its youth. After that it frees itself, emancipates itself, and goes off adventurously swimming and clambering along the coasts. Forgive me for this association of ideas, but like a modern sea lily you have freed yourself from your stem and are now off on a tour of inspection. One is tempted to give advice to this novice at locomotion. . . . Allow me: Kuckuck."

For a moment I thought something was the matter with

him, and then I understood. Although much older than I, he had introduced himself.

"Venosta," I hastened to reply with an oblique bow, as I was just then being served fish on my left.

"*Marquis* Venosta?" he asked with a slight raising of the eyebrows.

"At your service," I replied in a deprecatory tone.

"Of the Luxemberg line, I assume. I have the honour of knowing a Roman aunt of yours, the Contessa Paolina Centurione, born a Venosta of the Italian branch. And that line in turn is related to the Szechényis of Vienna and so to the Esterhazys of Galantha. As you know, you have cousins and connections everywhere, *monsieur le marquis*. You mustn't be surprised at my knowledge. Family history and the study of descent is my hobby, or rather my profession. Professor Kuckuck," he completed his introduction. "Paleontologist and Director of the Museum of Natural History in Lisbon, an as yet insufficiently known institution of which I am the founder."

He drew out his wallet and handed me his card, which prompted me to offer him mine—that is to say, Loulou's. On his I found his given names, Antonio José, his title, his official position, and his Lisbon address. As to paleontology, his conversation had given me some inkling of his connection with that subject.

We read the cards with mutual expressions of deference and pleasure. Then we put them in our pockets, exchanging short bows of acknowledgement.

"I feel free to say, *monsieur le professeur*," I added politely, "that I have been fortunate in my place at table."

"The pleasure is altogether mine," he replied. We had hitherto spoken in French; now he inquired: "I assume you speak German, Marquis Venosta? Your good mother, I believe, derives from Gotha—near my own native place—*née* Baroness Plettenberg, if I am not mistaken? You see I really do know my facts. So we can just as well—"

How could Louis possibly have failed to inform me that my mother was a Plettenberg! I seized upon this new fact as something with which to enrich my memory.

"But with pleasure," I replied, changing languages at his suggestion. "Good Lord, as though I hadn't babbled German all through my childhood, not only with Mama but also with our coachman, Klosmann!"

"And I," Kuckuck broke in, "have become almost entirely unaccustomed to my native tongue and am only too happy to seize this opportunity of moving once more within its framework. I am now fifty-seven. It was twenty-five years ago that I came to Portugal. I married a child of the country—*née* da Cruz, since we are speaking of names and families—of ancient Portuguese stock, and if a foreign language is to be spoken, French is far closer to her than German. And our daughter, for all her affection for me, does not share her Papa's taste in tongues, but prefers, after Portuguese, to chatter very prettily in French. A completely enchanting child. Zouzou, we call her."

"Not Zaza?"

"No, Zouzou. It comes from Susanna. What does Zaza come from?"

"I really can't say. I have encountered it occasionally—in artistic circles."

"You move in artistic circles?"

"Among others. I'm a bit of an artist myself, a painter and sketcher. I studied under Professor Estompard, Aristide Estompard of the Académie des Beaux Arts."

"Oh, an artist in addition to all the rest. Very gratifying."

"And you, professor, were certainly in Paris on museum business?"

"You have guessed it. The purpose of my trip was to secure from the Paleo-Zoological Institute a few skeletal fragments that are very important to us—the skull, ribs, and shoulder blade of a long-extinct species of tapir, from which through many evolutionary stages our horse has descended."

"What's that, our horse descended from the tapir?"

"And from the rhinoceros. Yes, your riding-horse, marquis, has passed through the most varied forms. At one time, when it was already a horse, it was of Lilliputian size. Oh, we have learned names for all its earlier and earliest stages, names that end in *hippos*, 'horse,' beginning with 'eohippos'—the original tapir, that is, which lived in the Eocene."

"In the Eocene. I assure you, Professor Kuckuck, I will make a note of the name. When do they believe the Eocene was?"

"Recently. It is, geologically speaking, modern times, a few hundred thousand years ago, when the ungulates first appeared. Moreover, it will interest you as an artist to know that we employ specialists, masters of their craft, to reconstruct these extinct animals in highly presentable and lifelike fashion from their skeletal remains, and the men of former times as well."

"The men!"

"The men as well."

"The men of the Eocene?"

"That is a bit early. We must admit that man's history is to some extent shrouded in darkness. He only emerged late, within the framework of the mammalian order, that much is scientifically well established. As we know him, he is a latecomer here, and the Biblical Book of Genesis is quite right in placing him at the pinnacle of creation. Only it abridges the process rather drastically. Organic life on earth, roughly speaking, has lasted some five hundred and fifty million years. It took some time to get to man."

"I am extremely thrilled by what you say, professor."

So I was. I was extremely thrilled—even then, and to an increasing degree thenceforth. I listened to this man with such intense, enthralled interest that I almost forgot to eat. Dishes were passed to me, I helped myself and started to eat, but then I would forget to move my jaws as I sat listening to his words, knife and fork idle in my hands, while I stared into his face and into his starlike eyes. I cannot give a name to the thirst with which my soul drank in all he had to say. However, without that concentrated and sustained receptivity, would I, after so many years, be able to repeat that conversation today, at least in its salient points, almost verbatim, indeed, I believe quite literally verbatim? He had spoken of curiosity, of the lust for the new, which makes up a good part of the longing to travel, and as he had done so, I recall, I had found something strangely challenging in what he said, something that impinged sharply upon my emotions. It was just this kind of provocation, this plucking of the inmost strings of one's being, that was to raise his edifying discourse to the height of infinite and intoxicating fascination, although he continued to speak calmly, coolly, in measured tones, at times with a smile on his lips. . . .

"Whether life has before it," he went on, "as long a period as it has behind it, no one can say. Its toughness is, of course, enormous, especially in its lowest forms. Would you believe that the spores of certain bacteria can sustain the uncomfortable temperature of outer space, minus two hundred degrees, for a full six months without perishing?"

"That's amazing."

"And yet the emergence and continuance of life are limited to certain clearly defined conditions which have not always existed and will not exist forever. The time within which a star is habitable is finite. Life has not always existed and will not always exist. Life is an episode, on the scale of the æons a very fleeting one."

"That predisposes me in favour of the same," I said. I used the phrase "the same" out of pure excitement and a desire to express myself formally and by the book. "There's a song, *Freut euch des Lebens*," I added, "with the line in it 'while the lamp still glows.' I heard it when I was very young, and I have always liked it, but what you say now about 'a fleeting episode' gives it a much profounder meaning."

"And how the organic world hurried," Kuckuck went on,

"to develop its orders and genera, exactly as though it knew the glorious lamp would not shine forever. That applies especially to the earliest phases. In the Cambrian—that's what we call the lowest level, the deepest formation of the Paleozoic period—plant life is, to be sure, meagre: seaweed, algæ, and nothing more. Life emerged from salt water, from the warm primeval sea, you must understand. But all of a sudden the animal kingdom is represented not just by the most primitive animals, but by cœlenterates, worms, echinoderms, arthropods—that is, by all the phyla except the vertebrates. It seems that less than fifty of the five hundred and fifty millions of years had passed before the first of the vertebrates came out of the water onto the land—some of which had emerged by then. And after that, evolution, the development of genera, went on at such a pace that in barely two hundred and fifty million years the whole Noah's Ark, including the reptiles, was present; only the birds and mammals were still missing. And all this thanks to an idea that Nature seized upon in the earliest times and which she has never tired of exploiting up to and including man—"

"Please tell me what that is."

"Oh, the idea is simple enough, just the cohabitation of cells, just the inspiration not to leave that slimy, glassy bit of primeval life, that elemental organism, by itself, but to construct, at first out of a few and then out of hundreds of millions, living designs of a higher order, multicellular creatures, great individuals—in short, to create flesh and blood. What we call 'flesh' and what religion deprecates as weak and sinful, as 'subject to sin,' is nothing but such an assemblage of organically specialized tiny individuals, a multicellular fabric. Nature pursued this precious basic idea of hers with true zeal—sometimes with too much zeal: once or twice she indulged in exaggerations of which she later repented. She was actually busy with the mammals when she permitted an exuberance like the blue whale to occur—as big as twenty elephants, a monster not to be sustained or nourished on earth. She sent it into the deep, where that enormous mass of blubber, with vestigial hind legs, fins, and oily eyes, still carries on a rather harried existence, nursing its young in an uncomfortable position, dodging the whalers, and devouring tiny shellfish. But much earlier than that, at the beginning of earth's middle ages in the Triassic period, long before a bird flew or a tree spread its leaves, we find true horrors, the dinosaurs, the giant reptiles—fellows that occupied more room than is seemly here below. One of those individuals was as high as a room and as long as a railroad train; it weighed forty thousand pounds. Its neck was like a palm tree, and its head, compared to its bulk, was ridiculously small. These creatures of exaggerated bodily size must have been dumb as a post. They were, however, good-natured—as often happens with those who are awkward and helpless."

"So they were not especially sinful, despite all that flesh?"

"Probably not, out of stupidity. What more shall I tell you about the dinosaurs? Perhaps this: they had a tendency to walk upright."

And as Kuckuck turned his starry eyes on me, I was overcome with something like embarrassment.

"Well," I said with pretended nonchalance, "these fellows, for all their upright gait, cannot have been much like Hermes."

"What makes you think of Hermes?"

"Excuse me, in the course of my education at the castle a good deal of attention was paid to mythology. It was my tutor's personal specialty."

"Oh, Hermes," he replied. "An elegant deity. I won't take coffee," he said to the waiter. "Bring me another bottle of Vichy. An elegant deity," he repeated. "And the golden mean of human stature, neither too large nor too small. I knew an old master builder who used to say that anyone who wanted to build must first recognize the perfection of the human figure, for in it are contained the profoundest secrets of proportion. Those who find a mystic significance in proportions maintain that man—and so the god in human form as well—occupies the exact middle point in respect of size between the very largest objects in the universe and the very smallest. They say that the largest material body, a red giant star, is exactly as much larger than a man as the tiniest element in an atom, something that would have to be magnified a hundred billion times to become visible, is smaller than he."

"That shows you how little it helps to walk upright if you don't maintain moderation in size."

"Highly ingenious, your Hermes must have been," my companion went on, "along with his perfect proportions, according to report. The fabric of cells in his brain, if one may speak of such a thing in connection with a god, must have assumed especially artful forms. But the point is this: if one pictures him as made of flesh and blood and not of marble or plaster or ambrosia, then a lot of natural history survives in him. It is remarkable how primitive, in contrast to the brain, human arms and legs still are. They retain all the bones you find in the most primitive land animals."

"That is thrilling, professor. It's not the first thrilling piece of information you have given me, but it is among the most thrilling. The bones in human arms and legs are like those in the most primitive land animals! I am not shocked at that; I am thrilled. I won't speak of Hermes' famous legs. But think of a shapely feminine arm, an arm that embraces us if we are lucky, what the deuce are we to make of that?"

"It seems to me, dear marquis, that you make a kind of cult of the extremities. That is perfectly understandable as the expression of a highly evolved creature's rejection of the footless structure of the worm. But as far as the shapely feminine arm is concerned, one should never forget that the limb is simply the hooked wing of the primordial bird and the pectoral fin of the fish."

"Good, good, I'll remember that in future. I think I can assure you that I'll remember it without bitterness or disenchantment, but rather with affection. But the human being comes from the ape, or at least that's what one always hears?"

"Dear marquis, let us rather say he comes from Nature and has his roots there. We should not be too much blinded by his anatomical similarity to the higher apes; too much fuss has been made about that. The pig with its little blue eyes, its eyelashes, and its skin, has more human qualities than any chimpanzee—think how often naked human beings remind us of swine. Our brain, however, in point of structural development, is closest to that of the rat. Echoes of animal physiognomy are to be found among people wherever you look. You see the fish and the fox, the dog, the seal, the hawk and the sheep. On the other hand, the whole animal world, once we have begun to take notice, strikes us as humanity disguised and bewitched. . . . Oh, indeed, men and animals are closely related! However, if we want to talk about descent, then we must say that men are descended from animals in just about the same way that the organic is descended from the inorganic. Something was added."

"Added? What, if I may ask?"

"The same sort of thing that was added when Being arose out of Nothingness. Have you ever heard of spontaneous generation?"

"I'm extremely eager to."

He glanced about briefly and then began in a confidential tone—obviously for no other reason than because I was the Marquis de Venosta:

"There have been not one but three spontaneous generations: the emergence of Being out of Nothingness, the awakening of Life out of Being, and the birth of Man."

Kuckuck took a sip of Vichy after this declaration. He held his glass in both hands, since we were careening around a curve. The dining-car was almost empty, and most of the waiters were idle. Having neglected my meal, I now drank cup after cup of coffee, but I do not ascribe to that the ever-increasing excitement that took possession of me. Bending forward, I sat listening to my strange travelling-companion, who spoke to me of Being, of Life, of Man—and of the Nothingness from which all this had been generated and into which it would all return. There was no question, he said, that life on earth was not only an ephemeral episode, but *Being itself was also*—an interlude between Nothingness and Nothingness. Being had not always existed and would not always exist. It had had a beginning and would have an end, and with it space and time; for they existed only through Being and through it were bound to each other. Space, he said, was nothing but the order of material things and their relationship to one another. Without things to occupy it, there would be no space and no time either, for time was only the ordering of events made possible by the presence of objects; it was the product of motion, of cause and effect, whose sequence gave time its direction and without which there would be no time. Absence of time and space, however, was the definition of Nothingness. This was extensionless in every sense, a changeless eternity, which had only been temporarily interrupted by spatio-temporal Being. A greater duration, by æons, had been vouchsafed to Being than to Life; but some time of a certainty it would end, and with equal certainty the end implied a beginning. When had time, when had events, begun? When had the first quiver of Being emerged from Nothingness in obedience to the words "Let it be," words that contained within themselves ineluctably those other words "Let it pass"? Perhaps the "when" of Being had not been so very long ago and the "when" of passing was not so very far ahead—possibly only a few billion years this way and that. . . . Meanwhile, Being celebrated its tumultuous festival in the measureless spaces that were its handiwork and in which it created distances congealed in icy emptiness. And he spoke of the gigantic setting of this festival, the universe, this mortal child of eternal Nothingness, filled with countless material bodies, meteors, moons, comets, nebulas, unnumbered millions of stars that swayed one another, were ordered by the effect of their gravitational fields into groups, clouds, galaxies, and super-systems of galaxies, each with enormous numbers of flaming suns, wheeling planets, masses of attenuated gas, and cold rubbish heaps of ice, stone, and cosmic dust. . . .

I listened in excitement, knowing well that to receive this information was a mark of distinction, a privilege I owed to one fact: that I was the Marquis de Venosta and that the Contessa Centurione in Rome was my aunt.

Our Milky Way, I learned, was one among billions; almost at its edge, almost like a wallflower, thirty thousand light years from its centre, was our local solar system with its gigantic but relatively insignificant ball of fire called "the" sun, although it only deserved the indefinite article, and its loyal retainers within its gravitational field, among them the earth, whose joy and labour it was to spin on its axis at the rate of a thousand miles an hour and to circle about the sun at the rate of twenty miles a second, thereby creating its days and years—*its*, be it observed, for there were other quite different ones. The planet Mercury, for example, nearest to the sun, completed its revolution in eighty-eight of our days and in the same period rotated once on its axis, so that for it year and day were the same. There you could see what time amounted to—it had no more general validity than weight. Take, for example, the white companion of Sirius, where matter was in a state of such density that a cubic inch of it would weigh a ton here. Material objects on earth, our mountains or our bodies, were, by comparison, the lightest, fluffiest foam.

While the earth wheeled around its sun, so I was privileged to hear, that earth and its moon wheeled around each other, and at the same time our whole local solar system moved, and at no mean pace, within the framework of a vaster but still very local star group. This gravitating system in turn wheeled with almost vulgar velocity within the Milky Way; the latter, moreover, our Milky Way, was travelling with unimaginable rapidity in respect to its far-away sisters, and they, the most distant existing complexes, were, in addition to all their other velocities, flying away from one another, at a rate that would make an exploding shell seem motionless—flying away in all directions into Nothingness, thereby in their headlong career projecting into it space and time.

This interdependent whirling and circling, this convolution of gases into heavenly bodies, this burning, flaming, freezing, exploding, pulverizing, this plunging and speeding, bred out of Nothingness and awaking Nothingness—which would perhaps have preferred to remain asleep and was waiting to fall asleep again—all this was Being, known also as Nature, and everywhere in everything it was one. I was not to doubt that all Being, Nature itself, constituted a unitary system from the simplest inorganic element to Life at its liveliest, to the woman with the shapely arm and to the figure of Hermes. Our human brain, our flesh and bones, these were mosaics made up of the same elementary particles as stars and star dust and the dark clouds hanging in the frigid wastes of interstellar space. Life, which had been called forth from Being just as Being had been from Nothingness—Life, this fine flower of Being—consisted of the same raw material as inanimate Nature. It had nothing new to show that belonged to it alone. One could not even say it was unambiguously distinguishable from simple Being. The boundary line between it and the inanimate world was indistinct. Plant cells aided by sunlight possessed the power of transforming the raw material of the mineral kingdom so that it came to life in them. Thus the spontaneous generative power of the green leaf provided an example of the emergence of the organic from the inorganic. Nor was the opposite process lacking, as in the formation of stones from silicic acid of animal origin. Future cliffs were composed in the depths of the sea out of the skeletons of tiny creatures. In the crystallization of liquids with the illusory appearance of life, Nature was quite evidently playfully crossing the line from one domain into the other. Always when Nature produced the deceptive appearance of the organic in the inorganic—in sulphur flowers, for instance, or ice ferns—she was trying to teach us that she was one.

The organic world itself had no clear divisions within it. The animal kingdom verged on the vegetable when it acquired a stem and circular symmetry like a flower; the vegetable on the animal when it caught animals and ate them instead of deriving its nourishment from the mineral kingdom. Man had emerged from the animal kingdom by descent, as people said, but in truth through the addition of something that was as impossible to define as the essence of Life or the origin of Being. And the point at which he had become a man and was no longer an animal, or no longer simply an animal, was hard to determine. Man retained his animal nature just as Life retained what was inorganic; for in its ultimate building-blocks, the atoms, it passed into what was no longer organic or not yet organic. Moreover, in its innermost sanctuary, in the invisible atom, matter took refuge in the immaterial, the no longer corporeal; for what was in motion there, the constituent parts of the atom, were almost below Being, since they occupied no definite position in space and did not have a definable mass as any reasonable body should. Being was formed from Not-Yet-Being and passed into Hardly-Still-Being.

Nature in all its forms, from the earliest, simplest, almost immaterial, to the most highly evolved and liveliest, had always remained collective and its forms continued to exist side by side—star cloud, stone, worm, and Man. The fact that many animal species had died out, that there were no more flying saurians and no more mammoths, did not interfere with the fact that contemporaneous with Man the original animal went on existing in unaltered form, the unicellular infusorian, the microbe, with one opening in its cell body for ingestion and another for egestion—no more was required to be an animal, and not much more to be a human being either, in most cases.

This was Kuckuck's jest, a caustic one. He felt he owed a young man of the world a bit of caustic wit, and I laughed, too, as with trembling hand I raised to my lips my sixth—no, probably my eighth—demitasse of sugared mocha. I have said, and I say again, that I was extremely excited, thanks to a feeling of expansion that almost burst the limits of my nature and was the result of my companion's conversation about Being, Life, and Man. Strange as it may sound, this vast expansiveness was closely related to, or rather was identical with, what as a child or half a child I had described in the dreamlike phrase "The Great Joy," a secret formula of my innocence used at first to denote something special, not otherwise nameable, but soon endowed with an intoxicating breadth of significance.

There was progress, Kuckuck said, passing on from his joke; without doubt there was progress, from Pithecanthropus erectus to Newton and Shakespeare had been a long and definitely upward path. But as with the rest of Nature, so too in the world of men everything was always present at the same time, every condition of culture and morality, everything from the earliest to the latest, from the silliest to the wisest, from the most primitive, sodden, barbaric to the highest and most delicately evolved—all this continued to exist side by side in the world, yes, often indeed the finest tired of itself and became infatuated with the primitive and sank drunkenly into barbarism. But no more of that. He would, however, give Man and me, the Marquis de Venosta, our due and not conceal what it was that distinguished Homo sapiens from all the rest of Nature, the organic and simple Being both, and which very likely was identical with the thing that had been added when Man emerged from the animal kingdom. It was the knowledge of Beginning and End. I had pronounced what was most characteristically human when I had said that the fact of Life's being only an episode predisposed me in its favour. Transitoriness did not destroy value, far from it; it was exactly what lent all existence its worth, dignity, and charm. Only the episodic, only what possessed a beginning and an end, was interesting and worthy of sympathy because transitoriness had given it a soul. But that was true of everything—the whole of cosmic Being had been given a soul by transitoriness, and the only thing that was eternal, soulless, and therefore unworthy of sympathy, was that Nothingness out of which it had been called forth to labour and to rejoice.

Being was not Well-Being; it was joy and labour, and all Being in space-time, all matter, partook if only in deepest sleep in this joy and this labour, this perception that disposed Man, possessor of the most awakened consciousness, to universal sympathy. "To universal sympathy," Kuckuck repeated, bracing his hands on the table as he got up and nodding to me as he looked at me with his starlike eyes.

"Good night, Marquis de Venosta," he said. "We are, I observe, the last people in the dining-car. It is time to go to bed. Permit me to hope that I shall see you again in Lisboa. If you like, I will be your guide through my museum. Sleep soundly. Dream of Being and of Life. Dream of the whirling galaxies which, since they are there, bear with joy the labour of their existence. Dream of the shapely arm with its ancient armature of bones, and of the flowers of the field that are able, aided by the sun, to break up lifeless matter and incorporate it into their living bodies. And don't forget to dream of stone, of a mossy stone in a mountain brook that has lain for thousands upon thousands of years cooled, bathed, and scoured by foam and flood. Look upon its existence with sympathy, Being at its most alert gazing upon Being in its profoundest sleep, and salute it in the name of Creation! All's well when Being and Well-Being are in some measure reconciled. A very good night!"

CHAPTER VI

No one will doubt me when I say that despite my innate love of sleep and the ease with which I usually returned to my sweet, refreshing homeland in the unconscious, on that night sleep eluded me almost completely until nearly morning. Not even my well-made berth in the first-class compartment was of any avail. What had possessed me to drink so much coffee before my first night on a train—a train, moreover, that raced, rocked, jolted, stopped, and then jarred into motion again? To have done so was deliberately to rob myself of sleep in a way that my new, unsteady bed could never have done alone. I shall not maintain, although I am as sure of it today as I was then, that six or eight demitasses of mocha could never have accomplished this by themselves if they had not been the purely automatic accompaniment to Profesor Kuckuck's thrilling table conversation, which was what had stirred me up so profoundly—I shall not maintain it because a reader of sensibility (and it is for such readers alone that I am setting down my confessions) will have realized it by himself.

Briefly, then, arrayed in silk pajamas (which protect the person better than a nightshirt against bed linen that may not have been thoroughly laundered) I lay awake that night until almost morning, sighing and twisting in an attempt to find a position that would lull me into Morpheus' arms; when slumber finally stole upon me unaware, I had a series of confused dreams such as often accompany shallow, restless sleep. Seated on the skeleton of a tapir, I was riding along the Milky Way, which was easily recognizable because it really consisted of milk or was covered with milk which splashed up around the hoofs of my bony mount. I sat awkwardly and uncomfortably on his backbone, holding on to his ribs with both hands and being badly shaken back and forth by his eccentric gait, which may have been a dream version of the hurrying and jolting of the train. I, however, interpreted it as a reminder that I had not yet learned to ride and must learn to without delay if I was to maintain my position as a young man of family. A brightly dressed crowd streamed toward me, passing to right and left of me, their feet splashing in the Milky Way, small men and women, graceful, of yellowish complexion, with merry brown eyes. They shouted to me in an incomprehensible tongue—representing Portuguese, no doubt. One of them, however, called to me in French: "*Voilà le voyageur curieux!*" Because she spoke French, I recognized that it must be Zouzou, whereas her shapely arms, bare to the shoulder, indicated to me that instead—or rather at the same time—it had to be Zaza. I tugged at my tapir's ribs with all my strength to make him stop and let me dismount, for I longed to join Zouzou or Zaza and begin a conversation about the antiquity of the bony structure in her charming arms. But my mount began to buck fiercely and threw me off into the milk of the Milky Way, at which the dark-haired people, including Zouzou or Zaza, broke into derisive laughter. At this my dream dissolved, only to give place in my sleeping but restless brain to equally silly imaginings. I was, for example, crawling on all fours along a steep chalk cliff above the sea, dragging after me a long liana-like stem, in my heart an anxious doubt as to whether I was animal or plant—a doubt that was not unflattering since it was associated with the name "sea lily." And so forth.

At long last, in the morning hours, my sleep deepened to dreamlessness, and it was only a little before our midday arrival in Lisbon that I awoke. Breakfast was not to be thought of, and I had but scant time to wash and avail myself of my beautifully fitted crocodile travelling-case. Professor Kuckuck was not to be seen in the confusion of the station platform or on the square in front of the Moorish-looking station whither I followed my porter. The latter found me an open carriage.

The day was bright and sunny, not too warm. The young coachman, who took charge of my steamer trunk and stowed it in the boot, might well have been one of the crowd who had laughed at my fall from the tapir on the Milky Way. He was of delicate build and yellowish complexion, exactly like Kuckuck's description; he had pointed moustaches and slightly Negroid lips, and was smoking a thin cigar; a round cloth cap clung to the side of his head, and his unruly dark hair was long at the temples. The alert expression in his brown eyes was not deceptive, for before I could name the hotel to which I had telegraphed for a reservation, he announced it himself, intelligently assigning me my place: "Savoy Palace." That was the sort of establishment where he thought I belonged, and I could only confirm his judgment with the words "*C'est exact.*" This he repeated, laughing, in murderous French as he swung himself into his seat and gave the horse a slap with the reins. "*C'est exact—c'est exact,*" he went on trilling happily during the short ride to the hotel. We had only a few narrow streets to negotiate before a broad, long boulevard opened before us, the Avenida da Liberdade, one of the most magnificent streets I have ever seen, a triple street indeed, with a path for carriages and riding-horses in the center and well-paved avenues on either side, splendidly adorned with flower beds, statues, and fountains. It was on this magnificent *corso* that my palatial quarters were situated.

How different my advent there from my distressing arrival in the hotel on the rue Saint-Honoré in Paris! Instantly there were three or four liveried grooms and green-aproned porters busy with my baggage, unloading my steamer trunk and bearing handbags, coat, and plaid roll ahead of me into the lobby as expeditiously as though I had not a moment to lose. Thus I could stroll in, carrying over my arm only my cane of Spanish bamboo with its ivory handle and silver ferrule, and approach the reception desk, where no one flushed with anger or commanded me to step back, all the way back. Instead, at mention of my name, there were only kind, welcoming smiles, gratified bows, and a deferential request to fill in the required information if it was altogether agreeable to me. A gentleman in a cutaway, warmly interested in whether my trip had been entirely agreeable, escorted me to the second floor and into the apartment I had reserved, a salon and bedroom with a tiled bath. The appearance of these rooms, whose windows opened on the Avenida, enchanted me more than I allowed myself to show. I translated my satisfaction, or rather delight, at this lordly magnificence into a demeanour of casual acceptance and thus I dismissed my guide. Left alone, however, and awaiting the arrival of my luggage, I hurried about, examining my regal living-quarters with more childish joy than I should really have permitted myself.

I took special pride in the walls of the salon, lofty expanses of stucco framed in gilded moulding, such as I have always greatly preferred to the more bourgeois wallpaper. Together with the white-and-gold doors, which were tall, too, and were set in niches, they gave the chamber a decidedly palatial, princely aspect. It was very spacious and divided by an open arch into two unequal parts, the smaller of which could serve, if desired, as a private dining-room. There, as well as in the larger section of the room, hung a crystal chandelier with glittering prisms such as I have always loved. Bright, soft rugs with wide borders lay on the floor, leaving exposed here and there stretches of the highly polished surface. Agreeable paintings hung above the magnificent doors, and on one wall hung a tapestry representing a legendary rape. Beneath it was a cabinet with a pendulum clock and two Chinese vases. Handsome French armchairs stood in comfortable elegance around an oval table with a lace cover and a glass top. On this, for the guest's refreshment, had been placed a basket of assorted fruits together with fruit knives and grape scissors, a plate of biscuits, and a polished fingerbowl–a courtesy on the part of the hotel management, as the card stuck between two oranges indicated. A cabinet with glass doors containing delightful porcelain figurines of cavaliers contorted into gallant postures, and ladies in crinolines, one of whom had suffered a tear in her dress so that the roundest part of her person was gleamingly revealed, to her great embarrassment as she looked back at it; standing lamps with silk shades, ornamental bronze candelabra on slender standards, a stylish ottoman with cushions and a silk cover completed the furnishings of the room. Its appearance delighted my starved eyes, as did the luxurious blue-and-grey décor of the bedroom, with its fourposter bed and upholstered easy chair, arms spread to invite reflective relaxation before sleep, the soft carpet from wall to wall absorbing every sound, the restful wallpaper, dull blue with long stripes, the tall pier glass, the gaslight in its milky sphere, the toilet table, the wide white closet doors with their glittering brass handles. . . .

My luggage arrived. I did not as yet have a valet at my disposal, as was occasionally the case later on. I put some necessaries in the drawers of the closet, hung up a few suits, took a bath, and made my toilet in the fashion that has always been peculiar to me. It somewhat resembles an actor's preparations, although the actual use of cosmetics has never tempted me because of the enduring youthfulness of my appearance. Arrayed in fresh linen and wearing a light flannel suit appropriate to the climate, I descended to the dining-room and there hungrily and enthusiastically made up for a dinner missed through listening and a breakfast missed through sleep. My lunch consisted of a ragout *fin*, a charred steak, and an excellent chocolate soufflé. Despite my pleasure in the meal, however, my thoughts still lingered on the conversation of the night before whose cosmic charm had made so deep an impression on my mind. Remembering it gave rise to a superior sort of joy not unrelated to my satisfaction in the distinction of my new existence. What occupied my thoughts more than the meal was wondering whether to get in touch with Kuckuck that very day—perhaps I should simply look him up at his home to make arrangements about visiting the museum and, more particularly, to make Zouzou's acquaintance.

That, however, might appear over-eager and precipitate. I succeeded in forcing myself to postpone my call until the following morning. Still far from rested, I determined to limit my activities for the day to a look around the city, and I set about this after my coffee. In front of the hotel I took a carriage to the Praça do Commércio, where my bank, likewise called Banco do Commércio, was situated; for I intended to make use of the letter of credit in my wallet to withdraw funds for my hotel bill and the various other expenses I would incur. The Praça do Commércio, a dignified and rather quiet square, is open on one side to the harbour, where the River Tagus makes a deep bend; the other three sides are lined with arcades, covered walks from which one enters the Customs House, the main Post Office, various ministries, and the bank for which I was bound. I was received by a black-bearded man of excellent manners and confidence-inspiring aspect, who respectfully examined my documents and set about carrying out my request with alacrity. He made the necessary entries with dexterity and then handed me his pen and a receipt, politely requesting me to sign it. I did not need so much as a glance at Loulou's signature in the document beside me to inscribe, with pleasure and affection, its exact copy, my lovely name, in sharp backhand letters encircled by the oval loop. "An original signature," the clerk could not refrain from saying. I shrugged, smiling. "A kind of heirloom," I said apologetically. "For generations we have signed ourselves that way." He bowed courteously, and I left the bank, my lizard-skin wallet bulging with milreis.

From there I betook myself to the near-by Post Office, where I dispatched to my home, Castle Monrefuge, the following telegram: "Arrived safe Savoy Palace and send warmest greetings. Brimming with new impressions of which I hope to write soon. Already observe some alteration in direction of my thoughts which have not always been what they should be. Your grateful Loulou." This accomplished, I went through a kind of arch of triumph or monumental gate on the side of the square opposite the harbour and into one of the smartest streets in the city, the Rua Augusta, where I had a social duty to discharge. I thought it would certainly be proper and in accordance with my parents' wishes if I were to pay a formal call at the Luxemburg Embassy, which was situated in the *bel étage* of a stately house. Without inquiring if the diplomatic representative of my native land and his wife were at home, I simply handed the servant who opened the door two of my cards, on one of which I had scribbled my address, with the request that he take them to Monsieur and Mme de Hüon. He was a man already well advanced in years, with stubbly grey hair, rings in his ears, rather broad lips, and a kind of melancholy animal expression, which led me to reflect upon the composition of his blood and evoked my sympathetic interest. I nodded to him with special friendliness as I left, for, in a certain sense, he belonged to the period of colonial splendour and the golden world monopoly in spices.

Returning to the Rua Augusta, I followed that busy and crowded thoroughfare toward a square which the porter at my hotel had recommended to me as the most important in the city; it is called Praça de Dom Pedro Quarto, or, familiarly, the "Rossio." For purposes of clarity let me say that Lisbon is surrounded by hills, some of them of considerable height, and on these the white houses of the better residential districts rise almost without a break, flanking the straight streets of the new part of town. I knew that Professor Kuckuck's home was located somewhere in those upper regions and so I kept glancing in that direction; indeed, I inquired of a policeman (I have always liked to talk to policemen) more by gesture than by words for the Rua João de Castilhos, the address I had read on Kuckuck's card. He pointed upward toward a street of villas and added in his tongue, which was as incomprehensible to me as the language I had heard in my dream, something about trams, cable cars, and *mulos*, obviously in reference to means of transportation. I thanked him repeatedly in French for this information, which was not of immediate importance to me, and he raised his hand to the brim of his summer helmet at the end of our brief but animated and pleasant interchange. How agreeable it is to receive such a mark of respect from these simple but smartly uniformed guardians of the public order!

I hope I may be permitted a general observation: that person is fortunate in whose cradle some good fairy has placed the gift of responding to pleasure, a perpetual responsiveness in even the most unlikely circumstances. No doubt this gift involves a heightening of responsiveness in general, the reverse of insensitivity, and therefore brings with it much pain which others are spared. But I cheerfully insist that the increase in joy more than compensates for that disadvantage—if it is one—and it is this gift of responsiveness to the smallest and even the most commonplace pleasures that has always made me consider truly appropriate my first and real Christian name, Felix, about which my godfather Schimmelpreester felt so bitter.

How right Kuckuck had been in saying that the principal ingredient in the desire to travel is a vibrant curiosity about as yet unknown human types! With warm interest I studied the people in the busy streets, those black-haired, alert-eyed men and women who accompanied their conversation with rapid southern gestures, and I made a point of getting into personal contact with them. Although I knew the name of the square I was approaching, I stopped a passer-by from time to time to ask the name—children, women, townsmen, sailors—simply to observe the play of expression on their faces while they gave their almost invariably courteous and detailed answers, to listen to their alien speech in their hoarse, exotic tones, and then to part from them with friendly gestures. I placed a gift, the size of which may have been a surprise, in the cup of a blind beggar who sat on the sidewalk, leaning against the wall of a house, with a cardboard sign beside him. To an elderly man who accosted me in a murmur, I gave an even more considerable sum. He was wearing a frock coat with a medal, but his shoes were broken and he had no collar. He was touched and even wept a little as he bowed his thanks in a way that showed me he had slipped into penury from some higher level of society, whatever his weakness of character may have been.

When I finally, then, reached the Rossio, with its two bronze fountains, its memorial columns, and its strangely wavy mosaic paving, there were many more occasions for asking questions of the strollers and the idlers sitting in the sun on the fountain edges—questions about the buildings that loomed so picturesquely in the blue above the houses bordering the square, the Gothic ruins of a church, and a newer structure that proved to be the Municipio or City Hall. Below, the façade of a theatre occupied one side of the Praça, while two other sides were lined with stores, cafés, and restaurants. And so when finally, on the pretext of desiring information, I had had my fun with various children of this alien spring, I sat down at a table in front of one of the cafés to rest and take tea.

Close to me sat a group of three distinguished-looking persons, also enjoying late-afternoon refreshment, and to them my well-bred and unobtrusive attention was at once attracted. There were two ladies, one considerably older than the other—mother and daughter, to all appearances; the third member of the party was a gentleman, just barely middle-aged, with an aquiline nose and spectacles. Below his Panama hat his hair fell in artistic fashion to the collar of his coat. He was hardly old enough to be the husband of the *senhora* and the father of the girl. As he ate his ice he held several neatly tied parcels on his lap, obviously out of courtesy, and two or three similar ones lay on the table in front of the ladies.

While I pretended to be interested in the play of the nearest fountain and in studying the architecture of the ruined church, I glanced surreptitiously at the trio. My curiosity and lively interest centred on mother and daughter—for such I considered them—and their disparate charms blended in my mind into an enchanting image of that relationship. This has been a characteristic of my emotional life. Earlier in this book, I reported the feelings with which, as a young sidewalk idler, I had drunk in the glimpse of a lovely brother and sister who appeared for a few minutes on the balcony of the Hotel Zum Frankfurter Hof. I remarked explicitly that such excitement could not have been aroused in me by either of the figures alone, either his or hers, but that their lovely brother-and-sister duality was what had moved me so deeply. The connoisseur of humanity will be interested in the way my penchant for twofold enthusiasms, for being enchanted by the double-but-dissimilar, was called into play in this case by mother-and-daughter instead of brother-and-sister. I, at all events, find it very interesting. I will just add, however, that my fascination was soon enhanced by a sudden suspicion that coincidence was here engaged in an extraordinary game.

At the very first glance the young person—eighteen, as I guessed, and wearing a simple loose summer dress of striped bluish material with a belt of the same stuff—reminded me startlingly of *Zaza*, but at once I am in honour bound to add "except that." Another Zaza, except that her beauty, or if that is too exalted a word and more applicable to her mother (this is a subject I shall return to directly)—except that her prettiness, then, was, so to speak, more demonstrable, more authentic, and more naïve than that of Loulou's friend, with whom everything was simply froufrou, a little *feu d'artifice* and an optical illusion not to be examined too closely. Here was dependability—if a word belonging to the moral order can be applied to the world of charm—a childish forthrightness of expression, of which in the sequel I was to receive disconcerting evidence. . . .

A different Zaza—so different, in fact, that on reflection I asked myself whether any actual similarity existed even though I thought I had seen it with my own eyes. Did I perhaps believe I had seen it only because I *wanted* to see it, because I, strange to say, was in search of Zaza's double? I am not altogether clear in my own mind on this point. Certainly in Paris my emotions had not been in competition with those of the good Loulou; I was not the slightest bit in love with Zaza, however much I liked to flirt with her. Can it have been that as part of my new identity I had assumed the obligation of falling in love with her? Had I fallen in love with her after the event and had I been hoping to meet another Zaza abroad? When I remember my sudden interest at Professor Kuckuck's mention of a daughter with so similar a name, I cannot entirely rule out this hypothesis.

Similarity? Eighteen years and black eyes constitute a similarity, if you like, although these eyes did not dart and flirt, but, narrowed a little by the thick lower lids, stared out with an expression of rather blunt inquiry when they were not sparkling with amused laughter. They were boyish—like the voice whose abrupt exclamations reached my ears a few times, a voice that was by no means silvery but rather brusque and hoarse, without any affectation, honest and direct, like a young boy's. In the nose there was no resemblance whatever: it was not a snub nose like Zaza's, but fine-bridged, although the nostrils were not particularly delicate. In the mouth, to be sure, even today I admit that there was a resemblance; in both instances the lips (whose lively red, in this case, was assuredly the work of Nature alone) were almost always parted, thanks to a habit of pursing the upper one, so that one saw the teeth between. The hollow under them, and the charming line of the chin leading down to the soft throat—these might well remind one of Zaza. Otherwise, everything was different, as memory shows me—transmuted from the Parisian to the exotic and Iberian, thanks especially to the tall tortoise-shell comb with which she held in place her high-piled hair. The hair was drawn back to leave her forehead bare, but at each temple there was a charming curl which again produced a foreign, southern, indeed Spanish effect. She wore earrings—not the long, swaying jet pendants her mother wore, but close-fitting and yet sizable flat opals surrounded by little pearls, which matched the exotic quality of her whole appearance. The southern tint of her ivory skin was something that Zouzou—I called her that immediately—had in common with her mother, whose type and *tenue*, however, were of a quite different order, more imposing, not to say majestic.

Taller than her attractive child, no longer slender but by no means too heavy, this lady, in the distinguished simplicity of cream-coloured linen, lace at throat and wrists, and long black gloves, was approaching matronly years without having as yet reached them. One would have searched in vain for grey in the dark hair under the wide, flower-trimmed, fashionable hat. A black neckband edged with silver became her well, as did her swaying jet earrings, and added a note of dignity to the noble carriage of her head. This quality characterized her whole appearance and was expressed almost to the point of sombreness, almost to severity, in her rather large face with its haughty, compressed lips, flaring nostrils, and the two deep creases between her brows. It was the sternness of the south, which many people fail to recognize, obsessed by the mistaken notion that the south is flattering and sweet and soft and that hardness is to be found only in the north, a completely erroneous idea. "Ancient Iberian stock, presumably," I thought to myself; "therefore with a Celtic admixture. And every sort of Phœnician, Carthaginian, Roman, and Arabic strain may be involved. No one to be trifled with." And I added in my mind that under the protection of such a mother, the daughter would be safer than with any possible male escort.

Nevertheless, it was reassuring that such an escort was present—as was only proper for two women in a public place. The respectable gentleman with the long hair sat nearest me of the three, almost shoulder to shoulder, since he had turned his chair sidewise to the table and his remarkable profile was exposed to me. I have never liked hair that falls to the collar, for, in the long run, it is bound to make the collar greasy. However, I overcame my repugnance and turned to this cavalier, throwing a glance of apology toward the two ladies, and addressed him in these words:

"Forgive, sir, the boldness of a stranger who has just arrived in this country and unfortunately has not yet mastered its language. I cannot converse with the waiter, who naturally enough speaks nothing else. Forgive, I repeat"—and once more my glance strayed to the ladies as though barely daring to touch them—"this unmannerly intrusion. But it is very important for me to gain certain specific information about this neighbourhood. I have the agreeable social duty, and the desire as well, to pay a call at a house in one of the residential streets of the upper city, the Rua João de Castilhos. The house in question—I add this in a sense to identify myself—is that of a famous Lisbon savant, Professor Kuckuck. Would you have the great kindness to tell me what means of transportation I might use for my little excursion?"

What an advantage it is to possess an easy and polished style of address, the gift of good form which that kind fairy thoughtfully laid in my cradle and which is so very necessary for the whole way of life I have adopted! I was satisfied with my speech, although toward the end I had become a little disconcerted because the girl, when I named the street and then mentioned Professor Kuckuck, had begun to giggle and had come close to bursting into laughter. This, I say, confused me a little—since it could only confirm the suspicion that had prompted me to speak. The *senhora* glanced at her child, shaking her head in regal reproof at this outburst of merriment—and then could not keep a smile from her own severe lips, of which the upper one was darkened by the faintest shadow of a moustache. The gentleman with long hair was naturally astounded, since he—unlike the ladies, I may say—had not hitherto been aware of my presence. However, he answered very politely:

"Certainly, sir. There are various possibilities—not all to be recommended equally, let me add. You could take a fiacre, but the streets that go up there are very steep, and the passenger usually finds himself obliged to walk beside the carriage at various points. The mule bus is preferable; it gets up the steep places very well. But best of all is the cable car. The entrance is near here in the Rua Augusta, which you certainly already know. It will take you conveniently and directly to the immediate neighbourhood of the Rua João de Castilhos."

"Splendid," I replied. "That's all I need. I can't thank you enough, sir. I shall follow your advice and I am very much obliged."

Thereupon I settled myself in my chair, indicating clearly that I had no intention of continuing to be a bother. However, the girl—whom I already called Zouzou—seemed not to have been impressed by her mother's admonitory glances and went right on displaying her merriment, until finally the *senhora* was compelled to explain her behaviour.

"Forgive this child's frivolity, sir," she said in harsh French, her voice an agreeable, husky contralto, "but I am Madame Kuckuck of the Rua João de Castilhos, this is my daughter, Susanna, and this is Dom Miguel Hurtado, a professional colleague of my husband. I can hardly be mistaken in assuming that I am addressing Dom Antonio José's travelling-companion, the Marquis de Venosta. My husband told us about his meeting with you when he arrived today."

"Enchanted, madame," I replied with sincere pleasure, bowing to her, to the young lady, and to Hurtado. "This is a charming coincidence! My name is indeed Venosta and I had the pleasure of your husband's company for a time on the train from Paris. I will make bold to say I have never travelled to greater advantage. The professor's conversation is inspiring—"

"You mustn't be surprised, *monsieur le marquis*," young Susanna broke in, "that your inquiry amused me. You inquire a great deal. I observed you on the square stopping every third person to inquire about something or other. Now you inquire from Dom Miguel about our own home—"

"You are forward, Zouzou," her mother interrupted her—and it was wonderful to hear her addressed for the first time by the nickname I had long since assigned to her.

"Excuse me, Mama," the girl retorted, "but when you are young everything you say is forward, and the marquis who is still young himself, hardly older than I am, it seems, was just a trifle forward too in beginning a conversation from one table to the next. Moreover, I have not told him what I wanted to say. First of all, I wanted to assure him that Papa did not burst out talking about him the minute he got home, as would almost appear from your words. He told us a great many other things first and then quite incidentally mentioned that he had dined the evening before with a certain de Venosta."

The lady who had been born da Cruz shook her head reproachfully. "Even when speaking the truth, my child," she said, "one must not be forward."

"Good God, mademoiselle," I said, "it's a truth I never doubted. I did not imagine–"

"That's good. That's good. That you did not imagine!"

The mother: "Zouzou!"

The girl: "A young man with a name like that, *chère maman,* who in addition happens to be so good-looking, is in danger of imagining all sorts of things."

After this there was nothing to do but join in the general merriment. Hurtado joined, too.

I said: "Mademoiselle Susanna must not overlook the greater danger she herself runs of imagining things because of her own appearance. Added to this there is the natural temptation to pride oneself on such a papa–and such a mama," bowing toward the *senhora.* Zouzou blushed–partly for her mother, who had not the slightest idea of blushing; but perhaps out of jealousy, too. She rescued herself in disconcerting fashion from this embarrassment by simply disregarding it and remarking with a gesture of the head toward me:

"What pretty teeth he has."

Never in my life had I encountered such forthrightness. But any awkwardness the speech might have caused was removed when the girl replied to the *senhora's* "*Zouzou, vous êtes tout à fait impossible!*" with the words:

"But he keeps showing them all the time. Clearly, he wants to have them mentioned. And besides, one ought not to be silent about something like that. Silence is unhealthy. A statement of fact is less harmful to him and to others."

An extraordinary creature. How extraordinary, how complete a personal exception to all the accepted conventions of her society and country, was to become clear to me only later. Only through experience was I to learn with what almost monstrous forthrightness this girl was capable of acting up to her remarkable principle that silence is unhealthy.

There was a somewhat embarrassed pause in the conversation. Mme Kuckuck-da Cruz drummed lightly on the table with her fingertips. Hurtado adjusted his glasses. I came to the rescue by saying:

"We should probably all do well to profit by Mademoiselle Susanna's pedagogical gift. She was completely right in the first instance in saying it would be ridiculous to assume that her honoured father began his account of his trip by mentioning me. I'll wager he began by the success of his mission, the acquisition in Paris of certain skeletal remains of a very important but unfortunately long-extinct species of tapir that lived in the ancient Eocene."

"You are entirely right, marquis," the *senhora* said. "That was exactly what Dom Antonio spoke of first of all, just as he seems to have spoken of it to you, and here you see someone who is especially pleased by this acquisition since it will mean employment for him. I introduced Monsieur Hurtado to you as my husband's professional colleague. He is, in fact, an admirable animal-sculptor. He has not only created all kinds of contemporary animals for our museum, but he is also able to re-create most convincingly, with the aid of fossils, creatures that have long since vanished."

That's the reason for wearing his hair down to his coat collar, I thought. It isn't absolutely necessary. Aloud, I said: "But, madame—but, Monsieur Hurtado—things couldn't have turned out better! In point of fact, the professor talked to me during the trip about your amazing abilities and now, as good luck will have it, I meet you on my first expedition into the city."

What did Miss Zouzou say to this? She had the presumption to say: "How delightful! Why don't you fall on each other's necks? Your acquaintance with us presumably amounts to very little in comparison with this meeting you are rejoicing over. And yet, marquis, you don't look in the least as though you were especialy interested in science. Your real interests probably lie more in ballet and horses."

One might well have disregarded these remarks. I replied, nevertheless: "Horses? In the first place, mademoiselle, the horse is really related, though at a distance, to the tapir of the Eocene. And even a ballet might prompt one to scientific reflection by awakening recollections of the primitive bony structure of the pretty legs one sees there. Pardon me for mentioning it, but it was you who brought the subject up. Moreover, you are at liberty to take me for an idler with the most banal interests and no feeling for higher things, for the cosmos or the three spontaneous generations or universal sympathy. That is your privilege, as I say, only it is possible you might be doing me an injustice."

"It's your duty, Zouzou," her mother said, "to explain that that was not your intention."

But Zouzou remained obstinately silent.

Hurtado, on the other hand, was visibly flattered by my enthusiastic greeting and politely took up the conversation.

"Mademoiselle," he said by way of apology, "is fond of teasing, *monsieur le marquis*. We men must put up with it, and which of us is not happy to do so? She teases me all the time, calls me the taxidermist because at the beginning that was indeed my occupation: I earned my daily bread by stuffing dead pets, canaries, parrots, and cats and providing them with bright glass eyes. From that, to be sure, I went on to higher things, to plastic reconstruction, from journeyman labour to art, and now I no longer need dead animals to create lifelike models. To do this requires more than manual skill; it requires long observation of Nature and long study, that I will not deny. My own abilities in this field have, for a number of years, been at the service of our Natural History Museum—moreover, I am not alone; there are two other artists working in the same department of the Kuckuck Foundation. For the reconstruction of animals of another geological period—the reproduction of archaic life, that is—one naturally requires a sound anatomical basis from which the whole creature can be logically deduced, and it is for this reason that I am so pleased that the professor has succeeded in acquiring in Paris the requisite skeletal remains of this early ungulate. I will be able to proceed from what we have. The animal was no larger than a fox and certainly still had four well-developed toes on the front feet and three on the hind. . . ."

Hurtado had grown quite warm while talking. I congratulated him heartily on his magnificent assignment, only regretting that I should not be able to see the result of his labours because my ship sailed in a week's time, the ship to Buenos Aires. But I was determined to see as much as possible of his earlier work. Professor Kuckuck had most kindly offered to be my guide through the museum. I had it very much in mind to make an appointment.

That could be done at once, Hurtado said. If I would come to the museum in the Rua da Prata, not far from here, next morning at eleven o'clock, the professor would be there as well as his unworthy self, who would consider it an honour to be allowed to take part in our tour of inspection.

Wonderful! I at once shook hands with him in agreement, and the ladies countenanced the arrangement with varied degrees of good will. The *senhora*'s smile was condescending, Zouzou's mocking. But even she joined with reasonable good grace in the short conversation that followed, although not without a trace of what Monsieur Hurtado had called teasing. I learned that "Dom Miguel" had gone to meet the professor at the station and had accompanied him home and had taken luncheon with the family. Escorting the ladies afterward on their shopping-tour, he had finally brought them to this place for refreshment. Without male escort, they would not, according to the customs of the country, have been allowed to appear there. There was talk, too, of my projected trip, the year-long journey around the world to which my dear parents in Luxemburg were treating me—their only son, for whom they happened to have a weakness.

"*C'est le mot*," Zouzou could not refrain from interjecting. "That certainly could be called a weakness."

"I see you are still worried about my modesty, mademoiselle."

"That would be a lost cause," she replied.

The mother reproved her: "My dear child, a girl must learn to distinguish between propriety and prickliness."

And yet it was just this prickliness that gave me hope that one day—few though my days were—I would be able to kiss those charming, pouting lips.

It was Mme Kuckuck herself who strengthened me in this hope by formally inviting me to lunch next day. Hurtado meanwhile launched into a consideration of the sights I must not fail to see during my limited stay. He recommended the exhilarating view of town and river from the public gardens in the Passeio da Estrella, spoke of an approaching bullfight, praised in particular the cloister of Belem, a pearl of architectural art, and the castles in Sintra. I, on the other hand, admitted that the object of interest I had heard about that had attracted me most was the botanical garden, where there were said to be plants belonging to the Carboniferous period rather than to the present day, specifically the tree ferns. That interested me more than anything else, and must be my first objective after the Museum of Natural History.

"A walk and nothing more," the *senhora* declared. It would be pleasant to undertake it. The simplest thing would be for me after my visit to the museum to have lunch *en famille* in the Rua João de Castilhos and to plan to make the botanical promenade in the afternoon either with or without Dom Antonio José.

She made this proposal and issued this invitation majestically; it goes without saying that I accepted it with polite surprise and gratitude. Never, I said, had I looked forward with more joyful anticipation than to the next day's program. After these arrangements had been made, we got up to go. Hurtado paid the waiter. Not only he, but Mme Kuckuck and Zouzou, too, gave me their hands. Everyone said: "*A demain, à demain,*" even Zouzou. But she added mockingly: "*Grace à l'hospitalité de ma mère.*" And then, dropping her eyes a little: "I don't like to say what I'm told to say. That's why I postponed telling you that it was not my intention to be unfair to you."

I was so taken aback by this sudden mitigation of her prickliness that I called her Zaza by mistake.

"*Mais, Mademoiselle Zaza—*"

"Zaza!" she repeated, bursting into laughter, and turned her back on me.

I had to call after her: "*Zouzou! Zouzou! Excusez ma bévue, je vous en prie!*"

While I made my way back to the hotel past the Moorish railroad station and through the narrow Rua do Príncipe, which connects the Rossio with the Avenida da Liberdade, I scolded myself for that slip of the tongue. Zaza! She had been simply herself, companioned only by her beloved Loulou—not by a proud, ancient Iberian mother—and that, after all, made an enormous difference!

CHAPTER VII

The Museu Sciências Naturaes of Lisbon, situated in the Rua da Prata, is only a few steps from the Rua Augusta. The façade of the building is unimpressive; there is neither gate nor staircase. One simply walks in, but even before passing through the turnstile next to the cashier's table with its array of photographs and picture postcards, one is amazed by the extent and depth of the entrance hall. The visitor is greeted from afar by a stirring scene from nature. Approximately in the centre of the room stands a dais, grass-covered, with a background of dark forest thicket, partly painted, partly constructed of real leaves and bushes. On slender legs, hoofs close together, a white stag stands as though just emerging, crowned by antlers with magnificent points and palms. His aspect is both dignified and alert as he cocks his ears forward and surveys approaching visitors with wide-spaced eyes, gleaming, calm yet wary. The ceiling light in the hall fell directly on the grassy plot and the shimmering figure of the proud and wary animal. One feared that if one moved so much as a single step he would disappear at a bound into the darkness of the thicket. And so I lingered, rooted to the spot by the timidity of the lonely creature there, without at once being aware of Senhor Hurtado, who stood waiting at the foot of the dais, his hands behind his back. He came toward me, signalling to the cashier that I was to be admitted without charge, and manipulated the turnstile himself, meanwhile expressing the heartiest welcome.

"I see, *monsieur le marquis*," he said, "you are captivated by our receptionist, the white stag. Quite understandable. A good piece. No, I didn't create him. That was done by someone before my time here. The professor is expecting you. May I take the liberty—"

But he had to give me smiling leave to go over to the magnificent animal, which fortunately could not flee, and examine it from close at hand.

"No fallow buck," Hurtado explained. "He belongs to the class of noble red deer, which at times are white. However, I am probably talking to an expert. You are a hunter, I assume?"

"Only occasionally, only when it is socially necessary. Here, nothing is further from my thoughts. I believe I would not be able to raise a gun against him. There's something legendary about him. And yet—I am right, am I not, Senhor Hurtado—and yet the deer is a ruminant?"

"Certainly, *monsieur le marquis*. Like his cousins, the reindeer and the elk."

"And like the ox and cow. You know, one can see it. There is something legendary about him, but one can see it. He is white, by exception, his antlers give him the look of a king of the forest, and his gait is delicate, but his body betrays the family—against which there is nothing to be said. If one examines the rump and hindquarters carefully and thinks about a horse—the horse is nervier, although one knows he is descended from the tapir—then the stag strikes one as a crowned cow."

"You are a critical observer, *monsieur le marquis*."

"Critical? Not at all. I have a feeling for the forms and representations of Life and Nature, that's all. A feeling for them. A certain enthusiasm. The ruminants have, after all, as I understand it, very remarkable stomachs. There are various compartments in them, and from one they regurgitate what they have eaten. Then they lie and chew their cuds thoroughly once more. You might say it is strange for anyone with such odd family customs to be crowned king of the forest, but I honour Nature in all her inventions and I can quite well put myself in the position of a ruminant! After all, there is such a thing as universal sympathy."

"No doubt," Hurtado said, taken aback. He was actually somewhat embarrassed by my exalted manner of speech—as though there were any less exalted way of saying "universal sympathy." Because he was stiff and nonplussed from embarrassment, I hastened to remind him that the master of the establishment was waiting for us.

"Very true, marquis. I would be wrong to keep you here any longer. To the left, if you please—"

Kuckuck's office opened off the long corridor. He got up from his desk as we entered, and removed his working-glasses from his starlike eyes, which I recognized as though I had first seen them in a dream. His greeting was cordial. He expressed his pleasure at the accident which had already brought me and his ladies together, and at the arrangements we had made. We sat around his desk for a few minutes while he inquired about my lodgings and my first impressions of Lisbon. Then he said: "Shall we make our tour of inspection now, marquis?"

This we did. Outside, in front of the stag, there now stood a school class of ten-year-olds to whom the teacher was lecturing about the animal. They glanced from it to him with equal respect. Then they were led off to inspect the glass cases along the walls which contained collections of beetles and butterflies. We did not linger over them, but at once turned to the right into a series of large and small rooms opening into one another and providing food enough and to spare for anyone with a taste for representations of Life such as I had boasted of possessing. Everywhere in room and hall the receptive eye was caught by forms that had poured uninterruptedly from Nature's womb. Next to the awkward first experiments were the most elaborately evolved, the most perfect of their kind. Behind a glass window was the replica of a patch of sea bottom where the earliest forms of organic life teemed in a kind of furious untidiness of design. Right beside it one saw cross-sections of shells from the lowest strata—of such minute workmanship inside that one could not but wonder at the meticulous artistry Nature had attained in that far bygone day. The soft, headless creatures whose homes these shells had been had mouldered away millions of years ago.

We encountered individual visitors, who had certainly had to pay the modest entrance fee, and were unescorted since their social position gave them no claim to special attention. They were obliged to garner their information from the labels attached to the exhibits, which were, of course, written in the language of the country. They gazed at our little group with curiosity, no doubt taking me for a visiting prince for whom the management was doing the honours of the establishment. I will not deny I found this pleasant; and there was the added charm of the contrast between my own fineness and elegance and the primitive crudity of many of the uncanny-looking fossils, the primeval crustaceans, cephalopods, brachiopods, tremendously ancient sponges, and entrail-less lily-stars—Nature's experiments, whose acquaintance I was briefly making.

All this inspired in me the moving reflection that these first beginnings, however absurd and lacking in dignity and usefulness, were preliminary moves in the direction of me—that is, of Man; and it was this that prompted my attitude of courteous self-possession as I was introduced to a marine saurian, a bare-skinned, sharp-jawed creature, represented by a five-metre-long model floating in a glass tank. This friend, who could have attained proportions much greater than those shown, was a reptile but had the shape of a fish and resembled a dolphin, which, however, is a mammal. Hovering thus between the classes, it ogled me from the side while my own eyes, even as Kuckuck was speaking, wandered ahead to farther distances where there appeared to be a life-sized dinosaur, extending through several rooms and protected by a red velvet cord. That is how it is in museums: they offer too much; the quiet contemplation of one or a few of the objects from their store would certainly be more profitable for mind and soul; as soon as you step in front of one, your glance is lured on to another whose attractiveness distracts the attention, and so it goes through the whole series of exhibits. I speak, however, from a single experience, for later I hardly ever visited such places of instruction.

As for the immoderate creature which Nature had abandoned and which was faithfully reproduced here on the basis of fossil remains, no single room in the building could have contained him—he was all in all, God save the mark, forty metres long—and although two rooms connected by an open archway had been set aside for him, it was only through skillful arrangement of his limbs that these met his requirements. We went through one room past the monstrous coils of his tail, his leathery hind legs, and part of his bulging rump; near his upper body, however, a tree trunk—or was it a short stone column?—had been erected and on this the poor creature supported himself with one foot, not without a kind of monstrous grace, while his endless neck and trivial head were bent down toward this foot in troubled meditation—or is meditation possible with a sparrow brain?

I was much touched by the appearance of the dinosaur and addressed it in my mind: "Don't be sad! It's true you have been cast out and cashiered for lack of moderation, but as you see, we have built a statue to you and we remember you." And yet not even this, the museum's most famous exhibit, completely held my attention, which was diverted by a simultaneous attraction. Hanging from the ceiling, its leathery wings outspread, was a flying saurian, the primordial bird with reptilian tail and claws on its wing tips. Near by were egg-laying mammals with pouches for their young, and, a little farther on, stupid-looking giant armadillos, whom Nature had considerately protected with a heavy armour of bony plates on back and flanks. But Nature had been just as solicitous of their ravenous boarders, the sabre-tooth tigers, and had provided them with such powerful jaws and rending teeth that they could handle the bony armour and tear great slices of no doubt tasty flesh from the armadillos' bodies. The larger and more heavily armoured the unwilling host became, the more monstrous grew the jaws and teeth of the guest who joyfully leaped upon him at mealtime. One day, however, Kuckuck informed us, climate and vegetation played a prank on the giant armadillos by depriving them of their innocent nourishment, and they became extinct. And there sat the sabre-tooth tiger, after that mighty contest, there he sat with his jaws and his armour-rending teeth and fell rapidly into despondency and gave up the ghost. He had done everything out of regard for the growing armadillo so as not to be left behind but to go on being able to crunch its bones. The latter, in turn, would never have grown so large or so heavily armoured if it had not been for that connoisseur of his flesh. But if Nature wanted to defend him by constantly increasing his coat of mail, why had she, at the same time, steadily strengthened the jaws and sabre teeth of his enemy? She had been on both sides–and so, of course, on neither–had only been playing with them, and when she had brought them to the pinnacle of their capacities she deserted them. What is Nature thinking of? She is thinking of nothing at all, nor can Man ascribe thoughts to her; he can only admire her busy impartiality when he strolls, as an honoured guest, among the multiplicity of her manifestations, of which such beautiful reproductions, in part the creation of Senhor Hurtado, filled the halls of Kuckuck's museum.

Further introductions were made: the hairy mammoth with its upward-curving tusks, now extinct, and the rhinoceros with its thick, flabby skin which looks extinct but is not. The half-apes gazed down at me from the branches they crouched on, with overlarge mirror eyes, and the nocturnal loris won a permanent place in my heart because, quite apart from those eyes, it had such delicate hands and slender arms–which concealed, of course, the same bony armature as that of the most primitive land animals. And the lemur with eyes like teacups and long, thin fingers clasped in front of its breast, and amazingly wide-spaced toes. These faces were like a trick of Nature to make us laugh; I, however, refrained from so much as a smile. For very clearly in the end they all prefigured me, even though disguised as in some sorry jest.

How can I name and praise all the animals the museum had on view, the birds, the nesting white herons, the surly owls, the thin-legged flamingos, the hawks and parrots, the crocodiles, the seals, the frogs, the moles and warty toads—in short, whatever creeps or flies? There was a little fox I shall never forget because of his witty face. I should have liked to pat them all on the head, the foxes, lynxes, sloths, omnivores, yes, even the jaguar in a tree with his slanting eyes, green and false, and his look of having been assigned a destructive and bloody role—I should have liked to pat them all, and here and there I did so, although touching exhibits was forbidden. But what freedom might I not allow myself? My guides were entertained to see me shake hands with a bear that was lumbering along on his hind feet, and give an encouraging slap on the back to a chimpanzee that had sunk down on his knuckles.

"But Man, professor!" I said. "After all, you spoke of Man. Where is he?"

"In the basement," Kuckuck replied. "If you have pondered everything here, marquis, we will descend."

"Ascend, you mean," I substituted in jest.

There was artificial illumination in the basement. Wherever we went, little theatres were let into the wall behind glass panes, with lifelike scenes from the early life of Man. We paused in front of each of them to listen to the commentary of the master of the establishment, and again and again, at my request, returned from a later to an earlier one, however long we might already have stood there. Does the kind reader perhaps recall how in my earlier days I had been at pains to search among the pictures of my forebears for some hint or indication of the source of my own striking physical perfection? Early experiences in life always recur in heightened form, and I now felt myself completely re-immersed in that activity as, with probing eyes and beating heart, I saw what had been striving toward me from the grey reaches of antiquity. Good God, what were those small, shaggy creatures squatting together in timid groups as though conferring in some cooing and hissing pre-language about the means of surviving and prospering on an earth already possessed by much better-equipped and more strongly armed creatures? Had the spontaneous generation of which I had been told, the separation from the animal, already taken place or had it not? It had, it had, if anyone asked me. There was proof of it in these shaggy creatures' obvious sense of strangeness and helplessness in a world which had been given to others and in which they had been provided with neither horns nor tusks, fangs nor bony armour nor iron jaws. And yet, it is my conviction that they already knew—and were discussing as they squatted there—that they already knew they were made of finer clay.

A roomy cave housed a group of Neanderthal people tending a fire—bull-necked, thick-set individuals, to be sure—but imagine anyone else, even the lordliest king of the forest, coming along and making a fire and tending it! That required more than a regal demeanour; for that, something had to be added. The head of the clan had an especially thick bull-neck; he was a short man with a moustache and rounded back, his arms too long for his stature; his knee had been bloodily gashed open, one hand grasped the antlers of a deer he had killed and was just dragging into the cave. Short-necked, long-armed, and stooped were they all, these people around the fire, the boy watching the provider and booty-bringer with hero worship in his eyes, and the woman emerging from the back of the cave with a child at her breast. But look, the child was just like an infant of today, a decidedly modern improvement over the state of the adults, but no doubt in growing he would regress to theirs.

I could not tear myself away from the Neanderthalers, but later I had equal trouble in leaving that eccentric who, many hundreds of thousands of years ago, crouched in his barren cavern and with mysterious diligence covered the walls with pictures of bison, gazelles, and other prey, with pictures of the hunters too. No doubt his companions were outside actually hunting, but he was here painting with coloured pigments, and the smeary left hand with which he leaned against the rocky wall as he worked had left numerous marks between the pictures. I looked at him for a long time and yet, after we had passed on, I wanted to return once more to that diligent eccentric. "Here we have someone," Kuckuck said, "who is scratching his imaginings in stone as best he can." And this fellow busily scraping away at his stone was very touching, too. Daring and valiant, however, was the replica of a man attacking a maddened and embattled wild boar with dogs and spear—the boar was daring and valiant, too, but at a subordinate level on Nature's scale. Two dogs—they were of a strange breed, now vanished, which the professor called bog hounds and which had been domesticated in the lake-dwellers' time—lay on the grass ripped open by the boar's tusks. There were others, however, and their master was taking aim with his spear. Since there could be no doubt about the outcome, we passed on, leaving the wild pig to its subordinate fate.

Then came a handsome seascape in which fishermen were carrying on their advanced and bloodless occupation by the shore, hauling in a good catch with their flaxen net. Next to them, however, something was going on quite different from anything else and more significant than the activities of the Neanderthalers, or the wild-boar hunter, or the fishermen hauling their net, or even the diligent eccentric. Stone pillars had been raised, a number of them; they stood unroofed, forming a hall of pillars with only the heavens as ceiling, and on the plain beyond the sun was just rising, flaming red, over the edge of the world. In the roofless hall a powerful-looking man stood with upraised arms presenting a bouquet of flowers to the rising sun! Had anyone ever seen anything like it? The man was not a greybeard and not a child. He was in the prime of life. And it was just the fact of his vigour and strength that lent his action its peculiar delicacy. He and those who, living with him, had for some personal reason chosen him for this office did not yet know how to build and to roof; they could only pile stones on top of one another into pillars, and with these construct a circle wherein to perform ceremonies such as this powerful man was enacting. The burrows of fox or badger, the splendidly constructed nests of birds showed far more art and ingenuity. But they were useful and nothing more—a refuge for themselves and their broods; beyond that, the creatures' thoughts did not go. The circle of piled stone, however, was something else; refuge and brood had nothing to do with it; they were below the attention of one who had freed himself from crude necessity and risen to a nobler need. Just let any other creature in Nature come along and hit on the idea of making a formal gift of flowers to the rising sun!

My head was hot and slightly feverish from my concentrated observations as I pronounced this challenge in my heart, the heart I had so freely bestowed. I heard the professor saying that we had now seen everything and could ascend again and go straight up to the Rua João de Castilhos, where his ladies were awaiting us for luncheon.

"One might almost have forgotten that amid all these sights," I replied. But I had by no means forgotten it; rather I regarded the tour through the museum as a preparation for my reunion with mother and daughter—exactly as Kuckuck's conversation in the dining-car had been a preparation for this tour of inspection.

"Professor," I said, wishing to make a short concluding speech, "I have not, as it happens, seen many museums in my brief life, but that yours is one of the most thrilling is beyond question. City and country owe you a debt of gratitude for establishing it, and I for being my guide. I thank you too most warmly, Senhor Hurtado. How accurately you have reproduced the poor, immoderate dinosaur and the tasty giant armadillo! Now, however, reluctant though I am to leave, we must not on any account keep Senhora Kuckuck and Mademoiselle Zouzou waiting. Mother and daughter—there is something thrilling about that, too. Very often great charm is to be found in brother and sister. But mother and daughter, I feel free to say, even though I may sound a trifle feverish, mother and daughter represent the most enchanting double image on this star."

CHAPTER VIII

And so it was that I was introduced into the home of the man whose conversation during the train trip had stirred me so profoundly. Often, peering up from the city, I had tried to search out his domicile, and it had now taken on even greater interest in my eyes through my unexpected encounter with the mother and daughter who lived there. Quickly and comfortably the cable car Hurtado had mentioned bore us upward and deposited us in the immediate vicinity of the Rua João de Castilhos. A few steps brought us to the Villa Kuckuck, a little white house like many others in that quarter. In front of it was a small lawn with a flower bed in the middle. The interior was furnished like the home of a modest scholar and was in such extreme contrast to the magnificence of my own lodgings in the city, both in size and in décor, that I could not forgo a feeling of condescension as I poured forth praises of the view and the cosiness of the rooms.

This feeling, however, was quickly moderated to one of timidity by another contrast that forced itself upon me: the appearance, that is, of the lady of the house, Senhora Kuckuck-da Cruz, who greeted us—and me especially—in that small, completely bourgeois living-room with a formality as extreme as though she were in a royal reception hall. The impression this woman had made upon me the day before was now definitely strengthened. She had chosen to appear in a different costume: a dress of very fine white moiré with a close-fitting ruffled coat, narrow ruffled sleeves, and a black silk sash worn high under her bosom. An antique gold necklace with a medallion circled her throat, whose ivory tint seemed several shades darker against the snowy whiteness of her dress. So, too, did her large, severe face framed by the trembling earrings. Today she was hatless, and a few threads of silver could after all be seen in the heavy dark hair that fell in curls on her forehead. But how perfectly preserved was that erect figure and how imperiously held the head, as the eyes looked down on you, almost weary with pride. I will not deny that this woman terrified me and, through the self-same qualities, strongly attracted me at the same time. The almost forbidding majesty of her demeanour was hardly justified by her husband's position as a meritorious scholar. There was some property of blood in it, a racial arrogance that had an animal quality about it, and was for that very reason exciting.

Meanwhile, I was on the lookout for Zouzou, who was closer to my own age and interests than Senhora Maria Pia—I heard her given names from the professor, who was pouring port wine for us from a carafe standing on the velvet-covered table in the living-room. I did not have long to wait. We had hardly begun to sip our *apéritif* when Zouzou entered and greeted first her mother, then, in comradely fashion, Hurtado, and last of all me—no doubt for pedagogical reasons, so that I would not begin to imagine anything. She had come from playing tennis with some of her young friends, whose names were something like Cunha, Costa, and Lopes. She pronounced favourable or unfavourable opinions of their individual performances on the courts in a way that showed she regarded herself as an expert. Looking at me over her shoulder, she asked whether I played, and although I had only been a sideline spectator of this diversion of gilded youth and had on a few occasions acted as ball boy on the courts in Frankfurt, I replied lightly that in the old days at Castle Monrefuge I had been a pretty fair player, but since then had got badly out of practice.

She shrugged her shoulders. How happy I was to see again the pretty curls beside her temples, the pouting upper lip, the gleam of her teeth, the enchanting line of chin and neck, the bold inquiring glance! She was wearing a simple white linen dress with a leather belt and short sleeves, which left her sweet arms bare—arms that, curving, gained in enchantment for me as she raised both hands to the slender golden snake she wore as an ornament in her hair. To be sure, Senhora Maria Pia's majesty of race impressed me to the point of terror; but my heart beat for her lovely child, and the idea that this Zouzou was or must become the travelling Loulou Venosta's Zaza implanted itself ever more firmly in my imagination, although I was fully aware of the enormous difficulties in the way of its accomplishment. How could the six or seven days till I took ship suffice, in these most difficult circumstances, for me to place even the first kiss on those lips, on that precious arm—with its primordial bony armature? It was then that the thought thrust itself upon me that I must absolutely prolong my too short stay, alter the program of my trip, arrange to take another ship, so as to give my relations with Zouzou time to mature.

What fantastic ideas shot through my mind! My alter ego, the stay-at-home, was determined to marry, and this now became part of my own thinking. It seemed to me as though I must betray the intentions of my parents in Luxemburg, give up the trip around the world they had prescribed to distract me, woo Professor Kuckuck's enchanting daughter, and stay in Lisbon as her husband—although at the same time it was painfully clear to me that the delicate ambiguity of my existence, its ticklish double aspect, completely ruled out any such excursion into reality. This, as I say, pained me. But how happy I was to be able to meet new friends on a social level corresponding to my own essential fineness!

Meanwhile we went into the dining-room, which was dominated by a walnut sideboard, too large, too heavy, and too ornately carved. The professor sat at the head of the table. My place was beside the lady of the house, opposite Zouzou and Hurtado. The fact that they sat together, combined with my, alas, forbidden dream of marriage, prompted me to observe the behaviour of the pair with a certain uneasiness. The thought that Longhair and the charming child might be destined for each other seemed only too probable, and it worried me. And yet the relationship between them showed such ease and lack of strain that my suspicions gradually evaporated.

An elderly maid with woolly hair brought in the food, which was excellent. There were hors d'œuvres with delicious native sardines, roast mutton, cream kisses for dessert, and afterwards fruit and cheese pastry. A quite strong red wine was served with all this. The ladies diluted it with water and the professor did not touch it at all. The latter saw fit to remark that his house could of course not rival the table at the Savoy Palace, whereupon Zouzou observed tartly, before I could answer, that I had chosen to have lunch here of my own free will and that I certainly could not expect anyone to take particular pains on my account. They *had* taken pains, but I passed over this point and remarked simply that I had no reason whatever to miss the kitchens of the hotel on the Avenida, and that I was enchanted to be lunching in so distinguished and winning a family circle, adding that I kept well in mind to whom I was indebted for this privilege. At this I kissed the *senhora*'s hand, with my eyes fastened on Zouzou.

She encountered my glance sharply, brows somewhat gathered, lips parted, nostrils dilated. I observed with pleasure that the calm which characterized her behaviour toward Dom Miguel was by no means duplicated in her attitude toward me. She hardly took her eyes off me, observed each of my gestures with no attempt at concealment, and listened just as openly, attentive and, as it were, incensed in advance, to each of my remarks, never altering her expression or showing any trace of a smile, but occasionally giving a short, contemptuous snort. In a word, my presence obviously aroused in her a prickly and characteristically combative irritability. Who will blame me for preferring this interest in my person, hostile though it was, to a passive indifference?

The general conversation was carried on in French, while the professor and I occasionally exchanged a few words in

German. We talked of my visit to the museum and of the insights I had acquired, which had inspired me with a feeling of universal sympathy, insights, I assured him, that I owed to him. We then discussed the proposed expedition to the botanical gardens and went on to the near-by architectural sights which I must not miss. I expressed my interest, saying that I kept in mind my honoured travelling-companion's advice not to look about Lisbon too hurriedly but to devote enough time to it. But it was just this that worried me; the plan for my trip allowed all too little time, and I was actually beginning to consider how I could lengthen my stay.

Zouzou, who loved to talk of me in the third person over my head, remarked cuttingly that it was wrong to urge thoroughness upon *monsieur le marquis*. In her opinion, this meant a misunderstanding of my habits, which were doubtless those of a butterfly, floating from flower to flower, sipping nectar wherever I went. It was charming, I replied, imitating her manner of speech, that Mademoiselle took such an interest in my character, even though she was mistaken about it—and it was especially nice that she did so in such a poetic figure of speech. At this she became even more cutting and said that, confronted by so splendid a personal appearance as mine, it was hard not to be poetic. There was anger in her words along with the conviction she had expressed earlier that one should call things by their right names and that silence is unhealthy. The two gentlemen laughed while the mother rebuked her rebellious child with a shake of her head. As for me, I simply raised my glass in homage to Zouzou, and she, in irritation and confusion, almost raised hers in return. However, she withdrew her hand in time, blushing, and covered her confusion with that short, disparaging snort.

We discussed plans for the rest of my trip, which was to curtail my stay in Lisbon so distressingly, and I mentioned particularly the Argentinian *estanciero* family whose acquaintance my parents had made in Trouville and whose hospitality awaited me. I told all I knew about them on the basis of the information I had received from the stay-at-home. Their name was Meyer, but the children, a son and daughter of Mrs. Meyer's by a former marriage, were named Novaro. She had been born, so I related, in Venezuela and at a very early age had been married to an Argentinian in government service, who had been shot in the revolution of 1890. After a year of mourning she had given her hand to the wealthy Consul Meyer. She and the children now stayed with him either in his town house in Buenos Aires or at El Retiro, his large estate in the mountains some distance from the city. It was there that the family spent most of its time. The substantial income Mrs. Meyer had inherited from her first husband had gone to the children when she married again, so that they were not only the eventual heirs of the wealthy Meyer but were already independently rich young people. Their ages were about seventeen and eighteen.

"Senhora Meyer is no doubt a beauty?" Zouzou asked.

"I do not know, mademoiselle. But since she found a husband so promptly I assume she is not ugly."

"One may assume the same of the children, those Novaros. Do you know their first names?"

"I don't remember my parents ever mentioning them."

"But I'll wager you're impatient to find out."

"Why?"

"I don't know, you spoke of the pair with unmistakable interest."

"I was not aware of it," I said, secretly taken aback. "As yet, I have no impression of them. But I admit that the combination of brother and sister, when they are attractive, has always held a certain fascination for me."

"I regret that I have to meet you so single and alone."

"In the first place," I replied with a bow, "what is single can hold fascination enough."

"And in the second place?"

"Second place? I said 'in the first place' quite thoughtlessly.

I have no second to offer. At most I might remark in the second place that there are other charming combinations besides that of brother and sister."

"*Patatípatatá!*"

"We don't say that, Zouzou," her mother broke in. "The marquis will commence to wonder about your upbringing."

I assured her that my high regard for Mlle Zouzou could not be so easily impaired. We rose from the luncheon table and went back to the living-room for coffee. The professor announced that he could not accompany us on our botanical excursion, but would have to return to his office. Accordingly, he simply rode down to the city with us and said good-by at the Avenida da Liberdade—parting from me with the utmost cordiality, in which I could detect a certain gratitude for the interest I had shown in his museum. He said I had been a most agreeable and valued guest and would be so regarded by him and his at any time during my stay in Lisbon. If I had the desire and the time to take up tennis again, his daughter would count it a pleasure to introduce me into her club.

Zouzou said with enthusiasm that she was quite willing.

With a nod of the head in her direction and a smile that expressed and solicited consideration, he shook hands with me.

From the point where he parted from us it is, in fact, but a pleasant stroll to the heights where lie the famous gardens with their ponds and lakes, grottoes and open slopes. We changed companions as we walked: sometimes Dom Miguel and I were at Senhora Kuckuck's side while Zouzou wandered on ahead. Sometimes I found myself alone beside that proud lady, watching Zouzou strolling ahead with Hurtado. Sometimes it happened, too, that I was paired with the daughter either in front of the *senhora* and the animal-sculptor, or behind. Frequently he joined me to impart information about the landscape and the marvels of the world of plants, and I admit that pleased me most—not because of the "taxidermist" or his explanations, but because then the "second place" which I had suppressed got its just due and I could see in front of me the enchanting combination of mother and daughter.

This is a fitting place to remark that Nature, however rare and interesting her guise, gets scant attention from us when we are engrossed with humanity. Despite all her pretensions, she plays no more important role than that of scenery, the background for our emotions, simple decoration. But as that, to be sure, she was worthy of every praise. Conifers of gigantic size claimed our amazed attention, half a hundred metres tall, at a guess. The domain abounded in fan palms and feather palms. In places it had the tangled aspect of a primeval forest. Exotic rushes, bamboos and papyri, lined the edges of the ornamental waters on which floated bright-hued bride and mandarin swans. We admired the palm lily with its dark-green tuft of leaves from which springs a great sheaf of white, bell-like blossoms. And everywhere were the geologically ancient fern trees, growing close together in wild and improbable little groves, with their massive trunks and slender stems spreading into crowns of fronds, gigantic leaves, which, as Hurtado explained to us, carry their spore capsules. There were very few places on earth, aside from this one, he observed, where there were still tree ferns. But, he added, primitive man had from time immemorial ascribed magic powers to ferns in general, which have no flowers and really have no seeds, especially in the concoction of love potions.

"*Pfui!*" Zouzou said.

"How do you mean that, mademoiselle?" I asked.

It is startling to encounter so emotional a reaction to a scientific and matter-of-fact term that calls up no specific image. "Which part of the phrase do you object to?" I inquired. "To love or to potions?"

She did not reply, but looked angrily at me, actually lowering in a threatening way.

At this point we chanced to be walking alone behind the animal-sculptor and the proud lady.

"Love is itself a potion," I said. "What wonder that primitive man, the fern people, so to speak, who still exist since everything on earth is contemporaneous and intermixed, were tempted to practise magic with it?"

"That is a disreputable subject," she said reprovingly.

"Love? How hard you are! One loves beauty. One's eye and soul turn to it like blossoms to the sun. You certainly wouldn't apply your disapproving exclamation to beauty, would you?"

"I find it the height of bad taste to bring the conversation around to beauty when one possesses it oneself."

To this forthrightness I responded as follows:

"You are unkind, mademoiselle. Should one be penalized for having a passable exterior by being forbidden to admire beauty? Isn't it instead culpable to be ugly? I have always ascribed it to a kind of carelessness. Out of an innate consideration for the world that was awaiting me, I took care while I was being formed that I should not offend its eyes. That is all. I'd call it a kind of self-discipline. Besides, people in glass houses shouldn't throw stones. How beautiful *you* are, Zouzou, how enchanting those ringlets in front of your little ears. I can't look at them enough; in fact, I have made a drawing of them."

This was true. That morning, while smoking a cigarette after my breakfast in the handsome alcove of my salon, I had supplied Loulou's nude studies of Zaza with Zouzou's ringlets.

"What! You have taken the liberty of drawing me?" she hissed through clenched teeth.

"Yes, I have, with your permission—or without it. Beauty is a freehold of the heart. It cannot prohibit the emotions it inspires, nor can it forbid the temptation of reproducing them."

"I wish to see that drawing."

"I don't know whether that's feasible—I mean, whether my drawing could stand your inspection."

"That's beside the point. I demand that you give me the picture."

"There are several of them. I will have to think about

whether I can lay them before you and also about just when and where."

"The when and where must be found. There is no question about the whether. What you have made behind my back is my property, and what you just said about 'freehold' is very, very shameless."

"It was certainly not intended to be. I would be inconsolable if I had given you reason to question my upbringing. 'Freehold of the heart,' I said, and is that not right? Beauty is defenceless against our emotions. It may be wholly unmoved and untouched by them, it need not pay the slightest attention to them. But it is defenceless against them."

"Will you please drop the subject once and for all?"

"The subject? With pleasure! Or, if not with pleasure, at least with alacrity. For example–" I went on in a louder voice and a caricature of a conversational tone: "May I inquire whether by chance your revered parents are acquainted with Monsieur and Madame von Hüon, the ambassador from Luxemburg and his wife?"

"No, what have we to do with Luxemburg?"

"You are right. I had to call on them. My parents would have expected me to. Now I can probably expect an invitation to luncheon or dinner."

"Much joy may you have of it!"

"I have a secret motive. It's my wish to be presented by Von Hüon to His Majesty the King."

"Really? So you're a courtier, too?"

"If you want to call it that. I have been living for a long time in a bourgeois republic. As soon as it turned out that my trip would take me into a monarchy, I decided to pay my respects to the King. You may think it childish, but it will satisfy a need that I feel and it will give me pleasure to bow as one bows only before a king and to make frequent use of the words 'Your Majesty.' 'Sire, I beg Your Majesty to accept my most humble thanks for the honour Your Majesty–' and so on. I would like even more to secure an audience with the Pope and I will certainly do so some time. There one even bends one's knee, which would give me great satisfaction, and says 'Your Holiness.' "

"You pretend to talk to me, marquis, of your need for devotion—"

"Not for devotion. For good form."

"*Patatípatatá!* In point of fact, you simply want to impress me with your acquaintances and your invitation to the Embassy and the fact that you have entrée among the great of the earth."

"Your mama has forbidden you to say *patatípatatá* to me. Besides—"

"Mama!" she called so that Senhora Maria Pia turned around. "I must report to you that I have said '*patatípatatá*' to the marquis again."

"If you go on quarrelling with our young guest," the Iberian replied in her sonorous, husky voice, "you can't walk with him any more. Come here and let Dom Miguel escort you. Meanwhile, I will try to entertain the marquis."

"I assure you, madame," I said after the change had been made, "that there was nothing resembling a quarrel. Who could fail to be enchanted by Mademoiselle Zouzou's charming forthrightness?"

"I am sure we have left you too long in that child's company, dear marquis," the regal lady replied, and her jet earrings vibrated. "Youth is generally too young for the young. In the end, association with those who are mature is, if not more welcome, at least more edifying."

"In any case, it is a greater honour," I observed, putting a cautious warmth into my words.

"And so," she went on, "we'll conclude this excursion together. Have you found it interesting?"

"In the highest degree. I have found it an indescribable pleasure. And I am perfectly certain that this pleasure would not have been half so intense, my responsiveness to the new impressions that Lisbon offers—impressions of things and people, or better, people and things—would not have been half so profound without the preparation which good fortune granted me by allowing me to fall into conversation during my trip with your honoured husband, *senhora*—if one may use the word 'conversation' when one's role has been simply that of enthusiastic listener—without, if I may say so, the paleontological loosening-up his discourse produced in the soil of my mind, making it a ready seed-bed for new impressions, racial impressions, for example, such as the experience of seeing the primordial race to which such interesting admixtures have been added at various periods, and which offers eye and heart a majestic image of racial dignity. . . ."

I paused to catch my breath. My companion cleared her throat sonorously and drew herself to an even greater height.

"There is no help for it," I went on, "I have to keep using the words 'primitive' and 'primordial.' They steal into all my thoughts. This is a result of that paleontological loosening-up I just mentioned. Without it, what would the tree ferns we have just seen have meant to me, even if I had been told that primitive man believed they were useful for love potions? Everything has become so significant since then—things and people—I mean, people and things—"

"The real reason for your responsiveness, dear marquis, is probably your youth."

"How charming it is, *senhora*, to hear the word 'youth' on your lips! You pronounce it with the kindliness of maturity. Mademoiselle Zouzou, it appears, finds youth annoying, quite in keeping with your remark that youth is usually too young for the young. In some measure it holds true for me as well. Youth alone could not have produced the enchantment I move in. My advantage is that I can behold beauty in a double image, as childlike blossom and as regal maturity—"

In short, I talked like a book, and my gallantry was not ungraciously received. For as I bade farewell to my companions at the bottom of the cable-car line which would take them back to the Villa Kuckuck, and was about to return to my hotel, the *senhora* casually remarked that she hoped there would be an opportunity of seeing me again before my departure. Dom Antonio had suggested that, if it pleased me, I should freshen up my neglected tennis with Zouzou's athletic friends. Not a bad idea, perhaps.

Not a bad idea indeed, but a foolhardy one! I questioned Zouzou with my eyes, and when she sketched with face and shoulders an attitude of neutrality that did not absolutely rule out my assent, an appointment was at once made for the third day following. We would play in the morning and after that I was to lunch with the family once more, a farewell lunch. When I had bowed over Maria Pia's hand and Zouzou's and had exchanged a cordial handshake with Dom Miguel, I went my way, speculating about what form the future would take.

CHAPTER IX

LISBON, 25 AUGUST, 1895

Dearest Parents, Beloved Mama, Beloved and Revered Papa:

These lines follow so long after the telegram I sent to announce my arrival here that I must fear your displeasure. That will be doubled—I am, alas, all too sure—because of the above address, which is not at all in accord with your expectation, our agreement, or my own intentions. For ten days now you have pictured me on the high seas, and yet here I am, still writing from the capital of Portugal, the first stop on my journey. Dear parents, I shall explain this state of affairs, which I myself could not foresee, together with the reason for my long silence, in a way that will, I hope, nip your displeasure in the bud.

It all began by my meeting on the train a distinguished savant named Professor Kuckuck, whose conversation, I am certain, would have fascinated and inspired you just as it did your son.

German by birth, as his name indicates, and coming from the district of Gotha like you, dear Mama, belonging moreover to a good family, though of course not of family, he is a paleontologist by profession and has been living for a long time in Lisbon, married to a lady of ancient Portuguese family. He is the founder and director of the Natural History Museum here, which I visited under his personal guidance and whose scientific exhibitions both paleo-zoological and paleo-anthropological (these terms will be familiar to you) made a deep impression on me. It was Kuckuck who first warned me not to take the beginning of my world tour lightly just because it was a beginning and not to apportion too short a time to my inspection of a city like Lisbon. This made me wonder whether I had not planned too brief a visit properly to see a place that has so impressive a past and so many contemporary wonders—I mention here only the tree ferns in the botanical gardens which really belong to the Carboniferous period.

When in your generosity and wisdom, dear parents, you arranged this trip for me, you probably intended it not only as a distraction from what were, I admit, silly fancies wherein my immaturity had been snared, but also as an educational experience, a kind of grand tour such as is appropriate to a young man of family. Well then, this intention has been promoted by my friendly intercourse with the members of the Kuckuck household. They are three in number—four at times, for one of the professor's professional colleagues, Senhor Hurtado, an animal-sculptor, is there on occasion. To be sure, they contribute to my education in very unequal fashion. I admit I have not succeeded in getting on very well with the ladies of the house. My relations with them have not really seemed to grow cordial in the past weeks nor does this appear likely within the foreseeable future. The *senhora*, *née* da Cruz and of ancient Iberian stock, is a woman of terrifying sternness, yes, severity, and of an unconcealed arrogance, the basis of which is, to me at least, by no means clear; the daughter, whose age is perhaps a little less than mine and whose first name I have still not been able to catch, is a young woman one would be inclined to number among the echinoderms, so prickly is her behaviour. Moreover, if in my inexperience I have not misjudged the situation, the above-mentioned Dom Miguel (Hurtado) is probably to be regarded as her presumptive fiancé and husband, although it is an open question in my mind whether he is to be envied on that account.

No, it is the head of the house, Professor K., to whom I am devoted, and his associate as well, who is so deeply versed in the whole world of organic forms and to whose ingenuity the museum owes so much. It is from these two, but principally of course from K. himself, that I receive the enlightenment and information that are so important to my education and that exert a far greater attraction than the study of Lisbon and the architectural delights of its environs. Quite literally they embrace all Being, including the spontaneous generation of Life—everything from stone to Man. These two extraordinary men quite rightly see in me something resembling a sea lily which has freed itself from its stalk—that is, a novice at motion and in need of advice. It is on their account that this prolongation of my stay here contrary to plan—for which, dear parents, I affectionately beg your approval—is especially pleasant and valuable, although it would be going too far to say that they were the authors of it.

The actual reason, rather, was this. I considered it only correct and in accord with your wishes not to go away without leaving cards on our diplomatic representative, Herr von Hüon, and his wife. I was at pains to discharge this formal courtesy on the day of my arrival here, but in view of the time of year I foresaw no further consequences. However, a few days later I received at my hotel an invitation to attend a bachelor party at the Embassy, an event that had obviously been arranged before my arrival. The date was very shortly before I was due to embark. Nevertheless, I was able to follow my inclination and accept without being forced to postpone my departure.

I went, dear parents, and spent a most enjoyable evening in the Embassy on the Rua Augusta, an evening that—I owe it to your love for me not to conceal this—can be put down as a personal triumph.

This, of course, must be attributed to the way you brought me up. The dinner was given in honour of the Roumanian Prince Joan Ferdinand, who is scarcely older than I and happens at the moment to be staying in Lisbon with his military preceptor, Captain Zamfiresku. It was a bachelor gathering because Frau von Hüon was at a watering-place on the Portuguese Riviera, whereas her husband had had to interrupt his vacation and return to the capital for business reasons. The number of guests was small, amounting to hardly more than ten, but the occasion was distinguished by great formality from the very first moment, when we were received by servants in knee breeches and lace-trimmed coats. In honour of the Prince, dinner clothes and decorations had been stipulated, and I took pleasure in seeing the ribbons and crosses and stars worn by these gentlemen, almost all of whom had the advantage of me in years and *embonpoint*—not, I admit, without a trace of envy at the enhancement of their costumes through these precious baubles. But I can assure you, without flattering you or myself, that from the moment I entered the salon in my unadorned evening dress I won the unanimous favour of the master of the house and his guests not alone because of my name but because of the easy courtesy and social grace that went with it.

At supper, which was served in the panelled dining-room, I felt, to be sure, a trifle bored in that circle of foreign and local diplomats, officers, and big industrialists, among whom an Austro-Hungarian councillor from the Madrid Embassy, one Count Festetics, stood out picturesquely because of his fur-trimmed Hungarian costume, top boots, and curved sabre. I myself was placed between the rude-mannered captain of a Belgian frigate and a Portuguese wine-exporter, who looked like a roué, and whose imperious behaviour suggested great wealth. For quite a time the conversation turned on political and economic matters I knew nothing about, and so my contribution was necessarily limited to a lively play of expression indicating warm interest. Presently, however, the Prince, who was sitting opposite me—a weary whey-face, by the way, afflicted with both a lisp and a stutter—drew me into a conversation about Paris. Who doesn't like to talk about Paris? Soon all had joined in, and I, encouraged by the gracious smiles and stuttering lisp of His Highness, allowed myself to take the lead. Well, after dinner, when people were making themselves comfortable in the smoking-room and sampling the liqueurs and coffee, the place beside the distinguished guest fell to me as though automatically; the master of the house sat on his other side. You are undoubtedly familiar with Herr von Hüon's unexceptionable but colourless exterior, his thin hair, watery blue eyes, and long, wispy moustache. Joan Ferdinand hardly turned toward him at all, but allowed himself to be entertained by me. This seemed to be all right with our host. No doubt the prompt invitation I had received had been due to his wish to offer the Prince the society of someone near his own age.

I can venture to say that I amused him very much, and with the simplest of means, which chanced to be just the right ones for him. I told him about my childhood and early youth back home in the castle, about the wobbling of our good old Radicule, my imitation of whom led him to outbursts of childish delight, since it reminded him exactly of the doddering and unprofitable zeal of a valet he had inherited from his father in Bucharest; about the incredible affectation of your Adelaide, dear Mama, whose gossamer swayings and glidings I likewise imitated, floating about the room to his vast amusement; moreover, about the dogs, about Fripon and the chattering of his teeth, induced at regular intervals by the condition of our tiny Minime, and of the latter's unhappy propensity, so inappropriate for a lap dog and on so many occasions so dangerous and damaging to your robe, Mama. In masculine society it was surely permissible for me to speak of this and of the chattering of Fripon's teeth—in elegant turns of phrase, of course; in any case, I found myself justified by the tears of laughter the royal scion kept wiping from his cheeks at the description of Minime's delicate condition. There is something touching in seeing a creature, handicapped by both a stammer and a stutter, abandoned to such boundless merriment.

Possibly it will be painful to you, dear Mama, that I exposed to public merriment the delicate constitution of your darling; but the effect I achieved by doing so would have reconciled you to my indiscretion. Everyone became boisterous. The Prince bent double and the Grand Cross, dangling from the collar of his uniform, perforce took part. Everyone joined him in demanding to hear more about Radicule, Adelaide, and Minime, and called for repeated *da capo*'s. The Hungarian in his fur-trimmed uniform kept hitting his thigh so hard it must have hurt, the great wine-dealer, who wore various stars as awards for his wealth, burst a button from his waistcoat, and our ambassador was greatly pleased.

The result of all this was that, at the end of the soirée when I was alone with the ambassador, he proposed that before my departure he should present me to His Majesty the King, Dom Carlos I, who chanced to be in the capital, as the flag of Braganza flying from the castle roof had already informed me. It was in a sense his duty, Herr von Hüon said, to present to His Majesty a son of Luxemburg's nobility who was passing through and who, as he put it, was in addition a young man of agreeable gifts. Moreover, the King's noble spirit—the spirit of an artist, for His Majesty liked to paint in oil, and the spirit of a savant too, for His Highness was a lover of oceanography, that is, the study of the sea and the creatures that live in it—was depressed by political cares which had begun immediately after his coronation six years before, through the conflict of Portuguese and British interests in Central Africa. At that time his conciliatory attitude had incensed public opinion against him and he had actually been grateful for the British ultimatum that made it possible for his government to give in, with a formal protest. Nevertheless, there had been awkward disturbances in the larger cities, and in Lisbon a republican uprising had had to be suppressed. But now it was the sinister deficit in the Portuguese railroads, which four years before had precipitated a serious financial crisis and had led to a declaration of state bankruptcy—that is, to a decree reducing government obligations by two thirds! That had given great impetus to the republican party and had facilitated subversion by the radical elements in the country. His Majesty had not even been spared the repeated and disturbing revelation that conspiracies to assassinate him had been discovered only just in time by the police. In the round of his daily routine audiences my presentation might perhaps have a diverting and refreshing effect upon this great gentleman. If the course of the conversation possibly allowed of it, would I please introduce the subject of Minime, to which poor Prince Joan Ferdinand had reacted so heartily?

You will understand, dear parents, that with my convinced and happy royalist inclinations and my enthusiastic desire (of which perhaps you have not been fully aware) to bow before legitimate royalty, this proposal by the ambassador held a strong attraction for me. What stood in the way of my acceptance was the sad fact that it would take some days, four or five, to arrange the audience and by then the time for my embarkation on the *Cap Arcona* would have passed. What was I to do? My desire to stand before the King, combined with the advice of my learned mentor Kuckuck not to devote too short a time to a city like Lisbon, led to the decision to change my plans at the last minute and take a later ship. A visit to the travel bureau informed me that the next ship of the same line, the *Amphitrite*, which was to leave Lisbon in two weeks, was already heavily booked and would not, in any case, afford me suitable accommodations. The most sensible thing, the clerk said, would be to await the return of the *Cap Arcona* in about six or seven weeks, counting from the 15th of this month, and to re-engage my cabin for the next trip, thus postponing my voyage until the end of September or perhaps the beginning of October.

You know me, dear parents, a man of quick resolves. I agreed to the clerk's proposal, gave the necessary orders, and, I hardly need add, informed your friends, the Meyer-Novaros, of the postponement of my trip, begging them in a courteously worded cable not to expect me until October. In this way, as you see, the period of my stay in this city has been prolonged almost beyond my own wishes. No matter! My lodgings here can without exaggeration be called tolerable, and I shall not lack edifying discourse until the moment I go aboard. So may I count your acquiescence as assured?

Without that, needless to say, my essential happiness would be destroyed. But I believe you will grant it all the more readily when I inform you of the altogether happy, indeed inspiring, course of my audience with His Majesty the King, which has since taken place. Herr von Hüon informed me that it had been graciously granted and came in his carriage to fetch me from my hotel to the royal castle in good time before the specified morning hour. Thanks to his being accredited and to the fact that he was wearing court uniform, we passed the inner and outer guards without formalities and with evidences of respect. We mounted the outer staircase, which is flanked at the bottom by two caryatids in overstrained poses, and came to a suite of reception rooms decorated with busts of former kings, portraits, and crystal chandeliers, and furnished mostly in red silk with period furniture. One makes slow progress from one room to the next. In the second, one of the chamberlain's functionaries desired us to be seated for a while. Aside from the magnificence of the scene, it is not unlike the waiting-room of any popular doctor, who gets further and further behind in his appointments and whose patients have to wait long past the hour of their appointment. The rooms were crowded with all sorts of dignitaries, local and foreign, in uniform and in formal dress; they stood in groups, chatting in low voices, or sat in boredom on the sofas. There were many plumes, epaulets, and decorations. In each new room we entered, the ambassador exchanged cordial greetings with this or that diplomat of his acquaintance and introduced me, so that through this repeated emphasis upon my station in life—in which I rejoice—the period of waiting passed very rapidly, though it could not have been less than forty minutes.

Finally, an aide-de-camp, wearing a sash and holding a list of names in his hand, asked us to take our places in front of the door leading to the royal study, which was flanked by two lackeys in powdered perukes. Out came an aged gentleman in the uniform of a General of the Guards, who, no doubt, had been paying a visit of thanks for some royal favour. The adjutant entered to announce us. Then the two lackeys opened the gold-panelled leaves of the door.

Although the King is only just over thirty, his hair is already quite thin and he is rather corpulent. He received us standing by his desk, dressed in an olive-green uniform with red facings and wearing on his breast a single star in the middle of which an eagle holds in his talons a sceptre and the imperial orb. His face was flushed from many interviews. His brows are coal-black; his moustache, however, which is bushy but waxed and turned up at the ends, is beginning to turn grey. He acknowledged our deep bows with a practised and gracious wave of the hand and then greeted Herr von Hüon with a wink in which he managed to convey a great deal of flattering intimacy.

"My dear ambassador, it is a real pleasure as always. You're in the city, too? . . . I know, I know. . . . *Ce nouveau traité de commerce. . . . Mais ça s'arrangera sans aucune difficulté, grâce à votre habileté bien connue. . . .* And the health of the enchanting Madame de Hüon . . . Is excellent. How delighted I am! How truly delighted I am! And so, then —who is this Adonis you bring to see me today?"

Dear parents, you must understand this question as a joke, a courtesy unjustified by fact. A tail-coat, to be sure, is advantageous to my figure, for which I have Papa to thank. At the same time, you know as well as I that with my cheeks like pippins and my little slit eyes, which I never see in the mirror without distaste, there is nothing mythological about me. And so I met this royal jest with an expression of merry resignation; and as though he were hastening to erase it from memory, His Majesty went on most graciously, holding my hand in his:

"My dear marquis, welcome to Lisbon! I don't need to tell you that your name is well known to me and that it gives me pleasure to greet a noble young scion from a country that maintains such cordial and friendly relations with Portugal, thanks by no means least to your companion here. Tell me—" and he reflected for an instant what I should tell him "—what brings you here?"

I will not sing my own praises, precious parents, for the engaging dexterity, courtly in the best sense, both serious and easy, with which I entered into conversation with the monarch. I will simply say for your reassurance and satisfaction, that I was not awkward and did not fall on my face. I informed His Majesty of the gift, which I owe to your magnanimity, of a year's educational travel around the world, a trip that had uprooted me from Paris, my place of residence, and brought me, on its first stage, to this incomparable city.

"Ah, so Lisbon pleases you, then?"

"*Sire, énormement! Je suis tout à fait transporté par la beauté de votre capitale, qui est vraiment digne d'être la résidence d'un grand souverain comme Votre Majesté.* I had the intention of spending only a few days here, but I realized the absurdity of this arrangement and completely changed my plans in order to devote at least a few weeks to a visit that one would like never to have to terminate. What a city, Sire! What avenues, what parks, what promenades and views! Because of personal connections I became acquainted first of all with Professor Kuckuck's Museum of Natural History—a magnificent institution, Your Majesty, not least interesting to me because of its oceanographic aspect, because so many of its exhibits instructively demonstrate that all forms of life emerged from the waters of the sea. But, then, the marvel of the botanical gardens, Sire, the Avenida-Park, the Campo Grande, the Passeio da Estrella with its incomparable view over city and river . . . Is it any wonder that, confronted by all these ideal vistas of a land blessed by Heaven and admirably cultivated by man's hand, tears should come to an eye which is a little—my God, how little!—an artist's eye? In short, I admit that I—very differently from Your Majesty, whose genius in the field is well known—have interested myself a little in Paris in the graphic arts, in drawing and painting, as an eager but, alas, ungifted pupil of Professor Estompard of the Académie des Beauz Arts. But that is hardly worth mentioning. What must be said is this: in Your Majesty one venerates the ruler of one of the most beautiful lands on earth, probably the most beautiful of all. Where else in the world is there a panorama to compare with the view over Estremadura offered the observer from the lofty royal palaces at Sintra, vaunting its wheat fields, vineyards, and orchards? . . ."

Let me remark parenthetically, dear parents, that I had not yet visited the castles of Sintra or the Monastery of Belem, whose delicacy of construction I went on to discuss. I have been prevented from paying those visits as yet because I devote a good deal of my time to tennis at a club for socially eligible young people, to which the Kuckucks introduced me. No matter! To the King I spoke in praise of impressions I had not yet received, and His Majesty was moved to remark that he appreciated my powers of observation.

This encouraged me to launch with all the fluency I possess, or with the fluency that this extraordinary situation inspired in me, on a speech in praise of the country and people of Portugal. One did not visit a nation, I said, on account of the country alone, but rather—and perhaps first of all—on account of the people, out of a love for the new, if I might so express myself, a love for human types never met before, a desire to look into alien eyes and alien faces. . . . I realized that I was expressing myself badly, but what I meant was a desire to rejoice in unfamiliar customs and attributes. Portugal—*à la bonne heure!* But the Portuguese, His Majesty's subjects, they were exactly what had first captivated my entire attention. This ancient Celtic-Iberian race, to which in historical times admixtures of blood from various sources, Phœnician, Carthaginian, Roman, and Arabic, had been added—what a charming, captivating human type it had little by little brought forth—its demure grace now and again ennobled by a racial pride of an imperious, indeed terrifying kind. "How warmly is Your Majesty to be congratulated on being the ruler of so fascinating a people!"

"Why, yes, why, yes, very pretty, very polite," Dom Carlos said. "Thank you, dear marquis, for the kindly view you take of the country and people of Portugal." And I had decided that he wished to end the audience with these words when he added, quite to the contrary: "But shan't we sit down? *Cher ambassadeur*, let's sit down for a while."

Unquestionably he had originally intended to conduct the audience standing and, as it simply concerned my presentation, to conclude it in a few minutes. If now it was extended and became more intimate, you may attribute that—I say this more to give you pleasure than to feed my own vanity—to the fluency of my speech, which perhaps entertained him, and the agreeableness of my general appearance.

The King, the ambassador, and I sat in leather armchairs in front of a marble fireplace with a screen before it. On the mantel there stood a pendulum clock, candelabra, and Oriental vases. We were in a spacious, handsomely furnished study, with two glass-front bookcases and a Persian rug of gigantic size. Two pictures in heavy gold frames hung on either side of the fireplace, one a mountain landscape, the other a painting of flowery fields. Herr von Hüon directed my attention to the paintings with his eyes, while gesturing toward the King, who was bringing over a silver cigarette box from a carved smoking-table. I understood.

"Will Your Majesty," I said, "most graciously forgive me if I divert my attention momentarily from your person to these masterpieces that irresistibly draw my eyes? May I examine them more closely? Oh, that is painting! That is genius! I can't quite make out the signature, but both of them must be by the first artist of your country."

"The first?" the King asked, smiling. "That depends. The pictures are by me. That on the left is a view from the Serra da Estrélla, where I have a hunting-lodge, the one on the right is an attempt to reproduce the mood of our marshy lowlands, where I often shoot snipe. You see I have tried to give some idea of the charm of the rock roses that in many places bedeck the plains."

"One feels as though one could smell their perfume," I said. "Good God, before such accomplishment, dilettantism must blush."

"Dilettantism is just what it is considered," Dom Carlos replied, shrugging his shoulders, while I, as though by a great effort, tore myself away from his works and resumed my chair. "People think a king capable of nothing but dilettantism. They at once remember Nero and his *qualis artifex* ambitions."

"Miserable creatures," I replied, "who cannot free themselves from such a prejudice! They should rejoice at a stroke of fortune that unites the highest with the highest, the grace of exalted birth with the gifts of the Muses."

His Majesty heard this with visible pleasure. He sat comfortably reclining in his chair, while the ambassador and I properly sat bolt upright in ours. The King remarked: "I take great pleasure, dear marquis, in your responsiveness, in the unconstrained enjoyment with which you observe things, people, the world, and its works, the engaging innocence with which you do this and for which you are to be envied. It is perhaps only at the social level which you occupy that this is possible. It is in the depths of society and at its highest pinnacle that one meets the ugliness and bitterness of life. Common men experience it—and the ruler of a state, who breathes the miasmas of politics."

"Your Majesty's observation," I replied, "is full of insight. Only I humbly beg you not to think that my own powers of observation are confined to a mindless enjoyment of surfaces without any attempt to penetrate to what is less agreeable inside. I offered Your Majesty my congratulations on the truly enviable lot of being the ruler of so glorious a country as Portugal. But I am not blind to certain shadows that threaten to dim your happiness and I know about the drops of gall and wormwood that malice has poured into the golden cup of your life. It is not unknown to me that here, too, even here—must I say, especially here?—certain elements are not wanting, elements that call themselves radical, no doubt because, like rats, they gnaw at the roots of society—horrible elements, if I may give moderate expression to my feelings of abhorrence, elements that welcome every embarrassment, every political or financial difficulty of the state, in order to make capital of them through their machinations. They call themselves men of the people, though their only connection with the people consists in perverting their sound instinct and robbing them, to their own sorrow, of their natural belief in the necessity of a clearly defined social hierarchy. And how? By dinning into them the wholly unnatural notion of equality, which runs counter to the people's interests just because it is unnatural, and by attempting to mislead them through vulgar oratory into a belief in the necessity and desirability—leaving out the possibility—of abolishing the distinctions of birth and blood, the distinctions between rich and poor, nobleman and commoner, distinctions in whose defence nature and beauty perpetually join hands. By his very existence the beggar, huddled in rags, makes as great a contribution to the colourful picture of the world as the proud gentleman who drops alms in his humbly outstretched hand, carefully avoiding, of course, any contact with it. And, Your Majesty, the beggar knows it; he is aware of the special dignity that the order of the world has allotted to him, and in the depths of his heart he does not wish things otherwise. It takes the instigation to rebellion by men of ill will to make him discontented with his picturesque role and to put into his head the contumacious notion that men must be equal. They are not equal, and they are born realizing that. Man comes into the world with an aristocratic point of view. That, young though I am, has been my experience. Whoever it may be—a minister, a member of the ecclesiastical hierarchy, or that other hierarchy, the Army, some honest noncommissioned officer in his barracks—he exhibits an infallible eye and instinct to distinguish the common substance from the fine, to recognize the clay of which one is made. . . . Fine friends of the people indeed, those who take away from the ill-born and lowly their joy in what is above them, in wealth, in the noble manners and customs of the upper strata of society, and who change that joy into envy, greed, and rebellion! They rob the masses of religion, which keeps them within pious and happy bounds, and, in addition, pretend to them that everything can be accomplished by changing the form of the state; the monarchy must fall, and with the establishment of a republic, human nature will be transformed and happiness and equality will appear automatically. . . . But it is time for me to beg Your Majesty not to take amiss this outpouring that I have allowed myself."

The King nodded to the ambassador with raised eyebrows, which greatly pleased the latter.

"Dear marquis," His Majesty then said, "you give expression to ideas that deserve only praise—ideas, moreover, that are not only appropriate to your origin but, allow me to say, do you personally and individually much credit. Yes, yes, I mean what I say. *A propos,* you mentioned the inflammatory rhetoric of the demagogues, their dangerous glibness. It is an unhappy fact that one encounters skill in speech principally among such people, lawyers, ambitious politicians, apostles of liberalism, and enemies of the established order. That order seldom finds defenders of intelligence and wit. It is a very comforting exception to hear the right side well and winningly presented for once."

"I cannot say," I replied, "how very much honour and happiness the word 'comforting' on Your Majesty's lips has given me. However ridiculous it may seem for a simple young nobleman to presume to think he could comfort a King, I confess that just this was my intention. And what prompted me to this attempt? Sympathy, Your Majesty. It is sympathy tinged with awe; if that is audacious, I should like to maintain that there is hardly any profounder combination of emotions than that of awe and sympathy. What I, in my youth, know about Your Majesty's troubles and about the enmity to which the principle you represent and even your exalted person are exposed, touches me deeply and I cannot refrain from wishing you every distraction possible from these troublous concerns and as much happy diversion as can be contrived. No doubt that is what Your Majesty looks for and finds in some measure in painting. Besides, I am happy to learn that you derive enjoyment from hunting."

"You are right," he said. "I am happiest, I admit, when I am far from the capital and its political intrigues, under the open sky in field or on mountain, stalking or standing in a blind with a few tried and true friends. You are a huntsman, marquis?"

"I cannot say that I am, Your Majesty. Beyond question the chase is the most knightly form of diversion, but, on the whole, I am no lover of firearms and participate only infrequently, when invited. The part that gives me the greatest joy is observing the dogs in action. A fine leash of pointers or setters, every muscle tense with excitement, noses to the ground, tails waving—the proud parade step and high-held head with which one of them brings back a bird or rabbit—these are things I delight in watching. I confess, in short, that I am a dog-lover and have associated since childhood with these ancient friends of man. The affection in a dog's eye, his open-mouthed laughter when you joke with him—after all, he's the only animal that can laugh—his awkward tenderness, the elegance of his play, the springy beauty of his gait if he's a thoroughbred—all this warms my heart. In most cases there is hardly any sign left of his descent from wolf and jackal. As little sign, usually, as of the horse's descent from tapir and rhinoceros. Even the bog hounds of the lake-dweller period had ceased to show any similarity. And who would think of a wolf when looking at a spaniel, a dachshund, a poodle, a Scotty, which seems to walk on its belly, or a kindly Saint Bernard? And what variety there is in the species! No other has so much. A pig is a pig, an ox an ox. But would one ever believe that a Great Dane, big as a calf, is the same animal as a griffon? At the same time," I chattered on, relaxing my posture now and leaning back in the chair—and the ambassador followed suit, "at the same time, one has the impression that these creatures are not aware of their proportions, whether gigantic or tiny, and do not take them into account in their relations with one another. Love—Your Majesty, I hope, will forgive me for touching on this subject—obliterates all sense of what is fitting and not fitting. At home in the castle we have a Russian wolfhound called Fripon, a great gentleman, reserved in manner and of a sleepy arrogance of demeanour, related, no doubt, to the trivial size of his brain. On the other hand, there is Minime, my Mama's Maltese lapdog, a little bundle of white silk hardly larger than my fist. One would think that Fripon would not be blind to the fact that in one particular relationship this trembling little princess would be no proper partner for him. However, at the times when her femininity asserts itself, although he is kept far away from her, his teeth commence to chatter from unrealizable love so that he can be heard rooms away."

The King waxed merry over the chattering teeth.

"Oh, Your Majesty," I hastened on, "I must tell you that this precious little creature Minime has a constitution that is very ill-suited to her role as lapdog."

And then, dear Mama, I re-enacted, much better and with more ludicrous detail, my performance of the other evening, the portrayal of the, alas, recurrent tragedy in your lap, the cries of alarm, the ringing of bells; I imitated Adelaide's fluttering entrance, her unexampled affectation only augmented by the crisis, her bearing away of the squirming and disgraced favourite, and the doddering attempts of Radicule to come to your assistance with fire shovel and ash bucket. My success was all that had been hoped for, the King held his sides with laughter—and it is really a profound joy to see a crowned head, oppressed by worry over a subversive party in his country, surrender himself to such self-forgetful merriment. I do not know what those waiting in the anteroom may have made of this audience, but it is certain that His Majesty enjoyed to a quite remarkable degree the innocent diversion I offered him. Finally, however, the latter remembered that my name and that of the ambassador (who showed visible signs of pride at having so well served His Majesty's interests by introducing me) were not by any means the last on the list, and gave the signal that the audience was over by rising, meanwhile mopping his eyes. As we were making our deep farewell bows I heard, though apparently I was not intended to, the repeated "*Charmant, charmant!*" with which the monarch expressed his appreciation to Herr von Hüon. And now, dear parents, here is something that will, I hope, make my small sin against piety and my arbitrary prolongation of my stay appear in a more favourable light. Two days later I received from the Court Chamberlain's office a little package that contained the insignia of the Portuguese Order of the Red Lion, second class, which His Majesty had been graciously pleased to bestow on me. This is worn around the neck on a crimson ribbon, and henceforth on formal occasions I shall not be forced to appear in unadorned evening clothes as I did at the ambassador's.

I know very well that one's true worth is not worn in enamel on one's shirt front, but deeper in the breast. But people—you have known them longer and better than I—people like to see the outward show, the symbol, the decoration worn in full view. I do not criticize them for this, I am full of kindly understanding of their needs. And it is my sympathy and love for my fellow men that make me rejoice at being able to gratify their childish love of show in the future by wearing the Red Lion, second class.

Nothing further for today, dear parents. Only a fool gives more than he has. Soon there will be more reports of my experiences and adventures in the world, all of which I shall owe to your generosity. And if I were to receive a letter from you at the above address, assuring me of your good health, that would be the most precious possible addition to the well-being of

Your affectionate and truly obedient son,

Loulou

This letter covered a great number of sheets of the Savoy Palace Hotel's best notepaper. It was composed partly in French and partly in German, in the carefully imitated stiff backhand and signed with the oval-encircled signature. Off it went to my parents in Castle Monrefuge in Luxemburg. I had taken pains with it, as my correspondence with this lady and gentleman who were so close to me was a matter of the deepest importance to me, and I awaited their answer with a tender curiosity, expecting it to come from the marquise. I had devoted several days to this little composition, which, by the way, aside from certain evasions at the start, was an altogether accurate report of my activities, even in the matter of Herr von Hüon's offering to present me to the King, thereby anticipating my request. The care I devoted to this report is all the more laudable because I had to steal time for it from my association with the Kuckuck family, which I had the greatest difficulty in keeping within the bounds of discretion. The occasion—who would have thought it?—was principally tennis, a sport in which I was as completely unskilled as in every other and which I played with Zouzou and her friends at the club.

My agreement to appear there was no small act of daring on my part. Betimes on the morning of the third day, however, I put in an appearance as agreed, wearing faultless sports attire—white flannels, snow-white shirt open at the neck, over which I wore a blue blazer, and those noiseless rubber-soled canvas shoes which give one a dancing movement. The well-kept double court not far from Zouzou's house was reserved for her and her friends by the day or hour. My mood was very much the same as when I had presented myself before the army medical commission: an adventurous though troubled determination filled my heart. Determination is all. Reassured by my convincing garb and winged shoes, I promised myself to play my part brilliantly in this game that I had watched and absorbed but had in fact never taken part in.

I arrived too early and found myself all alone at the scene. There was a small building where players could leave their coats and store their equipment. There I deposited my blazer and selected a racket and some of the lovely chalk-white balls. I began to practise playfully but self-confidently with these pretty objects. I bounced the ball on the surface of the racket, batted it to the ground, and scooped it up from the ground with the well-known light, shovelling motion. To limber up my arm and experiment with the force necessary in drives, I sent ball after ball over the net with forehand or backhand strokes—over the net when I could, that is, for most of the balls went into the net or far outside the opposite court; indeed, when I grew too enthusiastic they went straight over the backstop.

I was thus engaged in a singles match against no one, enjoying the feel of the handsome racket, when Zouzou Kuckuck came up with two other young people, also dressed in white, a boy and a girl who turned out not to be brother and sister, but cousins. If his name was not Costa, it was Cunha, and if her name was not Lopes, it was Camões—I no longer exactly recall. "Look at that, the marquis is practising solo. He looks very promising," Zouzou said derisively and introduced me to the charming young pair, whose charm, however, was far less than her own. After this, various other young folk arrived, members of the club, with names like Saldacha, Vicente, de Menezes, Ferreira, and so forth. There were, all told, probably a dozen players, including myself, most of whom immediately sat down on the benches outside the enclosure to look on. Four of us went onto the court, Zouzou and I on opposite sides of the net. A gangling youngster climbed up onto the high umpire's seat to keep track of the points and faults, the games and sets.

Zouzou took up a position close to the net, while I resigned that place to my partner, a girl with a yellowish complexion and green eyes, and kept to the back of the court in concentrated alertness. Zouzou's partner, the small cousin, served first, hard. Springing toward the ball, I managed, with beginner's luck, to return it with great speed and precision, so that Zouzou remarked: "Well, now!" After that I was guilty of a lot of nonsense—energetic leaping back and forth to conceal my total lack of skill—and this benefited our opponents; in a spirit of sheer bravado I also made sport of the game, seeming to take nothing seriously, and played jokes and tricks with the bouncing ball which aroused as much merriment in the onlookers as my hopeless errors. All this did not prevent my occasionally performing feats of pure genius which contrasted bafflingly with my obvious lack of skill and made the latter look like simple carelessness or an attempt to conceal my true abilities. Now and then I astonished the gallery by serves of uncanny speed, by returning a volley, by repeated impossible gets—all of which I owed to the physical inspiration of Zouzou's presence. I can still see myself receiving a deep forehand drive, one leg extended, the other knee bent, which must have made a very handsome picture, for it earned me applause from the gallery; I see myself leaping incredibly high, to the accompaniment of *bravo*'s and hand-clapping, to smash back a ball that had gone way over my partner's head—and there were other wild and inspired triumphs as well.

Zouzou played with skill and calm precision. She neither laughed at my blunders—as, for example, when I missed the ball I had tossed into the air when serving—nor at my uncalled-for pranks; on the other hand, she showed no reaction to my unexpected virtuoso feats and the applause they earned me. These occurred very infrequently and, despite my partner's solid play, Zouzou's side had won four games after twenty minutes and after another ten had taken the set. We left the court to other players and sat down on a bench to cool off.

"The marquis's game is amusing," said my yellow-and-green partner for whom I had spoiled so much.

"*Un peu fantastique, pourtant,*" replied Zouzou, who felt responsible for me because she had introduced me to the club. At the same time, I ventured to think that the fantastic nature of my play had done nothing to hurt me in her eyes. I apologized for myself on the ground of beginning over again and expressed the hope that I would quickly regain my lost skill and would then be worthy of such partners and opponents. After some chatter, while we watched the players and applauded their good strokes, a gentleman named Fidelio came over and addressed the two cousins in Portuguese. Presently he took them off for a conference of some kind. Hardly was I alone with Zouzou when she turned on me.

"Well, and what about the drawings, marquis? Where are they? You know that I wish to see them and take possession of them."

"But, Zouzou," I replied, "I couldn't possibly have brought them here. Where would I have left them and how could I have shown them to you? Every instant we would have run the risk of being caught at it."

"What a way to speak—'being caught at it'!"

"Well, yes, these imaginative products of my dreams of you are not for the eyes of a third person—leaving aside the question of your seeing them yourself. By God, I wish that circumstances here and at your house and everywhere else did not make it so hard to share secrets with you."

"Secrets! Please watch what you say!"

"But you insist upon secrets, which, like everything else, are very hard indeed to arrange."

"I simply said it was a challenge to your adroitness to find an opportunity of handing over those drawings. You are certainly not lacking in adroitness. You were adroit during the game—fantastic, as I said a moment ago by way of excuse, and often so blundering that one could easily believe you had never played tennis at all. But adroit you certainly were."

"How happy I am, Zouzou, to hear you say that!"

"How do you happen to be calling me Zouzou?"

"Everyone calls you that, and I love the name very much. I pricked up my ears the first time I heard it, and I have clasped it to my heart."

"How can one clasp a name to his heart!"

"The name is inseparable from the person who bears it. That's why it makes me so happy, Zouzou, to hear from your lips—how I love to talk about your lips!—a kindly, half-laudatory comment on my poor playing. Believe me, if in its bungling fashion it was in any way passable, that was because I was completely imbued with the consciousness of acting under your dear, bewitching black eyes."

"Very pretty. What you are practising now, marquis, is called, I believe, paying court to a girl. In this you show less originality than in your fantastic tennis. Most of the young people regard tennis as more or less of a pretext for this disgusting occupation."

"Disgusting, Zouzou? Why? A short time ago you called love a disreputable theme and said *pfui* to it."

"I say it again. You young men are all nasty, dirty-minded boys, interested in unseemly behaviour."

"Oh, if you are going to get up and go away, you deprive me of any chance of defending love."

"That's just what I intend to do. We have already sat here alone too long. In the first place, it's not proper, and in the second—for when *I* say 'in the first place' I am not accustomed to leave out the second—in the second place, you have very little taste for individual persons and wax much more enthusiastic about combinations."

She is jealous of her mother, I said to myself, not without pleasure, as she threw me an "*Au revoir*" and withdrew. May the queenly Iberian, in turn, be jealous of her daughter! That would dovetail with the jealousy my own devotion to one often provokes in my devotion to the other.

We made our way from the court to the Villa Kuckuck with the young people who had arrived with Zouzou, the two cousins, whose home lay in that direction. At luncheon, which was to have been a farewell meal but had already forfeited that name, there were only four of us, as Hurtado could not attend. It was spiced by Zouzou's scorn and derision for my tennis, in which Dona Maria Pia evinced a certain smiling interest, especially since her daughter prevailed upon herself to mention my occasional glorious feats. I say 'prevailed upon herself' because she spoke with brows knit and teeth clenched as though profoundly annoyed.

I pointed this out, and she replied: "Annoyed? Of course. You don't play well enough for that. It was unnatural."

"Say, rather, it was supernatural!" the professor laughed. "All in all, it seems to me that it amounts to this: the marquis was gallant enough to throw the victory your way."

"Dear Papa," she replied tartly, "you know so little about sport that you believe gallantry plays a part in it, and you provide a very kind explanation for the absurd behaviour of your travelling-companion."

"Papa is always kind," the *senhora* said, closing the subject.

We did not go for a walk after lunch that day, but I was to enjoy many more luncheons at the Kuckucks' home during the coming weeks, followed by excursions to places outside the city. More about that directly. Here I simply wish to mention the pleasure I derived from a letter from my dear mother which was handed me by the concierge upon my return from such an expedition about two weeks after I had dispatched my letter to her. It was written in German and read as follows:

VICTORIA MARQUISE DE VENOSTA *née* DE PLETTENBERG
CASTLE MONREFUGE, 3 SEPTEMBER, 1895

My dear Loulou:

Your letter of the 25th duly reached us, and both Papa and I thank you for its conscientious and undeniably interesting fulness of detail. Your handwriting, my good Loulou, always left much to be desired and is now as ever not unmannered, but your style has decidedly improved in smoothness and polish, a circumstance I attribute, in part, to the atmosphere of Paris, so friendly to word and wit, which you have breathed so long and which is making itself increasingly evident. Moreover, it is probably true that a sense for good and attractive form which has always been yours, since we implanted it in you, is an attribute of the whole man and is not limited to his corporeal deportment, but extends to all the personal manifestations of his life and therefore to the manner of his written and oral expression as well.

Besides, I assume that you did not really speak to His Majesty, King Carlos, in the oratorical and elegant fashion that you report in your letter. That is certainly a letter-writer's fiction. Nevertheless, you have given us pleasure by it, and most of all by the point of view you took the opportunity to express, which represents the sentiments of your father and myself just as accurately as those of the great man. We both completely share your conviction in the God-appointed necessity of distinctions between rich and poor, noble and commoner, on earth, and of the necessity of the beggar caste. Where would the opportunity be for Christian charity and good works if poverty and misery did not exist?

This by way of introduction. I will not conceal from you, and you expected nothing else, that your rather high-handed action in so considerably postponing your journey to Argentina at first troubled us a little. But we have accepted it and are reconciled, for the reasons you advance are sensible and, as you say with justice, the results of your decision have justified it. Naturally, I am thinking first of all of the acquisition of the Order of the Red Lion, which you owe to the grace of the King and to your own engaging behaviour and on which Papa and I send you our hearty congratulations. That is no inconsiderable decoration and is seldom attained by one so young; although it is of the second class, it is by no means to be considered second-class. It does the whole family honour.

This pleasant incident is mentioned, too, in a letter from Frau Irmingard von Hüon, which I received at almost the same time as yours, and in which, on her husband's report, she tells me about your social successes. She wished to warm a mother's heart and was completely successful in that purpose. Nevertheless, without wishing to offend you, I must say that her description, or that of the ambassador, was read here with some astonishment. Of course you have always been a prankster, but that you should possess such a talent for parody and such gifts of burlesque that you could set a whole company, including a prince of the blood, to laughing and were even able to move a care-laden monarch to almost unmajestic merriment—this we would never have believed of you. Well and good, Frau von Hüon's letter confirms your own report of the matter, and it must also be admitted here that the result justifies the means. You are to be forgiven, my child, for basing your representation on details of our family life which might better have been kept among us. As I write, Minime lies in my lap and would certainly endorse our attitude if the matter could be brought to her tiny attention. You have allowed yourself exaggeration and grotesque licence in your performance, and, in particular, you have exposed your mother in a ridiculous light through your description of her lying there in her chair, pathetically dirtied and half unconscious while old Radicule has to come to her assistance with shovel and ash bucket. I know nothing of any ash bucket—it is the product of your zeal to be entertaining. But as this has borne such pleasant fruits in the end, it doesn't greatly matter that you have rather arbitrarily detracted somewhat from my personal dignity.

No doubt it was for a mother's heart, too, that Frau von Hüon assured us that on all sides you are considered as pretty as a picture, a youthful beauty indeed. This announcement has once more caused us a certain degree of bewilderment. You are, to speak frankly, a nice boy, and unquestionably you underestimate yourself when you talk with engaging self-ridicule of your cheeks like pippins and your slit eyes. That is certainly unjust. But you could never be considered really beautiful or pretty, not that we know of, and compliments of this sort which are paid to me upset me a little, even though as a woman I am well aware that the desire to please can improve the exterior from within, can glorify it and, in short, prove a means *pour corriger la nature.*

But why am I talking about your exterior? Let people call it pretty or passable! The thing of importance is the safety of your soul, your social salvation, for which we at one time had to tremble. And it is this in your letter, as in your telegram, that has brought us a real lightening of the heart when we learned that in this trip we had hit upon the right means to free your soul from the spell of degrading wishes and projects, to cause you to see them in the right light—that is, as impossible and destructive—and to bid them farewell together with the person who, to our deep-felt concern, inspired them in you!

Wholesome circumstances, according to your letter, have contributed to this result. I cannot help regarding as a providential encounter your meeting with that professor and museum-director whose name, to be sure, sounds so funny, and your visits to his house as useful and conducive to your restoration. Distraction is good; but all the better when it is combined with a gain in education and brilliant information such as is so clearly evident in your letter in the simile of the sea lily (a plant unknown to me) and in your reference to the natural history of the dog and the horse. Such things are an adornment in any social conversation and, if they are woven in without pretension and with good taste, they will not fail to distinguish a young man of attainments from those who have no vocabulary beyond that of sports. Which does not mean that we were not glad to hear, in view of your health, that you have once more taken up the long-neglected game of lawn tennis.

As for your association with the ladies of that household, the mother and daughter, whose description you enliven with a few ironic lights, if this appeals less to you than your conversations with the learned head of the house and his associate, I hardly need warn you—however, I am now doing so—not to allow them to perceive your lower estimation of them and always to treat them with the chivalry that a cavalier owes in all circumstances to the opposite sex.

And now all good wishes, dear Loulou! When you embark in about four weeks, after the return of the *Cap Arcona*, our prayers will rise to Heaven for a smooth crossing that will not unsettle your stomach for so much as a single day. The postponement of your trip means you will arrive in the Argentinian spring and will probably have a taste of summer as well in that region where the seasons are the reverse of ours. You will provide yourself, I trust, with a suitable wardrobe. Light flannel is to be recommended because it is the best protection against chills, which, as is not generally known, are easier to catch in hot weather than in cold. Should the funds at your disposal prove inadequate, be assured that I am the woman to procure a reasonable supplement from your father.

Our kindest greetings to your hosts, Herr and Frau Consul Meyer.

Blessings,

Maman

CHAPTER X

When I recall the extraordinary and elegant equipages that later on were mine for a time—the gleaming victorias, phaetons, and silk-upholstered coupés—I am touched by the childish pleasure I derived, during those weeks in Lisbon, from a barely decent rented carriage. By arrangement with a local livery stable, it was kept constantly at my disposal, so that the concierge of the Savoy Palace had only to telephone for it when occasion arose. Actually, it was nothing more than a four-seated droshky with a folding hood, which had probably served as a family carriage before being sold to the stable. The horses and harness were at least presentable, and for a small premium I arranged for the coachman to have an appropriate personal uniform—a hat with rosette, blue coat, and top boots.

It was a pleasure to enter this carriage in front of my hotel with a page holding the door for me and the coachman bending down slightly from the box, as I had taught him, his hand at the brim of his top hat. A conveyance of this sort was an absolute necessity not only for outings and in order to take one's place in the procession of carriages in the parks and along the avenues—which I did for entertainment—but also in order to arrive with a certain elegance at those houses to which I was invited as a result of my evening at the Embassy and, no doubt, also as a result of my audience with the King. Thus, Saldacha, the rich exporter of wines, and his extraordinarily corpulent wife invited me to a garden party at their magnificent estate outside the city; Lisbon society was gradually drifting back from the summer resorts, and many of its representatives were there. These I encountered again, less numerous and with some substitutions, at two dinners, one of which was given by the Greek businessman Prince Maurocordato and his classically beautiful but astonishingly forward wife, the other by Baron and Baroness Vos von Steenwyk at the Dutch Embassy. On both these occasions I was able to display my Order of the Red Lion and received congratulations on all sides. On the Avenida I was kept busy bowing, for my distinguished acquaintances were increasing in number; nevertheless, all these relationships remained on a superficial and formal footing—or, to be more precise, I kept them so out of indifference, as my true interests were concentrated on the small white house on the hillside and on the double image of mother and daughter.

I need hardly say that these came first rather than last in my list of reasons for securing the carriage. With it, I could invite them to drive to such places of historic interest as, for instance, those whose beauty I had, by way of anticipation, praised to the King; and nothing gave me greater pleasure than to sit, my back to the driver, facing those two: that august representative of her race and her enchanting child. Sometimes Dom Miguel would sit beside me, for he was occasionally free to accompany us, and he liked to serve as our instructor on visits to castle or monastery.

These weekly or biweekly drives and excursions were regularly preceded by tennis and a family luncheon at the Kuckucks'. On the court I sometimes played as Zouzou's partner, sometimes as her opponent, and sometimes with others. My game quickly became more uniform: those sudden spectacular feats came to an end, and with them my laughable exhibitions of ineptitude. I played a decent medium sort of game, though the presence of my beloved gave me the advantage of a sort of physical inspiration—if I may call it that—beyond the average. If only it had been less difficult for us to be alone! The dictates of southern convention were explicitly and disturbingly in our way. To call for Zouzou at her house and accompany her to the courts was not to be thought of; we met there. Nor was there any chance of taking her home alone: it was understood that others must always be present. A tête-à-tête in the house before or after lunch, in the drawing-room or anywhere else, was out of the question. Only when we were resting on a bench outside the wire enclosure of the tennis courts was there now and again an opportunity for private conversation. On these occasions she always began by mentioning the portrait sketches and demanding that I show them to her or, rather, that I hand them over to her. Without contesting her stubborn theory that she owned the drawings, I kept evading her demand on the plausible pretext that there was no safe opportunity of submitting them to her. In truth, I doubted whether I would ever risk showing her those daring sketches, and I clung to this doubt as I did to her unsatisfied curiosity—if that is the right word for it—because the unrevealed pictures constituted a secret bond between us which delighted me and which I wished to preserve.

To share a secret with her, to have an understanding of our own—whether she liked it or not—seemed to me to have a sweet significance. And so I made a point of telling her about my social adventures before I recounted them to her family at table—and I also made a point of going into them more thoroughly, more intimately, and with more comment so that later on I could look at her and see in her smile the memory of what we had previously discussed. An example of this was my meeting with the Princess Maurocordato, whose divinely noble features and figure made her conduct so unexpected—conduct that was by no means divine, but more like that of a soubrette. I had told Zouzou how the lady from Athens had cornered me in her salon, had kept tapping me with her fan, showing the tip of her tongue between her lips, winking, and making the most wanton advances—wholly unmindful of that dignity of deportment which, one might think, the consciousness of classical beauty would naturally inspire in a woman. Sitting on our bench, we discussed for some time this contradiction betwen appearance and conduct, and we came to the conclusion that either the princess was at odds with her classical appearance, found it boring, and showed her rebellion against it by her behaviour—or that it was a matter of sheer stupidity and lack of awareness of, and respect for, oneself such as, for instance, a poodle might show, emerging snowy-white from its bath only to find a mud puddle and roll in it.

All this I passed over in silence when at luncheon I described my Greek evening and the princess's perfect figure.

"—Which naturally made a profound impression on you," said Senhora Maria Pia, sitting very straight as always, leaning neither forward nor back, her jet necklace and earrings vibrating slightly.

I replied: "Impressed me, *senhora*? No. On my very first day in Lisbon I was vouchsafed impressions of female beauty which I confess have made me unresponsive to further ones." At this I kissed her hand, smiling at the same time at Zouzou. That is what I always did. It was dictated by the double image. When I paid the daughter a compliment, I looked at the mother, and vice versa. The starry-eyed man of the house, sitting at the head of the small table, observed this byplay with vague benevolence, a testimony to the stellar distances from which he gazed. The reverence I felt for him was not one jot diminished by the realization that in my courtship of the double image, consideration for him was wholly superfluous.

"Papa is always kind," Senhora Maria Pia had accurately declared. I believe that the head of the house would have listened with exactly the same benevolent inattention and absent-minded kindliness to the conversations I carried on with Zouzou at the tennis court or on some excursion when we lingered behind alone—and these were unconventional in the extreme. They were so thanks to her axiom, "Silence is unhealthy"; to her phenomenal, altogether unconventional forthrightness; and to the subject to which this uneuphemistic bluntness was directed: the theme of love. To this, as we know, she had said: "*Pfui!*" I had trouble enough on that account, for I did indeed love her and let her see it in various ways; she understood it, too, but in what a fashion! This enchanting girl's idea of love was extremely odd and comically distrustful. She appeared to see in it something like the secret behaviour of nasty small boys, professed to ascribe the vice called "love" entirely to the male sex and to consider that the female sex had nothing to do with it, felt not the slightest natural inclination toward it, and believed that flirtations were begun exclusively by young men for the purpose of enticing girls into unseemly behaviour.

I would hear her say: "There you go again paying court to me, Louis." (Yes, it is true, she had begun to call me Louis sometimes when we were alone, just as I called her Zouzou.) "Murmuring sweet nothings and looking at me imploringly—or shall I say 'importunately'? No, I shall say 'lovingly,' but that is the name for a lie. You look at me with those blue eyes of yours and you know very well that they and your blond hair contrast so very strangely with your dark skin that one can't tell what to make of you. And what do you want? What is the purpose of your melting words and melting glances? Something that is unspeakably laughable and absurd, both childish and repugnant. I say 'unspeakably,' but of course it is not at all unspeakable, and I shall put it into words. You want me to consent to our embracing, to agree that two creatures whom Nature has carefully and completely separated should embrace each other so that your mouth is pressed upon mine while our nostrils are crosswise and we breathe each other's breath. That's what you want, isn't it? A repulsive indecency and nothing else, but perverted into a pleasure by sensuality—that's the word for it, as I very well know; and the word means that swamp of impropriety into which all of you want to lure us so that we will go crazy and two civilized beings will behave like cannibals. That's the purpose of your flirtatiousness."

She stopped speaking and managed to sit quite calm after this outburst of forthrightness, without any quickening of her breath or indication of fatigue. Moreover, it did not seem like an outburst, but rather like simple conformity to the principle of calling things by their right names. I was silent, shocked, touched, and troubled.

"Zouzou," I said finally, and for a moment I held my hand above hers without touching it, and then completed the gesture in the air, moving my hand above her head and downward, as though to shield her. "Zouzou, you distress me dreadfully when you use such words—what shall I call them, crude, cruel, exaggeratedly true, and for that very reason only half true, in fact not true at all—when you use such words to tear away the delicate mist in which my admiration for the charms of your person has enwrapped my heart and senses. Don't make fun of 'enwrapped'! I purposely, deliberately, and intentionally said 'enwrapped' because I must use poetic words to defend the poetry of love against your harsh, distorted version. I beseech you, what a way to talk about love and its purpose! Love has no purpose, it neither wills nor thinks beyond itself, it is entirely itself and entirely inwoven in itself—don't scoff at 'inwoven.' I have already told you that I am intentionally using poetic words—and that simply means more seemly ones—in the name of love, for love is essentially seemly, and your harsh words far outdistance it in an area that remains alien to love, however familiar it may be with it. I ask you! What a way to talk of a kiss, the tenderest exchange in the world, silent and lovely as a flower! This unforeseen occurrence, happening quite by itself, the mutual discovery of two pairs of lips, beyond which emotion does not even dream of going, because it is in itself the incredibly blessed seal of union with another!"

I pledge my word that is how I spoke. I did so because Zouzou's habit of discrediting love actually seemed to me childish and I regarded poetry as less childish than this girl's crudity. Poetry, moreover, came easily to me in my foundationless existence. It was simple enough for me to say that love has no ulterior object and does not think beyond a kiss at most, because in my unreal state I could not permit myself to come to grips with reality and, for example, to woo Zouzou. At best I could set myself the goal of seducing her, but there were serious obstacles in the way: not circumstances alone, but also her fabulous forthrightness and her exaggeratedly literal notion of the laughable impropriety of love. Just listen to the retort with which she met my poetic sally.

"*Patatípatatá!*" she exclaimed. "Enwrapped and inwoven and the lovely flowery kiss! All sugar to catch flies, a way of talking us into small-boy nastiness! *Pfui*, the kiss—that tender exchange! It's the beginning, the proper beginning, *mais oui*, or rather, it is the whole thing, *toute la lyre*, and the very worst of it. And why? Because it is the skin that all of you have in mind when you say love, the bare skin of the body. The skin of the lips is tender, you're right there, so tender that the blood is right behind it, and that's the reason for this poetry about the mutual discovery of pairs of lips: they in their tenderness want to go everywhere, and what you have in mind, all of you, is to lie naked with us, skin against skin, and teach us the absurd satisfaction that one miserable creature finds in savouring with lips and hands the moist surface of another. All of you do this without any feeling of shame at the pathetic ludicrousness of your behaviour and without giving thought—for it would spoil your game—to a couplet I once read in a book of spiritual instruction:

> However fair and smooth the skin,
> Stench and corruption lie within."

"That's a nasty little verse, Zouzou," I interrupted with a sad, disapproving shake of my head, "nasty, however spiritual it pretends to be. I'll accept all your crudity, but that verse you've just recited cries to high heaven. And do you want to know why? Yes, yes, I am sure you do want to know. And I am prepared to tell you. Because this villainous little verse is designed to destroy belief in beauty and form, image and dream, belief in every phenomenon that, because it exists in words, is necessarily appearance and dream. But what would become of life and what would become of joy—without which there can be no life—if appearance and the surface world of the senses no longer counted for anything? I'll tell you something, charming Zouzou: your spiritual verse is more blasphemous than the most sinful lust of the flesh, for it is a spoil-sport, and to spoil the game of life is not only sinful, it is simply and entirely devilish. What do you say now? No, please, I'm not asking that to invite an interruption. I let you talk, however crudely, and now I am talking nobly, and am inspired to do so! If things went according to that altogether malicious verse, then the only thing really and not just apparently admirable would be, at most, the inanimate world, inorganic Being—I say at most, for when you think of it critically there is a question about its soundness, too. One may well ask whether an Alpine sunset or a waterfall is especially admirable, more so than an image or a dream, whether it is as true as it is beautiful—that is, true in itself without us, without our love and admiration. Now, some time ago by the mysterious process of spontaneous generation organic life emerged from lifeless, inorganic Being. That its inward processes and essence are not of the cleanest goes without saying. Indeed, a smart aleck might say that all Nature is nothing but mildew and corruption on the face of the earth, but that is simply the wisecrack of a smart aleck and never, to the end of time, will it succeed in killing love and joy—the joy in images. It was from a painter that I learned that. He painted the mildew with devotion, and was highly respected for it in the end. He used the human figure, too, as a model, as a model for a Greek god. Once in Paris, in the waiting-room of a dentist who made a small gold inlay for me, I saw a picture book entitled *La Beauté humaine*. It was filled with pictures of the finest reproductions of the human figure painters and sculptors had made throughout the ages with devotion and with joy. And why did it contain so many of these glorious pictures? Because at all times the earth has been full of fellows who paid not the slightest heed to your spiritual rhyme, but saw truth in form and appearance and surface, and made themselves their priests and very often won dignity and fame by doing so."

I swear that's how I spoke, for I was inspired. And not just once did I speak thus, but repeatedly, whenever opportunity offered and I was alone with Zouzou. Sometimes it was on one of the benches beside the tennis courts, sometimes during a walk when four of us—including Senhor Hurtado, who would join us after luncheon—would stroll along the woody ways of the Campo Grande or between the banana plantings and tropical trees in the Largo do Príncipe Real. There had to be four of us so that I could walk alternately with the august half of the double image and then with her daughter. When I dropped back a little with Zouzou I could always find wise and noble words with which to combat her stupefying forthrightness and her childish notion that love was the unappetizing vice of small boys.

She clung stubbornly to this conception, though once or twice she betrayed by a silent, inquiring, sidewise glance fleetingly directed toward me that she had been struck by my eloquence and partly convinced—in short, that my zealous advocacy of joy and love had not completely missed its mark. There was one such moment, and I shall never forget it, when after many postponements we finally drove out in my carriage to the little village of Sintra. Under Dom Miguel's edifying guidance we had inspected the old castle in the village and then the citadels on the rocky heights with their far prospects. Finally we drove on to the famous monastery of Belem (that is, Bethlehem), erected by the pious but ostentatious monarch King Emanuel the Happy, in honour and memory of the highly profitable Portuguese voyages of discovery. To be honest, Dom Miguel's lectures on the architectural styles of the castles and monasteries—the Moorish, Gothic, Italian elements, with an unexpected epilogue on Hindu influence—went, as they say, in one ear and out the other. I had other things to think about: to wit, how I could make love comprehensible to the forthright Zouzou. When one is occupied with a human problem, nature and the oddest architectural monuments alike become nothing but decoration, nothing but superficially apprehended background for what is human. Nevertheless, I must admit that this fairyland of stone was not without its effect. The incredible, magic delicacy of the cloister of Belem, belonging to no time and like a child's enchanted dream, with slender towers and delicate columns in the niche-vaults, the lightly patinated white sandstone cut into such fairytale magnificence that it seemed as though the stone could be worked with the slightest of fretsaws to produce these gems of lacy openwork—all this, I say, truly enchanted me, imaginatively exalted my mind, and certainly contributed to the excellence of the words I addressed to Zouzou.

We four had lingered rather a long time in the fabulous cloister, wandering around it repeatedly, and as Dom Miguel had no doubt noticed that we young people were not paying very close attention to his lecture on the King Emanuel style, he stayed with Dona Maria Pia, going ahead, and we followed at a distance that I did all I could to augment.

"Now, Zouzou," I said, "I imagine that in respect to this edifice our hearts beat as one. A cloister of this sort is something I have never come across before." (I had not come across a cloister of any sort before, and it was just chance that my first one was this kind of child's dream.) "I am very happy to visit it with you. But let's come to an agreement about the right word to describe it. 'Beautiful'? No, that does not fit, though, of course, it is anything but unbeautiful. But 'beautiful'—the word is too severe and elevated, don't you think? We must take the meaning of 'pretty' and 'charming' at their best, raise it to the *n*th degree, and then we shall have the right term of praise for this cloister. For that's what it is: prettiness raised to the *n*th degree."

"There you go babbling again, marquis. It's not unbeautiful, but it is not beautiful either, but simply extremely pretty. After all, what is extremely pretty is certainly beautiful."

"No, there is a distinction. How can I make it clear to you? Your mama, for example—"

"Is a beautiful woman," Zouzou interrupted me quickly, "and I am pretty at most; that's what you mean, isn't it? You are going to use us to illustrate your silly distinction, aren't you?"

"You anticipate me," I replied after a measured pause, "and you somewhat distort my thought. It does indeed run along the lines you indicate, but not precisely. It delights me to hear you say 'we,' 'we two,' of yourself and your mother. But after I have enjoyed the combination, I divide you again and proceed to admire you separately. Dona Maria Pia is perhaps an illustration of the fact that beauty, to be perfect, cannot entirely dispense with prettiness and loveliness. If your mother's face were not so large and stern and such a terrifying example of Iberian racial pride but had instead a little of your loveliness, she would be a completely beautiful woman. As things stand, she is not altogether what she ought to be: a beauty. You on the other hand, Zouzou, are prettiness and charm to perfection, raised to the *n*th degree. You are like this cloister. . . ."

"Oh, thank you! I am a girl in the King Emanuel style, I am a capricious edifice. Many, many thanks. That's what I call gallantry."

"You're free to make fun of my sincere words, to distort them and to call yourself an edifice. But you mustn't be surprised that this cloister has touched my heart so profoundly that I compare you to it, for you, too, have touched my heart. I am seeing the cloister for the first time. You certainly have seen it often?"

"Yes, a few times."

"Then you should be happy to see it now in the company of a neophyte to whom it is all completely new. For that allows you to see the familiar with new eyes, the eyes of the neophyte, as though for the first time. One should always try to see everything, even the most commonplace, the most completely matter of fact, with new, astonished eyes as though for the first time. In this way it wins back its power to amaze, which has faded into matter-of-factness, and the world remains fresh. Otherwise, everything fades—life, joy, amazement. Take love, for example—"

"*Fi donc! Taisez-vous!*"

"But why? You, too, have talked of love, repeatedly, in accordance with your probably sound theory that silence is unhealthy. But you have expressed yourself so harshly about it, quoting nasty little spiritual verses, that you make one wonder how it is possible to speak so unlovingly of love. You have so grossly omitted sentiment in talking about the thing called love that what you say is unhealthy in its turn, and one feels obliged to contradict you and, if I may say so, to set you right. When one looks at love with new eyes, as though for the first time, what a touching and altogether amazing spectacle it is! It is nothing more nor less than a miracle! In the last analysis, seen in the most comprehensive possible way, all existence is a miracle, but, according to my estimation, love is the greatest. Recently you said that Nature had carefully separated and divided one human being from another. Very apposite and only too true. That's how it is and that's the rule. But in love Nature has made an exception—a very marvellous one if you look at it with new eyes. Notice carefully that it is Nature that admits this astounding exception, or rather, introduces it, and if you take sides in this matter for Nature and against love, Nature will not thank you in the least; it's a *faux pas* on your part, you are taking sides against Nature. I'll explain that, as I've undertaken to set you right. It is true: a man lives separated and divided from others inside his own skin, not only because he must, but because he does not wish it otherwise. He wants to be as separate as he is because essentially he wants to be alone and cares nothing at all about others. Anyone else, everyone else within a skin of his own, is actually repulsive. His own person is the only thing that is not repulsive. That's a law of Nature, I state it as it is. When he sits meditatively with his elbows on the table, his head in his hands, he may place a couple of fingers against his cheek and one between his lips. All right, it's his finger and his lips, and so what of it? But to have someone else's finger between his lips would be insupportable, it would actually fill him with loathing. Don't you agree? Loathing in actual fact is the essence of his relation to others. When their physical presence becomes oppressive, it is odious to him in the highest degree. He would rather suffocate than open his senses in proximity to alien bodies. Involuntarily he in his own skin takes every precaution, and it is only to spare his own sensibilities that he is considerate of others. Good. Or, at any rate, true. With these words I have sketched the natural over-all state of affairs briefly but accurately, and now I come to a paragraph in the speech I have specially prepared for you.

"For now something enters in through which Nature deviates amazingly from her basic design, something through which man's whole fastidious insistence upon separateness and being alone inside his own skin is annulled; the inflexible law that each is inoffensive only to himself is so completely wiped out that if one were to take the trouble to see it for the first time—and it is one's duty to do so—he might find his orbs overflowing with amazement and emotion. I use the words 'orbs' and 'overflow' because they are poetic and therefore appropriate to the subject. 'To shed tears' seems to me too ordinary in this context. One sheds tears when one gets a cinder in one's eye. But 'overflowing orbs' is on a higher plane.

"You must forgive me, Zouzou, if now and again I pause in this speech I have prepared for you and, as it were, begin a new paragraph. I am liable to digress, as here on the subject of orbs, and I must pull myself together again for the task of setting you right. Well, then! What is the digression on Nature's part that, to the astonishment of the universe, wipes out the division between one person and another, between the me and the you? It is love. An everyday affair, but eternally new and, carefully considered, nothing short of miraculous. What happens? Out of their separateness two glances encounter each other as glances never meet at other times. Startled and forgetful of the world, confused and a little shamefaced at their complete difference from all other glances, but not willing to surrender this difference for all the world, they sink into each other—if you wish, I will say 'plunge into each other,' but 'plunge' is not necessary, 'sink' is just as good. There is a trace of bad conscience as well—the reason for which I shall not ask. I am a simple nobleman, and no one can demand that I solve the riddles of the universe. In any case, it's the sweetest bad conscience in the world, and with this in their eyes and hearts these two who have suddenly been lifted above all classifications resolutely approach each other. They talk together in ordinary language about this and that, but both this and that are lies, just as the ordinary language is, and for this reason their lips as they speak have a slight mendacious twist and their eyes are full of sweet deceit. They glance at each other's hair and lips and limbs, and then the deceitful eyes swiftly drop or wander abroad somewhere in the world where they have no interest and see nothing at all, for these eyes are blind to everything except each other. These glances seek refuge in the world only to return promptly and all the more brightly to the other's hair and lips and limbs, for these, contrary to all usage, have ceased to be alien and worse than indifferent, unpleasant, repulsive because they are not one's own but another's, and have become the object of delight, longing, and a yearning desire to touch—an ecstasy of which the eyes anticipate, steal in advance, all they can.

"That's a paragraph in my speech, Zouzou, and I shall make an indentation. You are listening to me carefully? As though you were hearing about love for the first time? I hope so. Before long there comes the moment when these two privileged beings are sick to death of lies and all the to-do about this and that and the twisted mouths, and they toss all this aside as though they were already tossing aside their clothes, and they pronounce the one true sentence, the only true one for them, in contrast to which everything else has been simply garrulous evasion: the words 'I love you.' It is a true fulfilment, the boldest and sweetest there is. Thereupon, lips sink, or, as one might say, plunge into one another in a kiss, an occurrence that is so unique in this world of separateness and isolation that one's orbs might well overflow at it. I ask you, how crudely you talked about the kiss, which is, after all, the pledge of that marvellous release from separateness and from the fastidious refusal to be interested in anything that is not oneself! I admit, I admit with the liveliest sympathy, that it is the beginning of everything that is to follow, for it is the astounding, silent declaration that closeness, ultimate closeness, closeness as complete as possible, just that closeness that otherwise is oppressive to the point of suffocation, has become the essence of all that is desirable. Through lovers, Zouzou, love does everything, exerts itself to the utmost, to make this closeness complete, perfect, to raise it to the actual oneness of two lives, but in this, comically and sadly, it is never successful despite all its efforts. It cannot to this extent triumph over Nature, for Nature, despite the fact that it invented love, sides in principle with separateness. For two to become one is not something that happens to lovers; it happens beyond them, if at all, in a third being, the child, who emerges from their efforts. But I am not talking about the blessings of parenthood and the joys of family life; that goes beyond my theme and I shall not touch on it. I am speaking about love in new and noble words and trying to create new eyes for you, Zouzou, and awaken your understanding to its touching miraculousness, so that you will not again express yourself so crudely about it. I do this by paragraphs because I cannot say it all in one breath, and here I make another indentation in order to say in the following as follows:

"Love, Zouzou my love, does not consist simply in the state of being in love where, amazingly, one physically separate body ceases to be unpleasant to another. Everywhere in the world there are delicate signs and intimations of its existence. When a dirty beggar child on a streetcorner looks up at you and you not only give him a few centavos but run your ungloved hand over his hair, though very likely there are lice in it, and you smile into his eyes as you do so, and thereupon walk on happier than you were before—what is that but a delicate sign of love? I will tell you something, Zouzou: stroking that child's louse-infested hair with your bare hand and afterward being happier than before is perhaps more astounding evidence of love than the fondling of a beloved body. Look about you in the world and look at Man as though you were doing so for the first time. Everywhere you will see signs of love, intimations of it, confessions of it on the part of what is separate and disinclined to have anything to do with another physical body. People shake hands—that is something very ordinary, everyday, and conventional; no one thinks anything about it except those who are in love, and they enjoy this contact because as yet no other is allowed them. Others do it unfeelingly and without considering that it was love that originated the practice; but they do it. Their bodies remain at a measured distance—not too great proximity on any account! But across this space separating two closely guarded individual lives they extend their arms, and the strange hands meet, embrace each other, press each other, and there is nothing in this but what is most ordinary, there is nothing of any special significance, so it seems, so one thinks. In truth, however, carefully examined, it belongs in the domain of the miraculous, and it is no small testimonial to Nature's departure from itself, the denial of the aversion of stranger for stranger, a secret sign of omnipresent love."

My dear mother in Luxemburg would certainly never have believed that I could possibly have spoken thus and would no doubt have put down my report of it as nothing but a fine fiction. But I swear on my honour that is how I spoke, for it just came to me. Perhaps the fact that I succeeded in making so original a speech is to be attributed in large measure to the extreme prettiness and uniqueness of the Belem cloister through which we were wandering; let that be as it may. In any case, that is how I spoke, and when I had finished a very remarkable thing happened. Zouzou gave me her hand! Without looking at me, her head turned away as though she were inspecting the stone fretwork at her side, she put out her right hand—I, of course, was walking on her left. I took it and pressed it, and she responded to the pressure. In the same instant, however, she jerked her hand away and said, with brows gathered stormily:

"And those drawings you took the liberty of making? Where are they? Why don't you finally produce them and hand them over to me?"

"But, Zouzou, I have not forgotten. I have no intention of forgetting. Only you know yourself there has been no opportunity—"

"Your lack of imagination in finding an opportunity," she said, "is pitiable. I see that I must help out your ineptitude. With a little more circumspection and better powers of observation you would know without my having to tell you that behind our house—in the little garden at the rear, you understand—there is a bench surrounded by oleander bushes, more of a bower really, where I like to sit after luncheon. By this time you might know that, but of course you don't, as I have occasionally said to myself while sitting there. With the slightest degree of imagination and enterprise you would long ago have found an opportunity when lunching with us, after coffee, to act as though you were going away and actually to go a little distance, and then to turn about and come to find me in the bower, so that you could deliver your handiwork to me. Astonishing, isn't it? An idea of genius? Or so it would seem to you. And so in the near future you will be kind enough to do this—will you?"

"I most certainly will, Zouzou! It's really as brilliant as it is obvious. Forgive me for not having noticed the bench under the oleanders. It's so far at the rear I never paid any attention to it. So you sit there after lunch all alone among the bushes? Marvellous! I'll do exactly as you say. I will publicly take my departure, from you too, and appear to be going home; instead of that, however, I will come to you with the pictures. I give you my hand on it."

"Keep your hand to yourself! We can shake hands later on after we have returned home in your carriage. Meanwhile, there's no sense in pressing each other's hands all the time."

CHAPTER XI

Happy though this arrangement made me, I was understandably nervous at the thought of letting Zouzou see the pictures. It would be a rash act, an impossible act. By adorning Zaza's pretty body, portrayed in various poses, with Zouzou's highly characteristic cluster of curls, I had transferred to it Zouzou's identity. How she would take these impertinent portraits was a disturbing question. Besides, I asked myself why it was necessary to have luncheon at the Kuckucks' and go through the comedy of leave-taking before seeking her out in the bower. If it was Zouzou's habit to sit there alone after the midday meal, I could make my way to the bench among the oleanders on any convenient day, trusting to the protection of the siesta hour to escape discovery. If only I dared go to the rendezvous without those accursed and outrageous drawings!

Whether, through fear of Zouzou's wrath, which was unpredictable in the degree of its violence, I did not in fact so dare, or whether my volatile soul had been diverted from that desire by a new and thrilling experience—of which I shall speak directly—suffice it to say that day after day passed without my obeying Zouzou's command. Something intervened, I repeat, a distracting experience, a sombre celebration, that altered from one hour to the next my attitude toward the double image, reversing the emphasis by revealing one aspect, the mother, in the strongest light, blood-red in color, and putting the other, the enchanting daughter, a little in the shade.

Very likely I use the metaphor of light and shade because the contrast between them plays so important a part in the bull ring—the contrast, that is, between the sunny side and the shady side, with the shady side, where we people of distinction sat, having the preference, of course, while the small folk are banished into the sun. . . . But I speak too abruptly of the bull ring, as though the reader already knew that this very remarkable ancient Iberian institution was going to be my subject. Writing is not a conversation with oneself. Orderly development, self-possession, and an unhurried approach to the subject are indispensable.

To begin with, it must be said that my stay in Lisbon was now gradually drawing to a close; it was already late September. The return of the *Cap Arcona* was imminent, and there was barely a week until my departure. This inspired me with a desire to pay a second and final visit, alone, to the Museu Sciências Naturaes in the Rua da Prata. Before leaving, I wanted to see again the white stag in the entrance hall, the primordial bird, the poor dinosaur, the great armadillo, that delightful nocturnal monkey, the loris, and all the others—not by any means least the worthy Neanderthal family and the Dawn Man presenting his bouquet to the sun. And so I did. One forenoon, my heart flooded with universal sympathy, I wandered without any guide through the halls and galleries on the ground floor and the corridors in the basement of Kuckuck's institution. Nor did I fail to put in a brief appearance in the director's office, for I wanted him to know that I had been drawn back to his museum. As usual, he received me with great cordiality, praised me for my faithfulness to his institution, and then made the following announcement.

That day, Saturday, was the birthday of Prince Luis-Pedro, a brother of the King. In recognition of this, there was to be a *corrida de toiros*, a bullfight, next day at three in the afternoon, and the great man would be there. It was to be held in the big arena on the Campo Pequeno, and he, Kuckuck, was planning to attend this traditional spectacle with his ladies and Hurtado. He had tickets, seats on the shady side, and he had an extra one for me. For he considered it most opportune, in view of the educational purpose of my tour, that just before my departure I should have this opportunity of seeing a *corrida*. What did I think?

My thoughts were definitely unenthusiastic, and I told him so. The sight of blood made me somewhat queasy, I said, and, to my own knowledge, I was not the man for quaint national massacres. The horses, for instance–I had been told that the bull often ripped open their stomachs so that the entrails spilled out; I did not at all want to see this, not to mention the bull himself, for whom I should certainly feel sorry. One might suppose that if ladies' nerves were strong enough to stand this spectacle, I ought to be able to endure it if not exactly to enjoy it. But Portuguese ladies were born to these robust traditions, whereas he had in me a somewhat delicate foreigner–and so on, to the same effect.

But Kuckuck reassured me. I ought not to have too grisly an idea of the festival, he said. A *corrida* was, to be sure, a serious occasion, but not horrifying. The Portuguese were animal-lovers and would not permit anything horrible. As far as the horses were concerned, for a long time now they had been provided with protective padding so that hardly anything serious could happen to them, and the bull died a more chivalrous death than in the slaughterhouse. Besides, whenever I liked, I could glance away and turn my attention to the festive crowd and the view of the arena itself, which was picturesque and of great ethnic interest.

Very well, I could see that I ought not to scorn this opportunity or his considerateness, for which I thanked him. We agreed that my carriage and I would wait for him and his family at the foot of the cable railway in ample time to ride to the arena together. It would go very slowly, Kuckuck warned; the streets would be crowded. I found this confirmed when next day, to be on the safe side, I left my hotel at two fifteen. I had never seen the city in such a state, though I had been there on so many Sundays. Obviously, only a *corrida* could get everyone out. The Avenida in all its splendid width was crowded with carriages and people, teams of horses and teams of mules, people riding on asses and people walking, as were also the streets through which I rode to the Rua Augusta, kept to a walking pace by the density of the crowd. From every nook and cranny, from the old city, from the suburbs, from the surrounding villages, streamed city people and country people, mostly in holiday attire brought out only for such occasions. Hence, no doubt, the proud expectant, and yet dignified, even reverent expression of their faces. Their mood, so it seemed to me, was sedate; there were no shouts or uproar, no quarrelsome collisions, as they moved with one accord in the direction of the Campo Pequeno and the amphitheatre.

Whence the strange feeling of oppression, the mixture of awe, sympathy, and excitement tinged with sadness, that constricts the heart at the sight of a crowd exalted by a festival and informed and united by its meaning? There is something inarticulate, primordial, about it that inspires awe and a certain anxiousness as well. The weather was still midsummer's, the bright sun glinted on the copper ferrules of the long staffs the men planted before them like pilgrims. They wore bright-coloured sashes and hats with broad brims. The women's clothes were of snowy cotton, embroidered at breast, sleeve, and hem with gold and silver thread. Many wore high Spanish combs, often with the black or white veil called *mantilha*, which covers head and shoulders. There was nothing surprising about this in the case of farm women out for a holiday, but when Dona Maria Pia came to greet me at the cable-car station, not, to be sure, in the glittering national costume but in an elegant afternoon dress, wearing, however, just such a black *mantilha* over her high comb—I was surprised, yes, startled. She saw no reason for any smile of apology for this ethnic masquerade, and no more did I. Deeply impressed, I bowed with special reverence over her hand. The *mantilha* was particularly becoming to her. Through its fine fabric the sun threw a filigree pattern on her large, pale, stern face.

Zouzou wore no *mantilha*. And in my eyes, at least, the charming cluster of dark curls at her temples was ethnic mark enough. Her dress, however, was even darker than her mother's, a little as though she were going to church. And the gentlemen, the professor as well as Dom Miguel, who had arrived on foot and had joined us as we were exchanging greetings, were in formal attire, black cutaways and bowler hats, whereas I had selected a blue suit with bright stripes. This was somewhat embarrassing, but the ignorance of a stranger might perhaps excuse it.

I ordered my coachman to go by way of the Avenida-Park and the Campo Grande, where it was quieter. The professor and his wife sat on the back seat, Zouzou and I facing them, and Dom Miguel took the seat beside the coachman. The ride passed in silence or with very brief exchanges, due principally to Senhora Maria's extremely dignified, indeed stern, demeanour, which admitted of no chitchat. Once, to be sure, her husband calmly addressed a remark to me, but before answering I involuntarily glanced toward the sombre lady in the Iberian headdress and replied with reserve. Her black amber earrings oscillated, set in motion by the light jolting of the carriage.

At the entrance to the arena, the traffic was dense. Advancing very slowly between the other equipages, we had to wait patiently for our turn to dismount. Then the vast circle of the amphitheatre engulfed us with its barriers, pillared balustrades, and ascending rows of seats, of which only a few were still unoccupied. Beribboned officials directed us to our seats on the shady side at a convenient height above the yellow circle strewn with tanbark and sand. The huge arena filled quickly to the last seat. Kuckuck had not exaggerated the picturesque impressiveness of its appearance. It was a colourful collective portrait of a whole national society, an occasion on which the aristocracy, symbolically at least and somewhat shamefacedly, accommodated itself to the customs of the folk sitting opposite in the blazing sun. Not a few of the ladies, even foreigners like Frau von Hüon and the Princess Maurocordato, had provided themselves with high combs and *mantilhas;* indeed, some of them had imitated in their dress the gold and silver embroidery of the peasant costume, and the formal attire of the men seemed a mark of respect toward the folk—prompted at least by the popular character of the occasion.

The mood of the enormous circle seemed expectant yet subdued. It differed markedly even on the sunny side, or especially there, from the nasty vulgarity so common among crowds at ordinary sporting-events. Excitement, tension, I felt them myself; but as far as one could see in the thousands of faces staring down at the still empty battleground, whose yellow would soon be stained with pools of blood, these emotions seemed restrained, held in check by a certain air of consecration. The music broke off and changed from a Moorish-Spanish concert piece to the national anthem as the Prince, a lean man with a star on his frock coat and a chrysanthemum in his buttonhole, entered his loge. With him was his wife, wearing a *mantilha*. Everyone got up and applauded. This was to happen again in honour of a different individual.

These dignitaries had entered at one minute before three. On the stroke of the hour, to a continuing musical accompaniment, the procession moved out of the big centre gate, led by three men bearing swords, epaulets over their short embroidered jackets, colourful tight trousers extending to the middle of their calves, white stockings, and buckled shoes. Behind them strode the *bandarilheiros*, carrying their pointed, bright-coloured darts, and the *capeadores*, arrayed in similar style, their narrow black cravats dangling over their shirts, their short red capes across their arms. They were followed by a cavalcade of *picadores* armed with lances, their hats strapped beneath their chins, mounted on horses whose padding hung like mattresses on chest and flank. A team of donkeys adorned with flowers and ribbons brought up the rear. The procession moved directly across the yellow circle toward the Prince's box and there dispersed after each member had made a formal bow. I saw some of the *toireadores* cross themselves as they made their way to the protection of the barrier.

All at once the little orchestra again stopped in the middle of a selection. A single very high trumpet note rang out. The ensuing stillness was complete. Through a little gate which I had not noticed before and which had suddenly been thrown open, there breaks—I use the present tense, because the experience is so vivid to me—something elemental, running, the steer, black, heavy, mighty, a visibly irresistible concentration of procreative and murderous force, in which earlier, older peoples certainly saw a god-animal, the animal god, with little, threatening, rolling eyes and horns twisted like drinking-horns affixed to his broad forehead, bending a little upward at the points, and clearly charged with death. He runs forward, stops with forelegs braced, glares angrily at the red cloth that one of the *capeadores* has spread out on the sand in front of him with the gesture of a servitor, throws himself at it, rams one horn into it, and bores the cloth into the ground. Just as he is about to shift horns, the little human snatches the cloth away, springs behind him, and as this mass of power swings ponderously on itself two *bandarilheiros* plant their bright-coloured darts in the cushion of fat at the back of his neck. There they sit now; barbed, no doubt, they sway but hold fast, standing out at an angle to his body through the rest of the contest. A third man has planted a short feathered lance in the exact middle of his neck, and he carries this decoration, like the spreading wings of a dove, through the remainder of his deadly battle against death.

I sat between Kuckuck and Dona Maria Pia. In a low voice the professor provided me with an occasional commentary on the proceedings. I learned from him the names of the various passes. I heard him say that until that day the bull had led a lordly life in the open fields, cared for and attended with the greatest solicitude and courtesy. My neighbour to the right, the august lady, remained silent. She only took her eyes off the god of procreation and slaughter and what was happening to him long enough to direct a glance of reproof toward her husband when he spoke. Her pale, severe face in the shadow of the *mantilha* was expressionless, but her bosom rose and fell faster and faster and, certain of being unobserved, I watched that face and the ill-controlled surging of that bosom more than I watched the sacrificial animal with the lance in his back, the ridiculously tiny wings, and the blood beginning to streak his sides.

I call him a sacrifice because one would have to be dull indeed not to feel the atmosphere that lay over all, at once oppressive and solemnly joyous, a unique mingling of jest, blood, and dedication, primitive holiday-making combined with the profound ceremonial of death. Later in my carriage when he was at liberty to speak, the professor discoursed about all this, but his erudition added nothing essential to what my alert and subtle intelligence had divined. The jest, combined with rage, burst forth a few minutes later when the bull, obviously having reached the conclusion that things could not possibly turn out well for him, that force and wit were unequally matched, turned round in the direction of the gate through which he had entered with the intention of trotting back to his stall, the ribboned darts still hanging from his neck. There was a storm of outraged, scornful laughter. People sprang to their feet, on the sunny side especially, but on ours as well; there were whistles, shouts, catcalls, curses. My august companion jumped up, whistled with startling shrillness, made a face at the coward, and emitted a sonorous trill of disdainful laughter. *Picadores* dashed into his path and pushed at him with their blunt lances. New *banderillas* were rammed into his neck and shoulders, some of them equipped with firecrackers to enliven him; they went off with a bang and a hiss against his hide. Under such provocation the brief attack of reason which had so incensed the crowd was quickly transformed into the blind rage appropriate to his might and to this game of death. Once more he played his part and did not fail again. A horse and rider sprawled in the sand. A *capeador* who had stumbled was unhappily lifted on the mighty drinking-horns and hurled into the air. He fell heavily. While the wild beast was being drawn away from the motionless body by exploiting his prejudice against red cloth, the man was lifted and carried out amid honourable applause, which may have been for him or, equally, for the *toiro*. Very likely it was for both. Maria da Cruz joined in, alternately clapping her hands and crossing herself rapidly as she murmured in her own tongue what may have been a prayer for the fallen man.

The professor expressed the opinion that it would amount to no more than a couple of broken ribs and a concussion. "Here comes Ribeiro," he added, "a notable young man." From the group of actors there now emerged an *espada*, who was greeted with *ah*'s and cheers that testified to his popularity. While all the rest stood back, he occupied the arena alone with the bleeding, maddened bull. Even during the procession I had been struck by him, for my eye automatically selects from among the commonplace whatever is elegant and beautiful. This Ribeiro was eighteen or nineteen years old and extremely handsome. He wore his black hair smooth and unparted, brushed forward over his brow. On his finely chiseled Spanish face there was the trace of a smile, called forth perhaps by the applause or perhaps simply by his contempt for death and his awareness of his own prowess. His narrowed black eyes looked out with quiet earnestness. The short embroidered jacket with epaulets and sleeves narrowing at the wrists became him—ah, it was in just such a costume that my godfather Schimmelpreester had once dressed me—it became him as admirably as it had me. I saw that he was of slender build, with noble hands. In one hand he carried a bare bright Damascus blade, which he handled like a cane; in the other he held a red cape. Reaching the centre of the arena, which was already torn and blood-flecked, he dropped the sword and gestured with his cape at the bull standing some distance off shaking the *banderillas*. Then he stood motionless and watched with that barely perceptible smile and that earnest expression of the eyes the maddened charge of the frightful martyr, offering himself as a target like a tree standing bare to the lightning. He stood as though rooted—too long, it was certain; one would have had to know him well not to be horribly sure that in the next twinkling of an eye he would be hurled to the ground, gored, massacred, trampled to bits. Instead of that, something extremely graceful occurred, something casual and expert, that produced a magnificent picture. The horns already had him, they had ripped a bit of embroidery from his jacket, when, with a single easy gesture of the hand that communicated itself to the cape, he directed those murderous instruments to where he no longer was, as a graceful swing of the hips brought him up against the monster's flank, and the human figure, arm now extended along the black back to where the horns were plunging into the fluttering cape, blended with the beast in an inspired design. The crowd leaped up, shouting: "Ribeiro!" and "*Toiro!*" and applauding. I did so myself and so did the regal Iberian beside me. Back and forth I glanced, from her surging breast to the living statue of man and animal, now rapidly dissolving, for more and more the stern and elemental person of this woman seemed to me one with the game of blood below.

In his duet with the *toiro* Ribeiro performed various other virtuoso feats in which he was clearly intent on creating ballet motifs at instants of extreme danger, and on the plastic mingling of the awesome and the elegant. Once when the weakened bull, disgusted by the futility of his rage, turned away and stood brooding dully by himself, his partner was seen to turn his back and kneel in the sand, very slim and erect with raised arms and bowed head, spreading the cape behind him. That seemed daring indeed, but he was no doubt sure of the momentary lethargy of the horned devil. Once, running in front of the bull, he half fell on one hand while with the other he let the seductive red cape divert the raging beast to one side. In the next instant he had sprung to his feet and vaulted lightly over the creature's back. He never acknowledged the continual applause, for it was obviously meant for the *toiro* as well, who had no mind for applause or acknowledgment. I half feared the man might consider it unseemly to play such tricks on a sacrificial creature that had been raised with courtesy on the open plains. But that was just the point of the jest and, in this ancient folk ceremonial, was an element in the cult of blood.

To end the game, Ribeiro ran over to the sword he had dropped and stood, one knee bent, spreading his cape in the usual provocative fashion. With serious gaze he watched the bull charge at a heavy gallop with horns levelled. He let him come very close, almost upon him, and in the final instant snatched the sword from the ground and drove the slender, bright steel halfway to the hilt in the animal's neck. The bull crumpled, wheeling massively. For a moment he forced one horn into the ground as though it were the red cloth, then he fell on his side and his eyes glazed.

It was indeed the most elegant slaughter. I can still see Ribeiro, his cape under his arm, walking away on tiptoe as though fearful of making a sound, glancing back the while at the fallen creature that moved no more. Before that, during the brief death scene, the public had risen from their seats as one man and given the tribute of their applause to the hero of this game of death, who, but for his early attempt to flee, had conducted himself admirably. The applause lasted until he had been carted off by the colourful mule team and wagon. Ribeiro walked beside him as though to do him a final honour. He did not return. Later, under another name, in a different role, and as part of a double image, he was to reappear in my life. But of that in its proper place.

We saw two more bulls that were not so good as the first, nor were the *espadas*, one of whom drove in the sword so clumsily that the animal hæmorrhaged but did not fall. He stood there like someone vomiting, legs braced and neck extended, spewing out thick waves of blood onto the sand, an unpleasant sight. A heavy-set matador of vain deportment and exaggeratedly brilliant dress had to give him the *coup de grâce*, and so the hilts of two swords stuck out of his body. We left. In the carriage, then, Maria Pia's husband provided us with a learned commentary on what we had just seen—I, for the first time. He spoke of a very ancient Roman shrine whose existence testified to a deep descent from the high cult level of Christianity to the service of a deity well disposed toward blood whose worship, through the wide popularity of the rites, almost outstripped that of the Lord Jesus as a world religion. Its converts had been baptized not with water, but with the blood of a bull, who was perhaps the god himself, though the god lived too in the one who spilled his blood. For this teaching contained something that united its believers irrevocably, joining them in life and in death; and its mystery consisted in the equality and identity of slayer and slain, axe and victim, arrow and target. . . . I listened to all this with only half an ear, only in so far as it did not interfere with my absorption in the woman whose image and being had been so vastly enhanced by the folk festival, who had, as it were, been truly and completely herself for the first time, ripe for observation. Her bosom was now at rest. I longed to see it surge again.

I will not conceal the fact that Zouzou had gone completely out of my mind during the game of blood. For this reason I was all the more determined to follow her instructions at last and, for God's sake, to show her the pictures that she claimed as her own—those nude studies of Zaza with Zouzou's curls at the temples. I had been invited to the Kuckucks' for lunch the following day. A shower during the night had cooled the air; a light coat was in order, and in the inside pocket I put the roll of drawings. Hurtado, too, was there. At table the conversation turned on yesterday's spectacle, and to please the professor I inquired further about the religion that had been driven from the field, the cult that marked a long step down from Christianity. He could not add much, but answered that those rites had not been so completely driven from the field, for the smoking blood of a victim—the god's blood, that is—had always been a part of the pious, popular ceremonials of mankind, and he sketched a connection between the sacrament of communion and the festal, fatal drama of the day before. I looked at the lady of the house, curious to see whether or not her bosom was at rest.

After coffee I said farewell to the ladies, planning to pay a final call on my last day. I rode down on the cable car with the gentlemen, who were returning to the museum, and when we arrived I said good-by to them, with repeated thanks, leaving the question of seeing them again to an indeterminate future. I acted as though I meant to walk back to the Savoy Palace, but turning around and finding the coast clear, I took the next cable car up again.

I knew the gate in the fence in front of the little house would be open. The earlier chill had given place to a mild and sunny autumn day. This was the hour for Dona Maria Pia's siesta. I could be sure of finding Zouzou in the rear garden. With cautious but rapid strides I walked toward it along the gravel path that led around the side of the house. Dahlias and asters were blooming in the middle of the small lawn. The appointed bench stood off to the right, surrounded by a semicircle of oleander bushes. The dear child was sitting there half in shadow, wearing a dress very like the one in which I had seen her first, loose, as she liked a dress to be, blue-striped, with a belt of the same material around the waist and some lacework at the edge of the half-length sleeves. She was reading a book and although she must have heard my cautious approach, she did not look up until I was in front of her. My heart pounded.

"Ah?" she said. Her lips, like the beautiful ivory tint of her skin, seemed somewhat paler than usual. "Still here?"

"Here again, Zouzou. I have been down to the bottom of the hill. I came back secretly, as we planned, to fulfil my promise."

"How praiseworthy!" she said. "*Monsieur le marquis* has remembered an obligation—without undue haste. This bench has slowly become a kind of waiting-room—" She had said more than she intended and bit her lip.

"How could you imagine," I hastened to reply, "that I

would fail to live up to the arrangement we made in the beautiful cloister! May I sit down with you? This bench in the bushes is a good deal more private than the ones at the tennis court. I am afraid I shall have to neglect the game again and forget–"

"Not at all, the Meyer-Novaros across the ocean will certainly have a tennis court."

"Possibly. But it won't be the same thing. Leaving Lisbon, Zouzou, is very hard for me. I have said good-by to your esteemed papa. How memorably he talked at luncheon about the pious ceremonials of mankind! The *corrida* yesterday was, after all, I'll say this at least, a curious experience."

"I did not watch it very closely. Your attention, too, seemed to be divided–as you like it to be. But to the point, marquis! Where are my drawings?"

"Here," I said. "It was your wish. . . . You understand they are imaginative creations, produced, as it were, involuntarily."

She held the drawings in her hand and looked at the top one. It was an enamoured sketch of Zaza's body in such-and-such a posture. The flat button earrings matched, the cluster of curls matched even more exactly. There was little enough resemblance in the face, but what did the face count for here?

I sat as straight as Dona Maria Pia, prepared for anything, agreeable to anything, and thrilled in advance by whatever might occur. A deep blush suffused her face at the sight of her own sweet nakedness. She sprang up, tore the works of art into tiny pieces, and strewed them fluttering on the breeze. Of course, that was something that had to happen. What did not have to happen and yet did, was this: she stared for an instant with a bewildered expression at the scraps of paper lying on the ground, and the next instant her eyes filled, she sank back on the bench, flung her arms around my neck, and buried her glowing face on my breast. She gave little noiseless sighs that were nevertheless clearly perceptible, and at the same time–and this was most touching of all–she kept up a rhythmic hammering against my shoulder with her little fist, the left one. I kissed the bare arm around my neck, I raised her lips to mine and kissed them. They responded, just as I had dreamed, longed, determined they would when I had first seen her, my Zaza, on the Rossio. Who of you whose eyes peruse these lines will not envy me such sweet instants? And envy her as well, however hard the little fist might pound, for her conversion to love? But now what a peripeteia! What a reversal of fortune!

Zouzou suddenly threw back her head and tore herself from our embrace. In front of bush and bench, in front of us, stood her mother.

Silent, as though we had been struck on those lips so recently united, we looked up at the august lady, at her large, pale countenance, jet earrings quivering on either side, at the severe mouth, widened nostrils, and stormy brows. Or rather, I alone looked at her; Zouzou kept her chin lowered on her breast and went on with the rapid-fire pounding of her little fist, striking now against the bench on which we sat. And yet I ask you to believe that I was less cast down by this maternal apparition than one might have thought. However unexpected her appearance, it seemed fitting and necessary, as though she had been summoned, and in my natural confusion there was an element of joy.

"Madame," I said formally, rising, "I regret the interruption of your afternoon rest. What has happened has occurred almost accidentally and with complete propriety—"

"Silence!" the lady commanded in her marvellously sonorous, slightly hoarse voice. And turning to Zouzou:

"Susanna, go to your room and remain there until you are called." Then to me: "Marquis, I wish to speak to you. Follow me."

Zouzou rushed off across the lawn, which had obviously deadened the approaching footsteps of the *senhora.* Now she went along the path and, obeying her injunction to follow, I walked not beside her but behind her and a little to one side.

Thus we entered the living-room, from which a door led into the dining-room. Behind the opposite door, which was not entirely closed, there seemed to be a room of more intimate character. The austere lady closed that door.

I met her glance. She was not pretty, but very beautiful.

"Luiz," she said, "the obvious thing would be to ask you whether this is your way of repaying Portuguese hospitality—be silent! I shall spare myself the question and you the answer. I did not summon you here to give you an opportunity for witless apologies. They could not possibly exceed the stupidity of your conduct. That is unsurpassable, and all that is left for you, all you are entitled to, is to be silent and let more mature persons see to your interests and lead you back to the right path from the childish irresponsibility you were youthful enough to engage in. There's seldom more miserable childishness or more wicked nonsense than when youth associates with youth. What were you thinking of? What do you want of this child? With complete ingratitude you bring nonsense and confusion into a home that was hospitably thrown open to you because of your birth and other agreeable attributes, and where order, reason, and intelligent planning prevail. Sooner or later, probably within a short time, Susanna will become the wife of Dom Miguel, the worthy assistant of Dom Antonio José, whose unequivocal wish and will this is. You can thus realize what stupidity you were guilty of when, in your need for love, you followed a childish course and formed the capricious notion of turning a child's head. That was not choosing or acting like a man, but like an infant. Mature reason had to intervene before it was too late. Once when we were conversing you spoke to me about the graciousness of maturity and the graciousness with which it speaks of youth. To encounter it successfully requires, of course, a man's courage. If an agreeable youth only showed a man's courage instead of seeking satisfaction in childishness, he would not have to run off like a drenched poodle, uncomforted, into the wide world. . . ."

"Maria!" I cried.

And: "*Holé! Hebo! Ahé!*" she exclaimed in majestic jubilation. A whirlwind of primordial forces seized and bore me into the realm of ecstasy. And high and stormy, under my ardent caresses, stormier than at the Iberian game of blood, I saw the surging of that queenly bosom.

THOMAS MANN was born in 1875, in the ancient Hanseatic city of Lübeck, of a line of influential merchants. His father had been a senator and twice mayor of the Free City; his mother was of Germanic-Creole descent. An ideal boyhood was passed for the most part in the comfortable family home in Lübeck.

He was nineteen when he removed to Munich, where he worked in an insurance office. In 1894, after the publication of his first novelette, *Gefallen*, he gave up office work for the study of art and literature at the University of Munich. Then came one year in Rome, and from that time on, Thomas Mann devoted himself exclusively to writing. He was awarded the Nobel Prize for Literature in 1929.

After several visits to the United States, he settled temporarily in Princeton, New Jersey, where he lectured at the University. In 1941 he built a home in Pacific Palisades, California, and it was there that he wrote *Doctor Faustus* and *The Holy Sinner*. In 1949 Thomas Mann made a brief visit to Germany, his first contact with his native land in sixteen years; in 1952 he returned to Europe to take up permanent residence in Switzerland, where he expanded the early short story entitled "Felix Krull" into the *Confessions of Felix Krull, Confidence Man*. He died at Zurich on August 12, 1955.

Thomas Mann's *Confessions of Felix Krull*, *Doctor Faustus* and *Stories of Three Decades* are available in Modern Library editions. *Buddenbrooks*, *Death in Venice and Seven Other Stories*, *The Transposed Heads*, *The Magic Mountain* and Thomas Mann's *Essays* are available in Vintage Books.